The Lonesome Gun

A PERLEY GATES WESTERN

THE LONESOME GUN

WILLIAM W. JOHNSTONE
AND J. A. JOHNSTONE

THORNDIKE PRESS
A part of Gale, a Cengage Company

Copyright © 2023 by J.A. Johnstone.
The WWJ steer head logo is Reg. U.S. Pat. & TM Off.
Thorndike Press, a part of Gale, a Cengage Company.

ALL RIGHTS RESERVED
This book is a work of fiction. Names, characters, businesses, organizations, places, events, and incidents either are the product of the authors' imagination or are used fictitiously. Any resemblance to actual persons, living or dead, events, or locales is entirely coincidental. Following the death of William W. Johnstone, the Johnstone family is working with a carefully selected writer to organize and complete Mr. Johnstone's outlines and many unfinished manuscripts to create additional novels in all of his series, like The Last Gunfighter, Mountain Man, and Eagles, among others. This novel was inspired by Mr. Johnstone's superb storytelling.
Thorndike Press® Large Print Hardcover Western.
The text of this Large Print edition is unabridged.
Other aspects of the book may vary from the original edition.
Set in 16 pt. Plantin.

LIBRARY OF CONGRESS CIP DATA ON FILE. CATALOGUING IN PUBLICATION FOR THIS BOOK IS AVAILABLE FROM THE LIBRARY OF CONGRESS.

ISBN-13: 979-8-88579-528-9 (hardcover alk. paper)

Published in 2023 by arrangement with Pinnacle Books, an imprint of Kensington Publishing Corp.

Printed in Mexico
Printed Number: 1   Print Year: 2024

The Lonesome Gun

Chapter 1

"Becky, another hungry customer just walked in," Lucy Tate said. "I'm getting some more coffee for my tables. Can you wait on him? He looks like trouble." She looked at Beulah Walsh and winked, so Beulah knew she was up to some mischief.

"I was just fixing to wash up some more cups," Becky said. "We're about to run out of clean ones. Can he wait a minute?"

"I don't know," Lucy answered. "He looks like he's the impatient kind. He might make a big scene if somebody doesn't wait on him pretty quick."

"I don't want to make a customer mad," Beulah said as she aimed a mischievous grin in Lucy's direction. "Maybe I can go get him seated."

"Oh my goodness, no," Becky said. "I'll go take care of him." She was sure there was no reason why Lucy couldn't have taken care of a new customer instead of leaving Beulah to do it. Beulah was busy enough as cook and owner. Becky dried her hands on a dishtowel and hurried out into the hotel dining room. Lucy and Beulah hurried right after her as far as the door, where they stopped to watch Becky's reaction.

"Perley!" Becky exclaimed joyfully, and she ran to meet him. Surprised by her exuberance, he staggered a couple of steps when she locked her arms around his neck. "I thought you were never coming home," she said. "You didn't say you were gonna be gone so long."

"I didn't think I would be," Perley said. "We were just supposed to deliver a small herd of horses to a ranch near Texarkana, but we ran into some things we hadn't counted on, and that held us up, pretty much. I got back as quick as I could. Sonny Rice went with Possum and me, and he ain't back yet." She started to ask why, but he said, "I'll tell you all about it, if you'll get me something to eat."

"Sit down, sweetie," she said, "and I'll go get you started." He looked around quickly to see if anyone had heard what she called him, but it was too late. He saw Lucy and Beulah grinning at him from the kitchen door. Becky led him to a table right outside the kitchen door and sat him down while she went to get his coffee. "I was just washing up some cups when you came in. I must have known I needed a nice clean cup for someone special."

He was both delighted and embarrassed over the attention she gave him. And he wanted to tell her he'd prefer that she didn't do it in public, but he was afraid he might hurt her feelings if he did. Unfortunately, Lucy and Beulah were not the only witnesses to Becky's show of affection for the man she had been not-so-secretly in love with for a couple of years. Finding it especially entertaining, two drifters on their way to Indian Territory across the Red River spoke up when Becky came back with Perley's coffee.

"Hey, darlin'," Rafer Samson called out, "bring that coffeepot out here. Sweetie ain't the only one that wants coffee. You'd share some of that coffee, wouldn't you, sweetie?"

"Dang, Rafer," his partner joined in. "You'd best watch what you're sayin'. Ol' sweetie might not like you callin' him that. He might send that waitress over here to take care of you."

That was as far as they got before Lucy stepped in to put a stop to it. "Listen fellows, why don't you give it a rest? Don't you like the way I've been taking care of you? We've got a fresh pot of coffee brewing on the stove right now. I'll make sure you get the first cups poured out of it, all right?"

"I swear," Rafer said. "Does he always let you women do the talkin' for him?"

"Listen, you two boneheads," Lucy warned, "I'm trying to save you from going too far with what you might think is fun. Don't force Perley Gates into something that you don't wanna be any part of."

"Ha!" Rafer barked. "Who'd you say? Pearly somethin'?"

"It doesn't matter," Lucy said, realizing she shouldn't have spoken Perley's name. "You two look old enough to know how to behave. Don't start any trouble. Just eat your dinner, and I'll see that you get fresh coffee as soon as it's ready."

But Rafer was sure he had touched a sensitive spot the women in the dining room held for the mild-looking young man. "What did she call him, Deke? Pearly somethin'?"

"Sounded like she said Pearly Gates," Deke answered. "I swear it did."

"Pearly Gates!" Rafer blurted loud enough for everyone in the dining room to hear. "His mama named him Pearly Gates!"

Lucy made one more try. "All right,

10

you've had your fun. He's got an unusual name. How about dropping it now, outta respect for the rest of the folks eating their dinner in here?"

"To hell with the rest of the folks in here," Rafe responded, seeming to take offense. "I'll say what I damn well please. It ain't up to you, nohow. If he don't like it, he knows where I'm settin'."

Lucy could see she was getting nowhere. "You keep it up, and you're liable to find out a secret that only the folks in Paris, Texas, know. And you ain't gonna like it."

"Thanks for the warnin', darlin'. I surely don't want to learn his secret. Now go get us some more coffee." As soon as she walked away, he called out, "Hey, tater, is your name Pearly Gates?"

Knowing he could ignore the two no longer, Perley answered. "That's right," he said. "I was named after my grandpa. Perley was his name. It sounds like the Pearly Gates up in heaven, but it ain't spelt the same."

"Well, you gotta be some kinda sweet little girlie-boy to walk around with a name like that," Rafer declared. "Ain't that right, Deke?"

"That's right, Rafer," Deke responded like a puppet. "A real man wouldn't have a name like that."

"I know you fellows are just havin' a little fun with my name, but I'd appreciate it if you'd stop now. I don't mind it all that much, but I think it upsets my fiancée."

Perley's request caused both his antagonists to pause for a moment. "It upsets his what?" Deke asked.

"I don't know," Rafer answered, "his fiant-cee, whatever that is. Maybe it's a fancy French word for his behind. We upset his behind." He turned to look at the few other customers in the dining room, none of whom would meet his eye. "We upset his fancy behind."

"I'm sorry, Becky," Perley said. "I sure didn't mean to cause all this trouble. Tell Beulah I'll leave, and they oughta calm down after I'm gone."

Beulah was standing just inside the kitchen door, about ready to put an end to the disturbance, and she heard what Perley said. "You'll do no such thing," she told him. "Lucy shouldn't have told 'em your name. You sit right there and let Becky get your dinner." She walked out of the kitchen then and went to the table by the front door, where customers deposited their firearms while they ate. She picked up the two gun belts that Rafer and Deke had left there,

12

took them outside, and dropped them on the steps. When she came back inside, she went directly to their table and informed them. "I'm gonna have to ask you to leave now, since your mamas didn't teach you how to behave in public. I put your firearms outside the door. There won't be any charge for what you ate if you get up and go right now."

"The hell you say," Rafer replied. "We'll leave when we're good and ready."

"I can't have you upsettin' my other customers," Beulah said. "So do us all the courtesy of leaving peacefully and, like I said, I won't charge you nothin' for what you ate."

"You threw our guns out the door?" Deke responded in disbelief. He thought about what she said for only a brief moment, then grabbed his fork and started shoveling huge forkfuls of food in his mouth as fast as he could. He washed it all down with the remainder of his coffee, wiped his mouth with his sleeve, and belched loudly. "Let's go, Rafer."

"I ain't goin' nowhere till I'm ready, and I ain't ready right now," Rafer said, and remained seated at the table. "If you're through, go out there and get our guns offa them steps."

"Lucy," Beulah said, "step in the hotel lobby and tell David we need the sheriff."

"Why, you ol' witch!" Rafer spat. "I oughta give you somethin' to call the sheriff about!" He stood up and pushed his chair back, knocking it over in the process.

That was as far as Perley could permit it to go. He got up and walked over to face Rafer. "You heard the lady," he said. "This is her place of business, and she don't want you and your friend in here. So why don't you two just go on out like she said, and there won't be any need to call the sheriff up here."

Rafer looked at him in total disbelief. Then a sly smile spread slowly across his face. "Why don't you go outside with me?"

"What for?" Perley asked, even though he knew full well the reason for the invitation.

"Oh, I don't know. Just to see what happens, I reckon." Finding a game that amused him now, he continued. "Do you wear a gun, Perley?"

"I've got a gun on the table with the others," Perley answered. "I don't wear it in here."

"Are you fast with that gun?" When Perley reacted as if he didn't understand, Rafer said, "When you draw it outta your holster, can you draw it real fast?" Because of Perley's general air of innocence, Rafer assumed he was slow of wit as well.

"Yes," Perley answered honestly, "but I would only do so in an emergency."

"That's good," Rafer said, "because this is an emergency. You wanna know what the emergency is? When I step outside and strap my gun on, if you ain't outside with me, I'm gonna come back inside and shoot this place to pieces. That's the emergency. You see, I don't cotton to nobody tellin' me to get outta here."

"All right," Perley said. "I understand why you're upset. I'll come outside with you, and we'll talk about this like reasonable men should."

"Two minutes!" Rafer blurted. "Then if you ain't outside, I'm comin' in after you." He walked out the door with Deke right behind him.

Becky rushed to Perley's side as he went to the table to get his gun belt. "Perley, don't go out there. You're not going to let that monster draw you into a gunfight, are you?"

"I really hope not," Perley told her. "I think maybe I can talk some sense into him and his friend. But I had to get him out of here. He was gettin' too abusive. Don't worry, I'll be all right. He oughta be easier to talk to when he doesn't have an audience."

He strapped his Colt .44 on and walked outside to find Rafer and Deke waiting. Seeing the expressions of gleeful anticipation on both faces, Perley could not help a feeling of uncertainty. If he had looked behind him, he would have seen everyone in the dining room gathered at the two windows on that side of the building. Everyone, that is, except Becky and Beulah. All the spectators were confident of the unassuming young man's gift of speed with a handgun. As far as Perley was concerned, his lightning-fast reactions were just that: a gift. He never practiced with a weapon, and he honestly had no idea why his brain and body reacted with no conscious direction from himself. Because of that, he was of the opinion that the talent could just as easily leave him with no warning. That was one reason he tried to avoid pistol duels whenever possible.

He took a deep breath and hoped for the best.

"I gotta admit, I had my doubts if you had the guts to walk out that door," Rafer said when Perley came toward them. In an aside to Deke, he said, "If this sucker beats me, shoot him." Deke nodded.

"Why do you wanna shoot me?" Perley asked him. "You've never seen me before today. I've done you no wrong. It doesn't make any sense for you and me to try to kill each other."

"The hell you ain't done me no wrong," Rafer responded. "You walked up to my table and told me to get outta there. I don't take that from any man."

"If you're honest with yourself, you have to admit that you started all the trouble when you started makin' fun of my name. I was willin' to call that just some innocent fun, and I still am. So we could just forget this whole idea to shoot each other and get on with the things that matter — and that's just to get along with strangers on a courteous basis. I'm willing to forget the whole trouble if you are. Whaddaya say? It's not worth shootin' somebody over."

"I swear, the more I hear comin' outta your mouth, the more I feel like I gotta puke. I think I'll shoot you just like I'd shoot a dog that's gone crazy. One thing I can't stand is a man too yellow to stand up for himself. I'm gonna count to three, and you'd better be ready to draw your weapon when I say three, 'cause I'm gonna cut you down."

"This doesn't make any sense at all," Perley said. "I don't have any reason to kill you."

"One!" Rafer counted.

"Don't do this," Perley pleaded, and turned to walk away.

"Two!" Rafer counted.

"I'm warnin' you, don't say three."

"Three!" Rafer exclaimed defiantly. His six-gun was already halfway out when he said it — and he staggered backward from the impact of the bullet in his chest. Deke, shocked by Perley's instant response, was a second slow in reacting and dropped his weapon when Perley's second shot caught him in his right shoulder. He stood, helplessly waiting for Perley's fatal shot, and almost sinking to his knees when Perley released the hammer and returned his pistol to his holster.

"There wasn't any sense to that," Perley said. "Your friend is dead because of that foolishness, and you better go see Bill Simmons about your shoulder. He's the barber, but he also does some doctorin'. We ain't got a doctor in town yet. You'd best just stand there for a minute, though, 'cause I see the sheriff runnin' this way."

Deke remained where he was, his eyes still glazed with the shock of seeing Rafer cut down so swiftly. Perley walked over and picked up Deke's gun, broke the cylinder open, and extracted all the cartridges. Then he dropped it into Deke's holster.

"Perley," Paul McQueen called out as he approached. "What's the trouble? Who's that?" He asked, pointing to the body on the ground before giving Perley time to answer his first question.

"I think I heard his friend call him Rafer," Perley said. "Is that right?" He asked Deke.

Deke nodded, then said, "Rafer Samson."

"Rafer Samson," McQueen repeated. "I'll see if I've got any paper on him, but I expect you could save me the trouble," he said to Deke. "What's your name?"

"Deke Johnson," he replied. "You ain't got no paper on me. Me and Rafer was just passin' through on the way to the Red."

"I don't expect I do," McQueen said. "At least by that name, anyway. You were just passin' through and figured you might as well cause a little trouble while you were at it, right?" He knew without having to ask that Perley didn't cause the trouble. "How bad's that shoulder?"

Deke nodded toward Perley. "He put a bullet in it."

"You musta gone to a helluva lot of trouble to get him to do that," the sheriff remarked. "Perley, you wanna file any charges on him?" Perley said that he did not. "All right," McQueen continued. "I won't lock you up, and we can go see Bill Simmons about that shoulder. Bill's a barber, but he also does some doctorin', and he's our undertaker, too. He's doctored a lotta gunshots, so he'll fix you up so you can ride. Then I want you out of town. Is that understood?"

"Yessir," Deke replied humbly.

"Perley, you gonna be in town a little while?" McQueen asked. When Perley said that he was, McQueen told him he'd like to hear the whole story of the incident. "I'll tell Bill to send Bill Jr. to pick up Mr. Samson." He looked around him as several spectators from down the street started coming to gawk at the body. "You mind stayin' here a while to watch that body till Bill Jr. gets here with his cart?"

"Reckon not," Perley said.

Bill Jr. responded pretty quickly, so it was only a few minutes before Perley saw him come out of the alley beside the barbershop, pushing his hand cart. Perley helped him lift Rafer's body up onto the cart. "Sheriff said he called you out," Bill Jr. said. "They don't never learn, do they?" Perley wasn't sure how to answer that, so he didn't.

Chapter 2

When he turned back toward the dining room again, Perley saw the folks inside still crowded up at the two small windows, and he thought maybe he'd just skip his dinner. But then he saw Becky standing in the open door, waiting for him to return. He truly hated that she'd seen the shooting. The incident she'd just witnessed was the kind of thing that happened to him quite frequently. There was no reason for it that he could explain. It was just something that had been attached to him at birth — the same as his natural reaction with a handgun, he supposed. He often wondered if when the Lord branded him with the cow-pie stigma, He thought it only fair to also grant him lightning-fast reactions. Perley had his brother John to thank for the saying, "If there wasn't but one cow pie in the whole state of Texas, Perley would accidentally step in it."

Becky broke into his fit of melancholy at that point when she became impatient and stepped outside the door. "Perley, come on in here and eat your dinner. It's almost time to clean up the kitchen." He reluctantly responded to her call.

Inside, he kept his eyes focused on the space between Becky's shoulder blades, avoiding the open stares of the customers as he followed her to the table by the kitchen door. "Sit down, Becky said, "and I'll fix you a plate." She picked up his coffee cup. "I'll dump this and get you some fresh."

When he finally looked up from the table, it was to catch Edgar Welch's gaze focused upon him. The postmaster nodded and calmly said, "Attaboy, Perley." His remark caused a polite round of applause from most of the other tables. Instead of feeling heroic, Perley was mortified. He had just killed a man. It was certainly not his first, but it was something he was most definitely not proud of.

Becky returned from the kitchen with a heaping plate of food. She was followed by Beulah, coming to thank him for taking the trouble outside her dining room. "There ain't no tellin' how many of my customers mighta got shot if you hadn't gone out there with him. He was gonna come back in here if you hadn't. There certainly ain't gonna be no charge for your dinner. Becky, take good care of him."

"I will," Becky said, and she sat down at the table with him. She watched him eat for a few minutes after Beulah went back into the kitchen before she asked a question. "Before all that trouble started, when you first came in, you said you came by to tell me something. Do you remember what it was?"

"Yeah," he answered. "I came to tell you I've gotta take a little trip for a few days."

"Perley," she fussed, "you just got back from Texarkana. Where do you have to go now?"

"Rubin wants me to take a contract he signed down to a ranch somewhere south of Sulphur Springs. It's for fifty head of Hereford cattle. Him and John have been talkin' about crossbreedin' 'em with our Texas longhorns to see if they can breed a better meat cow."

"Why can't one of them go?" Becky asked.

"John and Rubin both work pretty hard to run the cattle operation for the Triple-G. I never cared much for workin' on the ranch, and there wasn't anything tyin' me down here till I found you. So I have always been the one to do things like takin' this contract, and takin' those horses to Texarkana." He saw the look of disappointment on her face, so he was quick to say that there would surely be a change in his part of running the Triple-G after they were married. Judging by her expression, he wasn't sure she believed him. Their discussion was interrupted at that point, when Paul McQueen walked in the dining room and came straight to their table.

"Mind if I sit down?" Paul asked.

"Not at all," Becky answered him. "I've got to get up and help Lucy and Beulah. Can I get you a cup of coffee?" She knew he had been in earlier to eat dinner.

"Yes, ma'am, I could use a cup of coffee," he said. When she left to fetch it, he said, "Bill's workin' on that fellow to get your bullet outta his shoulder. I asked him how it all happened, but I swear, he seemed to be confused about how it did happen. I asked him why he pulled his weapon, if it was just you and his partner in a shoot-out. He said he wasn't sure why he pulled it. Said maybe he thought you might shoot him and damned if you didn't. I don't think he really knows what happened, but I can pretty much guess. Anyway, I don't think you have to worry about him. I told him I wanted him outta town as soon as Bill's finished with him, and I think he's anxious to go. Bill Jr. was already back with the body before I left there."

"If you're wonderin' about that business at all, you've got plenty of eyewitnesses," Perley suggested. "Everybody you see sittin' in here now was at those two windows up front. So they can tell you better than I can. I'm a little bit like the one I shot. It happened so fast, I ain't sure I remember what happened."

"Don't get me wrong, Perley, I don't doubt you handled it any other way than you are about everything, fair and square. I just wanted the whole picture in case the mayor asks me."

McQueen didn't have to wait long before he received the first eyewitness report. It came when Edgar Welch finished his dinner. Before leaving, he walked over to the table. "That was one helluva bit of shootin' you done today, Perley. Sheriff, you shoulda seen it." He then took them through the whole encounter. "Perley wasn't even facing that devil when he drew on him, and he still beat him."

"Maybe it ain't such a good idea to tell too many people about it, Edgar," McQueen said. "You might not be doin' Perley or the town any favors if we talk about how fast he is with that six-gun of his. We might have the kind of men showin' up in town that we don't wanna attract, like them two today."

"I see what you mean," Edgar said. "And I agree with you. We might have more drifters like those two showing up in town. Point well taken. Well, I'll be gettin' back to the post office."

The sheriff left soon after the postmaster, leaving Perley to finish up his dinner with a brief word here and there from Becky as she helped Lucy and Beulah clean up the dining room. He promised her that he would stay in town the entire day and eat supper there that night, before going back to the Triple-G. She gave him a key to her room on the first floor of the hotel, right behind the kitchen, so he could wait for her to finish her chores. She would have a couple of hours before it was time to prepare the dining room for supper. He was concerned about Buck, so he took the bay gelding to the stable so he could take his saddle off and turn him loose in Walt Carver's corral.

He suspected that Possum was going to give him a goodly portion of grief for slipping out that morning without telling him where he was going. He was halfway serious when he wondered what he was going to do with Possum after he and Becky were married.

It was after two o'clock when Becky showed up at her room. They embraced briefly before she stepped away, apologizing for her sweaty condition, the result of having just cleaned the kitchen. She seemed strangely distant, he thought, not like her usual lighthearted cheerful self. "Maybe I ought to go on back to the ranch now," he suggested, "and let you get a little bit of rest before you have to go back to the dining room."

"I guess I'm just a little more tired than I thought," she said. "But I don't want to rush you off. I know you stayed in town because of me." She didn't want to tell him that the incident that took place right outside the dining room had made a tremendous impact upon her. She had sought the counsel of Beulah Walsh, the closest person to a mother she had. Her own mother had passed seven years ago, leaving her father a widower living alone in Tyler. While they had worked cleaning up the kitchen, Beulah, and Lucy, too, had tried to help her understand the man she had fallen in love with.

"The thing that happened in the dining

room today is not that unusual in Perley's life," Beulah had told her. "His skill with a firearm is a curse that he has to live with," she said. "To Perley's credit, he tries to avoid it, but it always finds him sooner or later. And like you saw today, even his name is a curse and an open invitation to a troublemaker. So you have to be prepared for that day when Perley's not the fastest gun."

"I know how you feel, honey," Lucy had suggested. "But why don't you wait to see if he's gonna be working full time at the ranch before you marry him? The way it is now, him and Possum are gone who knows where most of the time. You said he's leaving tomorrow to go somewhere for a few days, and that ain't good for a marriage. You don't wanna spend your life wondering if your children's daddy is coming home or not."

Those words were still ringing in Becky's mind as she tried to sort out her true feelings, and she could see the confusion in Perley's eyes as they searched hers. This was the first time since she had met Perley that she wondered if she was about to make the wrong decision. In spite of her love for the man, she reluctantly decided that Lucy's advice might be best. "Perley," she finally managed to say, "you're leaving tomorrow to take that contract for the cows. Why don't we wait till you get back to talk about any plans we want to make? I must confess, that business today really got to me. And working in the kitchen afterward just seemed to drain all the energy I had. I hope you understand. I love you."

He didn't understand at all, but he said that he did. She seemed to be a Becky he had never met before. "That's a good idea," he said. "I'm gonna go now, so you can rest up before you have to go back to work tonight. We'll talk about everything when I get back. I love you, too." She stepped up to him and gave him another brief embrace, a fraction longer than the one she had greeted him with. He reached in his pocket and pulled out her door key. "Here," he said, "I don't reckon I'll be needin' this."

She stood in the doorway and watched him walk down the hallway to the back door. "Perley," she called after him, "be careful." He acknowledged with a wave of his hand.

"That last kiss felt more like a goodbye kiss," he told Buck as he followed the trail back to the Triple-G Ranch. "It sure didn't seem like Becky a-tall. I feel like I just got fired."

Walt Carver was sure surprised when he showed up at the stable to get Buck. Perley gave him no reason for returning so soon, other than the simple fact that he had changed his mind. Without pushing Buck, he arrived at the ranch in plenty of time to get supper at the cookshack, which was where he generally ate his meals. His eldest brother, Rubin, and his family lived in the original ranch headquarters. His other brother, John, had built a house for himself and his family. Perley was welcome to eat at either house, but he found it more to his liking to eat with the cowhands at the cookshack. He always felt that he was imposing, even though he knew he was a favorite with his nephews and nieces. Now, since he had time, he decided to stop by the house and pick up the contract and money for the Herefords from Rubin.

"Howdy, Perley," Link Drew greeted him when he rode up to the barn. Young Link had grown like a weed since Perley had brought him home with him after the brutal death of Link's mother and father in the little store they operated. Link was nine when he came to the Triple-G. Looking at him today, Perley couldn't remember if he'd had one or two birthdays since he had arrived. "You want me to take care of Buck for you?" Link asked.

"I think Buck would appreciate it," Perley replied. "If you'll do that, I'll run up and get something at the house, and I'll see you at supper." He climbed down from the saddle and handed Link the reins. He hesitated half a minute to watch the boy lead the big bay gelding away before turning to walk up to the house. "Knock, knock," he called out as he walked in the kitchen door. In reality, the house was as much his home as it was Rubin's, but being practical, he didn't want to surprise anybody.

"Oh, hello, Perley," Lou Ann, Rubin's wife, greeted him. "If you're lookin' for Rubin, he's in the study."

"Thank you, ma'am," Perley said, and headed for the hallway door.

"You stayin' for supper?" Lou Ann asked. "You're welcome, you know."

"No, thank you just the same, Lou Ann. I'm just gonna pick up a paper and some money from Rubin, and I'll be outta your way."

Just as Lou Ann said, he found Rubin at his desk in the study. "You got that contract and the money for those cattle?" Perley asked as he walked in.

"Thought you weren't comin' back till

after supper," Rubin said as he opened a drawer and pulled out a big envelope. "What happened? Becky kick you out?" he joked. "When are you gonna bring her down here to officially meet the family?"

"I don't know," Perley answered. "Might be a while. There ain't no hurry."

"Well, you might be wise to take your time and be sure it's what you really want. You stayin' for supper?"

"Nope," Perley answered. "I just came to get this." He picked up the thick envelope and tested its weight. "You got a thousand dollars in here?"

"Plus a contract that Weber has to sign, sayin' he got the money," Rubin answered. "He wouldn't deal with anything but cash. Take Possum with you. That's a lot of money you're carrying."

Perley couldn't help chuckling when he thought of the remote possibility of getting away without Possum. "I'll tell him you said to take him. That way he'll feel like he has a right to complain if something doesn't suit him. We'll leave right after breakfast in the mornin'." He turned and headed for the door.

"You take care of yourself, Perley," Rubin called after him.

"I will," Perley replied, and went out the

front door in time to hear Ollie Dinkler banging on his iron triangle to announce supper was ready.

"Beans is ready, Perley," Ollie said when Perley walked past him.

"Right," Perley replied. "I'll be right back, soon as I put this in the barn. He folded the thick envelope Rubin gave him, took it into the barn, and stuck it in his saddlebag. When he returned to the cookshack, he found Possum waiting for him.

"I thought you said you was gonna eat supper in town with Becky," Possum said. "What's wrong? And I know somethin' is, so tell me what happened."

"What makes you think somethin's wrong?" Perley asked. "She just had a hard workin' day, and I thought she could use a little rest. Besides, we gotta get an early start in the mornin', and I didn't wanna get back too late tonight."

"You stickin' with that story?" Possum asked.

"I reckon," Perley answered. "Let's eat while there's still some beans in the pot."

Possum followed him inside where Ollie was serving. "You think you can find that Weber Ranch?" he asked Perley.

"I expect so," Perley answered. "I wouldn't think it would be too hard." He paused to let that simmer a little while in Possum's brain until he saw him working up his argument for the wisdom of accompanying him. "Oh, and Rubin said it might be a good idea to take you along." Possum sighed as he exhaled his argument.

"That brother of yours knows what's what," Possum said.

They carried their plates and cups of coffee to the table and sat down across from Fred Farmer, who at forty-four was the oldest of the cowhands. Were it not for the fact that Perley's brother John filled the role as foreman, Fred would most likely have been the best candidate. "Did I hear Possum say you and him are ridin' down below Sulphur Springs in the mornin'?" Fred asked.

"That's a fact," Perley said. "So, it might be a little hard to keep things runnin' smooth without Possum and me," he joked.

"That's true," Fred came back. " 'Course, you two are gone somewhere half the time, anyway, so we're kinda used to it. Besides, we picked up another man today."

"Is that right?" Perley asked. Fred nodded toward the door and Perley turned to look. "Well, I'll be. . . ." he uttered when he saw Sonny Rice walk through the door. He looked at Possum. "Did you know?"

"Yeah, I was fixin' to tell you Sonny came

back. I just ain't had a chance to," Possum said.

Sonny filled a plate and brought it and a cup of coffee to join them. Fred slid down the bench to make a place for the young man. "Howdy, Perley," Sonny greeted him.

"Sonny," Perley returned. "I swear, I never expected to see you again. Are you back for good or just a visit?" The last time he saw Sonny was when they were on their way back from Texarkana. Sonny had left him and Possum to escort pretty young Penny Denson and her brother to their farm on the Sulphur River.

"I'm back for good," Sonny answered. "You know there ain't no way I could ever be a farmer."

"The way the sparks were flyin' between you and that young girl, I thought love conquers all, even walkin' behind a plow," Perley commented. "She was hangin' on you like a new pair of curtains on the window."

"I reckon I thought so, too," Sonny confessed. "And things was lookin' pretty good there till the feller she's engaged to marry came to supper the next night after we got back. She introduced me as her brother, Art's, new friend. I started back to the Triple-G the next day. End of story."

"Sonny, you're better off in the long run," Fred told him. "You'da missed all this good companionship you get at the Triple-G."

"The mistake you made was goin' back to that farm with her and her brother," Possum remarked. "If you was so danged struck by her, you shoulda just picked her up and run off with her."

"Now, there's some good advice," Perley declared sarcastically. "What would you do with a wife right now, anyway? You're better off without the responsibility."

"I reckon that could apply to everybody settin' here," Possum said.

The remark was not lost on Perley. He knew it was aimed at him, and Possum wasn't buying the story he'd told about coming back early to give Becky some rest.

Chapter 3

They started out right after breakfast the next day, each man leading a packhorse, since they weren't really sure how long they might be gone. Their path was to be directly south, so the first portion of their trip was a short eight miles to the town of Paris and a stop at Henderson's General Store to pick up the supplies they needed for the four to five days they anticipated they would be gone. They didn't waste much time because they knew what they needed to survive on their own cooking. After Perley paid Ben Henderson, Possum asked him if he wanted to stop by the hotel dining room for a quick visit with Becky.

"No, reckon not," Perley said. "I expect they're still pretty busy with the breakfast customers, and we've already killed some time gettin' on the trail to Sulphur Springs."

Possum didn't respond for a few seconds while he studied Perley with a suspicious eye. Then he asked, "When are you gonna tell me what's goin' on between you and Becky? Or should I say what ain't goin' on?"

Perley knew he was going to have to tell Possum sooner or later, so he decided to go ahead and get it over with. "I think we were movin' too fast, and Becky needs to give herself time to think it over a little more."

"What?" Possum exclaimed. "She ain't thought about nothin' but marryin' you for at least the past two years."

"Something happened yesterday in the dinin' room that got her upset, and I expect it made her wanna think about what she might be gettin' into. I can't really blame her. It shook me up a little bit, too."

"What happened?" Possum asked. "Somebody japin' you about your name?"

"Yeah, you know how they like to get on me about it. Well, these two fellows got kinda nasty about it, and one of 'em challenged me to a shoot-out." He went on to tell Possum that he was ultimately given no choice but to face the man.

"Are you tellin' me you shot two men yesterday in front of the dinin' room? Killed one of 'em and wounded the other'n, and you ain't said a mumbly word about it till now?"

"The subject never came up till now," Perley answered.

"I swear, if you ain't the damnedest . . . !" Possum exclaimed, scarcely able to believe Perley hadn't seen fit to even mention it. "Who were they?"

"You know, in all the excitement goin' on, I never got around to askin' their names," Perley said with a generous helping of sarcasm. "Two drifters passin' through on their way to the Nations is all I know."

"I knew I shoulda come into town with you yesterday," Possum fretted. "I don't wonder that Becky was shook up." He tried to picture the altercation in his mind. "Did she see you shoot those two fellers?"

"I think so," Perley said, "but I can't say for sure."

"That's bad," Possum declared.

"Well, what happened, happened, and I couldn't stop it yesterday," Perley said. "And I sure can't change it now, so I reckon it'll be up to Becky to decide. I can't hold it against her if she calls it off."

"Hell, you ain't ready to get married, anyway," Possum decided. "Let's get started to that ranch. I can't believe there's a ranch of any size where this Weber spread is supposed to be located. Rubin said it wasn't far from Sulphur Springs. Southwest of the town is what he told me. He said a while back a couple of families was tryin' to start a little settlement there and hopin' to build a church. But the last time I was down that way, there weren't much of anything left of that little settlement. A couple of empty houses, that was about all there was."

"But that was back in biblical times," Perley joked. "I expect a lot has changed since you were there. Maybe this fellow Weber wanted to be near Sulphur Springs."

Leaving Paris, they followed a commonly used wagon road between the towns of Paris and Sulphur Springs. After a ride of approximately fifteen miles, they struck the north fork of the Sulphur River at a little after noon and decided to rest the horses there. Considering the time it took to make the ride from the Triple-G to Paris, added to the time spent in Henderson's store, they were ready to eat something, too. So Perley got a fire going while Possum unwrapped the slab of bacon they had purchased at the store and started slicing strips to cook over Perley's fire. "It's taking these little trips like this that causes me to get a hankerin' for Ollie Dinkler's grub," Possum declared. "At least we'd have some beans and biscuits to go with this bacon."

"We'll stop in Sulphur Springs long enough to buy us a meal," Perley said. "We ought to get there somewhere around mealtime tomorrow."

While the horses grazed beside the river, Perley and Possum ate their dinner of bacon and slapjacks and washed it down with strong coffee. They decided they would rest the horses again when they reached the south fork of the Sulphur River, which was only about ten miles farther. Then they would decide whether to go on a little farther before making camp, or camp there by the river. Since the horses were going to get a rest again after another ten miles, they increased their pace a little, alternating between a walk and a trot. The result was the sighting of the trees outlining the river in the distance after less than an hour and a half. "Yonder's the river," Possum announced. "Looks like somebody's already campin' there."

"Right where the two trails meet," Perley said, referring to the east-west trail that followed the river. Two covered wagons looked to be parked about where that trail crossed the one he and Possum were following. Thinking it was probably two families heading for Dallas or Fort Worth, he said, "I expect we'll ride a-ways upriver to rest our horses."

As they approached a little closer they realized that one of the wagons appeared to have a broken wheel. "Uh-oh," Possum said. "They've got some trouble there. Reckon we oughta check on 'em? I don't see no men around. Do you?"

"No, I don't," Perley replied. "Looks like four or five women down near the water with the horses, but I don't see any men. I expect we'd better stop."

The party of five women weren't aware they had company until Perley and Possum rode past their wagons and came down to the water. Their reaction at seeing the two men was one of alarm at first, and four of them quickly gathered behind one formidable-looking woman dressed in a pair of men's pants and wearing a pistol. "Looks like you've had a little bad luck," Perley said in greeting. "Mind if we step down? We were planning to water our horses here, but we can ride on up the river a-ways if that would suit you better."

"Don't make no difference to us," the woman said. "Water 'em here, if you want to."

Perley and Possum stepped down. "Where are your menfolk?" Possum asked. "Gone to Sulphur Springs to get another wheel?" He asked the question, knowing that, if that were the case, they would have jacked the wagon up, removed the broken wheel, and taken it to town to get it fixed.

"Yeah," the woman replied. "They went to get a new wheel. I expect they'll be back any minute now."

Perley looked at Possum and gave him a slight shake of his head. Then he turned back to the woman and said, "Ma'am, you ladies don't have to be afraid of us. We're not gonna cause you any problems. By the look of that fire you've got goin', I'd say you've been stuck here with that broke wheel for at least two days, and you're gonna stay stuck here till that wheel gets fixed." Having had a chance to get a look at the other women with her, he felt safe in saying, "There ain't no men with you. Where are you headin'?"

She smiled and said, "Saw right through me, didn't ya? You're right, it's just us girls and we're headin' for Nacogdoches. I've got a friend there who's build a new saloon, and he wrote me to come help him run it."

Perley and Possum exchanged a quick look of puzzlement. "If you keep traveling in the direction your wagons are pointed, you might eventually see Dallas, but you ain't never gonna see Nacogdoches." When that caused her to blink, he said, "You're close to a hundred and fifty miles from Nacogdoches, and it's that way." He pointed south. "It's not that way." He pointed west. "Where did you start out from?"

"Well . . ." She hesitated. "That's kind of complicated. This trip, we started out from Texarkana."

"Texarkana?" Possum interrupted. "Do you know this river you're followin' is the Sulphur?"

"We were pretty sure it was," she answered. "And that's another part of the story. You sure you wanna hear the whole story?"

"You got me hooked," Possum said. "I know I wanna hear how you wound up here on the way to Nacogdoches."

"Might as well start at the beginning," she said.

Perley could see that it was going to be quite lengthy, so he interrupted. "It looks like we're gonna camp here tonight, so we'd best take care of our horses first, then we'll be better listeners."

They unloaded their horses and set up their camp a little way up the river from the wagons. While they were doing that, Perley and Possum talked over the situation they had ridden into. "They ain't goin' anywhere until that wheel gets fixed," Perley said.

"That's a fact," Possum replied. "I wonder

how many people have passed by here since those women have been broke down. Looks like we're gonna be the ones who have to help." Neither of them said it, but both were thinking that Perley had found another cow pie to step in.

Perley looked around at the abundance of trees. "They stopped at a good spot for wood to make spokes," he said. "I know how to fix a wheel, but I ain't ever done it."

"Well, I have," Possum said, "but it's a helluva job. I wonder if they've got any tools in those wagons."

When they went back to the wagons, the woman who was obviously the boss lady asked them if they could fix the broken wheel. "Yes, ma'am, we can," Possum answered her. "But it ain't an easy job, and it'll take a little time."

"I can pay you for fixin' it, if you don't charge too much," she said.

"Tell you what," Perley said. "Why don't we take it out in trade?" When she turned to grin at the other women, he quickly explained. "We'll fix your wheel if you'll do the cookin' while we're here. We can provide some cookin' supplies."

"There ain't no problem there," she said at once. "We've got plenty of supplies. That's one of the reasons we couldn't ride on off and leave the broke-down wagon. We couldn't get all our stuff in one wagon. So that's a deal. You fix that wheel so we can move that wagon, and we'll fix the meals for you. Since we're gonna be campin' together, I think we oughta get to know who we're campin' with. Gather around again, girls." When the women lined up beside her she introduced everybody, starting with herself. "I'm Elmira Miller. This young one here is my daughter, Junie. Next to Junie, with the curly red hair, is Ruby. Then comes Viola, with the gap between her front teeth. Smile, Viola, and show 'em that gap. Last, but you can see not least, is Nellie. Ruby, Viola, and Nellie are all workin' girls. My daughter, Junie, ain't in the business. Now, who do we have the pleasure of dining with?"

"I'm Perley and he's Possum," Perley answered.

"Two P's outta the same pod, huh?" Elmira asked.

"Some folks think so, don't they, Possum?"

"I expect so," Possum answered, but his mind was already on the broken wheel. "You know, Elmira, we didn't come with workin' on a wagon wheel in mind. Have you got any tools in those wagons?"

"I know there's a box on the underside of both wagons that's supposed to hold tools, but I ain't never had any reason to look in it," she answered.

"Like I said, it's gonna be a job fixin' that wheel," Possum told her. "It's gonna take some time. We have to make new spokes, so we're gonna need a saw and a chisel. We've got a small axe, but we're gonna need something like a hammer to tap those spokes in the hub. We'll look in the toolboxes and maybe we'll be lucky."

Nellie Butcher turned out to be the cook of this outfit of soiled doves. She fixed a fine supper that included biscuits baked in an oven she fashioned in the bank of the river. While they ate, Elmira continued the story of what brought them to their predicament. "Like I started to tell you, we came here from Texarkana, but that's not where the story starts. . . .

"I owned a saloon and dance hall in Shreveport for six years, and I sold it when I got a good offer for it. I got this letter from an old friend of mine who built a new saloon in Nacogdoches. He wanted me to come help him run it. But I heard that the town of Texarkana was booming, and I might be missin' a big opportunity there. Nellie will tell you, people in Shreveport were sayin' that was the place to go 'cause the railroad was gonna put it on the map."

"That's what they were sayin'," Nellie confirmed.

"And I'd never heard of Nacogdoches," Elmira continued. "So we decided to check on the rumors. Ruby and Viola wanted to go with us, so I bought another wagon, and we drove sixty-five miles north to Texarkana. And that was a big mistake. That town wasn't nowhere near ready for a new saloon and dance hall. So that's where I made my biggest mistake. I met a fellow up there named Otis Welker who said he knew where Nacogdoches was, and he'd lead us there for fifty dollars and a roll under the covers with one of the girls every other night."

"He didn't have no more idea where Nacogdoches was than we did," Nellie remarked.

"That's right," Elmira said. "We rode into Texas a little way, and we came to this river. Otis said Nacogdoches was on this river, and he was gonna leave us because all we had to do was follow the river."

"So he just rode off and left you?" Perley asked. "Was that before or after you broke the wheel on the wagon?"

"That was before. No, he said he was gonna leave, but he didn't," Elmira said.

"That's his paint horse over yonder, with the others."

"He's still around somewhere?"

"No, he ain't around here. He's dead. We left him at the last place we stopped before we broke that damn wheel."

"Dead?" Possum reacted. "What happened to him?"

"I shot his sorry ass," Elmira answered.

"For runnin' out on you?" Possum asked.

"No, for not runnin' out like he said he was. That low-down dog sneaked back that night and attacked my thirteen-year-old daughter when she went to the bushes to relieve herself. He deflowered my baby. He was always eyein' her every chance he got." She looked over at Junie, and the young girl hung her head, ashamed. "It ain't no fault of yours, honey. I cleaned your slate when I shot him. It's the same as if it never happened."

"That's a fact, honey. You're as good as new," Viola said, and put her arm around Junie, whose chin was still resting on her breast.

It was difficult to know what to say after hearing Elmira's brazenly frank accounting for the fate of one Otis Welker, so neither Perley nor Possum felt the urge to offer any comment. The conversation returned immediately to the subject of repairing the wagon wheel, and the women followed Perley and Possum when they went to inspect the wheel close up. "It's a good thing you didn't try to drive it on that wheel," Possum said. "The iron rim still looks in pretty good shape, but we still might have to chop up some of those spokes that ain't broke, just so we can get the rim off." He looked at Perley and shook his head. "I expect we'd best pick us out the right size pine to jack that wheel off the ground and cut it down tonight, while we've still got some daylight left. We'll be workin' on that wheel all day tomorrow."

"I reckon you're right," Perley said. "We'll look in those toolboxes and see if there's a better axe in one of 'em." He was really thinking about the envelope with the money and the contract in his saddlebag and wondering how long they were going to be delayed in delivering them.

Possum gave him a curious look and asked, "Why don't we just use the one hangin' on the side of the wagon?"

Perley chuckled, embarrassed to have made a remark while his mind was elsewhere. "Yeah, I reckon that would work just as well. We'll still take a look inside the toolboxes to see if there's a good saw and maybe a chisel and a hammer, 'cause we're gonna need 'em."

Luck was with them when they opened the toolboxes, so they felt sure they could build a good enough wheel to make it to Sulphur Springs, which was about sixteen miles from there. Then the women could have the blacksmith make them a permanent wheel. They picked out a tall young pine tree to use as a lever for their jack and cut it down with the bow saw they found in one of the toolboxes. The base of the trunk was large enough to use as a fulcrum when three pieces were sawed off to be stacked like a pyramid. The next task was to find wood for the spokes of the wheel. There was no hickory, which would have been best, but there were some small oak trees, which would be second best. They worked until it was too dark to see, cutting small trees and limbs from larger ones. When they finally stopped for the night, they felt they were ready to start making new spokes first thing in the morning. Then Viola came to say they had made a pot of coffee to go with some corn cakes, and she invited the men to join them. When Possum told her that was to his liking, she smiled and showed them her gap. They followed her back to their campfire.

"What time do you want your breakfast in

the morning?" Nellie asked.

"Just whenever you have yours," Perley answered. "It doesn't make that much difference to us. Right, Possum?"

"That's right," Possum said. "We'll most likely get at it as soon as we can see what we're doin'. To start with, we'll be down the river a little ways, where that patch of oak trees is, so if we're early, maybe we won't make enough noise to bother you ladies from your beauty rest."

"I declare, we sure were lucky when you two came along," Ruby said. "Viola and I were talkin', and we don't know how you boys are fixed for money. But if you've got a hankerin' to chase the rabbit, there won't be no charge for it."

" 'Preciate the kind offer, ma'am," Possum replied. "But I'm too old and Perley's made a promise, so we won't be botherin' you nice ladies. And we can all get a good night's sleep. We've got a lotta work to get done tomorrow."

Chapter 4

Perley and Possum were up at first light the next morning, took a few minutes to put some wood on the women's fire, then went downriver to the oak trees they had talked about before. To begin with they concentrated on the size and general length of the limbs they cut to be whittled down to exact size using one of the original spokes as a pattern. "We'll use the rest of this oak to build that fire up good and hot when we're ready for the rim," Possum said.

They had enough pieces of oak to complete the wheel by the time they saw the women getting up, so they went back to the wagons and dumped their wood on the ground. "Is there some way we can help?" Elmira asked.

"Yes, ma'am," Perley answered, "just as soon as we put these three pine chunks in place." He and Possum placed two of the thick sections under the axle, then put the third on top of them. After making sure they were solid and not going to move, they brought the rest of the long pine they had cut the night before and laid one end across the three chunks. It just barely fit under the wagon, but they didn't have to raise it much to clear the wheel. "All right, ladies, help me raise the wagon so Possum can pull that wheel off the axle." The women eagerly rushed to help, and when they all put their weight on the end of the pole, they lifted the wagon up enough to free the wheel. Possum didn't waste any time in removing the broken wheel from the axle. Then Perley told the women, one by one, to let go of the pole letting the wagon drop slowly down again until the axle was supported by the pine fulcrum.

"That don't look like it's goin' anywhere," Possum declared, and laid the wheel on the ground to remove the broken pieces of spokes. There were still enough unbroken spokes to make the removal of the iron rim difficult, so a couple more good spokes had to be broken before Possum managed to get the rim off. Once the rim was off, he pulled one more of the good spokes out of the hub to be used as the pattern. "Now, we gotta skin the bark off these oak pieces and whittle 'em down to look just like this one, especially this end that fits into the hub."

In the toolboxes under each wagon they had found a couple of chisels, one mallet-type hammer, and a hatchet, so they started chiseling away the bark from the oak. "Shoot," Ruby exclaimed, "I can do that." She went to the wagon and came back with a sharp knife. Then she picked up one of the limbs and started whittling the bark away. Not to be outdone, Viola followed her lead, while Nellie and Elmira started preparing breakfast. Junie was left to fret because she didn't know what to do to help.

"You can help me cut these to the right length," Perley said, holding up one of the new spokes. "We've gotta cut each one of the new ones the same length as this pattern, but we need to find a better place to cut 'em, something flat to hold 'em to."

"I know where," Junie said. "Come on!" She ran around to the back of the wagon and climbed up in it. She pulled a wooden chest around sideways, and when Perley followed her, she put the sawn end of the oak against the flat side of the chest. "Gimme the pattern," she said, and when he did, she held the end of it against the chest beside the piece to be cut.

"Perfect," Perley said, and cut the new spoke off at exactly the same length as the pattern. By the time Nellie announced that breakfast was ready, half of the new spokes were cut to length. The wagon wheel crew went back to work after breakfast, and before it was time to even start thinking about dinner, all the spokes were cut to size and ready for the important step in the process: fitting the ends into the hub. That was a little more precise, and consequently, slower work. Here again the women proved to be adept at the task. When that was all done, Possum found a flat place on the ground and dug a small hole for the hub to fit in so the wheel would lie flat on the ground. Anticipating a critical part in the process, Perley was building up the fire and placing some large pieces of oak in the middle of it.

After Possum laid the wheel on the ground, he took the iron rim and placed it carefully on top of the wheel. "Uh-oh," Elmira uttered. "We messed up. It's too big for the rim to fit." She was right; the iron rim laid on top of the spokes, just a little too small to slide down over the ends.

"Looks perfect to me," Perley said to Possum. Possum agreed. He picked up the rim again and took it to the fire. This was the part that the two of them were concerned about. The best tools they could find for the final stage of the repair was two shovels. "Let's see how we're gonna do at this," Perley said. Possum dropped the rim on the ground, then he and Perley got on opposite sides of it. They slipped the shovels under the edge of the rim and very carefully picked it up, holding the shovel handle as far from the blade as they could. Then, moving ever so slowly, so as not to let the rim slide off their shovels, they walked it over and lowered it in the middle of the fire, then withdrew their shovels.

"Whaddaya say we let the ladies take it outta the fire when it's ready?" Possum joked. There was nothing to do now but wait for the fire to expand the rim. Everyone gathered around to watch. After close to half an hour, Possum decided it was time to try it. "You ready?" he asked Perley, and Perley nodded. They stood on opposite sides of the fire with their shovels and picked the rim up again, this time even more carefully. Careful to keep the rim level on the two shovels, they inched slowly over to the wheel on the ground and laid the hot rim down on the spokes. Using the hammer and the hatchet, they tapped the rim into position until it slid down over the ends of the spokes, some of which were scorching and smoking from the hot iron. A couple of little flames erupted on two of the spokes before they got the rim down evenly all the way around. Then Possum poured one bucket of water he had ready on the wheel, went back down to the water's edge and refilled the bucket and dumped that on the wheel. As the iron rim cooled, it tightened around the spokes, holding them securely in place.

"Well, if that ain't something," Elmira declared as she stood looking at the finished repair. "I gotta admit, I thought you were gonna end up with some god-awful creation, and I thought it was gonna take a helluva lot longer."

"That's because we had so much help," Possum said. "Otherwise, it woulda took a helluva lot longer. We'll let it cool all the way down before we put it back on your wagon. It oughta work all right for you, but there's a blacksmith in Sulphur Springs. You might feel better if you have him take a look at it. That ain't but about sixteen miles south of here, and it's the direction you oughta be headin' in, if you really wanna go to Nacogdoches."

"Do you know how to get to Nacogdoches?" Elmira asked.

"Yes, ma'am, I do," Possum answered. "And I know what you're thinkin', but Perley and me are headin' somewhere on business, and we're gonna have to take care of that. We'll be glad to tell you how to get there."

"I'd be willing to pay you," she insisted. "Both of you, fifty dollars, and we'd feed you, just like today."

"I'm just as sorry as I can be," Possum said. "But Perley ain't gonna do it. It's his family's business we're on, so he's got to do that."

"Let him take care of the family business and you take us to Nacogdoches," she persisted. "Can't he handle it by himself? He seems pretty capable."

"I'm afraid he needs me with him," Possum pleaded. "Besides, I work for his family, and if we don't get back when we're supposed to, I might find myself on the grub line."

"I wouldn't have even asked you, but I know what kind of men you and Perley are. The kind that wouldn't run off and desert five helpless women in the middle of who knows where we are."

"Ah, you ain't fightin' fair now," Possum complained. "We just can't do it right now. Talk to Perley." He called to Perley, who was standing on the other side of the fire. "Perley! Come talk to Elmira."

Preparing to start all over, Elmira gave

Perley a big friendly smile when he walked over to them. "Possum and Perley," she pronounced, "I can't tell you how much I appreciate you two coming to our rescue when we were in such trouble. I don't even know your last names."

"Well, that's not important, anyway," Perley said. "Remember Possum. His last name's Smith. That's easy to remember, Possum Smith."

"What's yours?" Elmira asked.

"Gates," he answered very quickly, hoping to move on before she started repeating it.

"Possum Smith and Perley Gates," she said, then paused when it struck her. Her lips parted in a wide smile. "Perley Gates," she repeated. "I knew it! Is it spelled P-e-a-r-l-y?"

"No, ma'am, it's spelled P-e-r-l-e-y, and it ain't got nothin' to do with the Pearly Gates up in heaven."

"Maybe not to you," she said, "but it does to me. I was in a terrible fix and heading into more trouble. I needed a miracle, and up you popped. You can't tell me that it was all a coincidence. Somebody up above sent you and Possum to rescue me and my girls."

"You really believe that?" Perley exclaimed in frustration. "And right after you just shot a man dead?"

"Otis Welker?" she replied. "He was an evil man who needed killing. I think maybe you were my reward for riddin' the world of Otis Welker. And now, you're gonna lead me and my girls to Nacogdoches."

"Say what?" He turned to look at Possum. "Possum . . . ?"

"Don't look at me," Possum replied. "I told her we can't go to Nacogdoches. We've got important papers to deliver for the Triple-G."

Perley turned back to face Elmira. "That's right, what Possum said: We've got to deliver some important papers. We'll put your wheel back on and head you in the right direction to Tyler, and when you get to Tyler, anybody there can show you the road to Nacogdoches." He knew it wasn't quite that simple, but someone would probably tell her how to get there.

"How far is Tyler from Sulphur Springs?" Elmira asked.

"About fifty miles, I'd say," Perley looked at Possum "Wouldn't you say?"

"That's about right," Possum confirmed. "Two and a half, three days, you oughta get there by then."

"How far is Nacogdoches from Tyler?" Elmira asked then.

"Nacogdoches . . ." Possum repeated. "We

ain't been down that way for quite a spell, but I'd have to say it's a little farther than from Sulphur Springs to Tyler. Maybe about sixty-five or seventy miles," he speculated. "But like Perley said, somebody in Tyler could probably tell you better."

It was obvious that their answers to Elmira's questions were nothing less than upsetting to the five women gathered around the two Samaritans. Ruby and Viola began to fret about their decision to leave Shreveport in the first place, fearing that they would perish in the Texas wilderness. "Don't despair, girls," Elmira said. "Maybe there'll be some other Good Samaritan that'll hear our prayers for help."

Possum looked at Perley, already worried about the expression he could see on his young friend's face. He was afraid if he heard much more of that kind of talk, he was going to commit the two of them to something he definitely did not want. He was too late, however. Perley swallowed the bait. "Well Possum and I won't leave you right away. We'll go to Sulphur Springs with you, and to the blacksmith to make sure you've got a good wheel on your wagon. Then we might be able to go a-ways with you south of there, till I have to go see a fellow named George Weber. After I get the business done we came down this way for, we'll see if we can help you get started in the right direction."

"Anybody gonna eat this mess I fixed?" Nellie interrupted. "Iron rim ain't the only thing cookin' on this fire."

"That's a good idea," Possum said. "Everybody fill your bellies up and after dinner you can lift that wagon up again, and I'll put the wheel on. I wanna eat first 'cause if that wheel don't work, you might quit feedin' me and Perley."

"Not a chance," Elmira told him, and gave him another big smile. "You came to take care of us, so we're gonna take care of you."

Possum cringed and thought, *You just ain't gonna give up, are you?* They had already lost a day's travel by fixing the wagon wheel. And they were going to lose another by going to Sulphur Springs with the wagons. He was afraid that Rubin and John, Perley's older brothers, might think something terrible happened to them and send somebody to look for them. *Well, ain't no different than usual,* he told himself.

When Possum decided the iron rim was totally cold and had shrunk back all it was going to, they raised the wagon again, and he put the wheel back on. It performed just like the original. So they decided to go ahead and pack up and start out for Sulphur Springs that afternoon, hoping to find a spot to camp after about eight miles. That would put them in town around midday the following day. Perley planned to stop in the post office there to see if he could get directions to George Weber's ranch. If they weren't sure in the post office, he thought the sheriff might tell him how to find Weber. He planned to do that while the women were at the blacksmith.

The first part of the trip worked out all right because they came upon a nice little creek about halfway to Sulphur Springs and made their camp there for the night. The women were accustomed to having breakfast before they started out for the day, but they still arrived in the town before noon, in time to catch Wyatt Jordan before he went to dinner. He took a look at Possum and Perley's handiwork and pronounced it a first-rate job. "It's hard to say how that wheel will hold up. It looks pretty good to me. If you folks got a-ways to go yet, you might wanna buy a little insurance. I sell wagon wheels that size. I make 'em myself, and I keep four of 'em on hand. I could put a new wheel on that wagon, and you could keep the one you just fixed in case you broke another one.

Whaddaya say?"

"That sounds like a good idea to me, but you'll have to talk to the lady about it," Perley replied. "She owns the wagons. My partner and I just happened to come up on 'em back at the south fork of the Sulphur River, where they broke that wheel." When Jordan turned and looked at the women out by the two wagons, Perley said, "She's the one wearin' a handgun. She'll talk business with you.

"Do you know a fellow named George Weber?" Perley asked then. "He owns a cattle ranch somewhere south of here." Jordan said that he wasn't familiar with the name, so Perley called to Elmira. "Come talk to Mr. Jordan. He's got a suggestion you might be interested in."

When Elmira heard the blacksmith's suggestion, she accepted it at once — so quickly, in fact, that Perley had to chuckle. She was evidently not that confident in a wheel that he and Possum had made out of some tree limbs. This in spite of Wyatt Jordan's praise for the job. He could hardly blame her. "While you're waitin' for your wagon to be fixed, I'm going to the post office," Perley told her. "Possum will probably go with me 'cause that's what he does. But we'll be back. All right?"

"All right," she said, "but I'm counting on you."

"We'll be back," he repeated. "Our packhorses are tied to the back of your wagon."

"Oh, that's right." She grinned.

Perley went back to the horses and climbed up on Buck. As he expected, Possum climbed on Dancer and asked, "Where we goin'?"

"I'm just goin' to the post office to get some directions to Weber's ranch, I hope. You don't have to go with me, if you'd rather stay here."

"I'll go with you," Possum said, "in case you get in trouble."

"I'm just goin' to the post office," Perley insisted. "How could I get in trouble?"

"You'd find a way to get in trouble if you was goin' to church," Possum replied.

They started out at a trot toward the stores a short distance from the stable and the blacksmith shop, slowing to a walk when they reached the sheriff's office. "Post office is farther up the street," Perley said, "but we might as well ask the sheriff. He oughta know how to get to Weber's." So they pulled up before the sheriff's office and dismounted. "Virgil Cooper," Perley said aloud, recalling the sheriff's name while he looped Buck's reins over the hitching rail.

He had never had occasion to personally meet the sheriff, but he was familiar with the name.

Sheriff Cooper was sitting on the corner of his desk drinking a cup of coffee when they walked in. He took a quick look at each of them, obviously strangers, before asking, "Somethin' I can do for you fellers?"

"Yes, sir," Perley answered. "I'm hopin' you can tell me how to find a rancher near here named George Weber."

Cooper gave them another look. "Whaddaya lookin' for George Weber for?"

"My name is Gates," Perley said. "I'm from the Triple-G Ranch, north of Paris. We're buyin' fifty head of Hereford cows from Mr. Weber, and I'm takin' him the bill of sale to sign. We ain't ever been to his place, so I don't know how to get there."

"The Triple-G," Cooper said. "That's the Gates brothers' outfit, right?"

"Right," Perley replied. "The three Gates brothers."

"Which Gates are you?"

"Perley. I'm the youngest, that's why I'm the one ridin' around lookin' for places we don't know how to find."

"Perley Gates," Cooper said. "You're the one with the name like you came from Saint Peter with a fast draw like a streak of lightning, right?"

"Oh, I don't know about that," Perley stumbled. "I wouldn't know who woulda spread something like that around."

"Hot damn!" Cooper exclaimed, seemingly delighted by Perley's embarrassment. "You're just like they said." He grinned then and looked at Possum. "And who might you be?"

"Possum Smith, Sheriff," he said, and stepped forward to shake Cooper's hand. "I'm Perley's partner, and if I had to guess, I'd say you heard about some face-off Perley was in from somebody who actually saw it."

"As a matter of fact," Cooper replied. "The fellow that told me is a Baptist preacher down in Bison Gap. Name's Harvey Poole, my wife's brother. He saw you gun down a feller named Quirt somethin'."

"That was a while back," Possum said.

"He didn't give me any choice," Perley said. "There was no cause for it." His honest reaction was distress that someone outside Bison Gap knew about it. "Can you tell us how to find the Weber Ranch?" he asked, anxious to change the subject.

"Sure can," Cooper answered. "It's easy enough to find. You know the trail you rode in on from Paris goes straight out the other end of town to Tyler, right?" Perley nodded yes. "Well, you take that road outta town, and you'll come to a sizable creek in about three miles. There's a trail off to the right, follows the creek all the way to Weber's place, about four and a half miles. Shouldn't have any trouble finding it."

"Much obliged, Sheriff," Perley said. "We'll get outta your way now."

"No trouble at all," Cooper said. He held his coffee cup up toward them. "You can see what I was busy doin' when you came in. Now, I'm thinkin' about goin' to get me some dinner. Come along with me if you're ready for dinner. I'm partial to a little eatin' place up near the bank. Varner's Vittles, that's what they call it. Feller named Jake Varner owns it, and it's his wife, Polly, who does the cookin'. It'll be my treat. Whaddaya say?"

"That surely appeals to my appetite," Perley said. "But Possum and I kinda got ourselves hung up with a party of workin' gals — two wagons of 'em. That sounds like a lot, but there ain't but four and a young girl." He saw the sheriff's expression turn from one of amusement to one of concern. So Perley quickly explained how he and Possum happened to become involved, summing it up by saying, "They won't be in

Sulphur Springs any longer than it takes Wyatt Jordan to put a new wheel on that wagon. Then they're headin' to Nacogdoches. Possum and I will take 'em on out of your town and put 'em on the road to Tyler. And we hope that's the last we see of 'em. Thanks for the invitation to join you for dinner, but I reckon we'd best get back to the blacksmith."

"Well, I was glad to meet you, Perley. You too, Possum. Stop by when you're back in town." He chuckled and added, "When you ain't with your whores."

"We might do that," Perley said. "I'd like to try that Varner's Vittles."

70

Chapter 5

Elmira looked relieved when they returned to the blacksmith's shop. "He's all done with my new wheel," she said. "Right now, he's fixin' me a couple of hooks on the bottom of one of the wagons to carry my spare wheel that you and Possum made."

"Good," Perley said. "You oughta be ready to roll pretty quick then. I expect you ladies are thinkin' about findin' you a good spot to rest your horses and cook a little dinner."

"As a matter of fact," Nellie said, having overheard his comment.

"If you can wait for another three miles, I might know a good spot for you. The sheriff just told me about a creek three miles south of here on the Tyler road. Since that's right on the way all of us are headin', Possum and I'll go down there with you. There's a trail headin' west at that spot that'll take Possum and me to the ranch we have to go to, and you'll be on the road to Tyler, and that's on your way to Nacogdoches."

Neither Nellie nor Elmira seemed especially excited about that, but it was thirteen-year-old Junie who put it into words for him. "Mama wants you to take us all the way to Nacogdoches."

"I'm aware of that, Junie," Perley tried to explain. "But you see, Possum and I ain't just free to go where we please. We've got responsibilities back at the Triple-G Ranch. We have to deliver some official papers to a ranch here, and then we have to get back to work at the Triple-G. We've got people dependin' on us." He could see the disappointment in the young girl's face, but he didn't know what else to tell her. Still, he tried. "You're headin' in the right direction now. You ain't lost anymore, and accordin' to what your mama says, you've got somebody waitin' for you in Nacogdoches. Nothin' to worry about."

He glanced from Junie to her mother's face, looking for help, but Elmira remarked, "What she said."

He exaggerated a shrug of his shoulders and said, "I expect we'd best get started. Are you gonna need to buy any more supplies before you leave Sulphur Springs?"

"No, I think we're fixed pretty good till we get to Tyler, anyway, even if you and

Possum were to change your mind and take a little ride with us," Elmira said. "So as soon as Mr. Jordan gives me my bill, we'll go find that creek and cook some dinner."

They pulled out of Sulphur Springs with Perley and Possum in the lead, their packhorses behind them, and the two wagons following after the packhorses. Otis Welker's paint gelding on a rope trailing behind Elmira's wagon served as testimony to the woman's resolve. As they walked their horses along the street, Perley called Possum's attention to a small building wedged in between the hardware store and a saloon. "That's where Sheriff Cooper went," he said. Then he read the name on the small sign over the door. "Varner's Vittles. I like the sound of it."

"Maybe we'll try it out, if the timing's right on our way back, after we see Weber," Possum replied.

"You know Elmira's gonna try to get us to eat with them when we get to that creek," Perley said. "But I'd rather go straight to Weber's. That woman just doesn't take no for an answer."

"Even sicced the young'un after you, didn't she?" Possum said and chuckled.

"Do you really think that? She seemed

sincere to me, like she was worried about her mama and herself. I don't think Elmira put her up to it."

"I swear, Perley, that's the reason it's important for me to go with you on things like this. You trust too many folks."

"I reckon I oughta be more like you," Perley countered, "and trust nobody."

"Help you live longer," Possum maintained.

They rode on out the Tyler road until reaching the creek the sheriff had described after close to three miles. It was a nice little creek bordered by small oaks and clumps of willows. The women pulled their wagons up parallel to each other, leaving plenty of room for a fire to be built between them. Perley and Possum declined the invitation to eat with them, giving as their reason a desire not to arrive at the ranch too late in the afternoon. As the women watched the two ride off up the creek, Elmira said, "We're gonna wait right here till they come back; I don't care how long they're gone."

"Hell, Elmira," Nellie insisted, "they flat-out ain't gonna go with us to Nacogdoches. We ain't gonna see 'em no more, and you know it. They won't come back this way. They'll just cut across and strike this road somewhere between here and Sulphur

Springs. And you know you can't really blame 'em. You can't expect a couple of strangers to happen along and just up and decide to take us a hundred miles."

"I can't really argue with you about that, but I just wanna wait to see if they come back this way. If they do, I think it'll be because they do give a damn about whether we get to Nacogdoches or not." She shrugged. "That's all I'm sayin'. They're a strange pair. Sometimes strange things happen."

Nellie shook her head in disagreement. "Well, whatever — let's get a fire goin', so I can cook somethin' to eat."

Four and a half miles west of the two wagons, Perley and Possum spotted the barn and ranch house of George Weber. There was no gate or fencing around the barnyard, only two posts, one on either side of the path, that served as an entrance. On one of the posts, there was a small sign that read, *Lazy-W Ranch*. "Lazy-W," Possum announced. "I reckon that means we're more likely to find Mr. Weber at the house than the barn."

"Maybe so," Perley said. "We'll try the house first." So they rode on into the yard and dismounted at the front steps.

They walked up on the porch and Perley knocked on the door. There was no response right away, so he knocked again, this time much louder. Seconds later, the door opened, and a tall, thin man with streaks of gray in an otherwise dark-brown head of hair and beard stood silently frowning at them. He had a large napkin tied around his neck. Since he said nothing, Perley asked, "George Weber?"

"I'm George Weber," he replied.

"Well, Mr. Weber, it appears we've interrupted your dinner," Perley said, adding together the napkin under Weber's chin and the frown on his face. He couldn't help wondering, however, what good the napkin was doing, since it seemed certain any gravy dripping would be caught by the beard before it reached the napkin. "We can wait and come back a little later, after you've finished your dinner."

"What do you want?" Weber asked abruptly.

"My name's Perley Gates and I wanna give you a thousand dollars."

"What?" Weber responded, confused at first, then, "Gates! You're from the Triple-G, about the cattle!"

"That's right," Perley replied. "I'm Perley Gates and this is Possum Smith. We've brought the money and a bill of sale for you to sign. But we can wait till you finish your dinner. We got a little bit behind with some business in town and didn't realize it was time to eat."

"No, no," Weber insisted. "Come on in the house. Sounds to me like you ain't ate yet. Come on back to the kitchen and my wife will scare up somethin'. I gotta apologize for the way I answered the door. We've had a little trouble with some drifters knockin' on the door at all hours. I thought you mighta been some more of 'em. I got the message from your brother, Rubin," Weber said, getting back to the subject of cattle as he led them down the hallway. "He said you'd be bringin' cash money. I appreciate it. I don't trust the banks no more." He led them into the kitchen where they found a trim little woman, startled to see two strange men behind her husband. "Hon," Weber announced, "these fellows are from the Triple-G, come to pay for the cattle they're buyin', and they ain't ate yet. Fellows, this is my wife, Lydia."

Perley stepped forward and said, "Perley Gates, ma'am. My friend here is Possum Smith, and we didn't expect to pop in on you unannounced, lookin' for dinner. You folks just go right ahead and finish your dinner, and Possum and I'll go back to the parlor and wait till you're done."

"Nonsense!" Lydia responded. "You'll do no such a thing. Set yourselves down at the table. I just baked a big cake of cornbread and a pot of beans. I expect you want coffee. I'll put on a fresh pot."

"That's awfully nice of you, ma'am, but we don't wanna eat up your food," Perley protested. "Just a cup of coffee will do us just fine, won't it, Possum?" He gave Possum a wink.

"Sure will," Possum responded. "We don't wanna put you out none."

"We've got plenty," Lydia insisted, and went to the cupboard to get a couple of plates and cups. "It'll be nice to have some company for a change. I'm not used to anybody for the noon meal. George usually takes dinner with the boys at the bunkhouse. You're just lucky I cooked up plenty of food. Sometimes, he brings Robert Wells with him."

"Robert's my foreman," Weber explained.

"Looks like the lady ain't gonna give us no choice, Possum," Perley joked. "Might as well sit down. I'm gonna go get that envelope outta my saddlebag and bring it in here, just in case Buck gets a notion to run off somewhere."

78

When he came back into the kitchen, Lydia was filling the coffeepot with water. "Never can tell who might come knockin' on your door, can you Mrs. Weber?"

"Call me Lydia," she said. "I ain't that much older than you. You're right about folks knockin' on your door, though — especially recently. Did George tell you about that?"

"I started to," Weber said, "when we were at the door. This past week my men have noticed three riders on three or four occasions, lookin' like they might be scoutin' our herd. We ain't got that big a herd, five hundred and fifty thereabout, and I've got a big enough crew to keep a pretty good watch on 'em if we have to. A couple of days ago, two fellows came knockin' on my front door, wantin' to talk to the owner. Said they might be interested in buyin' some cattle. I wasn't here; I was out with the cattle. Lydia told 'em they could talk to the foreman, and they asked where he was. Well, Lydia didn't like the looks of them, so she was smart enough to tell 'em Robert was right there in the barn with the rest of the men. 'Course he was by himself in the barn. What was it you told 'em, hon?"

"I told 'em all I had to do was to blow the whistle I had in my apron pocket, and they'd come right away," Lydia said. "And I said they'll probably come up here anyway when they see the horses at the front of the house. They said they'd wait and come back another day when they could catch George here." She shook her head slowly, picturing the two men in her mind, and said, "They were mean-lookin' men, and they certainly didn't look like any cattle buyers. One of 'em wore a black hat with what looked like a rattlesnake skin for a hatband. I still get the shivers when I think about 'em. It's the main reason George is eating dinner at the house."

"That's who I thought you and Possum might be when you came knockin' on the door," Weber said with a chuckle. "But we haven't seen any sign of 'em since that day, so I hope they've given up any idea about stealing cattle."

"See there, Possum, it's a good thing you didn't wear your snakeskin hatband today, or we wouldn't be gettin' this fine dinner," Perley joked.

When they finished eating, Lydia cleared away the dishes and poured more coffee. Perley opened the envelope and pulled out the bill of sale Rubin had prepared. "You can read this over, but it's a pretty simple bill of sale that says we gave you one thousand dollars for fifty head of Hereford cattle in prime condition to be delivered to the Triple-G Ranch.

Without waiting to be asked to, Lydia went to the study to get pen and ink. When she came back, Weber signed the papers, and she signed where Rubin had put a line for a witness. Perley took a copy and left one for them and he counted out the stack of one hundreds and fifties. "I don't have any reason not to trust you, so I'm givin' you the money now. Just so I don't have to lie to Rubin, I'd like to ride out and take a look at the cattle I just bought. Can we do that this afternoon?"

"That's a good idea," Weber said. "We've got the whole herd in pretty close to headquarters right now, since this business with those cattle thieves we were tellin' you about. So you can see the condition of the herd. I'm just gonna cut fifty head out and drive 'em up your way. We'll start 'em day after tomorrow. Is that all right?" Perley said that it was. "Good," Weber said, "You can sleep in the bunkhouse tonight, if you want to. There's several empty beds in there."

"That's mighty neighborly of you," Perley said. "We'll do that."

"And I'll expect the three of you for supper tonight," Lydia said.

"Yes, ma'am, whatever you say," Possum said.

"What kinda shape are your horses in?" Weber asked. "Do you need to leave 'em here to rest? We can throw your saddles on a fresh one."

"They really haven't been ridden very far since they were rested," Perley said. "How far will we be ridin' to take a look at our cows?"

"Quarter of a mile, maybe as much as a half mile," Weber estimated. "Like I said, we pulled the herd in pretty close since we spotted those buzzards nosin' around them."

"Our horses will be fine for that short a ride," Possum said. So after Weber put his money away in a safe in his bedroom, the three of them rode out a short way from the headquarters buildings to find the majority of Weber's cattle grazing in a small valley. They could see a couple of his men herding some strays up from a gully to join the main herd.

"I need to move these cows outta this valley," Weber declared, "else they'll have it grazed down to the roots in another day. That's why I'm hopin' those drifters have moved on." He gestured with his arm, sweeping an imaginary arc across the valley. "There they are. When we're ready, I'll just have the boys cut out fifty head and move 'em up to your range."

"They look in pretty good shape, considerin' they ain't got no horns to brag about," Possum remarked.

Weber laughed and replied, "Yeah, but they've got a lot more meat on 'em, and they're a helluva lot easier to lasso than your longhorns."

"Can't argue with that," Perley said. There wasn't really more that he needed to see. The whole herd looked to be in fine condition, so any fifty would be acceptable. They rode around the herd anyway, and Weber signaled one of his cowhands to come to him.

"This is Bill Davis," Weber said when the man pulled up beside them. "Bill, these fellows are from the Triple-G — Perley Gates and Possum Smith." Bill gave them each a howdy, and Weber continued. "Have you seen any sign of those men sneakin' around the cattle?"

"No, sir," Bill answered. "I think they mighta changed their minds about whatever they were thinkin' about doin'. I sent a couple of the boys to ride a wide circle around this whole valley to see if they could run up on 'em. They found an old campsite way down on the south end, but they said it was at least two days old. That's the only sign they could find."

"I expect they decided they wouldn't get very far with a bunch of these cattle before we caught up with 'em," Weber said. "Best keep doublin' up on the night herders for a few more nights, just to be safe."

Most of the rest of the afternoon was spent with Weber's herd, and Perley and Possum met all but a few of Weber's cowhands. They returned to the headquarters wondering why he needed so many for the herd of only five hundred and fifty cows.

Four and a half miles from the Lazy-W Hereford cow ranch, Nellie Butcher walked over close to the creek where Elmira was rinsing out some stockings. "It's time I started fixin' some supper," Nellie said. "You still think those two will come back this way? You want me to cook enough to feed them?"

"Might not be a bad idea," Elmira answered. "I think Perley ain't gonna ride back home without checkin' to see if we're still here. And when he does, it'll give me a chance to work on his conscience some more. We're liable to end up with an escort to Nacogdoches before all's said and done."

"Maybe you think so," Nellie responded,

"but I think there ain't a chance in hell of it." She sighed and said, "But I'll cook extra, so if he does show up, we can feed him before he heads for home."

Elmira was about to disagree with her when they heard Junie call out, "They're comin' back!" She looked up to see her daughter running back to the wagons from a log she had been sitting on close to the east-west trail Perley had left on. "They came back!" Junie gushed excitedly. "I knew they would!"

"I thought they would, too," Elmira said. She gave Nellie a smile and started out toward the road to join Ruby and Viola, who heard Junie yelling and walked out by the road. "They comin' back, huh?"

"Somebody's comin'," Ruby answered, "but it ain't Perley and Possum."

"Oh," Elmira replied, disappointed. "Well, I reckon we'll just wait and see who it is." She looked up the road to see the men approaching. She saw right away that it was not the two she hoped for. There were three riders, not two, and they were each leading a packhorse. "Maybe they're somebody from that ranch they went to. If it is, they can tell us if Perley is still at the ranch." So, they went back to the wagons and waited.

"Are we open for business?" Viola asked.

"I reckon that'll be up to you," Elmira answered, "just like always." She turned to speak to her daughter. "If they stop here, you just get yourself back in the wagon and stay there till they're gone."

"Why, Mama?" Junie asked. "Can't you just tell 'em that I ain't in the business? I wanna hear what they say about Perley."

"I don't know what kind of men they are, so it's just a good idea for you to stay outta sight, in case one of them is as sick in the head as Otis Welker was. You ought to be able to hear what's bein' said from the wagon."

"Yes, ma'am," Junie said, reluctantly.

Chapter 6

"What the hell . . . ?" Snake Dalton drew out when he looked up ahead. "Somebody's set up a camp at the crossroads. There's a couple of wagons pulled over by the creek."

"Damned if it ain't," Luther Rainey said. "Might be worth lookin' into. Maybe a couple of families headin' out for new country with all their possessions and money packed in them wagons." They were in need of a source of easy money. The plan they originally had to make some fell through when they decided the herd of cattle they wanted to raid was too well guarded. Then, when they figured every man on the place was out watching the cattle, Snake and Luther rode up to the house and knocked on the door while Lester hid out in the trees with the packhorses, waiting for his signal. And bad luck jumped up and bit them again. The woman that answered the door said her foreman and all the men were right there in the barn.

When they got closer to the crossroad, Lester Blunt said, "I don't see no men around. I see some women between the wagons by the fire. Wonder where the men are?"

"Let's go find out," Luther said. "Maybe they're back at that ranch guardin' those cattle," he joked.

"Let's just make sure they ain't hidin' out somewhere, hopin' we'll walk in," Snake said. "They might be in the same business we're in." They pulled up even with the wagons, and Snake called out. "Howdy in the camp! Mind if we come in?"

"Not if you're peaceful," Elmira called back. "Come on in."

The three men rode up in front of the wagons, looking all around them before they dismounted. "Where's your menfolk?" Luther asked Elmira, since she looked a little older than the others, and she was dressed in a pair of men's trousers and wearing a pistol and holster.

"Who needs menfolk?" Elmira answered.

Luther didn't answer right away, but Snake blurted, "Well, I'll be.... They's whores. I swear, set up your business right here on the creek. Right?"

"Well, no, that ain't exactly right," Elmira

said. "We're just stopped here for the night. We're on our way south of here. I have three ladies who are trained to entertain payin' customers, and they're free to do business on their own until we get to our permanent place. So if that's what you're interested in, you can talk to them."

"We might be interested in that. Ain't we, boys?" Luther looked at each of his companions, grinning, and they all dismounted. He walked over and took a look at Nellie, by the fire. "Looks like she's gittin' ready to fix supper. We'd be interested in that, too. Make sure you fix plenty of it 'cause we're hungry."

"Is that a fact?" Elmira asked. "You ain't even asked any of the ladies how much it'll cost you to spend time with 'em. As for supper, that might cost you more than you wanna spend for it."

"Oh, that ain't gonna be no problem," Luther said, " 'cause we ain't plannin' on payin' you nothin' for it. It's gonna be your privilege to take care of us three outstandin' men at no charge. And for doin' that, we're gonna let you live. How's that for a good deal?"

"First thing you need to do is to hand over that gun you're wearin'," Snake said. "We wouldn't want it to go off accidentally and shoot you in the leg."

Elmira realized she was in a helpless situation, but she was not willing to give in to the three worthless-looking bullies. "I'm not givin' you my gun. Now you can get your trashy behinds back on those horses and get outta my camp."

"Ain't you the sassy one?" Snake retorted. "Against three of us with our guns. How fast are you with that gun? Let's see if you can beat me, all right? When I count to three, draw and fire. One, two, three," he said and whipped out his six-gun. She didn't bother to try drawing hers, knowing she didn't have a chance. He didn't pull the trigger but continued to hold the gun on her until he walked up to her. Then he dropped it back in his holster and backhanded her hard across her face. She staggered a couple of steps but did not go down. Nellie started toward him, but he pulled Elmira's gun from her holster and pointed it at Nellie. "You want some? Just keep comin'," Snake taunted. She thought better of it. "If you don't get somethin' cooked up to eat, I'm gonna put a hole in your head, right between your eyes." This was enough to halt her advance upon him. "Now, get busy. I'm hungry." When she backed away, he said, "Lester, you and Luther take a look and see what's inside them wagons."

"There ain't nothin' in the wagons but women's clothes," Elmira yelled at him. "Ain't no need for you to go messin' 'em up."

"Is that a fact?" Snake replied. "Lester, go look in them wagons. If they've got any money, it'll be in a trunk or jewelry case or somethin' like that." He remained where he was, watching Elmira closely in case she hadn't really given up. It was only a few moments, however, before they were both startled by a loud shout from Lester, followed immediately by the discharge of a shotgun. They both ran around to the back of Elmira's wagon to discover Lester holding the barrel of the shotgun in one hand and Junie's ankle in the other. "What the hell?" Snake demanded.

"This little weasel was hidin' in the wagon!" Lester exclaimed. "Woulda blowed my head off if I hadn't grabbed the barrel of this shotgun. I'm fixin' to break the damn gun across her backside now." He backed away from the wagon, dragging Junie out by her ankle.

Elmira tried to get to Junie, but was too late to catch her before she hit the ground. "Leave her alone!" she cried out when she got to her. "She's sick."

"What's wrong with her?" Lester asked.

"She's got the weepin' sickness," Elmira said.

"What the hell is that?" Snake demanded. "She cry all the time?"

"No, she don't cry," Elmira replied. "She's got the weepin' sickness, down there, in her lower parts. That's why she has to stay in the wagon 'cause it's catchy and the rest of us don't wanna get it." He gave her a look like he wasn't sure he believed her. "That's why we're on our way south. They ran us out of Texarkana."

"Have the rest of you women got it?" Luther asked.

"We ain't sure yet," Viola spoke up. "The doctor in Texarkana said we most likely would, but it ain't been long enough to know for sure. But we figure we might as well work as long as we can, at least till it shows up like she's got it."

"Dang," Lester mumbled, "I was thinkin' about trying you out after supper."

"Maybe you won't catch nothin' if you give yourself a good bath in the creek after we're done," Viola said. "The doctor said it don't usually kill ya, you just wish you was dead."

"There's a chance we ain't caught it from Junie," Ruby offered. "But we all drank outta the same bottle and used the same washrag, and the doctor said you ain't supposed to do that."

"They're just makin' that stuff up," Snake said, "just to keep us from havin' our way with 'em."

"Maybe so," Luther replied. "You might be right, but I ain't that desperate right now."

"Me either," Lester said. "Besides, I ain't willin' to risk gittin' a knife in my back. You go ahead and enjoy yourself, though. And if you don't come down with any weepin' sickness, you'll have the laugh on us."

"I ain't studyin' that now," Snake declared. "Let's get in them wagons and tear 'em apart. They've got some money hid somewhere, and we need to find it. And look for any more guns they got hid in there." He turned and pointed Elmira's gun at Nellie again. "And you get to cookin' my supper. What are you fixin'?"

"Beans, bacon, and biscuits," Nellie answered. "The three B's. Does that suit your royal highnesses?"

"I'll let you know when I see it," he said.

With Lester in one wagon and Luther in the other, the women sat on the ground by the fire, listening to the plundering of their possessions, while Nellie cooked supper.

When supper was just about ready, Ruby and Viola got up off the ground and fixed the coffee and fetched plates and cups. "Come eat," Snake yelled, and Lester and Luther climbed down from the wagons with nothing to show for their efforts beyond the total disarray of the women's possessions. "Nothin'?" Snake asked when they came to the fire.

"Nothin'," Luther echoed.

"Not a dad-blamed thing," Lester expounded. "I dug all the way to the side boards. Nothin' but clothes and bedclothes and cheap jewelry."

"They've got money hid somewhere," Snake declared, "and if we can't find it, then we're just gonna have to get it outta them women, one way or another. Fill your plates and we'll let the women have whatever's left." He cocked an eye in Elmira's direction. "It might be the last meal they'll ever eat. I'm tired of bein' easy on 'em." He sat down then to concentrate on the plate of food he had dished out. As he sat there on the ground eating, he was thinking about the pleasure he was going to have beating the location of the hiding place out of Elmira. Then he glanced over at the wagon where the young girl had been hiding, and it struck him. "Both of those wagons have got toolboxes under 'em. One of 'em's got somethin' behind the toolbox."

"That's my spare wheel," Elmira volunteered at once. "We had to fix a broken wheel. I had to spend the last of my money for a new wheel, so the blacksmith fixed it so we could carry the old wheel with us."

Snake cast a look of curiosity in her direction, surprised by her voluntary explanation and inclined not to believe that all her money was spent on a new wheel. "So all your money went to a new wagon wheel, did it? You must think I ain't got no sense a-tall. Where, exactly was you headin'?"

"Nacogdoches," Elmira replied reluctantly.

"And you didn't have no more money than just enough to buy one wheel? That musta been one helluva fancy . . ." He stopped abruptly when another thought struck him. He turned to Lester and said, "She might be tryin' to help us find her money after all. She said her money's in the wheel, but she didn't say which wheel. Crawl under that wagon and take a look at that extra wheel rigged under it."

Lester put his plate aside and crawled under the wagon at once, and Elmira's heart sank, for only a minute passed before Lester howled like a hound on the scent of a wild hog. "I found it! There's a metal box wedged up between the wheel and the wagon bed!"

"Well, bring it out from under there and let's see how much we've got," Snake said, while favoring Elmira with a smug grin.

"It ain't that easy," Lester said. "It's wedged in here pretty good, and there's a couple of screws holdin' it to the bottom of the wagon. I need a screwdriver."

"Oughta be one in the toolbox," Luther said.

Still smiling at Elmira, Snake asked, "How much is in that box? Save us the trouble of countin' it." He knew by the look of distress in her eyes that it was a lot.

"I don't remember," she answered, even though she knew the exact amount. It was money from the sale of her business in Shreveport, and money she planned to expand her friend's business in Nacogdoches with. She had other money, a much smaller sum, that they would have to strip off her clothes to find. She had hoped that the three would ride off and leave them after they had abused them and eaten half their food supply. But now she despaired that with the discovery of her money, the amount of it would tend to make them reluctant to leave any witnesses alive.

Lester's discovery captured the attention

of all three outlaws, so Nellie took the opportunity to tell the women to fill their plates while there was still plenty to eat. "You may need your strength for whatever happens tonight." Like Elmira, she was not confident they had a future once their captors found out the amount of their prize. None of the five had any appetite, but they dished out the remains of the pot of beans and divided up the bacon and forced themselves to eat.

While they ate, the three outlaws huddled back behind Elmira's wagon to witness the opening of the metal container. Inside the box, they found the money wrapped in a square cut from an old rain slicker. "Hot damn!" Luther fidgeted excitedly. "Dump it out on the tailgate, Lester!"

Lester dumped it out, and all three stared in disbelief at the pile of paper money, banded in individual little packs. Snake picked up a pack and fanned it like a deck of cards. "Boys," he said, "we ain't never had a payday like this one."

"Let's count it," Luther said. "I wanna know how rich I am."

"Keep your eye on them women over by the fire," Snake warned. "They mighta had another pistol hid somewhere."

"Whadda we gonna do about them?"

Lester asked. "We just gonna leave 'em?"

"We can't just leave 'em," Snake said. "With this much money, we can't take a chance on anybody knowin' we got it. It'll be better for us if all five of 'em are dead when we leave here."

"I reckon you're right," Lester replied. "They ain't nothin' but ol' whores, anyway. Ain't nobody gonna miss 'em."

"That's right," Luther said. "They've all got the blame weepin' sickness anyway. Probably gonna die before long. You wanna go ahead and do it now, so we don't have to keep an eye on 'em?"

"I don't know," Lester said. "It's gonna be dark pretty quick, kinda late for us to be startin' out somewhere. We've already got a camp right here, and we might as well let them cook breakfast for us in the morning."

"I don't wanna take a chance on gittin' my throat slit while I'm sleepin' tonight," Snake declared. "And now that we got their money, they'd sure as hell try it."

"We got plenty of rope," Lester suggested. "Just tie 'em up tonight and let 'em loose in the mornin'. Then shoot 'em."

"After they cook breakfast," Luther said. "We can tell 'em we're gonna let 'em keep half the money if they don't give us no trouble. Now, let's count the money." That seemed to suit Snake and Lester.

They started counting, but it turned out to be a longer job than they had anticipated. They finished up by the light of the fire as the frightened women watched and waited — for they knew not what. "I swear," Snake commented when the counting was done. "Thirty-two-thousand." He looked quickly at Elmira and asked, "Is that right?"

"Within five hundred," she said.

"More or less?" he asked.

"Less," she answered. "Now that you've got all my money, what are you gonna do with us?"

"Like we told you, we're gonna take a little piece of your money to pay for us protectin' you tonight, and you get to keep the rest. That's fair enough, ain't it? Then, after we all have a good breakfast, we'll be movin' along in the mornin' and hope you have a nice trip."

"What do you mean by a *little piece*?" she asked.

"Why, we'll just let you decide how much it's worth to know your money is safeguarded for sure tonight, even if it ain't but for one night."

Elmira didn't bother responding to that comment. She knew for certain that their only hope for survival was to escape that night, while the three men were asleep. She couldn't plan how best to do that until she knew where they were going to sleep. She hoped that Ruby and Viola were not fooled by Snake's change in attitude, from threats and plundering to talk of protection. She knew that Nellie believed they would never leave them alive, and she had already told Junie to stay close to her. She was afraid, however, that she would die trying to protect her daughter. *If only we had some whiskey,* she thought, *and the possibility of getting them all dead drunk.* But there was no alcohol, and it didn't appear the outlaws had any, either.

As the evening wore on, their captors became more and more conscious of what the women were doing, watching their every move, even escorting them to a clump of laurel bushes to answer nature's calls. But the cruelest order of all came when Snake announced, "Bedtime," and he and Lester drew their six-guns and ordered the five captives to stand in a group. Then Luther took each woman and tied her in the wagon, hand and foot, until he had all five of them tied helpless in the two wagon beds. "That's just so you don't go gittin' no crazy ideas in the middle of the night," Snake told them. "Don't worry, we'll untie you when it's time to make breakfast in the mornin'."

"That's right," Luther said, "and we're gonna want some more of them biscuits." They left the women then and went back to the fire to finish another pot of coffee. To their hostages, it seemed like forever before the three men decided they'd had it for the night. Snake took one last check on the women to satisfy himself that Luther had done an acceptable job of securing them. Then he spread his blankets by the fire and went to sleep. Luther and Lester had already picked a spot and were well on the way. They were three wealthy men when compared to the night before, when there wasn't as much as two dollars between them. Pretty soon a snoring contest began to compete with the night creatures that dwelled in the creek.

As the sounds of snoring increased to a steady drone, soft sounds of crying came to Elmira's ears from the other wagon. She guessed it was Ruby, and she felt sick inside to know that she could not help her, and she regretted her decision to let her and Viola, too, come with her when she left Shreveport. She did not forget to send another silent curse in Otis Welker's direction for his part in starting them out on this ill-fated journey. These were the last thoughts that registered in her mind before she fell asleep in the early morning hours.

Chapter 7

Elmira blinked her eyes, confused by the morning light and not sure where she was until she became aware of someone untying her hands. "Time to get up. Go make some coffee," the voice she recognized as Snake's said. "Your hands are free. You can untie your feet." She could not believe she had actually gone to sleep, tied as she was, facing the side of the wagon. She was more surprised that the outlaws were untying them. They had said the night before that they would be untied, but she expected that possibly Nellie would be the only one freed, so she could cook their breakfast and the rest of them would be executed as they lay helpless in the wagons. *It's a waste of time trying to read those twisted minds,* she told herself. Snake backed away from the wagon then, when Junie approached. Elmira was puzzled by his move, then it occurred to her that he feared Junie's *weeping sickness.* She had been tied up in the other wagon with Ruby and Viola. Elmira turned toward the other side of the wagon and discovered that Nellie was already gone.

"She's buildin' the fire up," Junie said when she saw her mother looking for Nellie.

"Damn," Elmira swore. "Am I the last one up? I can't believe I went to sleep at all." She worked at the hard knot in the rope around her ankles until she was finally free. "Are you all right, honey?" she asked her daughter.

"I don't know," Junie answered. "They're lettin' us walk around free right now, but I'm afraid of what they're gonna do with us. Do you think they're gonna kill us?"

Elmira wasn't sure what she should tell her daughter at this point. "I don't know, honey, but if they try to, I'm gonna grab anything I can get my hands on to fight 'em. And I want you to take off through those laurel bushes and run as fast as you can if they make the first move toward any of us. They've got the money. Maybe they'll just ride off and leave us alone."

Junie fought to keep the tears from forming in her eyes. "I wish Perley hadn't gone off and left us."

"I do, too, honey," Elmira said, "but I

don't know how much help he woulda been against these three devils." She thought about the pleasant, unassuming young man and his older companion with the graying ponytail hanging down his back. *No, I don't think they would have been of much use against the three hardened killers,* she thought. "Come on, let's go help Nellie fix a nice breakfast for our guests."

"Lookee yonder," Possum said. "Our sportin' ladies are still here. I swear, I was hopin' they'd be gone by the time we came back. We shouldn'ta followed this trail back. We shoulda cut across and picked up the road to Sulphur Springs north of this creek."

"I reckon," Perley responded. They continued on a little closer, and Perley said, "There's some extra horses down by that creek. Some of 'em are saddled, and there's some packhorses, too. They've got company. Maybe that's the reason they're still here. They set up for business right there by the creek."

"Well, I'll be. . . ." Possum commented. "Looks that way, don't it? 'Course that's one thing about the business they're in: You can set up shop anywhere, and there's customers waitin'." Perley didn't say anything more and Possum suspected what he was thinking about, so he said, "Don't reckon there's any need for us to stop in. Looks like they're doin' all right."

"I don't know, Possum, I've got a feelin' we oughta just check on 'em to make sure everything's all right. They were awful worried about gettin' to Nacogdoches."

"Yeah, reckon you're right," Possum conceded. "I didn't think you'd be able to ride on by without stoppin'."

The first to spot them was Junie. "Perley!" she exclaimed, alerting everyone.

"What? Who?" Snake reacted, just then seeing the two riders approaching. He put his plate aside and got to his feet, as did his two companions. He looked around for Elmira. "They friends of yours? If they are, you better get rid of 'em right now, or they're dead men."

"Perley," Junie repeated, this time more softly. "I knew you'd come back."

Snake heard her and said to Lester, "Get hold of her. She's fixin' to run out there."

Lester walked over beside Junie and put his hand on her shoulder. "You just stay right close to me, you little witch, or I'll smack you down."

"You come with me," Snake told Elmira. "The rest of you women just stay where you are and keep your mouth shut." Back to

Elmira then, he said. "Now me and you are gonna go say howdy to your friends and tell 'em you're busy." With one hand on her elbow, he walked her out to meet them.

Perley and Possum pulled off of the trail and Perley dismounted, watching the man with Elmira carefully. The first thing he noticed was the man's hat. He was wearing a rattlesnake skin for a hatband. Perley remembered George Weber's wife, Lydia, describing the man who knocked on her front door with such a hatband. He felt sure he was looking at one of the would-be cattle rustlers. The question to be answered now — was he and his two friends paying customers of Elmira's? He doubted it. The man's first words to him increased that doubt.

"Nobody's invited you to step down," Snake said. "This is a private party here."

"Oh?" Perley responded. "Then I reckon I owe you an apology. Is that right, Elmira? Is this a private party?"

She didn't have time to answer because Junie thought he was going to get back on his horse. "Perley!" she shouted, and tried to run to him, but Lester managed to grab her arm and stopped her.

"I told you!" Lester roared, and drew his hand back to slap her, only to howl in pain when the bullet tore through the palm of his hand. Snake's first reaction was to draw his six-gun, but he thought better of it with Perley's already in his hand. Possum, meanwhile, still in the saddle, had drawn his rifle from the saddle sling and was drawing a bead on Luther.

"Hold on, damn it!" Snake demanded. "Ain't no need to do no shootin'. There's just been a misunderstandin' here. Put the guns away. Come on over by the fire and we'll straighten this out."

"He busted my hand!" Lester howled.

"Get a rag or somethin' to wrap his hand in," Snake told Nellie, then back to Perley, he said, "That was pretty good shootin', if you was aimin' at his hand. You can put it away now and we'll talk like civilized people." Perley dropped his Colt .44 back in the holster and walked toward the fire with Snake.

Junie ran to meet him. "I knew you'd come back to take care of us," she said.

"We thought you'd be gone by now," Perley told her, not noticing that Snake had stopped while he walked on.

"Perley!" The shout from Possum was the only warning he had when Snake reached for his gun. Perley turned and put a bullet in the center of Snake's chest before Snake's weapon cleared the holster. He spun back toward the fire when Possum's rifle discharged, in time to see Luther drop his six-gun and clutch his belly. Possum put a second round in his chest. "Ain't no use to make him suffer," Possum said. That left Lester with a hole torn all the way through his right hand. Still shocked by the ease with which Snake was dispatched to hell, Lester figured he was next. He reached down with his left hand, unbuckled his gun belt, and let it drop to the ground. He stood there, his head down, a piece of an old bedsheet wrapped around his right hand, waiting for his execution.

"What's your name?" Perley asked him.

"Lester Blunt," he answered.

"Well, what about it, Lester?" Perley asked. "Is the fight over, or are you wantin' to avenge your two partners?"

"I reckon it's over for me. I can't do much with my right hand tore up. At least I got to see the fastest gun in Texas before I died. I'd appreciate it if you'd go ahead and get it over with quick. I've done some bad things in my life. I reckon this is what comes of a life like that."

"Well, I stopped you from doin' one of the worst things you coulda done," Perley said. "And that was when you started to hit that young girl. You don't wanna go to meet your maker with something like that on your record."

"No, I reckon not. I'm sorry about that." He raised his chin high enough off his chest to glance at Junie. "I'm sorry about that, miss, and I hope you get over the weepin' sickness."

Puzzled by Lester's last remark, Perley continued. "I believe you mean it, Lester. I'll tell you what — we ain't gonna execute you. You're gonna inherit all your two partners' belongings. And it looks like the horses are all saddled, packed up, and ready to go. So you need to get on your horse and lead 'em outta here right now. Possum and I will put your partners' bodies over the saddle for you so you can take 'em somewhere to dump 'em." Perley reached in his pocket and pulled out some money. "Since I messed up your hand, here's ten dollars. There's a doctor in Sulphur Springs. He ought not charge more than that to fix it."

Elmira interrupted then. "First we'll need to recover that metal box with my money in it," she said.

"Right," Lester said. "Snake put it on his packhorse. We counted it, but we didn't split it up. It's all in the box."

When Perley gave Elmira a puzzled look,

Elmira said, "I'll tell you about that later." She went with Lester to Snake's packhorse, and he showed her where it was packed. Perley and Possum picked up the bodies and laid them across the saddles. Then they tied the horses up on a single lead rope for Lester. It was going to be difficult for him, what with one hand bandaged up, but he assured Perley that he would manage, at least until he got to Sulphur Springs.

"Ain't no way he's gonna be able to handle all that," Possum remarked as they watched Lester ride off toward the road to town. "At best, he'll dump them two bodies on the side of the road, and ain't no tellin' what he'll do with all his horses."

"Hard to say what a man can do when life don't give him but two choices: *do* or *don't*. If he wants it bad enough, he'll pick *do*," Perley said. "He oughta be able to sell his extra horses and saddles, plus the guns he don't need, for enough money to get him a little start in some direction. Better than the one he was headin' in before, I hope."

"Well, I hope you're right, Reverend Gates," Possum commented sarcastically.

They turned back toward the wagons to find Elmira standing there, waiting for them. Junie was standing by her side. "I don't think I can find the right words to thank you two angels for comin' back to save us," Elmira said. "They were fixin' to ride off with all the money I had from sellin' my business — money I need to start up again in Nacogdoches. And I don't believe for a minute that they were gonna leave us alive. I don't know that I woulda let Lester go, if it'd been me in your shoes, but I reckon that was enough killin'. The main thing is you came back when we needed you." She placed her hand on her daughter's shoulder. "Junie said you'd come back for us. She said you wouldn't leave us women unprotected." Her revelation caused Possum to roll his eyeballs skyward, certain of the effect it was bound to have on Perley. Elmira continued, "This whole experience has taught me that a group of women needs protection from who knows how many predators might be waitin' between here and Nacogdoches. Maybe I shouldn't have shot Otis Welker. He might have been better than nothin', even if he did de-flower my baby."

Possum interrupted her at that point. "Before we all break down and start bawlin', let me say we're wastin' a lotta time with this tongue waggin'. You women need to get them wagons hitched up and break this camp down if me and Perley are gonna lead you to Nacogdoches anytime soon."

"Ha!" Perley couldn't help reacting, having expected to have a long, drawn-out argument with Possum on the right and honorable thing to do in respect to the prostitutes' problem. One look at Elmira and her daughter, and the way their eyes suddenly lit up, told him Possum's statement wasn't lost on them. Their happy smiles followed immediately.

"We'll get right to it!" Elmira exclaimed, and she turned to issue the marching orders to the other women, who all cheered when she told them they had two new guides.

"Now you see what you caused," Perley commented to Possum. "Look how happy you made those women. Don't it make you feel good that you could cheer up all of 'em like that?"

"Yeah, it's hard to keep from gigglin'," Possum said sarcastically. "Rubin's gonna be tickled, too. Whaddaya gonna tell him?"

"What am I gonna tell him?" Perley asked. "I don't have to tell him anything. You're the one that made the decision. What are you gonna tell him? 'Course, I didn't say I was goin' to Nacogdoches, so I just might ride on back home."

"If you hurry, you can catch up with Lester," Possum responded. "I expect he'd appreciate the help. But what are you gonna do about Rubin?"

"I reckon I can wire him when we get to Tyler. That's gonna be about three and a half or four days, countin' today." He paused to picture his brother's reaction to the news. "I could tell him that we spent the thousand dollars to take the women to Nacogdoches. Then when his Hereford cows showed up, he wouldn't care about us being gone so long."

Although they joked about it, they knew the time they would be away would surely be cause for concern for his brothers. It would depend on how soon Weber got the fifty cows started toward the Triple-G, but if he started right away, the cows might arrive about the same time the telegram did. Perley thought about this, and the thought of having stepped in another cow pie, and simply shrugged. This was just the way things generally happened for him. "It is, what it is, partner. Let's go help the ladies get movin'."

The women were already hustling around the campsite, getting their wagons back in order after the plundering by the three outlaws. Perley and Possum got the horses hitched up to the wagons and the packhorses loaded, and before long, they were ready to roll. The two men led the little wagon train back to the crossroads and turned to the south on the road to Tyler, their packhorses and Otis Welker's saddle horse trailing along behind the wagons. There was no guiding necessary, since the road went all the way to Tyler. Other than protection, the job for the men was to scout ahead to find good places to stop to rest the horses and eat.

Nellie Butcher climbed up to sit on the wagon seat beside Elmira while Junie walked along beside the horses. "I used to enjoy walkin' when I was as young as she is," Nellie remarked.

Elmira laughed. "I reckon I probably did, too. I don't remember if I really enjoyed it, but I know I didn't mind it."

"Were you feelin' lucky when you woke up this morning, with your hands and feet tied to the side of the wagon?"

"Are you japin' me?" Elmira replied. "In the first place, I couldn't believe I was still alive when I first woke up. Then, when I realized I was, I had a sinkin' feelin', 'cause I knew what was comin' as soon as those devils were through usin' us."

Nellie lowered her voice a little to make sure Junie couldn't hear what she was saying. "Do you think you know what an angel looks like?"

Elmira gave her a look as if she was crazy before she said, "No, I don't reckon I do. Do you?"

"Junie does," Nellie answered.

"Fiddle," Elmira grunted. "Are you talkin' about Perley? She's just got herself a little warm spot for Perley, something that don't surprise me for a thirteen-year-old."

"Maybe so, maybe not," Nellie maintained. "Elmira, those three outlaws weren't gonna be satisfied to take your money and go. They weren't gonna leave us alive to tell anybody. I know that, and you know that."

"I know that," Elmira confirmed. "There ain't no doubt in my mind."

"Well, I ain't never had no religion of any kind," Nellie continued. "But last night I prayed. I prayed as hard as I could, and I asked the Lord to please send us an angel, or a miracle of some kind. And this mornin', Perley Gates shows up. A man with a name like that, Perley Gates. That's a giveaway right there." She paused and gave Elmira a smug look while Nellie thought about that. "Were you lookin' when Perley shot Snake?" She didn't wait for Elmira's answer. "Perley was in front of Snake, with his back to him, when Snake went for his gun. Perley turned and shot him through the heart before Snake even got his gun all the way outta his holster."

"That's why I'm so doggone thankful him and Possum decided to go with us," Elmira said. "They've got guns, and they know how to use 'em."

"You must not have been lookin' when he actually shot Snake," Nellie said. " 'Cause if you had, you woulda seen that Perley was faster than an ordinary man can move. How come we never heard of Perley Gates? A man that fast with a six-gun would be known all over Texas, and I doubt he'd be the polite, innocent-lookin' man that Perley is."

"I swear, Nellie, maybe you oughta get off the wagon and go walk with Junie. How 'bout Possum? He killed that one named Luther. Maybe he's an angel, too."

"He was right there when he was needed," Nellie allowed. "But he had time to pull his rifle out and take aim at Luther. And then he had to shoot him again to make sure he was dead, like a man killin' a dog gone mad. With Perley, it was more like snappin' his fingers and Snake never knew what hit him."

"Well, Nellie, this is a free country, so you can believe whatever you want to. And I'm your friend, so I ain't gonna judge you by what ideas you come up with. I think there ain't no way you can prove he's an angel, and there ain't no way I can prove he ain't. And I'm still your friend."

"But see, that's where you're wrong," Nellie said.

"About what?"

"About not being able to prove he is an angel. We've already got the proof," Nellie insisted.

"Where?"

"You," Nellie said, "and me, and Junie, and Viola, and Ruby — all of us on our way to Nacogdoches, instead of layin' dead back on that creek bank."

"You're right," Elmira surrendered. "I give up. He's an angel. Don't forget to thank the Lord when you go to bed tonight."

"Wouldn't hurt you to do the same," Nellie told her.

"One thing you gotta give Elmira credit for," Possum commented when he pulled up even with Perley again, "she bought pretty good horses to pull those wagons." He had dropped back to see how the horses were doing after he and Perley had estimated they had probably driven about ten miles. "Those wagons ain't loaded down that heavy. They might make close to fifteen miles."

"I think I'll go on up ahead and see if

there's any good spots to camp in the next few miles. You wanna go with me?"

"No," Possum said. "Ol' Dancer has got too comfortable walkin' this slow pace with the wagons. I don't wanna start him to complainin'."

"All right, then, I'll let Buck kick up his heels a little bit. I don't want him to get the idea that he's retired." He nudged the big bay gelding into a gentle lope and moved on out in front of the two-wagon train. In a few minutes time he was out of Possum's sight as he followed the wagon road that showed evidence of a fair amount of use. He passed over several tiny streams and continued on a couple of miles before he came to a healthy creek and knew this was what he was looking for. So he turned Buck off the road and followed the creek upstream a short distance before deciding it was as far as the wagons could easily be driven. Satisfied, he turned Buck around and went back to the road to wait for Possum to catch up.

When Possum and the wagons came into sight, Perley rode out to meet him and led him back to the spot he had picked to park the wagons and make camp. They guided the women driving the wagons into the camp. Then Perley and Possum took care of all the horses while the women gathered wood for the fire, and the meal was started. This became the usual routine for the days that followed.

CHAPTER 8

They came to the first buildings on the north side of the town of Tyler in the early afternoon after a three and a half-day drive. They decided to drive straight through the main street so they could see where everything was located. Then they drove on out of town and made their camp half a mile south of the town. While they were driving through the town, they attracted a fair amount of attention from the people they passed along the street, which was no surprise to Perley. A couple of wagons driven by women usually meant rolling sin to a town with several churches. "I wouldn't be surprised if we got a welcome visit from the sheriff before suppertime," Possum told Perley.

"I hope so," Perley replied. "Maybe he can tell us the best way to get to Nacogdoches from here. I saw the telegraph office when we rolled through. I expect I'd best go get that taken care of first thing."

"Elmira says she needs to go to that general store on this end of town to pick up some more supplies if we're gonna have anything to eat between here and Nacogdoches," Possum said. "Reckon one of us oughta go with her before we unhitch her wagon?"

"I don't know that she needs one of us," Perley said. "I expect she's always bought her supplies without any help before — maybe Nellie — but I expect the storekeeper will be glad to load 'em in her wagon for her. Might be best if you stayed here with the younger girls while she's gone to the store."

"You're probably right," Possum said.

"I shouldn't be long at the telegraph office," Perley said. "I'll check by the general store to see if she's still there when I'm done." They left it at that, and Perley rode back into town to the telegraph office. Trying to be as brief as possible while explaining the whole situation, he wrote his message out for the operator to read. "Does that make sense to you?" Perley asked the operator.

"I reckon," the operator replied, "if the person at the Triple-G knows what you're talkin' about. A lot of telegrams don't make any sense to people who ain't involved in what's going on."

"It'll have to do," Perley said. "I've gotta start watchin' my money. When I left home, north of Paris, a few days ago, I didn't have any idea I was goin' to Tyler."

"Is that a fact?" the operator responded, not really interested in Perley's financial situation as long as he paid for the telegram." He took the money and gave Perley his change. " 'Preciate it," he said, and returned to his desk, leaving Perley standing at the window.

Back outside, he climbed up on Buck and wheeled the big horse toward Rinehart's General Store. He could see Elmira's wagon in front of the store, so he decided to stop to see if she needed any help. When he went inside the store, he saw Elmira and Nellie standing at the counter talking to two men — one behind the counter, the other on the same side with the two women. When Elmira turned and saw him, she said, "Perley, come tell these fellows it ain't against the law for a woman to buy lard, flour, bakin' soda, and such." The man standing in front of the counter with them turned when she spoke, and Perley saw that he was wearing a badge. He almost smiled when he recalled Possum's remark earlier. The sheriff was already making his visit.

"Are you with these women?" the sheriff asked Perley.

"Yes, sir, I am," Perley answered. "What law have they broken?"

The sheriff hesitated. "Well, I'm just gettin' down to that. It's a moral question, and I have to ask you: What's your intended business here in Tyler?"

"Our business in Tyler is to ride through it from the north end and out the south end, on our way to Nacogdoches, stoppin' only long enough to send a telegram and to buy supplies for our journey."

The sheriff was not quite sure he heard right. "So you're just passin' through?" Perley nodded, and the sheriff turned to the store owner. "They're just passin' through, Ross." Back to Perley then, he said, "I reckon I owe you an explanation. The town of Tyler is founded on a solid base of religious folks. There's three churches in town, and Mr. Rinehart here is a deacon in the Methodist church. We just had a bad time with one of the saloon owners, who brought in a bunch of prostitutes and wanted to set up a dance hall. Don't get me wrong — there's whores in Tyler, but not like he was fixin' to bring into town. So when some of the folks saw two wagons roll into town with women drivin' 'em, they just naturally wondered how many women were ridin' in the back of those wagons. Then when two of the women came into the store wantin' to buy a whole lot of supplies, Mr. Rinehart sent for me. I'm the sheriff here. John Talbot's my name."

"You thought they were prostitutes?" Perley responded, looking shocked. He turned to look at Elmira. "Oh, Mrs. Miller, I'm so sorry. I or Reverend Smith should have come with you and Miss Butcher to get these supplies. I never thought you needed a chaperone just to go to a store. Please don't tell the other ladies that the folks here thought they were whores."

"I'm sorry if . . ." the sheriff sputtered, embarrassed. "I was just goin' by what Ross said."

"For your information, Sheriff Talbot," Perley said. "You have a grand total of five females ridin' in those two wagons: these two ladies here, two young women who are working with them, and this lady's thirteen-year-old daughter. The two ladies here in your store are counselors for the Sulphur Springs Christian Academy. The two younger women have just recently completed a trainin' program on helpin' other young women who have started on the wrong path in life to find the right path. We stopped to make camp about half a mile south of town, if you have no objection, and we plan to move on first thing in the mornin'. We've a-ways to go yet, so we need those supplies. Mrs. Miller has the money to pay for them."

All four people standing at the counter were stunned for a few moments after Perley's statement. Among the first to recover, Elmira smiled and said, "I was just waiting for Mr. Rinehart to tell me the total cost."

"Yes, ma'am," Rinehart blurted. "I certainly hope you didn't think I thought . . ." He was too embarrassed to finish.

"Not at all," Elmira said. "I'll take the blame for it. I mean, with the way I'm dressed, wearing trousers and a gun. I have to admit, I'm a little uncomfortable myself, but I do it to discourage any wrong notions someone might have, if Perley or Poss— I mean, Reverend Smith is not around."

"I reckon I oughta apologize if I offended you ladies in any way," Sheriff Talbot offered then. "I hope you don't get a bad impression of our town from our mistake. It ain't the way we usually like to greet strangers to Tyler, is it, Ross?"

"No, it sure isn't," Rinehart replied. "Here's the total for the supplies, and I'd like to throw in another sack of flour and a sack of dried apples at no charge. My wife makes a real tasty apple pie with those apples. You ladies might enjoy one, too."

"Why, thank you, sir," Elmira said. "That is most kind of you."

"I'll carry some of this out to the wagon for you," Perley said, and he picked up a couple of the larger sacks and went out the door with them.

"What was his name?" Sheriff Talbot asked.

"Perley Gates," Nellie said, "and he always shows up when you need him." She looked at Elmira and grinned.

"Pearly Gates," the sheriff repeated, not sure he had heard correctly. When neither one of the women corrected him, he picked up a couple of sacks and carried them out to the wagon.

"Much obliged, Sheriff," Perley said when he saw Talbot bringing the supplies. "Maybe you could tell me if this road outta town we're camped on will take us to Nacogdoches. I've never come down this way before."

"Yep, you're on the right road to Nacogdoches," Talbot said. "Least, it'll take you most of the way. When you get about fifty miles south of here, there's a crossroad you gotta look for at a little place called Alto. Used to be an old fort or somethin' there a long time ago. I don't know what it was, but there was a sign there that says Nacogdoches to the east. I reckon it's still there. That road will take you on across the Angelina River to Nacogdoches." He paused, then asked, "You and the preacher gonna work at the mission down there, or whatever you call it, with the women?"

"Gracious, no," Perley said. "Me and the preacher are just responsible for gettin' the ladies down there safely, then we'll be headin' back to Sulphur Springs. That's what I had to send a telegram about, to let them know where we are, and that everything's all right."

"Well, have a good trip," Talbot said. "And if you come back this way, we'll try to give you a little better welcome."

"Thanks, Sheriff, but I don't think the ladies got their feelin's hurt. They'll most likely be laughing about the misunderstandin'." Perley went back inside the store when the sheriff walked back to his office. He picked up the last packages that the women couldn't carry and said so long to Ross Rinehart. Then he rode along beside the wagon as Elmira drove it out of town. The last statement he had made to the sheriff turned out to be accurate, because the two women busted out laughing as soon as they were well away from the store.

"What was it you said we was?" Nellie asked as they headed out of town.

Perley had to take a moment to remember. "Counselors," he said then. "Counselors for the Sulphur Springs Christian School." He paused, "No, academy. Sulphur Springs Christian Academy." That brought another round of coarse guffaws from the two women, and they joked about the scene all the way back to the camp.

"Give us a hand loadin' some of this stuff into the other wagon, Reverend Smith," Elmira called to Possum when she pulled her wagon up beside the other.

Possum gave her a puzzled look, wondering what was so funny that they were cackling over it. "You didn't catch them in the saloon, did you?"

"Nope," Perley answered. "I found 'em in the general store talkin' to Mr. Ross Rinehart and the sheriff. Both gentlemen were a little concerned that we might have come to Tyler to stay. But they were both all right when they found out we were just passing through."

"Well, what's so funny about that?" Possum wanted to know.

"I'll tell you," Elmira answered him. "Wait till I get these horses unhitched. I want Viola and Ruby to hear it, too. It might make 'em strut a little more like high-class ladies."

"I'll take care of your horses for you," Perley said. "I don't wanna hold you up from makin' supper."

Back at the Triple-G headquarters, north of Paris, Texas, John Gates rode into the barnyard where he found his elder brother, Rubin, talking to Ollie Dinkler about some repairs to the cookhouse. "Seen any sign of Perley and Possum?" John asked as he stepped down from his horse.

"Not a sign," Rubin answered, and released a deep sigh.

"Well, I just came from the south range," John told him, "and we just got fifty head of Hereford cows, delivered by some boys from the Lazy-W."

"No foolin'?" Rubin replied. "Where in the hell is Perley? Him and Possum have been gone a damn week."

"I don't know, Rubin," John said, genuinely concerned at that point. "They oughta have been back here before now. Maybe we oughta head up that way to see if something's happened to him." They both turned then when a team of horses pulling a wagon came in the front gate with Fred Farmer and young Link Drew in the seat. Link was driving the horses. Fred's fourteen-year-old son, Jimmy, was standing up behind the seat.

"I swear," Rubin commented, "I believe Fred and Alice are gonna adopt that orphan Perley brought home with him." Fred's wife, Alice, worked in the kitchen helping Rubin's wife, Lou Ann.

"We went into town to get a keg of nails and some things Lou Ann needed," Fred said, thinking he needed to tell Rubin why he drove the wagon to town. "Grover Jones's boy told me you had a telegram come in for you today. I got it right here." He reached in his back pocket and handed it to Jimmy. Jimmy jumped down from the wagon and brought it to Rubin. Then Fred, John, and the two boys all waited for Rubin to open it and read it.

Rubin opened the wire. "It's from Perley," he said, and read it.

"Well, what's it say?" John asked. Rubin just shook his head slowly and handed it to him.

John read it, then as if to make sure he understood, read it again, this time out loud. "Bought cows STOP Got paper signed STOP Cows should be there soon STOP

Ran into five women in trouble STOP Have to take them to Nacogdoches STOP Be back soon as possible STOP." He exchanged helpless looks with his brother. "Five women in trouble — that could mean anything." He stared at the telegram again, in case he had misread it. "Nacogdoches," he read. "How far is that?"

"I don't know, a helluva long way. I'm not surprised, though," Rubin declared. "I swear, I am not surprised. I'd be surprised if nothin' had happened."

"If there ain't but one cow pie in the whole state . . ." John started but didn't bother to finish. "You think we ought to say anything to Mama?"

"Lord, no" Rubin said at once. "She worries enough about him when he's right here at home. We won't do her any good to put that on her mind. Besides, he'll show up. He always does, and he's got Possum with him."

"That just means he's probably got into twice as much trouble," John declared.

"What about George Weber's men?" Rubin asked then, getting back to the business of the ranch. "Are they comin' in here to headquarters to eat supper and sleep tonight?"

"Nope," John replied. "They brought a

chuckwagon with 'em. Said they were just gonna turn right around and go home. I told 'em they were welcome here tonight, but they thanked me just the same."

"How'd the cows look?" Rubin asked. "Think they were worth what we paid for 'em?"

"Yep, they looked in good shape. Looked like a lot more steaks on 'em than our longhorns like to tote."

The women were still laughing about Perley's performance in the general store after supper that night. "They sure changed their attitude after Perley told 'em who we were," Nellie crowed. "For a while there, I thought they was gonna refuse to sell us what we needed. And by the time we left, they gave us extra flour and a sack of these apples at no charge. I ain't built me an oven here, but I'll make a fried pie, and we'll have some before we go to bed tonight." So they celebrated Perley and Possum's return to the party with coffee and fried apple pie, and the next morning, they set out once again on the road to Nacogdoches.

On the third day after leaving Tyler, they came to a settlement called Jacksonville, according to the sign nailed to a tree. It offered little more than a post office and a small store. There was a creek close to a blacksmith shop, so they stopped and watered the horses there. As usual, the wagons being driven by women attracted the attention of the few souls available to witness them. It no doubt was enough to talk about after the wagons moved on down the road.

The days that followed were pretty much the same, meeting only an occasional traveler on the road. It seemed to Perley and Possum that the directions were simple enough to follow, and there was no need for protection for the women after the one encounter with Snake Dalton and his two partners. It was hard not to second-guess their decision to take them to Nacogdoches, but they both felt they were too far invested in their commitment to leave the women on their own at this point. At what they estimated to be about fifty miles, they reached the crossroads at Alto, just as Sheriff Talbot had said. There was a small store and a sign on a post that read, *Nacogdoches,* but the post had rotted and broken off just above the ground. Someone had leaned it up against a tree. "I'm gonna stop in that store and see if I can buy me some smokin' tobacca," Possum said. "You need anything?" Perley said no. Possum asked Elmira if they did and got the same answer, so he said,

"I'll catch up."

Perley led the wagons onto the road heading east to Nacogdoches. The horses were not due a rest yet, but it was getting along late in the afternoon, so he was hoping to find a good camping spot for the night. After several minutes, Possum caught up with them. "Fellow back there in the store said it's about twenty-four miles to Nacogdoches. I reckon that's about what we figured." He turned to Elmira and Nellie on the wagon seat and said, "Two more days, ladies."

"It's a good thing," Nellie replied, " 'cause we'll have about used up most of the supplies we bought in Tyler."

"I reckon we'd best take the first decent place we come to and camp," Perley suggested.

"That fellow said it ain't but seven or eight miles to the river," Possum said. "The horses ain't had time to get very tired. They oughta make it all right, then they can rest all night and they'll have plenty of water."

"That sounds like a good idea to me," Perley agreed. "Then we'll have a short ride into town the next day." With that as their plan, they told Elmira, who had no objections, so they continued on until reaching the Angelina River and selecting a spot for their camp.

The mood was cheerful and light at supper that night, with a fair amount of excitement on the part of the women. Their journey, starting out from Shreveport, detouring through Texarkana, then west to Sulphur Springs before turning south to this camp on the bank of the Angelina River, had at times seemed destined to failure. Now, thanks to Perley Gates and Possum Smith, it seemed certain they were going to reach their destination. As far as Perley and Possum were concerned, there was a feeling more akin to relief and eagerness to get back to the Triple-G.

To show her appreciation, Elmira wanted to pay her two heroes for their service and at least to make sure they had ample supplies on their packhorses for their trip back home. Perley told her that neither he nor Possum came with them for the money, so they wouldn't accept any. "We only did it because we wanted to make sure you got down here safe and sound. So we appreciate the offer, but we can't accept it." Elmira was insistent upon reimbursing them for their time and effort, so it turned into the only real argument they ever had. Finally Perley agreed to let her pay for any supplies he and Possum needed for their return trip.

There was one member of the party who was melancholy in anticipation of the sun coming up in the morning. Junie Miller knew that she was going to miss Perley when he rode away from them tomorrow. She had sensed something special about him from the first day he came into their lives. She knew for certain that there was not a mean bone in his body, even though she had seen him kill a man and wound another. If she lived to be one hundred, she would never forget how he had reacted to strike the hand that threatened her. She knew that he cared for her. Not in the way grownups cared for each other, but in a more spiritual way. And she believed that he was sent to keep her safe by a power that even her mother didn't understand. When there was an opportunity to speak to him without fear of someone interrupting, she asked. "Do you think you'll ever come back to see us after you leave tomorrow, Perley?"

"Why, I don't know," he answered, "but I'm hopin' I get an invitation to your weddin' when you get a little older. I'd truly like to see that."

CHAPTER 9

After fording the river, they made one more stop to rest the horses before entering the town limits of Nacogdoches. They were all surprised to find it a busy little town. "I've gotta admit it," Elmira commented as their wagons moved slowly down the street of shops and businesses, "I expected a town about the size of that little town called Jacksonville."

Perley and Possum pulled back beside her wagon, no longer leading. "Where to, boss?" Possum joked.

"The Shamrock Saloon," Elmira exclaimed, trying hard to control her excitement. "I see it up ahead, there." She gave her horses a slap with the reins and headed for the saloon. The street was crowded with horses and wagons, but there was an alley between the Shamrock and a hardware store, so Possum suggested pulling the wagons around to the back of the saloon.

When they got back there, they discovered a two-story addition on the back of the saloon and parked the wagons behind it. He and Perley left their horses there as well. Elmira was anxious to see the saloon from the entrance, so they walked back up the alley to the front. The entire party of travelers pushed through the batwing doors of the Shamrock at the same time, then stopped to take it all in. It was busy, much to Elmira's delight. She looked around from the long bar to the tables at the back of the room. Then she walked up to the bar to face a curious bartender, who was staring at the group standing together in the doorway.

"Can I help you, ma'am?" The bartender asked.

"Who owns this place?" Elmira insisted.

"Walter Tatum," the bartender answered.

"Well, where is he?" Elmira demanded. "I wanna see him."

"He's in his office. He's busy right now." The bartender was beginning to feel his temper rising. "What is it you want?"

"I told you, I wanna see Walter Tatum and I wanna see him right now, or I'm gonna raise such hell as you ain't never seen before. Where's his office? I'll go get him myself. He's gonna have to deal with me one way or another." She turned as if starting toward the back.

"No, no! Hold on! I'll get him. You wait right here." The bartender hurried out from behind the bar and went through a door in the back of the saloon. Perley looked at Possum and they both blinked, never having seen a side of Elmira like this. The steady hum of noise that hung over the room when they walked in suddenly went silent.

After a couple of minutes the bartender reappeared, followed by a large, heavyset man with wide shoulders and a broad face wearing a nasty, irritated expression. He stopped dead still when he saw the woman standing defiantly, feet spread, hands on hips, staring him down. For a split second, the silence in the saloon deepened, and then he exploded, threw his head back, and roared with laughter. "Elmira Miller!" he howled, and hurried to greet her. She met him halfway, and he wrapped his arms around her and picked her up off the floor. "I swear," he exclaimed, "I thought you'd changed your mind. Hell, I told Ernie if you didn't show up pretty soon, I was gonna go get you." He looked then at the group of baffled people standing in the entrance and put Elmira back down on the floor. "Are these your people?" She nodded excitedly.

"Well, bring 'em on in and let's get 'em something to drink." He looked at the bartender and said, "Ernie, see what they need to drink."

Then he led them to a small room off the main saloon where there was one long table in the middle. "Have a seat, everybody. Ernie's gonna bring a couple of bottles in, but if you want something different, just tell him, and he'll get it if we've got it." His eyes stopped on Junie then. "I know who this young lady is. Junie, the last time I saw you, you were about three feet tall. And now look at you. You're as pretty as your mama." Junie blushed appropriately. He continued then. "I'm gonna guess that this lady is Nellie Butcher, and I ain't gonna lie to ya, I've really been hopin' nothing had happened to her. We've been without a cook for a month, and I can tell you, it's hurt my business. But you're gonna have to introduce me to these other two young ladies."

"Viola Swan," Elmira said, "and this is Ruby Jones. They're both professionals. Now before you ask me about the two men, I'll tell you they ain't stayin'."

"Glad to hear that," Walt said, "I was wonderin' what I was gonna do with them. No offense, gentlemen." He chuckled in appreciation of his own humor.

"These two men are true friends of mine," Elmira said. "If it wasn't for these two, none of the rest of us would be sittin' at this table today talkin' to you. After savin' our lives, they escorted us I don't know how far, but it was close to a hundred and fifty miles down here, just to make sure we got here all right. I'll tell you the whole story later. Perley Gates and Possum Smith," she introduced them. "Everybody, this is Walt Tatum. He owns this joint."

Walt leaned over the table to extend his hand. "I expect I owe you gentlemen my thanks for bringing these ladies down here. This lady and I have been talking about going into business together for years."

"That's what I understand," Perley said. "Right now, though, I think I'd like to get those wagons of hers and our horses taken care of." He gave Elmira a sideways glance and said, "Especially that wagon with the spare wheel under the bed."

"Damn, that's right." She looked at Walt and said, "If anything happens to that wagon, I won't have the money I told you I had to invest in this business."

"We've got two wagons and the horses that pulled 'em, plus an extra saddle horse that belongs to Elmira," Perley said. "They're behind the saloon right now. We'll need to get 'em unloaded before we take 'em to a stable. And I need to get that box that's wedged under the spare wheel."

"We can unload them right now," Walt said. "Bring all their stuff in the back door. I've got the empty rooms ready and waiting for you. That back addition ain't been finished all the way, but the rooms are ready for you ladies," he said as Perley walked out to the back door. Walt bent down close to Elmira. "Did you say his name was Pearly?"

She laughed and answered, "That's right, Perley Gates."

Everybody jumped to the task at hand, and the wagons were soon emptied. The only things left were the few supplies for cooking, which Elmira told Perley to help himself to, if there was anything he could use. She said to leave pots and pans and such in the wagons. Perley crawled under the wagon and crawled back out with the metal box, which he gave to Elmira. She turned to Walt and said, "This goes in your safe right away."

When the unloading was done, Walt told Perley where the stable was located. "Just take the wagons to the stable. Gil Porter's the owner. Just tell him that it all belongs to me, and he'll take care of it. Then I expect it's gonna be about suppertime, so you fellows will be wanting to eat. There's a couple of good places to eat in town. When you get back, you can decide."

They tied Buck and Dancer, along with Otis Welker's horse and their packhorses, to the backs of the wagons and drove the wagons to the stable Walt had directed them to. Gil Porter was very accommodating when he heard Walt had sent them. They made arrangements for their horses and packhorses and paid a little extra to sleep in the stall with their horses. Then they returned to the Shamrock where they found Walt showing Elmira and the other women around the saloon, introducing them to some of the regular customers, and showing Nellie the kitchen. They really didn't see any further need for their services, so they pulled Elmira aside and told her that her wagons and horses were all taken care of. "Reckon that just about does it," Perley said. "We hope your business goes as well as you're expectin' it to. From what I've seen of the town, it looks like you've got plenty of customers to go after."

She realized they were saying goodbye then. "Wait," she said, "ain't you stayin' around tonight? We'll get some supper, and you know the drinks for you and Possum will be on the house tonight. Walt might even have another empty room in that new section where you could spend the night."

"No need to bother you folks about that. We're already fixed up for the night, and we'll be starting out for home before breakfast in the mornin'."

Elmira suddenly felt at a loss for words. "I declare, I feel like there's so much I need to say to you two, and I don't know where to start."

"You don't need to say nothin'," Possum said. "We just hope everything turns out like you want it."

"Tell Junie goodbye for me," Perley said.

"Tell her yourself," Elmira replied. "She's standin' right behind you."

Perley turned around to find the young girl waiting patiently. "You sneaked up on me there. I wondered why I didn't see you anywhere. You take care of yourself, young lady, and your mama, too. We all expect big things outta you."

"Are you leavin' right now?" Junie asked.

"Yep. Possum and I have to get back to the Triple-G."

She stepped closer and gave him a hug. "I'll never forget you and Possum. You be real careful on your way back to where you came from, even if you call it the Triple-G." She released him and stepped back again.

"Right," he replied, confused by her comment. "We'll never forget you, either." He turned to find Nellie grinning at him, so he nodded to her as he and Possum walked out the door. As they did, Possum told him what Junie had meant. "Oh," he exclaimed. "How could a kid as old as she is get a crazy idea like that?"

"Beats me," Possum said. "Let's go find something to eat."

"Walt never gave us those suggestions on where to eat. Wanna just see if we're lucky?"

"Let's go ask Gil Porter where to eat," Possum said. "This'll be our last good meal for a spell. I druther not risk pickin' a bad place to buy it."

So they walked back to the stable and Gil didn't hesitate. "Thornton's," he said, "you'll get a good meal there every time." Following his directions, they walked halfway down the main street and turned on a side street by the bank. A few doors down, they saw the sign: *Thornton Family Restaurant.*

"Welcome, gentlemen," Edna Thornton greeted them when they came in the door. "Can I ask you to hang your gun belts over there on the wall, please?"

"Yes, ma'am," Possum answered, and he and Perley removed their belts and hung them on two in a row of hooks for the purpose. "I reckon they don't care if you've got a pocket pistol," he mumbled to Perley when they returned to the door where she waited for them.

The restaurant was about half filled, so Edna asked, "Any particular table you want to sit at?" They had no preference, so she seated them at a table not far from the kitchen door. "Maureen will be your waitress," she said. "You have a choice tonight of stew beef or pork chops. While you're deciding, I'll tell Maureen what you want to drink. Coffee?" She asked then, playing the odds. They both nodded.

A couple of minutes later, a young girl came to the table carrying two cups of coffee. "My name's Maureen," she said. "I'll be waiting on you today."

"We know," Possum commented, "your mother told us." She looked so much like the lady who welcomed them that it was an easy guess.

Maureen blushed and giggled. "That's not my mother. That's my sister. My mother's in the kitchen doing the cooking."

"I'll take the pork chops," Possum blurted, anxious to change the subject.

"I'm gonna tell Edna what you said," Maureen declared, still giggling delightedly.

"Don't you tell your sister that," Perley said. "His eyesight is so poor in his old age I have to lead him around to keep him from bumpin' into things. No sense in hurtin' Edna's feelings when he's as blind as a bat."

"All right," she said, "I won't tell her. What are you gonna have?"

"I'll take the pork chops, too," Perley said, and she hurried off to the kitchen to place the order. He looked at Possum and said, "It's gonna be kinda hard to gnaw on a pork chop with your foot in your mouth, ain't it?"

"I swear that woman looks a lot older than Maureen," Possum replied. "And they looked so much alike I thought she was her mother."

"I did, too," Perley confessed, "but I had better sense than to say something like that."

Maureen returned shortly with two plates, each with two pork chops, beans, and rice and gravy in generous portions. While she placed them on the table, another customer walked in, spoke to Edna, then proceeded to a table near the kitchen door. He was wearing an army model Colt .45, and Edna make no mention of it. He spoke to Maureen as well when he passed by. "I know you fellows are strangers here," Maureen informed them, "and you may have noticed he's wearing a gun."

"Figure he's the sheriff," Perley said, "and the gun rule doesn't apply to him."

"I know he's the sheriff," Possum declared. "When he came in the door, his coat pulled aside just enough to see there was a badge on his vest."

Maureen gave him a suspicious look and grinned. "And this is the man who's blind as a bat, right?"

Possum was speechless for a moment, then he said, "Well, it's a big badge, and it's real shiny."

Perley and Maureen laughed. "Don't tell your sister," Perley told her. "It might hurt her feelings."

"I won't," Maureen said. "I promise."

They took their time eating the supper that lived up to Gil Porter's recommendations, and they were finishing off their coffee when all the diners were interrupted by a man who burst into the restaurant yelling for the sheriff. "Sheriff Steel! Monk Tarpley got the jump on Eddie and laid him out cold! He's broke outta jail!"

Sheriff Clayton Steel jumped up immediately. "He'll be headin' for the stable!" His statement was punctuated by the sound of two gunshots coming from that direction.

The sheriff wasn't the only one who reacted instantly to the alarm. Perley and Possum jumped to their feet and rushed to the hooks on the wall to get their weapons. Almost as an afterthought, Perley reached in his pocket and pulled out some money. He didn't take time to ask how much they owed; he just slapped a couple of dollars in Edna's hand as he rushed by her and ran after the sheriff.

There were already about a dozen people gathered in front of the stable door. The man who sounded the alarm in Thornton's was one of them, having outrun the sheriff and Perley and Possum. "They say he's already got a couple of horses and took off, Sheriff," the man said.

The sheriff pushed through the spectators and went into the stable, with Perley and Possum right behind him. "Gil!" Steel called out. "Gil, you in here?" He held up his hand for silence when he thought he heard something. "Where are you, Gil? Are you hurt?"

"I'm in here." His weak call came from the tack room, so they rushed in to find him lying on the floor. "He put a couple of bullets in me," Gil managed to say.

"Don't worry, we're gonna get Doc up here as soon as we can." He turned to Perley then and said, "Go see if Eddie's all right and go get Doc."

"I don't know Eddie," Perley said. "And I don't know where the doctor is."

The sheriff paused to take a closer look at the two men accompanying him. "Who the hell are you, anyway?"

"We're strangers here and our horses were in this stable," Perley answered.

"For the love of —" Steel started but was too frustrated to complete. "Go out there and tell somebody to go get Doc Collins and tell somebody to check on my deputy."

"I'll do it," Possum said to Perley. "You stay here and ask Gil if our horses are stolen."

The sheriff turned his attention back to Gil Porter. "How bad is it, Gil? Can you sit up, or is it better there on your back?"

"I think I can sit up a little," Gil said. "It was that Monk Tarpley. He put one in my shoulder and one in my side, but I don't think he hit no organs or serious stuff."

"How many horses did he take with him?" Perley asked.

"He took three. Yours was one of 'em."

That was news Perley didn't want to hear. "Are you sure?" Perley asked. "Of all the horses you've got in here, how'd he come to pick ours?"

"Just bad luck," Gil groaned, starting to feel the pain from his wounds by then. "They were the last ones I brought in from the corral, so they were the first ones he saw in the stalls."

"I don't reckon you know which way he headed, you bein' shot and all," the sheriff asked.

"It sounded like he went south," Gil groaned.

"That figures," the sheriff replied.

"Why does that figure?" Perley asked the sheriff, anxious for pursuit to begin.

" 'Cause that's where that Tarpley bunch hangs out most of the time," Steel said. "I take it I can count on you in the posse."

"Oh, you sure can," Perley responded. "But I'll have to borrow a horse to ride." He turned back to Gil then. "You're sure he took my bay, and Possum's gray?"

"He took your bay, but he didn't take the gray or that paint you brought in. The other horse he stole was a sorrel."

"You said he took three horses," Perley pressed, since Gil seemed able to talk all right.

"That's right," Gil said. "The other one was that dun he rode into town on. That's the first one he looked for. That's the one he threw his saddle on and rode outta here on."

Possum rushed back in at that point. "Somebody's gone for the doctor and another fellow is goin' to the jail to see if your deputy is all right," he announced, then asked Perley. "Did he get our horses?"

"He took Buck," Perley said, "but he didn't take Dancer, and I've gotta find him before he finds out he can't ride Buck and ends up shootin' him."

"Damn the luck," Possum swore. "Let's look at all the horses in here and make sure Buck ain't one of 'em before we go chasin' after that feller. Buck weren't the only bay horse in here."

"Good idea," Perley said, and they split up and ran back through the stalls, only to confirm Gil Porter's report. When they got back to the front of the stable, the doctor had arrived and was examining Gil's wounds. The group of spectators outside the stable had grown into a small crowd, and a handful of them had pushed inside to get a closer look. Doc Collins promptly drafted four of them to carry Gil back to his office for some surgery. "We're goin' after my horse," Perley tried to tell Gil as he was being carried out. "We've paid you for tonight, but we'll just call it even." Gil responded with only a weak wave of his hand, not really caring what Perley was trying to tell him. He was more worried about leaving his stable with no one tending it.

The sheriff walked outside with the doctor and announced to the crowd of spectators that he was calling for volunteers to ride a posse. "We've still got more than an hour of daylight left, so I need you in a hurry. Everybody who wants to ride meet in front of the jail as fast as you can get ready." Perley recognized the man who had alerted them in the restaurant, so he asked if he knew which way Monk Tarpley had fled. The man said Tarpley had left town on the road south. Perley was satisfied then, since everyone was of that opinion.

"Let's get saddled up," he said to Possum. "Might as well load our packhorses, too, 'cause we ain't likely to be comin' back here. I'm gonna throw my saddle on that paint that belongs to Elmira. I don't think she'd care if I took it."

"She kept trying to pay us for helpin' 'em," Possum replied. "It oughta make her happy. She'd probably just as well get shed of any reminders of Otis Welker, anyway."

At least Monk Tarpley hadn't gotten into the stall where their packs and saddles were, so they packed everything up, and Perley put his saddle on the paint. The horse showed no resentment toward the new rider. They figured that after hauling Otis for a while, the horse wasn't particular. When they got to the jail, Sheriff Steel was again calling for volunteers for his posse. Beside him on the steps to his office, his deputy, Eddie Price, stood. There was a rag tied around his head as a bandage covering the cut left there by the edge of the washbasin when Monk had caught him by surprise. Steel was admonishing the crowd for their lack of enthusiasm to go after Monk Tarpley. When Perley and Possum rode up, Steel used their example as responsible citizens to motivate his fellow townsmen. "We owe our thanks to these two volunteers. Strangers to our town, they are only here for one day, yet they feel it their duty to help the citizens of Nacogdoches." He didn't mention the fact that Monk stole Perley's horse. With daylight in limited supply, he had to cut his recruitment short and settle for the four men who answered the call, in addition to Perley and Possum. Since his deputy was still somewhat shaky after the blow to his head, he was left to watch the office.

Sheriff Steel led his six volunteers out the south road on a trail already growing cold.

There was no attempt to search the road

for tracks. since it was generally assumed that Monk would be heading back to the general domain of the Tarpley family as quick as he could. It was about eight miles to the Angelina River, so the sheriff held the posse to an easy lope. He reasoned that they should try to pick up Monk's tracks on the other side of the river; that would likely be the point where he would try to disguise his trail. The problem, however, was the same one they started with: Even holding the horses to a steady pace, daylight was rapidly slipping away. And by the time they reached the river, it was already difficult to distinguish one set of tracks from another. To add to their problems, the horses were tired, so they had to rest them. It only became darker as they waited, until one of the volunteers spoke what the others were thinking.

"I don't know about the rest of ya, but when my horse rests up a little, I'm turnin' around and goin' home. It's too damn dark to see any tracks on the other side of the river now. So it don't make no sense to even cross over in the dark."

Sheriff Steel didn't waste his time trying to convince them to continue because he was of much the same opinion. He knew what they knew: There was little chance of running Monk to ground after he crossed the river. It was wild country between the Angelina and the Neches rivers, stretch of pine woods and bushy creeks, with a lot of places for individuals or gangs to disappear. "Well, there ain't no use to set around here in the dark," Steel said. "He got away, and that's that. I ain't got no jurisdiction outside the city limits, anyway. But I appreciate you fellers volunteerin' to try to catch him. I'll stand for a round of drinks when we get back to town."

A couple of the men decided their horses were rested enough to go back to town, but just to make sure, they decided to walk and lead their horses about halfway. The other two decided to wait a little while longer before starting back. "What about you two?" Steel asked Perley.

"I expect we'll make our camp right here," Perley replied. "Then we'll cross on over in the mornin' and see if we can find some tracks that might be a rider leadin' two horses."

"I understand how you can feel about losin' a good horse," Steel said. "But I wouldn't feel right about it if I didn't warn you about this little piece of Texas. There's a lotta good folks tryin' to make a livin' off the land in Angelina County. But there's some bad people that have found this piece of Texas to their likin', too. And that feller you're trying to track, Monk Tarpley, is one of dozens in that Tarpley clan that's hidin' out from some holdup or bank robbery in Houston, or San Antonio, or somewhere else. And they ain't too friendly with anybody who comes looking for one of 'em. So, young feller, if there ain't somethin' extra special about that horse you lost, you'd be well advised to just accept the loss and find you another horse."

"I 'preciate the warnin', Sheriff," Perley said. "But that horse has took care of me for quite a while now. And he expects me to take care of him. So he's gonna be awful disappointed if I don't come after him."

Steel didn't reply at once. Instead, he looked at Perley as if he were talking to a crazy person. He looked at Possum for support, but Possum merely responded with a helpless shrug of his shoulders. "Well, I reckon you think you know what you're doin', but I don't think you really do."

"There is one thing that's gonna be a problem for us," Perley said. "And that's the fact that I ain't ever seen Monk Tarpley. I wouldn't know him if he walked up to me and said howdy."

"Well, that ain't gonna be no problem," Steel said. "He's got a big scar about five inches long, right across his left cheek. The story I heard was that one of his cousins did it in a fight over a chicken leg. Monk killed him for it is what I heard, but I ain't sure about that last part. Anyway, if you see that scar, you'll know it's Monk. It looks like a blacksmith sewed it up for him."

"That sure helps, if I get close enough to see his face," Perley said. "What about if I was to see him down the street, comin' toward me?"

"He's a heavyset man about your height, I reckon, but he's built like a bull. He ain't got no neck. His head's just settin' on his shoulders. I think you'll know him, if you see him." He watched Perley's reaction to the description of Monk Tarpley. Then he asked, "You still wanna go after him, just the two of you?"

"Oh, there ain't any doubt about that," Perley answered. "Buck would never forgive me if I didn't come get him."

CHAPTER 10

When the sheriff and the remaining two members of his citizen posse decided their horses were rested enough to ride, one of the men felt an obligation to speak to Perley and Possum. "You sure you fellows wanna go after Monk by yourselves? The sheriff weren't lyin' when he told you it was damn risky going into that country to get one of them Tarpleys. Everybody between here and the Neches River is a Tarpley, or married to one, and they ain't friendly to outsiders." Perley thanked him for his concern but told him the horse was too good to abandon. The fellow wished him good luck and started back to town with Steel and the other man.

Perley had not mentioned his main concern for the bay gelding: the fact that Buck would not permit any man but Perley to ride him, hence the inspiration for his name. And as a consequence for that disposition,

Perley was afraid Buck would end up getting shot after Monk had been thrown a few times. After the sheriff's warning against going into Tarpley country, and then another by one of the posse men, he realized that he was endangering Possum's life as well as his own. He had no right to do that, nor did he want to. So he told Possum what his plans were while they gathered wood to build a fire. "We can set up our camp here on this side of the river and go across in the mornin' to see if we can find his trail. If we find it, I don't wanna fool with a packhorse, so you can come back here to this camp and watch the packhorses to make sure nobody comes along and runs off with 'em." Possum didn't respond at once. He just stared at Perley as if he had suddenly began uttering meaningless phrases of nonsense. Finally Perley asked, "Did you hear what I said?"

"Yeah, I heard you," Possum answered. "I was just wonderin' if you heard what you said. 'Cause it sounded like a crazy man talkin'."

"Maybe I am crazy for wantin' to go into that hornet's nest of relatives, and that's up to me. But I ain't got no right to drag you into it and risk gettin' you killed just for the sake of my horse. If those Tarpley people are as bad as they say, you're liable to get picked off by one of his cousins before we ever saw Monk. If we find a trail to follow, me and ol' Paint, here, can slip in there and track Mr. Tarpley to his hideout. If I can find him, I might trade him the paint for Buck. He oughta be ready for a trade if he's tried to ride Buck."

"I expect he'd just keep both horses and thank you for bringing him the paint," Possum said. "Then he'd shoot you for your trouble. If you're through talkin' like a crazy man, let's get this fire goin' and make us a pot of coffee."

"You know, I would like to know that if I didn't come back, you could ride back to the Triple-G to tell 'em what happened to me."

"Yeah, I can see that," Possum replied. "John would most likely shoot me for comin' back without you. Now, quit talkin' nonsense. It hurts my ears." They continued to argue the subject throughout the rest of the evening until Perley gave up trying to talk Possum out of going with him.

Morning found a heavy mist lying low upon the water. Perley was the first to awaken, so he crawled out of his blanket and went down to the river's edge to fill the coffeepot. When it was filled he shifted it to his left hand, as was his habit. At that instant he heard the faint rustle of leaves in the bushes on the bank behind him. Without conscious thought, he reached for his .44 as he spun around, but his hand found nothing but air. His gun belt was lying beside his blanket. The moment of panic passed when the nose of a small mule deer pushed through the bushes and stopped, equally surprised by the man's presence. The meeting was brief, however, because the deer bolted, followed by two more behind it, and disappeared into the mist. Perley decided it a good thing that he was not armed. It might have been too tempting to pass up a chance for fresh venison, even though they had no time to butcher and cook a deer. It would have been hard to explain that to Buck.

Possum was awake and stirring up the fire when Perley returned to the camp. Before going to sleep the night before, they had decided to have coffee and beef jerky before starting the hunt for Monk Tarpley. "While you enjoy your breakfast of jerky, let me tell you about what you mighta had, if the situation was a little different," Perley said, and told him about being surprised by the deer.

"Boy, that woulda made a fine breakfast," Possum commented. "I wouldn't mind takin' a little time to deer hunt after we find

Buck. There ain't much use to hurry back home now. After we've been gone this long, they've most likely broke both our dinner plates, anyway."

They didn't take much time with their breakfast and were packed up and ready to leave as soon as there was enough daylight to scout the opposite bank for tracks. There were none at all in the road on the other side. They decided not to split up to search for Monk's exit from the river, figuring they might have ended up so far apart that the one who found the exit would have to fire a shot to signal the other one, and they preferred not to announce their presence if possible. So for no reason other than it would be easier riding with the current than against it, they started downstream. They only rode about one hundred yards before coming to a small stream. Monk had figured to leave the river there, likely thinking his tracks would still be hidden in the water. But he was leading two horses that were not that particular about disguising their tracks, plus it was getting dark by the time he reached the stream. Consequently, there were plenty of hoofprints here and there along the sides of the stream.

Monk had stayed with the stream through a thick pine forest, and when it crossed a small clearing, he left it and picked up a game trail on the other side of the clearing. Perley and Possum followed that trail for what they estimated to be at least two miles before coming to a good-sized creek and a narrow wagon road running along beside it. The tracks of the three horses were the only ones on the road, and there appeared to be no further efforts to hide them. " 'Pears to me he feels safe now that he's got this far," Possum commented.

"Hold up!" Perley cautioned softly, and pulled the paint to a stop. When Possum pulled up beside him, Perley pointed up ahead of them. "Looks like a cabin sittin' back in the woods a-ways."

"Might be a good idea to cross over to the other side of the creek and pass by in the trees over there," Possum suggested. Perley thought this a good idea, so they crossed to the other side of the creek, then rode past the cabin, stopping only long enough to rule it out as Monk's destination. It was a very small, roughly built cabin with only a large shed behind it with a small corral attached. There was not even an outhouse for convenience. It looked to be typical for someone living catch-as-catch-can. There was no sign of life in or around the cabin, although they definitely felt that they were being watched as they passed. When they went back across the creek, they saw that Monk's tracks were still following the road. "I swear," Possum said, "if we had to run for it all of a sudden, I'm danged if I'd know which way to head."

"Well, it looks like we might be comin' out of these thick woods up ahead," Perley said. "I can see more daylight through the trees." They came to a wide branch from the stream flowing across the road. A path left the road before the branch, but it disappeared into the trees. On the other side of the branch, there appeared to be a clearing. When they came to the edge of the trees, they stopped to look at a rustic house in a section of the woods that had been cleared to some extent. There was a barn behind the house, and a pasture dotted with the stumps of the trees that had possibly been used for the buildings. Leaving the road again so they could remain in the trees, they moved forward until they could see the other side of the house and the barn behind it. To get a better look, they dismounted and tied their horses on some pine limbs, then moved closer to the edge of the woods. The next thing they saw almost caused Perley to speak out. A couple of men were standing in front of the barn when another led a horse out of the barn. Both Perley and

Possum froze. The man leading the horse fit the description Sheriff Steel had given of Monk Tarpley. The horse he led was Buck, and he was saddled.

"Easy, partner," Possum cautioned Perley. "Let's see what they've got in mind."

"I'm going to get my rifle," Perley said, thinking to take Monk out if he started to harm the horse.

"Wait a minute," Possum said. "He's bringin' Buck out for one of the other fellows to look at. He's trying to sell him."

"That fellow is gonna try to ride him," Perley said. They knew what was coming but were too far away to do anything to prevent it without starting a shooting war. While they watched, the man took the reins from Monk and stepped up into the saddle. Nothing happened until the man gave Buck a gentle kick with his heels. The horse exploded, throwing the man violently over his neck, then rearing up on his hind hooves, showing his dominance. This suddenly gave Perley an idea. He ran back and jumped on the paint.

"What the hell?" Possum gasped. "Where are you goin'?"

"It's time to trade horses," Perley said. He grabbed the reins of his packhorse and rode back through the trees until reaching the road again.

"Lord help us!" Possum prayed, and with no other choice, he jumped on his horse and followed.

Perley rode up the middle of the road and pulled into the path to the barn, surprising the three men standing there, the would-be rider having regained his feet. "Howdy," Perley offered as he rode into the barnyard. "Looks like you've got an unmanageable horse there."

"A what?" Monk responded.

"A horse that's hard to manage," Perley said.

"What if I have?" Monk asked, his face reflecting a blank mind. "Who the hell are you?"

"I'm the fellow who rides unmanageable horses, that's who," Perley answered. "Did you ride him?"

"Maybe I did and maybe I didn't," Monk answered, still bumfuzzled by the sudden appearance of a complete stranger. "Who the hell are you?" he repeated.

"Let's see you ride him now," Perley challenged, ignoring the question.

"He's my horse. I'll ride him when I want to. Who's that?" Monk demanded when Possum rode in.

"He's with me," Perley said. "We were just

passin' by when we saw your friend take a ride. I like the look of that horse. I might trade you this paint I'm ridin' for that buckin' horse."

"What makes you think you can ride him?"

" 'Cause I can ride any horse. I told you; that's what I do. And the horse knows I can ride him. Look at him." Upon seeing Perley, Buck started whinnying and snorting and bobbing his head up and down. "He knows I can ride him and there ain't nothin' he can do about it."

When Monk saw Buck's behavior, he laughed and said, "He's wantin' to bust your behind. Go to it, bigshot. Let's see you ride him."

Perley climbed down from the paint and walked over to Buck. He stroked the big bay's face a couple of times, then stepped up into the saddle. As before, when the other man climbed on him, Buck just stood there. "You'd better grab on to that saddle horn," the man just thrown warned, snickering in anticipation. Perley touched Buck lightly with his heels and the horse loped around the barnyard at a gentle pace. Then he galloped up to the wagon road and back, pulling the horse to a sliding stop.

Perley stepped down. "Whaddaya say?

Trade ya even. My paint for the buckin' horse. And I'll guarantee you the paint won't buck you off."

Monk wasn't sure if what he saw wasn't some kind of trick. He knew that horse had landed him on his back the two times he tried to ride him. And he just did the same thing to Monk's cousin. "No," he decided. "I don't know what it was you done, but you broke that horse, so he don't buck no more. I don't wanna trade him now."

"Is that right?" Perley replied. "Well, why don't you step up on him and ride him?"

"I might do that," Monk declared, and started toward Buck. The horse dropped his head and snorted several times as his front hooves pawed the ground. Monk hesitated but decided to see if he was right. He grabbed the reins and put his foot in the stirrup, but Buck sidestepped away from him. They went around and around in a circle, Monk with one foot in the stirrup, and rapidly wearing out, hopping on the other foot. He made a desperate move to throw a leg over the saddle, only to be thrown all the way over the other side of the horse to a painful landing on his back. Furious, Monk fumbled around, trying to pull his gun out of his holster.

Perley stepped in front of Buck. "I ain't

gonna trade you a good paint for a dead horse. You want a good ridin' horse? Give that paint a try." Still fuming, Monk stood for a long moment staring at Buck. Then he took the reins Perley held out for him. Still a bit leery, he stepped up onto the paint and gave him a kick. The horse immediately responded, and Monk galloped him up to the road and back, ending with a sliding stop also. "Deal?" Perley asked.

"Deal," Monk replied.

"Well, let's pull the bridles and saddles off of 'em. I'm just tradin' horses. I'll keep my own tack."

Monk watched Perley as he pulled his saddle off the paint and decided to sweeten his deal. "This bay's worth more than that paint. To make it a fair swap, you need to give me the paint and twenty dollars for this bay." He only glanced in Possum's direction, giving no thought to the fact that he was still sitting on his horse, his rifle laying casually across his thighs.

Perley hesitated, as if reconsidering the trade just agreed upon. He dropped his saddle on the ground. "A horse ain't worth no more than what he can do," he said. "You can't ride that bay, so he ain't worth nothin' more than what you'd pay for a packhorse. Lookin' at it from my side, I'm thinkin' the paint is worth more than the bay, but we already agreed on a swap. We're tradin' even, or we ain't tradin'."

"Ha," Monk grunted while he pulled his saddle off the bay. "A deal's a deal, we'll swap, but I ain't so sure you'll like that devil when whatever that was you rubbed on his nose wears off." Perley was puzzled by the remark until he remembered that he had stroked Buck's face a couple of times before climbing on him. He gave Monk a smile then, and Monk remarked, "I ain't as dumb as you think."

Possum continued to sit on his horse and watch a trade that he never could have imagined taking place. His job, he decided, was to remain silent and watch the proceedings in case they suddenly went sour. And if they did, he was ready to open up with his rifle, knowing Perley would probably react like greased lightning as usual. The third man, who seemed to be no more than an interested witness to the horse sale, turned around and went back to the house. Possum wasn't sure if Perley noticed, but it gave him some concern. Monk's cousin, still rubbing his back after trying to ride Buck, asked Perley, "Your partner don't say much, does he?"

Perley glanced at Possum. "No, he never has said anything. Fact is, I ain't sure if he can talk or not. He just motions."

The cousin found that interesting but only for a moment. Then his mind was back to buying a horse. "Now I reckon it's the paint that I'll decide on," he said to Monk.

"Yeah," Monk replied, "but the price has gone up. The paint's worth more than that bay I was gonna sell you. A good saddle horse like that'd cost a hundred and fifty to two hundred dollars."

"Maybe so," the cousin retorted. "But you didn't pay that much for it. You didn't pay a dime for it."

"That's why I was gonna let you have that bay for forty dollars," Monk said. "I oughta get at least fifty for the paint."

While the two of them were haggling over the price of the paint, Perley busied himself changing the saddles and bridles. He got Buck saddled and ready to go first, then he laid Monk's saddle close to the paint. Monk and his cousin still seemed locked in their pricing of the paint horse, so Perley stepped up into the saddle and nodded toward Possum. Possum nodded back. "Well, it was a pleasure doin' business with you. We'd best be gettin' along." He wheeled Buck around and started up the path to the road without waiting for Monk's response.

Behind them, Monk's father, Clyde Tarpley came out the back door of the house, followed by the man who had been watching the swap before. "Monk!" Clyde yelled. "Who the hell was that?"

Monk, still distracted by his price haggling with his cousin, seemed just then aware that Perley and Possum were gone. He looked toward the wagon road in time to see them turn onto it from the path. "Him? He's the feller that fixes unmanageable horses. The feller with him don't talk."

"What's he doin' ridin' off on that bay you stole? I thought you was gonna sell that bay to Bud." Monk's answer just then registered with him. "He's the feller that fixes what?"

"You know, horses you can't ride — he fixes 'em," Monk explained.

"You mean he breaks horses? What'd he want here?"

"He don't break 'em like you're talkin' about. He fixes 'em from bein' wild by rubbin' some kinda secret stuff on their noses. I swapped that bay for this paint, and if Bud's got any sense, he'll gimme fifty dollars for him."

Clyde came storming toward them. "I swear, Monk, I wish to hell I'd put a strap around your ma's belly to hold you in there till your brain had a chance to grow. What kinda trade did you make for this paint?"

"Even trade, Pa," Monk answered proudly. "Didn't give him any money."

"You dang fool," his father scolded, "you just let him slick you good. That bay is twice the horse this paint is. Who the hell is he, anyway? You ever see him anywhere before? Anybody from Nacogdoches?" He looked from Monk to Bud. They both responded with a blank look and a shake of the head.

"They was both leadin' packhorses," Bud offered. "So most likely they ain't somebody from Nacogdoches. And they're followin' the creek road on out that way. They most likely was just passin' through here."

"I'll bet they're lost right now. They mighta been ridin' some of these old woods trails, lookin' for folks like Monk they can slick outta somethin'. Monk, go saddle my horse, I want that bay horse back, and we'll see what else they've picked up on their little ride through Tarpley country."

"Hot damn!" Cousin Bud yelped. "Let's go show 'em who owns this part of Texas! Go get your horse, Lonnie." Lonnie ran after Clyde and Monk, eager to get in on the fun.

Perley and Possum held their horses to an easy lope, hoping to put as much distance behind them as they could without tiring their horses too soon. They could only guess what the reaction would be after the older man they glimpsed storming out of the back door of the house took charge. If what they had been told about the Tarpley clan was true, they might expect some violent response. For that reason, there was no need for talk about what they should do. The only option was to put distance between them. They didn't even know if they might be followed by the four they saw back in the yard, or if there were more in the house that might increase their posse. After loping for some time, they slowed the horses to a walk. Perley reined Buck back until Possum pulled up beside him so they could talk.

"I swear," Possum spoke first, "that was the doggonedest thing I ever saw. I'da never thought you coulda got your horse back without somebody gettin' shot." He paused, then added, "So far."

"If we can just keep ahead of them until we reach the Neches River, we might have a better chance of holdin' 'em off, if we have to," Perley said. "How far you reckon we are from that river?"

"It's hard to guess," Possum confessed. "I ain't sure how far we've come from the Angelina after followin' all these little game trails and this wagon track. Steel said it was twenty miles between the two rivers at the point we crossed the Angelina. I just hope the horses don't give out. They don't show no signs of it. I am glad of one thing, though. When you took off and rode right down there in their backyard, I was afraid you were thinkin' about arrestin' Monk Tarpley."

"Arrest him?" Perley responded. "You must really think I'm crazy. I'm not a lawman, and you and I ain't a posse. I think if I'da tried something like that, I'da had a good chance of gettin' us both killed. If we had run back the way we came in, I woulda been happy to tell Sheriff Steel where he could find Monk Tarpley. But I'd leave it up to him to get him arrested."

Possum laughed. "Well, I'm glad to hear you ain't lost all your reasonin' powers. And you got your horse back without firin' a shot."

"I'm not sure we're gonna get outta here without firin' a shot, if they're comin' after us. I have to say, I'll be relieved if there's only the four of 'em that chases us. If that's what happens, our best chance is to set up in ambush and not even let 'em get close. Because I think we can assume they won't be comin' to apologize for stealin' my horse."

"If we get out of this mess alive, you think we ought to circle back to Nacogdoches to tell Sheriff Steel where Monk Tarpley is holed up?" Possum asked.

"I think if we get out of this mess, when we strike the Neches River, we ought to follow it north to Tyler. Then head straight to Paris and the Triple-G. If we went back and drew Clayton Steel a map to Monk Tarpley's house, Steel wouldn't go in there to arrest him. That ain't his job, just like it ain't our job. He'd contact the U.S Marshals or the Rangers, and they'd be the ones to go in there after Monk. If it ain't Steel's job, it sure as hell ain't yours or mine. I don't know what to tell you, Possum. Maybe you feel like Monk's an escaped prisoner and we oughta try to bring him in to justice. I don't know what he did to get put in jail, although it was a pretty good lick he put on that deputy's head to escape."

"Well, I'll tell you what I think about it. If you had decided to go back to Nacogdoches and lead the sheriff back in that cow pie to get that worthless lamebrain back there, I was gonna tell you you were gonna have to do it without me."

"Good, then we're agreed on it," Perley said. "Let's pick up the pace a little bit." He nudged Buck with his heels and the big bay started to trot.

Chapter 11

They continued the increased pace for a while longer before dropping back into a walk again, the horses now showing signs of fatigue. "Thank the Lord!" Possum exclaimed. "Yonder's the river." They could see the thicker ribbon of trees that marked the course of the river about one hundred yards ahead. When they reached the river, they rode the horses on into the water and stopped to let them drink. When the horses were satisfied, they rode on across to the other side to select the best place to rest them. The spot they decided upon was upriver from the road crossing, about half a mile north of it, where a narrow gully ran down into the river. It offered a small patch of grass for grazing the horses, just north of the gully. "We'd be smart to rest these horses," Possum said, "and we ain't likely to find a better place than this."

A question to be decided in light of their

special circumstances was whether or not they should take the loads off the packhorses to give them better rest. The horses might rest quicker with them off, but there was a distinct possibility that the whole Tarpley nation might pop up on their trail, forcing them to jump on their horses and run. In that case, it would be better not to have to load them again. That time might mean the difference between life and death.

There was another possibility that Perley had considered but had not brought up with Possum because he did not want to generate false hopes. He remembered Sheriff Steel talking about the Tarpley clan thinking they owned that piece of territory south of Nacogdoches, between the Angelina and the Neches Rivers. If they really felt that territory was theirs by claim, then maybe the two rivers were like fences to them. Maybe they would give chase to strangers until they reached the river boundary but stop at that point, satisfied that they had chased the trespassers out. Perley had not given that as his reason for saying they might be able to hold them off once they reached the Neches, but he hoped that would be the case. And with that in mind, he relieved his packhorse of its burden.

"Looks like you made up your mind,"

Possum commented.

"I think, in the long run, we'll have a better chance if the horses ain't forced to stand around under a load," Perley explained.

"And you figure it's every man for hisself now, right?" Possum asked, seeming more than a little disappointed that Perley hadn't consulted him first.

"I figure we might find ourselves in a shoot-out here in a very short time, so we need to make it as easy on our horses as we can. And when the time comes when we have to run, I'll cover you while you load your packhorse. And you'll cover me while I load mine. I don't have the right to tell you how to get ready for whatever pops over that riverbank, though. So if you don't want to unload your horse, I'll just try to hang back and cover your behind when your horse is too tired to take another step."

"Well, if that ain't somethin'," Possum snorted. "I thought we was partners in this deal. If you're gonna strip your horse down, then I reckon I'm gonna strip mine down, too. 'Course, we're liable to be ridin' the rest of the way home bareback without no packhorses."

"That's a possibility," Perley allowed with a grin.

■ ■ ■ ■

It was fully half an hour before they showed up on the western side of the river. Perley spotted them when they approached within a hundred yards of his and Possum's position by the gully. Perley was at once disappointed that his belief that they might stop at the river didn't turn out to be the case. But at least there were no more than the four he had seen in the yard. "Well, we'll see just what they've got in mind," Possum remarked.

"Yonder they are!" Bud Tarpley exclaimed at about the same time Perley spotted them. Out in front of the others, Bud reined his horse back and waited for them to pull up around him. "Yonder," he repeated, and pointed to Perley and Possum standing next to the gully, about a hundred yards distant. "Whaddaya gonna do, Uncle Clyde?"

"We'll get a little closer, so I can talk to 'em," Clyde said. "Spread out a little bit and get your guns ready. I wanna see how much starch they've got in 'em. When the shootin' starts, be mindful of them horses. There's four good horses I wanna pick up back there behind 'em." He rode out in front of the three younger men, walking his horse to within talking distance before pulling up again. "Howdy strangers," he called out. "You fellers has got a horse that belongs to my son. We've come to take it off your hands. See, it's a horse I bought for him for his birthday, and he didn't really have no thought about tradin' it for that paint. So I expect you two fellers wanna do the right thing and turn that bay horse back over to us. We'll give you back the paint, and everything will be right again."

"I expect that's as close as you'd better come," Perley called back to him. "In the first place, that bay you're talking about was stolen by your son, Monk. And the reason I know he stole him is because he's my horse. If you gave your son a bay horse, it had to be a different one than this one I'm ridin'. If he told you he didn't want to swap it for the paint, he's lyin'. And if you say you gave this one to him for his birthday, that would make you a liar, too. Best you turn around and go on back across the river and leave us be. We don't have anything that belongs to you or your son. And there's no sense in anybody gettin' hurt over a misunderstandin'."

"There ain't no misunderstandin' on my part," Clyde said. "You're a fast-talkin' horse thief that talked my son outta that bay horse, and I'm gonna take the horse back one way or another."

"If you really believe that, then the best thing to do is send Monk back into Nacogdoches to report Monk's stolen horse to the sheriff," Perley suggested. "I'm sure Sheriff Steel will be glad to take care of him. And the sheriff knows how to get hold of me."

"You're makin' a big mistake, young feller. I might be willin' to cut you and your partner some slack. If you just leave that horse and ride on outta this territory, we'll let you go peacefully."

"Mister," Perley said, "I'm tired of wastin' my time with you. This is the last warnin' I'm gonna give you. Monk made a mistake. The horse belongs to me, and there ain't any sense in anybody getting' shot over it."

"All right," Clyde said, "ain't no sense in anybody gittin' shot. We're goin'." He turned his horse around and started back toward the three behind him. "Pick your target boys and we'll all cut loose when I turn back around."

"Back up to the edge of the gully," Perley told Possum. "I don't trust that old buzzard. If those other three don't turn around and go with him, they're gonna throw down on us. If he starts to turn back to face us, drop down in the gully. I'll start on the right side, you take the left. Okay?"

"Okay," Possum responded, edging closer to the gully behind them. With their rifles at the ready, they watched Clyde Tarpley as he rode back to his anxious assassins. When he wheeled his horse around, their rifles came up to fire, and Perley and Possum took one step back at the same moment and dropped into the gully. As the four shots snapped over their heads, both men in the neck-deep gully popped back up to return fire. Almost as fast with his Henry rifle as he was with his Colt handgun, Perley knocked Clyde and Monk out of the saddle. Possum hit Lonnie but was not quite fast enough to hit Bud before the sudden explosion of gunfire caused the horses to bolt. Possum took dead aim on the fleeing assassin and sent a final shot that ended the threat.

There were no shouts of celebration as the two partners crawled up out of their gully. Their first concern was to see if the horses were all right. They appeared to be okay, so they went to check on the four victims to make sure there was no last desperate shot for revenge waiting for one of them. Clyde and Monk were both dead, as was Lonnie. Possum went to check on Bud, who had remained in the saddle for about fifty yards before hitting the ground.

He was alive, but barely. Possum's bullet had struck him in the back and evidently punctured his lung. Determining no hope for him to make it, Possum cranked another cartridge into the chamber and ended Bud's misery. Possum was glad it was his task to do and not Perley's. Perley would no doubt be in a melancholy fog over four useless killings, so Possum prepared to make him work through it. "Come on," he said when he returned to the gully. "We've got a lot of work to do. We're gonna have to round up their four horses, see if we wanna keep 'em all or turn some of 'em loose. Gotta collect all their weapons and ammunition, see if their saddles and bridles are worth foolin' with. We gotta do somethin' with the bodies. It'd be easy to just throw them in this gully, but every time it rained, it would wash some of their evil into the river. And I expect it wouldn't take many rains before those four ruined the river for good."

"And after we do all that," Perley suggested, "I reckon it might be a good idea to move on up the river a-ways to find us another place to camp. This one's got too many signs about what happened here. Might be hard to explain if another gang of Tarpley kin stops by." He looked around him, then threw up his hands. "Well, we might as well get to it." It was early enough in the afternoon to get all they had to get done and still move their camp by suppertime.

They rounded up the four extra horses they now had and put them north of the gully with their horses. Next priority was checking the four bodies for weapons and money. By this time, they had been gone from the Triple-G so long, Perley was almost out of money, and Possum was broke. They didn't find much on their victims. "When we get to Tyler, we might be able to sell a couple of horses and saddles," Perley suggested.

"Right now, I'd give one of 'em for a plate of food," Possum quipped.

"That's right," Perley was reminded, "we didn't have any dinner, did we?"

"Maybe tonight we'll eat one of those horses," Possum remarked.

They looked around until deciding on a final resting place for the four Tarpley men. It was a hole left by a large, uprooted tree, evidently blown over in a windstorm. Then they each took one of their horses, and with ropes around their boots, dragged the bodies to the spot well away from the river to await the buzzards. They packed the rifles and ammunition that had belonged to their adversaries on their four extra horses, as well as some of the load their packhorses had been carrying. With all the horses rested, watered, and grazed now, they started following the river to the north, anticipating a ride of around two and a half or three hours before they would go into camp for the night. Being old ranch hands, they decided to drive the extra horses instead of leading them on ropes. The horses seemed content to be adopted by their new party and were enjoying their freedom.

They camped that night in a little bend in the river that almost formed a half circle. From their fire, they could see the end of a cotton field on the opposite side of the river, just north of the bend. It was the first sign of a farm they had seen. When the horses were all taken care of, they boiled some coffee and cooked some bacon and hardtack, frying the hardtack in the bacon grease and sprinkling brown sugar on it to eat it like dessert. "It's times like these that I truly miss Nellie Butcher," Possum lamented.

"Amen to that," Perley replied.

They went to their blankets that night with a queasy feeling in their bellies, vowing never to fix their hardtack like that again. Morning brought a repeat of another morning not long before. Perley woke up first, as he usually did, and went down to the river to fill the coffeepot. On the bank behind him, he heard a rustling in the bushes, and he reacted without having to think, drawing the Colt he had strapped on as he spun around, ready to shoot. He thought he was dreaming, so he blinked his eyes rapidly, but the vision didn't go away. The bushes parted to reveal a young mule deer. Perley swore it was a dream because it looked like the very same deer he had seen on the Angelina. This time, however, he felt no restrictions. He pulled the trigger and the deer fell, shot through the head.

The sound of the .44 brought Possum scrambling out of his blanket, trying to find his gun. "Perley!" He yelled when he saw Perley's empty bedroll.

"Down by the water," Perley answered.

Possum came running down to him in his stocking feet, yelping with each stick or stone he stepped on. "What is it? What was that shot?"

"You ain't gonna eat no hardtack and bacon for breakfast," Perley said, pointing his pistol toward the bushes where the deer lay dead.

Possum walked back to the bank of bushes he had just run past. "You shot him with your pistol?"

"That's the only weapon I took with me to fill the coffeepot," Perley said. "You ain't gonna believe this, but I think it's the same deer that spooked me on the Angelina."

"You're right, I ain't gonna believe you. Shot him with your pistol," he repeated, surprised that the deer had fallen right there. "Where'd you hit him?"

"In the head," Perley replied.

"You shot him in the head," Possum said again.

"That's all I could see to aim at," Perley said.

Possum shook his head as he tried to create a picture of Perley drawing his six-gun and nailing the deer in the head. *Only Perley,* he thought. *Anyone else would most likely have emptied the gun trying to hit the deer in the head with a pistol.* Had it been him instead of Perley, he would have probably just fired into the bushes, trying to guess where the deer's body might be, then hope that one or two of his shots had done enough damage to eventually bring the deer down. He cleared his mind of the likelihood of Perley's shot and brought it back to the treat it provided. "Hallelujah!" he cried out then. "Fresh deer meat! Let's hang him up in a tree and butcher him."

So instead of getting an early start toward home, they spent half the day skinning and butchering their deer. With strips of the fresh meat roasting constantly over the fire, they filled their bellies as they worked. Some strips were laid on green branches over another fire to be smoked and eaten when the fresh meat was gone. The choice cuts of the meat were wrapped in the deer's hide. Even though they knew the meat would start to turn within a day or two, they still wrapped large portions of it in the hide. When they were finished, they left the remains for the buzzards, packed their fresh meat supply on the horses, and set out once again for home.

As they continued up the river and closer to Tyler, they began seeing more evidence of small farms. When they finally decided to stop and make camp for the night, they could once again see signs of land being cleared. A little beyond that, they could see pasture and grazing cows. "Who says there ain't no cattle ranches down in this part of Texas?" Possum asked in jest. "Them things in that pasture over yonder sure look like cows."

"I reckon somebody has to raise meat for the cotton farmers to eat," Perley said as he got his fire going. They soon had their horses taken care of and more fresh venison roasting over the fire. "Another day and a half oughta see us in Tyler."

Possum started to respond but instead grunted, "Uh-oh, we got company."

Aware at almost the same time, Perley said, "From both sides."

"You gonna stay hid back there in the trees, or are you gonna come on in?" Possum called out.

"Evenin', boys." A man stepped out of the shadows. He was holding a rifle at the ready. "Come on out, Elam." A second man emerged from the trees on the other side of their camp. He appeared to be younger and was also holding a rifle. They both closed in a little more on Perley and Possum. Caught at a disadvantage, sitting by the fire, there was nothing they could do but wait to see what might happen. "What's that you got cookin' on the fire, there? Smells like some fresh beef."

"Is that what you came sneakin' in here to find out?" Possum asked him. "Are you hungry? Or have you got somethin' more than that on your mind?"

"Get on your feet," the older man ordered, "and back away from that fire."

They both got up very slowly and stepped back toward the younger man. When they did, the older man moved up to take a closer look at the piece of meat roasting over the fire. When he straightened up again, it was to see Perley's .44 aimed at him and his son struggling with Possum to pull his rifle barrel back down from the vertical position Possum had forced it into. The struggle ended when the young man felt Possum's six-gun pressed into his side.

"I advise you to drop the rifle on the ground," Perley told the older man. "I guarantee you I can fire this .44 before you can even bring your rifle around to aim it at me again."

He could see that Perley was not bluffing, so Lucien Russell reluctantly laid his rifle on the ground. When he did, his son released his rifle and Possum pulled it away then stepped back, his pistol still aimed at Elam. When both intruders were standing subdued under the two guns now held on them, Perley said, "Suppose you tell us what you came here for."

Perley dropped his pistol back in the holster and waited while the frustrated man shifted his weight nervously from one foot to the other. It was obvious that he had been outfoxed, and his attempt to stop them had failed, but he decided to have his say, anyway. "Damn it, why don't you pick on somebody else for a change? This is the second one of my cows you had for supper. You ride in here with all the horses you stole somewhere. Why don't you eat one of them?"

"Believe me, we thought about it," Possum couldn't resist saying with a chuckle.

"Whoa," Perley said. "Is that what you think? That we killed one of your cows? Possum, cut a slice of meat for our guest."

"My pleasure," Possum said, enjoying the presumption now. "This your son?" Lucien said that it was. "I'll cut him a slice, too." He cut one for each of them. When Elam hesitated, Possum said, "Put it in your mouth. It ain't gonna hurtcha."

They both chewed up a bite and swallowed it. "Well, whaddaya think?" Perley asked.

"I don't know," Lucien hesitated. "It's awful lean. I reckon it tastes more like venison than beef," he finally admitted.

"Most deer meat does," Perley said. "We shot this deer this mornin', so it's still fresh and we've got plenty of it. I'd offer you some coffee with it, but we're runnin' short on coffee and a few other things. Possum and I work for the Triple-G cattle ranch, just about six miles this side of the Red River. We raise cattle, and we don't steal another fellow's. If we're on your land, here, we'll be goin' first thing in the mornin', and we'll try to leave it like we found it."

"I swear, fellows, I don't know what to say," Lucien stammered. "I feel like a dad-blamed fool. I was just so sure those other fellows were back to hit me for another cow."

"Natural mistake," Perley said. "I'da thought the same as you did."

"I apologize for everything I said," Lucien insisted. "Especially that crack about eatin' one of the horses you stole."

"We didn't steal 'em," Perley replied. "The previous owners are deceased, and like Possum said, before we shot that deer, we were thinkin' about eatin' one of 'em. You got more family back at the house?" Lucien said he had a wife and two daughters. "Maybe they'd like some fresh venison. We'd consider it a favor if you took some of this deer meat off our hands. I hate to see it wasted, and Possum and I aren't gonna be able to eat it before it goes bad. I figure it's got another day or two before it starts to turn. You can look at it and decide for yourself. We plan on eatin' it all day tomorrow, then it might start to go bad. You might know better than me. You can even take the hide it's wrapped in. I can wrap what we need in my rain slicker. It doesn't look like I'm gonna use it for anything else on this trip, anyway."

Lucien's son found it hard to believe what was taking place. He couldn't help laughing and commenting, "I declare, Pa, we sure showed these rustlers what's what, didn't we?" They all decided the best thing to do was to laugh about it and enjoy the fresh deer meat. Lucien and Elam stayed a little while and ate some more of the roasted venison before wishing them a good trip back to the Triple-G and saying goodnight. It wasn't the last they saw of the family, however. About half an hour later, Elam showed up again with a little sack of ground coffee and four biscuits from supper. "Pa said he didn't want you to run out of coffee before you got back home. And Ma said you might wanna eat a couple of cold biscuits when you get up in the morning. And she said to thank you for the generous amount of venison you gave us."

Chapter 12

"Who is it, Ma?" Broadus Tarpley asked his wife when she told him somebody was coming up the path from the creek.

"I can't tell yet in this light," Hannah answered. "He's on foot, and it's already too dark down in them trees to tell."

Broadus got up from the kitchen table where he had been sitting and drinking coffee. He went over to the back door beside his wife and peered out across the back yard. "Looks like Elmo," Broadus said. He knew it had to be one of his brother's boys, coming from that direction.

"I wonder what he wants," Hannah said.

"I reckon you'll find out when he gets here," her husband said. "Yup, it's Elmo," he confirmed when the boy walked out of the trees.

"Uncle Broadus!" Elmo yelled. "Aunt Hannah!"

"What is it, boy?" Broadus called back.

"Come in the house and stop that hollerin'."

"It's Pa and Lonnie and Monk and Bud!" Elmo exclaimed. "Ma sent me to get you. They're gone! And we don't know where!"

"Whaddaya mean, they're gone?" Broadus demanded. "Calm yourself down and tell me what you're talking about.

"They went after two fellers that took off with a horse that Monk had stole," Elmo said. "And that was way before dinnertime, and they ain't never come back! Ma said I best come tell you 'cause she thinks they musta run into trouble."

"Did you see the two fellers?" Broadus asked, concerned himself, since his brother's wife was. He and his brother, Clyde, had married sisters, Hannah and Atha, and had built identical houses on either side of a branch that ran off the creek and connected by a footpath across the branch. Of the two families, Elmo was the youngest at age fourteen. A skinny young'un with a big head, he was always being offered something to eat by mothers of both families, in hopes of growing his body in better proportion to his head.

"Yes, sir, I seen 'em," Elmo replied, taking the biscuit Hannah offered him. "They didn't pull no gun on 'em or nothin' like that. It was mostly just one of the men. He just talked Monk into tradin' for a paint he was ridin'. Then them two fellers just rode off. Lonnie was out there with Bud and Monk. He came in the house and told Pa about it, and Pa went out the door to stop 'em, but they took off. So Pa and Monk, and Lonnie and Bud got saddled up and took off after 'em. I didn't go with 'em 'cause I didn't have no horse."

"And they ain't got back yet?" Broadus asked. He didn't ask why Elmo said he didn't have a horse. The boy was not known for thinking straight, and Clyde had quite a few horses. Elmo shook his head and accepted the second biscuit Hannah offered him. "Which way was they headed?" Broadus asked.

"Toward the Neches," Elmo answered.

"They musta run into some trouble," Hannah said.

"There was just them two strangers?" Broadus asked. "You sure there weren't some more riders waitin' back up on the road? Was these two fellers wearin' badges?"

"If they was, you couldn't see 'em," Elmo said. "And if there was anybody else with 'em, they musta been way round the bend, 'cause I couldn't see 'em."

"Damn," Broadus swore, "that don't sound too good." He was trying to think if there was anything he could do right away, but darkness was already settling in. "There ain't nothin' we can do tonight. We can't track 'em in the dark. But I'll get the word to my boys tonight, and we'll start lookin' for 'em first thing in the mornin'. Might not be no need to worry, anyway. They might still be trackin' them two fellers and just got caught by the dark. Your ma need somebody to set with her tonight?"

"No, sir, I'll take care of Ma," Elmo said.

"All right, you tell her I'll get the boys and we'll go find Clyde in the mornin', when we can see which way they went." He walked back to the door with Elmo and stood there watching until the boy disappeared into the darkness of the trees. Then he looked back at his wife and said, "I'm gonna go over to Cletus's place and tell him to take the word to Marvin." He stuck his hat on his head and went out the door, heading toward the barn. Cletus's cabin was just a short distance back up the road, so he didn't bother with a saddle. He put a bridle on his almost solid-black Morgan gelding, jumped on his back, and rode up from the yard to the narrow wagon track that followed the creek.

When he got to the cabin, he pulled up in front of the door and called, "Cletus!"

After a few moments, the door opened, and a young man stepped out on the stoop wearing nothing but his underwear. "Pa?"

Broadus slid off the Morgan. "Was you in bed?"

"I was fixin' to," Cletus said. "What you doin' ridin' around in the dark?"

"It's your Uncle Clyde and the boys," Broadus said. "Is that little gal waitin' for you in there?"

"Bonnie?" Cletus replied. "No, she run off again, couple of days ago. I hope she stays away this time. What about Uncle Clyde and the boys?" Broadus told him the story Elmo had told him about the two mysterious strangers that ran off with a horse Monk had stolen. "I saw them two fellers when they passed by the cabin." Cletus said. "They crossed over on the other side of the creek, ridin' through the woods to keep me from seein' 'em. Nah, there weren't nobody else with 'em," he said in answer to Broadus' question. "I figured they was runnin' from somebody, but I didn't never see nobody else on the road after 'em." He paused and asked, "You wanna come inside the house?"

"No," his father replied. "Out here is fine." He preferred not to see the mess he knew the inside of the cabin would be.

"And Elmo said Uncle Clyde and the boys went after them two?" Cletus continued. "And they still ain't come back?"

"That's right," Broadus answered. "So I'm goin' lookin' for 'em as soon as it's light enough to see in the mornin'. I want you and your brother to go with me, in case we run into some trouble somewhere." Cletus nodded his head in obeyance. "I was gonna get you to go tell Marvin, but I didn't know you was goin' to bed."

"Ain't no trouble, Pa," Cletus insisted. "I'll yank some clothes on real quick and ride over to Marvin's. Maybe I oughta just go like this," he japed, "so Amy Lou can see what she coulda had if she'd waited to meet the rest of the family."

"Tell him to come to our house for breakfast in the mornin' at about sunup," Broadus said, ignoring the crack about Marvin's wife. "I'll tell your ma that you boys will be there for breakfast. Then if Clyde and the boys still ain't come back, we'll get on their trail and find out why."

"All right, Pa, I'll put some clothes on and get on over to Marvin's. I expect they've already turned in, so I'll get there as quick as I can. But it takes about twenty minutes to get there after I've got my horse saddled. If Marvin weren't so blamed henpecked, he'da built a house down at this end of the creek instead of up at the other end with Henry Jessup's crowd. He most likely needs to be reminded that he's a Tarpley once in a while."

"Don't be too hard on your brother," Broadus said. "He's just trying to keep a little gal happy that don't wanna get very far away from her mama." He jumped back on the Morgan and said, "See you in the mornin'."

As their father requested, both boys arrived at his house when the early rays of light were just extending their fingers through the dense clusters of leaves. "Mornin', Ma," each son said in turn when they walked in the kitchen door. She turned to inspect them, hands on hips.

"I declare, Marvin, don't that little Jessup gal give you nothin' to eat? You'll be startin' to look like poor little ol' Elmo before long if she don't start feedin' you."

"Good to see you, too, Ma," Marvin responded. "Amy Lou gives me all I want to eat."

"If she could cook like you, Ma," Cletus japed, "maybe he'd want more to eat."

"Well, set yourselves down and we'll see what we can do to fatten you both up,"

Hannah said. In a few minutes, she set a big platter of scrambled eggs down on the table. "Now don't disappoint my hens. They worked hard to make sure you don't go ridin' off hungry this mornin'." She went back to the stove to fetch a big pot of grits.

They didn't waste any time putting their mother's offering away because they both knew their father was not one to linger at the table when there was a chore to be done. And this chore was not one to be taken lightly. They were all anxious to find out if Clyde and the boys had ever returned home during the night, so Hannah did not attempt to encourage them to finish up every scrap. With breakfast finished, they made all the appropriate compliments on the quality of the food, then went to their horses. With Broadus leading the way, they rode out to the wagon road and followed it the short distance to the other side of the branch and the path to Clyde's house.

Atha Tarpley met them at the front door after Elmo told her they had arrived. She appeared drawn and haggard from lack of sleep, her eyes red from weeping. "Oh, Broadus," she cried out to him, "they ain't come back. Somethin' terrible has happened to 'em."

"I know, Atha," he said. "We're goin' to

try to find 'em right now. I'm just as sorry as I can be we had to wait so long, but there weren't no way we could track 'em in the dark. If they left one solitary track, we'll find 'em. Hannah's gonna come over here to stay with you when she cleans up after breakfast."

"I wanna go with you, Uncle Broadus," Elmo said.

"No, you stay here," Atha said before Broadus could answer. "You're all I've got left of my family right now!"

"She's right, son," Broadus said as kindly as he could. "And we ain't got a horse for you. You need to stay here and take care of your mama. She's dependin' on you." Looking back to the stricken woman he said, "We'll not waste any more time. Let's go boys," he said, and they turned their horses back to the wagon road.

The tracks were a day old, and there were a lot of them, but they felt sure they were all left by the people they were after. According to what Cletus had seen and Elmo's account as well, there were two strangers and two packhorses. So, with Clyde and the boys after them, they had a trail of eight horses to follow. And that wasn't a difficult trail to follow until they reached the Neches River. To their surprise, the tracks they followed went into the water and came out on the other bank, then turned north. "That don't look like they were trying to hide their trail," Cletus commented.

"No, it don't," Broadus agreed. "It might even mean they was fixin' to ambush Clyde and them." They rode on farther along the riverbank until they spotted a gully ahead.

"Look at the ground!" Marvin exclaimed, pointing under his horse's feet. "Somethin' happened when they got here." Looking down, the others could see what he meant. It appeared that the horses had spread out and moved around frantically. Marvin pulled his horse to a stop and jumped down to look closer. "That's blood! There! And there!" He exclaimed, pointing to dried-up blood spots on the ground. "They was ambushed!" All three looked quickly around to try to determine from where they were shot.

"That gully, I'll bet," Cletus said, catching his brother's excitement. He gave his horse a kick and galloped up to the gully where he found plenty of evidence that the two killers had done their work there. He signaled for his father and brother to come and showed them the footprints in the bottom of the gully and the spent cartridges. It was plain to see that was the end of the story.

"I'm awful sorry, Pa," Marvin said. "I know you was hopin' we wouldn't find somethin' like this. They just waited for 'em to catch up and then they just shot 'em down."

Broadus dropped down on one knee, hung his head, and shook it slowly back and forth. "They never had a chance. I can't let somebody get away with a lowdown trick like this. I can't face my brother in hell if I can't tell him I got the sorry dogs that done this." He looked up at his two sons. "I've gotta tell your Aunt Atha how Clyde was gunned down." He hung his head again for a minute before he thought of something more to be done. "We've gotta find their bodies and give 'em a decent burial." He got on his feet again. "Let's spread out and see if we can find where they left 'em."

"Back there, where they was shot off their horses — remember that track that looked like somethin' was dragged?" Marvin asked. "That somethin' mighta been a body."

"You're right," Broadus replied, and they all hurried back to the spot. They didn't have to look long before finding two more tracks like the first one. But they didn't find a fourth one. "That's gotta be what them marks are," Broadus said. "Maybe one of 'em got away."

"Well, whaddaya reckon happened to him?" Cletus asked. "He never came home."

"Look at this," Marvin said. "I'm lookin' at them three draggin' marks, and to me, it looks like they're all pointin' in the same direction."

"I'll swear . . . you're right," Broadus said. "They're all pointin' over that way. Let's go see if that's where they took the bodies." They spread out a little and starting walking toward a low rise where an uprooted tree lay on the ground.

It was Cletus who walked closest by the hole left in the ground. As he passed, he took a quick glance into the hole side and was startled by the glassy gaze he received in return from his Uncle Clyde's corpse. His involuntary yelp of surprise called the others. "What is it?" Broadus asked. "You find 'em?" Cletus nodded vigorously. "Well, nobody got away," Broadus declared when he got there. "They's all four in that hole. We've gotta dig 'em some graves."

"With what?" Cletus asked. "We ain't got no shovels."

"We'll just have to scratch out some graves with our knives and our hands, I reckon," his father said. "We can't just leave 'em for the buzzards to pick apart."

"I don't mean no disrespect, Pa," Marvin said. "But it looks to me like they're already in a hole. And I don't see why they have to have separate holes. They's all one family, ain't they? All we need to do is cover 'em up so nothin' gets to 'em, don't you reckon?"

"I reckon that would be all right," Broadus said. "I'm sure Clyde and the boys would think that was all right, as long as they're covered up to keep the critters out." With no tools but a couple of hand axes and their knives, it still took a lot of work. But using their shirts as sacks, they hauled enough dirt and sand to fill in over their kinfolk.

When the burial was done, they declared it time to sit down and rest. They regretted that they had not foreseen the need to bring a coffeepot with them, but there was a river full of water to wash down the beef jerky and biscuits Hannah had put in Broadus's saddlebags. While they rested and ate, the conversation naturally shifted to what to do now that they had found their dead. Should they try to pick up a new trail that might lead them to the men who shot their family members, or to go home and prepare for a long tracking? First of all, they decided, they should see if the killers left a trail to follow. It was useless to just ride north in hopes of stumbling upon the two men who performed the massacre. It would help if they knew who the two men were. They had never really seen them up close enough to identify them on a street or in a saloon. It was discouraging to think about their chances of success. The killers already had a day's start on them. And by the time Broadus and his sons got home to take the sorrowful news to Atha and Hannah, then prepared for a long search, they would likely be two days behind in the chase. Marvin reminded Broadus that he would also have to ride home to tell Amy Lou, which might delay the search even more.

Still, to satisfy his conscience, Broadus insisted on scouting the riverbank beyond the gully where they found the many tracks of the eight horses — moving at a fairly rapid pace it appeared. "The way them tracks is spread out like that, it don't look like they had them extra horses on a lead rope," Cletus observed.

"They know them horses will follow their own horses," Broadus said. "And they're movin' fast. We ain't got much of a chance to catch up with 'em." No one wanted to admit it, but all three knew there wasn't one chance in a hundred that they could ever catch up with the two men who had just wiped out all the men in Atha Tarpley's family except the boy, Elmo. The fact that Clyde Tarpley and his three sons went after the two men, clearly intending to kill them, had nothing to do with the right or wrong of the massacre. Their lot on this day, however, was to return home with the news of the tragic loss and to swallow the bitterness of no revenge.

Chapter 13

Perley and Possum left early the next day with plans to eat breakfast when they stopped to rest the horses. They each ate one of the biscuits Elam brought them to curb their hunger until that time. When they stopped, they ate their fill of deer meat again, along with the other biscuit and coffee. The meat still smelled all right, but Perley was afraid that as the day wore on, it might take on a stronger aroma, and they might have to decide whether or not to chance it. "I hope Lucien's family ate all theirs for breakfast," Perley commented.

"You worry too much," Possum told him. "That meat can take on a little strong scent and still eat good."

"I'll eat it again for dinner," Perley decided, "but I don't think I'll chance it for supper tonight. I'll eat that jerky we smoked, or some sowbelly, but you can have the raw deer meat."

"Suit yourself, partner," Possum said.

When they stopped for the noontime meal, they roasted more of the meat, and Perley suggested that they go ahead and cook it all. He figured the meat would last a lot longer if it was cooked. But Possum insisted on keeping a portion of the meat raw, claiming that it held the fresh flavor better that way. So when they made their camp that night, each man ate what he decided wouldn't kill him for supper. For Perley, that was smoked deer jerky accompanied by some serious japing from Possum about his sensitive stomach. They figured they were no more than twelve miles from Tyler, and that it might be shorter than that if they left the river at that point and angled over to strike the road they had ridden out on the trip to Nacogdoches. They were still planning to replenish their almost depleted supplies in Tyler, but they were going to have to sell at least a couple of horses to pay for the supplies. The stable was the place to go to sell them, and it was located on that road just south of the town.

The morning started as it usually did when the two of them were traveling. Perley woke up first, grabbed the coffeepot, and went down to the edge of the river to fill it. When he walked back up to the camp, however, Possum was not rebuilding the fire as usual. "Hey, sleepyhead," Perley roused him, "you plannin' to sleep all day? You ain't even got the fire started up." Possum continued to lie there, making no motions toward getting up. "What's the matter with you?" Perley asked. "Are you all right?"

"I don't feel so good," Possum answered. "I didn't sleep much, and I'm sick to my stomach."

"That damn deer meat," Perley said at once. "I was afraid of that. You got food poisonin'. Are you gonna be able to ride?"

"Hell, yeah, I ain't gonna stay here. It'll pass, soon as I get my body stirrin' up a little and get some coffee in me." He rolled over and slowly rose up on his hands and knees and remained that way for a few minutes.

"You gonna make it?" Perley asked, doubtful that he would.

"It'll pass," Possum insisted, still on his hands and knees. "Uh-oh," he uttered then. "Somethin's fixin' to pass right now!" He crawled off his blanket as fast as he could before emptying the contents of his stomach on the ground. Perley grabbed the blanket and jerked it away, in case Possum needed more room to repeat the process. He wondered then if food poisoning could kill you, because Possum looked close to death's door. He didn't have more time to think about that prospect before a panicked call for help. "Perley! Help me pull my britches off! It's fixin' to come out the other end!" Possum flopped down from his hands and knees to land on his side where he unbuckled his belt and unbuttoned his pants. "Hurry!" he pleaded and Perley grabbed the cuffs of his pants and pulled them off.

"Unbutton the back door!" Perley yelled.

"I can't reach 'em!" Possum cried.

Perley reached over and unbuttoned the back flap of Possum's underwear for him, then jumped back before the exodus. "Damn," he uttered, feeling a little queasy, himself. "I'm gonna get you a wet rag and a dry one so you can clean yourself up some. I'd try to do it, but I'd rather shoot you before I did that."

"I'd shoot you if you tried to," Possum groaned. "I'll manage, thank ya."

Perley rummaged through their packs until he managed to find some old washcloths and rags they carried for no specific purpose. He wet one of them in the river and took them to Possum. "I'll build a fire and make some coffee. Maybe that'll help you feel a little better." He paused before japing, "Then I'll cook you some more deer meat, if you feel like you're hungry."

"You've got a mean streak in you that nobody knows about," Possum managed between groans of pain. "I ain't sure I'm over this yet. I still feel sick as a dog."

Perley proceeded to build a new fire, a good bit farther away from the first one, for reasons unnecessary to explain. He got a pot of coffee working, and when Possum thought he could handle it, he brought him a cup of it. Possum sipped about half the cup down but complained that it was threatening to come back up. About a minute later, he threw up again, although there was nothing left but the little bit of coffee he had just downed. It was as if his stomach was no longer accepting deliveries of any kind. Perley was at a loss as to what he should do. Possum looked in no condition to ride, but if he didn't get more supplies pretty soon, they would be living on the smoked jerky. He felt really sorry that Possum was so sick and mad at him at the same time for insisting on eating the tainted meat.

As miserable as he now felt, Possum was also aware of the problem his sickness was causing. And he believed he would just have to be determined to make it to Tyler, where

Perley might sell some horses and buy the supplies they needed to get home. So after he thought he had recovered enough, he struggled out of his underwear and gave it to Perley to wash in the river. Luckily, they had saved his outside garments from any damage, so he pulled them back on. Then, when he felt he was up to it, he told Perley he thought he was ready to ride. "You sure?" Perley asked. " 'Cause you sure don't look like it."

"I can make it," Possum answered, so Perley packed up the horses and put out the fire. Then he tied Possum's long johns on one of the four extra horses to dry. He saddled Buck and Dancer and when he was ready to go, he tied Possum's packhorse behind Dancer's saddle, so Possum wouldn't have to lead the packhorse by the reins. Then he helped Possum up into the saddle. They rode away from the river at an angle to intercept the road east of it, and after a two-hour ride, struck the road at a nice little creek about three miles south of the town. Perley decided it might be wiser to put their four extra horses on lead lines now that they were going to be on the road. The creek looked like a good spot to do it. He turned to tell Possum what he had decided, only to find his partner lying on his horse's neck.

"Doggone it, Possum, why didn't you tell me you were 'bout to fall off your horse?" Perley scolded.

"I was hopin' I could make it to town," Possum gasped, "and maybe find a doctor to give me something to settle my belly down. But I swear, Perley, I can't make it no farther."

"Then we'll just make camp right here," Perley said. "Ain't no reason to make you go any farther today. There's water and plenty of wood for a fire, and it ain't that far to town. Looks like folks have camped here before."

After he got Possum settled comfortably on his bedroll, Perley relieved the packhorses of their burdens and rigged up a rope line down at the creek to tie them. When he was about to pull Buck's saddle off, Possum spoke up. "Why don't you go ahead and take those horses into town and see what you can get for 'em? Ain't no use in both of us wastin' time. If you can sell 'em, you could go ahead and buy the stuff we need to get us home. I'll be all right here."

"I don't wanna leave you by yourself in case you start feelin' worse again," Perley said.

"Wouldn't make no difference if I did,"

Possum insisted. "Wouldn't be nothin' you could do about it whether you was here or not."

"I reckon I could do that. I need to pick up some bacon and beans, coffee and flour and some molasses to get your strength back. You can prop yourself up on that tree with your rifle and your six-gun right beside you. I'll stack some firewood up beside you, so all you have to do is reach over and throw a piece on the fire if you need it." They decided to sell all four horses if he could for whatever the man who owned the stable wanted to give him for them. They were in no position to try to drive a hard bargain. In fact, the man who owned the stable might not buy the horses at any price. Perley might have to try to sell them to anybody on the street who couldn't pass up a good horse at a low price. If he really thought a doctor could immediately relieve Possum's suffering, he would have encouraged him to hang on his horse for just three miles more. But Possum was not the first person he had seen with food poisoning, and they had all recovered within a day or so with complete bed rest. And they all got it from eating tainted meat. So he was sure Possum would gradually feel better. "All right," Perley said when he was ready to go. "Don't run off anywhere while I'm gone."

"Don't worry. Anything that starts runnin' will be between my chin and my fanny."

Perley rode up to the front of the barn at the stable, leading his four horses, all of which were saddled. He dismounted as the owner of the stable walked out to meet him. "Howdy," Perley said. "Are you the owner?"

"I am," he said. "Calvin Tully, what can I do for you?"

"Mr. Tully, when I last rode through Tyler, Sheriff John Talbot told me that you bought and sold horses, and that I could depend on you to give me a fair price." When Perley and Possum had passed through Tyler, he had met the sheriff, but there was no discussion about the sale of horses. He decided the sheriff would be a good reference in this particular case, however. He thought he already detected a look of suspicion on Tully's face.

Tully then looked surprised. "John Talbot said that?" Perley didn't answer, he just smiled at Tully, not wishing to compound the lie. "You lookin' to sell those horses? Looks like they was recently occupied," he said, referring to the saddles. "Where'd you get 'em?"

"Nacogdoches," Perley answered. "The

previous owners are deceased, so you don't have to worry about anybody coming to claim them. My partner and I were workin' with Sheriff Clayton Steel on a posse down there. We were going to take the horses back to Sulphur Springs, but we ran into a little hard luck. My partner came down with a bad case of food poisonin', and we've had to hang around down here till our money ran out. So we decided to sell 'em for what we can get. I looked 'em over before we took 'em, and they're in pretty good shape. To be honest with you, one of 'em is a little older than the other three. If you take a look at their teeth, I'd guess three of 'em are about four and a half. They've already got their canines growin' in. But the other one, that dun, he's got a full mouth and a lot of wear. But I reckon I'm tellin' you your business. So if you're interested in 'em, tell me what you'd give for 'em, and I'll throw the saddles in for nothin'."

"Well, to tell you the truth," Tully responded, "I weren't plannin' to do no buyin' this month, till I can catch up a little bit." From the way he was craning his neck to look at them, however, Perley knew he was interested. He looked each horse over thoroughly and when he was through, he said. "I think you're pretty close on their age. But I declare, I really got no business buyin' any horses this month. How much were you thinking about askin'?"

"Well, I know what I can get for 'em when we get home. But like I said, my partner and I find ourselves in need of cash money right now. And we're a long way from home. So we're not looking for the goin' rate for a good saddle horse, a hundred and fifty dollars. We want this sale to be a good deal for you, too. So whaddaya say to seventy-five dollars a head?"

Tully shook his head and said, "I say fifty dollars a head, but I don't want the dun. I ain't sure I could get my money back on him."

"All right," Perley said. "You kinda got me over a barrel, but I reckon I'm desperate enough to take it. So, for a hundred and fifty dollars, the price of one good saddle horse, you got yourself three young horses."

"The saddles come with 'em, you said," Tully reminded him.

"Yes, sir, I did," Perley admitted. "A deal's a deal." He turned around and stroked the dun on his neck. I reckon you'll be goin' home with me, Grandpa." He waited outside then while Tully went into his tack room where his money was hidden. He was back in a few minutes to count the money out into Perley's hand. They shook hands then, and Perley untied the dun from the lead rope, climbed on Buck and led the dun up the street to Rinehart's General Store. He was more than satisfied with the money he got for the horses. He hadn't expected to get that much for all four of them.

"Mr. Gates, I believe it is," Ross Rinehart greeted him when he walked into the store. "Sheriff Talbot said you might be coming back through town on your way back to Sulphur Springs. I trust you got the ladies safely settled in Nacogdoches."

"That we did," Perley replied. "Thank you for askin'. Reverend Smith and I are on our way back home, and I'm goin' to need to replenish our supplies. And by the way, Mrs. Miller made a real tasty pie with those dried apples you gave us. I wanna thank you again for that."

That seemed to please Rinehart quite a bit. "I'll tell my wife. Is the reverend with you today?"

"Not right here in town. He's waitin' for me at our camp about three miles south of town, trying to get over a bad case of sick stomach from eatin' some deer meat that had turned."

"That can be a nasty thing, all right," Rinehart said. "You say you're gonna need some things?" Perley started calling out the items he wanted to buy, and when they were done, Rinehart provided some sacks so Perley could hang most of it on Buck's saddle and the dun's. Rinehart thanked him for another good order and wished him a safe trip home.

He was thinking that he was just as happy that he had not seen Sheriff Talbot on his way out of town, especially since he had used him as a reference when he sold the horses. He was also hoping that when he got back to the camp, Possum might possibly be feeling a lot better, and they could get started toward home again. He could imagine that Rubin and John were wondering where in the world he could be. It seemed that things like this were always happening to him, and he wondered why. Then he wondered what Becky must be thinking, after no word from him in weeks. *I hope you're ready to ride, Possum,* he thought. *Because I'm going to have a lot of explaining to do.*

When he reached the creek, he turned Buck upstream, but before he reached their camp, he had a feeling that everything was not right. There was no whinny of recognition from Buck or the horses in the camp. That was unusual, especially between Buck and Dancer. He pushed on through the laurel bushes that hugged the bank of the creek just before the little clearing where they had made their camp. Startled, he stopped cold, pulling Buck back so hard that he was standing in the stirrups. Possum's body was lying face down beside the dying fire. The horses were gone. Articles of spare clothes and cooking utensils were scattered about on the ground. He looked right and left before riding on in and jumping down to run to the body. "Possum!" He cried out in despair, and the body rolled up on its side, causing him to jerk back in surprise. "I thought you were . . ."

"I was playin' dead," Possum interrupted. "When I heard you comin' through the bushes, I thought it was them comin' back."

"Thank the Lord you're not," Perley exclaimed. "Your head! What happened? You're bleedin' pretty bad! Lemme get something to wrap around your forehead and slow that bleedin' down."

"I got knocked in the head," Possum said as Perley got a piece of an old sheet out of his saddlebag. "It's all my fault. I reckon I deserved it."

"That's gonna leave you a nice little scar," Perley said as he wrapped the bandage around Possum's head. "We'll see if that doesn't stop the bleedin', then I'll take another look at it to see if we're gonna need to find a doctor. Now, tell me what happened."

"It was my fault," he repeated. "I was still sicker'n I let on this mornin', but I didn't wanna hold you up. You left me all fixed up with my rifle and my six-gun right beside me. Trouble is, I started throwin' up again right after you left. I didn't wanna throw up right there by the fire, so I crawled over to the bushes. If I'da took my gun with me, I mighta had a chance, but I was so sick I didn't think about my gun. Next thing I knew, somebody grabbed my boots and dragged me back over by the fire. There was two of 'em. I was still so sick I was havin' trouble seein' 'em plain. But one of 'em was a tall, lanky feller. The other one weren't as tall, and he looked like he had a face full of whiskers. I heard him call the tall one Slim."

"Damn, Possum," Perley apologized. "I shouldn'ta left you, as sick as you were. What'd they hit you with?"

"My rifle butt, when they asked me where my money was hid and I told 'em I didn't have any money, I reckon it knocked me out for a minute or two 'cause the next thing I knew, I was layin' on my belly again and my pockets was turned inside out. I know I was hopin' they'd go ahead and shoot me. And they was goin' to, but the short one was afraid they was too close to the road and somebody might hear the shot. Slim said it didn't matter nohow 'cause it looked like I was dyin', anyway, and they better get the hell away from here. I couldn't see much layin' flat on my belly like that, but it looked like they tore all the packs open, and they stole my horse. But I don't think they took the packhorses. It sounded like they just run 'em off. There was a time when I could have stopped them, but they had my guns, so I just kept playin' dead."

Perley shook his head slowly as he listened to his friend's accounting of the attack upon the camp. He held himself responsible for Possum's unfortunate encounter with the two assailants who cruelly took advantage of a sick man. The anger that burned like a fire in his veins was not going to be subdued until Slim and his furry-faced partner paid the price for what they did to Possum. But the immediate problem was what to do about his friend if he tried to track the two men down. Possum must have sensed what his young friend was thinking, because he said, "I can ride, Perley. I still feel weak as hell, but I'm finally over bein' so sick.

Maybe all I needed was a knock in the head."

"I don't know, Possum, you look pretty bad. You might be suffering from that knock on the head more than you think. I sold three of the horses, so I've got enough money to put you in the hotel for a few days now."

"I'm tellin' you the truth now, Perley. I can ride. My head hurts, but it's on straight. And my belly's sore, but it ain't turnin' upside down no more, and there ain't nothin' left in my behind but bad memories. I've gotta go after my horse. I feel the same way you did when those buzzards took Buck."

"All right, partner," Perley conceded. He could understand that. "I reckon there was a reason that fellow at the stable didn't want the dun. He ain't Dancer, but he's saddled and ready to go. You sit there a few minutes while I take a ride a little way up this creek to see if our packhorses mighta come back to the creek, if you're sure those two didn't take 'em."

"I know they didn't," Possum insisted. "They didn't wanna mess with 'em. I heard 'em run 'em off."

"I won't look long, but we need those packhorses to carry all this stuff I just bought." He was afraid to leave Possum for very long, in case Slim and the other one came back. He took a couple of minutes to unload the supplies from the saddles of the two horses. Then he pulled his Henry rifle from his saddle scabbard and handed it to Possum. "Just in case," he said. He shook his head when he thought about not only Possum's rifle and pistol, but also the four rifles and handguns they had carried on the packhorses. With the ammunition they picked up, the two assailants were ready for a war. He stepped back up into the saddle and turned Buck upstream.

He knew that time was not his friend, and the longer it took for him and Possum to get on the trail of the two, the more time they would have to cover their trail, as well as time to get rid of Possum's horse. So he was quick to thank whatever saint was in charge of things like that when he saw both packhorses drinking from the creek less than half a mile from the camp. They paused to watch him as he rode in front of them and grabbed both reins, then led them back to the camp where he would try to put their camp back together.

Chapter 14

Perley gathered as much of their scattered packs as he could find strewn along the creek bank, especially their coffeepot and frying pan, and packed everything away with the supplies just purchased. It was past time to eat dinner, but Perley didn't want to take the time at this stage of their hunt. As for Possum, he still had no desire to eat yet. So as soon as the horses were ready to travel, they started searching for tracks that would show them which way to start. Perley got down and scanned the creek bank carefully, trying to determine the freshest tracks leading in the direction of the road to Tyler. "Look for a print with three notches filed in the base of the shoe," Possum said. When he received a curious look from Perley in response, he said, "Dancer's got three notches filed into his right front shoe. Ralph cut 'em in that one shoe last time he shoed him."

"Well, that'll help, if we find any distinct prints after they hit the road," Perley said. Ralph Johnson, who did all the blacksmith work on the Triple-G, had offered to do the same for Buck, but Perley had not been that worried about somebody stealing Buck. Now he thought about Buck's recent abduction by the Tarpley family and wondered if that would have been of any help in finding his horse. "Nah," he scoffed but continued scouring the ground for a horseshoe with notches. He kept looking, even though his common sense told him he had less than a slim chance of following the stolen horse once it struck the road. It was a well-traveled road with many hoofprints. He might be able to determine if the thieves went north into town or south to who knew where. Still, he had to try. He felt he owed it to Possum.

After about fifteen minutes, Perley called out, "I got one! I found a clear print with three notches. It's headin' toward the road." That was hardly a surprise, but the next one he found was. "Wait a minute! These tracks are from at least two horses, and the three notches shoe is goin' with 'em."

"That's the way it oughta be," Possum said, "their two horses and they're leadin' Dancer."

"Yeah, but they ain't headin' for the road," Perley said. "They're crossin' the creek. At least they're goin' into the water. I reckon they're crossin' to the other side." He turned Buck down the bank and into the water. There were no tracks coming out on the other side. "They didn't come straight across. I'll see if I can find where they came out." He rode up out of the water and walked Buck slowly along the bank, looking for the exit tracks. When he reached the road with still no sign of tracks, he turned Buck around and went back to the camp where Possum was waiting patiently, as he had been ordered to do. "There ain't no tracks coming out of the creek all the way to the road," Perley reported.

"Then they came back out on this side," Possum said. "Who knows why? If you'da been lookin' for 'em, you mighta seen where they came out on this side."

"Maybe," Perley allowed, "but I wanna check back up the other way on this side first. Maybe, for some reason, they turned around and went upstream instead of goin' to the road. Do you remember if they came in from the road?"

"Nah," Possum replied. "I'm sorry, Perley, I was flat on my belly, pukin' my guts out when they grabbed me. They coulda dropped from the trees as far as I knew."

"I might as well make sure they didn't come at you from back up the creek," Perley decided, and continued up that side. In about twenty-five yards he found what he was looking for. He reined Buck to a stop and stared up the creek bank ahead of him. He wasn't sure they had come into their camp from that direction, but they sure as hell left it that way. He turned around and went back to get Possum.

"What did you find?" Possum asked when he saw the concerned expression on Perley's face, not realizing the concern was for him.

"I found where they came outta the creek, and they didn't come back this way. They kept goin' upstream. I ain't so sure you're up to what we might find if we follow this creek upstream," Perley told him.

"The hell I ain't," Possum replied. "What are you talking about?"

"I mean with the condition you're in, you just ain't ready to take this on right now. You ain't got a gun. And a few hours ago you couldn't even sit up straight. I know you ain't scared of anything, but right now, they got all the guns. What I'm sayin' is it would be a damn good idea if I go on up this creek by myself, just to see if there's another way outta here, or if there might be a camp farther up the creek. And if there is, it'd be the smart thing to find out if it's just the two that jumped you, or a gang of 'em."

Possum hesitated to comment at once. He realized that if there was a gang of outlaws hiding out up the creek, it would be suicide for the two of them to show up, him with Perley's rifle, and Perley with his six-gun. "You're right," he finally conceded. "I can't argue with that. But you've got to promise me you'll just scout that creek to see if there's anybody up there or not. And then we'll decide what we can do about it."

"I promise," Perley said. "I ain't lookin' to commit suicide, even for your horse."

"And you take your rifle with you," Possum insisted.

"I don't wanna leave you without a weapon," Perley said.

"You'll be a lot better off with both your weapons, and you're fast enough to move like three men when you've got both. I'll wait here, but if I hear a whole lot of shootin', I'll run like hell. All right?"

"All right," Perley said, and he wheeled Buck around and headed back up the creek.

He held Buck to a fast walk until he reached the point where he discovered the tracks leaving the water. Then he reined the obedient bay gelding to an easy walk and listened as well as watched the bank ahead of him. He continued on for at least half a mile before he heard the first sound up ahead of him. It sounded like a Jew's harp. He thought surely he must be wrong. He rode a dozen yards farther before he decided it was better to leave Buck and continue on foot. He noticed a thin thread of smoke drifting up through the trees ahead of him, and he wondered why he had not seen it before or smelled it, even. But then he noticed the slight breeze blowing away from him. He had to wonder now how many were in the camp. The size of the fire would indicate not many, maybe just the two who attacked his camp. But that didn't make any sense if that was the case. After striking their camp and leaving Possum for dead, anyone with half a brain would not go back to a camp just a little over half a mile away. Then he remembered something Possum had said right after he had come back. He said the two assailants had started to shoot him while he was lying there playing dead. They decided not to because the camp was so close to the road, and someone might hear the shots. It made sense now that they were afraid it might have drawn attention to their own camp, farther up the creek. Their concern saved Possum's life.

He knew he had to get a closer look at the camp, so he moved away from the creek and circled through the trees until he came to within thirty yards of the campfire. What he saw fit Possum's blurry description of his two assailants. A tall, lanky man stood next to the fire where a chunky man with a full whiskered face sat Indian-style, playing a Jew's harp. Just from what he could see from his vantage point, Perley decided there was only the two men in the camp. And it looked as if they had been camped there for longer than just a few days, for they had set up a tent. Beyond the tent, he saw Possum's gray horse down at the edge of the creek, tied to a tree by a rope long enough to let it drink. There were four more horses with Dancer, but they were not tied. So, there were only the two of them. The question now was what to do with them.

"I wish to hell you'd throw that damn thing away," Slim Dickson complained. "You ain't never gonna learn how to play it. It ain't nothin' but a noise."

Fuzzy Taylor took the Jew's harp out of his mouth long enough to reply. "It keeps me from hearin' all your complainin'."

"If you weren't so damn lazy, I wouldn't

have so much to complain about. We got stuff to do, and I ain't gonna do all the work while you set around foolin' with that thing. There's them two packhorses we chased outta that camp down yonder. Like as not, they mighta wandered back to that camp. We oughta go back down there and make sure that old man is dead. Oughta bury him."

"He was half dead before you knocked him in the head," Fuzzy said. "I was fixin' to shoot him to make sure, but you was afraid somebody might hear it on the road."

"You coulda cut his throat," Slim said. "They wouldn'ta heard that from the road."

"I didn't think of that," Fuzzy declared. "Why didn't you say somethin'?"

"I didn't think of it, either, till just now," Slim admitted. "But that don't matter now, anyway. We need to find them other two horses, pack up them rifles and six-guns, and take 'em over to Dallas and sell 'em. We been hangin' around here too long since that sheriff . . . what's his name . . . Talbot, ran us outta Tyler. We can't even go into town to get a drink of likker."

"Well, it's too late today to pack up and leave," Fuzzy said. "It'll be suppertime before you know it. Best wait till mornin'."

"I reckon you're right," Slim said.

"Never do today what you can put off till tomorrow, right, boys?" Perley called out as he walked up behind them, causing both men to jump, startled. Fuzzy almost swallowed his Jew's harp. Slim reached for his six-gun, only to drop it when Perley's bullet smashed his hand. Fuzzy, still sitting Indian-style, found it too awkward to even try for his gun. He also found it an awkward position when he attempted to quickly get to his feet. "Just sit right there," Perley told him, and reached down and pulled Fuzzy's gun out of the holster. "Now, I believe you fellows have got quite a bit of stuff that belongs to my partner and me. You remember my partner, don't you? He's the fellow you knocked in the head and left for dead. You'd best thank the devil, or whoever you worship, that he ain't dead. Else I wouldn't be in the kind mood I'm in right now."

He looked at Slim then, who was holding his bleeding hand and writhing with the pain of it. "Pull your bandanna off and wrap it around your hand."

Slim pulled the bandanna off from around his neck and wrapped it around his bleeding hand. "I can't tie it on," he complained. "You'll have to tie it for me."

"You're gonna have to give me credit for more brains than that, Slim," Perley told him. "It doesn't need to be tied on. Just close your fist. It'll stay on."

"Whaddaya gonna do with us?" Fuzzy asked.

"To tell you the truth, I think you deserve hangin'," Perley answered. "But if you behave yourselves, I'll take you into town and let the sheriff deal with you. If you don't behave, I'll shoot you."

"We'll behave," Slim said, and winked at Fuzzy. He figured it was going to be difficult for Perley to tie one of them up while still keeping an eye on the other.

All three were surprised then when Possum walked out of the trees, leading Buck. "Looks like you could use a spare hand, partner." He didn't hesitate when he had heard Perley's pistol shot.

Perley smiled because he was just wondering how he was going to get each one of them securely tied up while still guarding the other. "Always there when needed," he remarked. "I can sure appreciate the help. I reckon you don't need any introductions. I think you've already met Slim and No Name."

"Yep," Possum responded, and reached up to feel the rag around his head. "They made quite an impression on me. Whaddaya plannin' to do with 'em?"

"Well, I figured it ain't really my job to punish people who break the law, so I figured we'd tie 'em up, put 'em on their horses, and take 'em into town, to the sheriff's office. That's if they don't give us any trouble. If they make trouble, then I think we oughta just go ahead and shoot 'em. Whaddaya think?"

"Sounds like a good plan to me," Possum said.

"You look like you're movin' around pretty good now. You feelin' like you're gonna make it?"

"Yeah, I am," Possum replied. "Just seems like all of a sudden I felt a whole lot better. I'm even a little bit hungry."

"That's really a good sign. Take a look inside that tent there and see if you can find your guns. I expect that's where they put all the weapons they stole from us. Dancer's tied to a tree down by the water."

Possum went inside the tent and found all the weapons and ammunition. He picked up his pistol and the Winchester 73 he had traded his old rifle for just prior to their trip. Then Perley left him to guard the prisoners while he went down to the creek to bring all the horses up to the camp. Although Possum swore that he was feeling well enough to do some of the work, Perley insisted that he was better suited to guard the prisoners. When Possum asked "How so?" Perley said, " 'Cause you've got more reason to wanna shoot 'em after what they done to you."

"Well, you're right about that. As a matter of fact, if it'd been me that sneaked up on this camp, I mighta just shot 'em right off and been done with it."

"I'll tell you what," Perley suggested. "I'll make it easier on you to watch 'em while I'm gettin' 'em ready to go." He picked out a couple of small trees and tied each one of the prisoners with their backs to the trees and their hands behind the trees. Then he and Possum loaded all the weapons on their packhorses. When it got down to saddling their horses, they gave the two outlaws the option of riding their own horses, and Perley saddled them. When everything was set and Possum's horse was saddled as well, Perley untied the prisoners, one at a time from the tree, then retied their hands behind their back and helped them up into the saddle. Then, as a precautionary measure, Perley cut a short piece of rope and tied their feet together under their horses' bellies. When all was ready, Possum led the parade back down the creek toward the road, with Perley riding rear guard.

They made one last stop, and that was when they reached their camp. They transferred all the weapons and ammunition that belonged to them from the prisoners' packhorses to their packhorses, leaving only what actually belonged to Slim and Fuzzy on their horses. After packing up all their other things, they rode out to the road and headed to town.

As they rode up the street toward the sheriff's office, it occurred to Perley that they seemed to be creating almost as much interest from the gawkers as they had when they drove Elmira's wagons through town. In the sheriff's office, Leon Shoat, Sheriff John Talbot's general handyman around the jail, peered out the window at the column of riders approaching. "Well, I'll be. . . ." Leon started but didn't finish. A moment later, he drawled, "Forever more."

Irritated more than curious, Sheriff Talbot finally asked, "What are you mumblin' about, Leon?"

"It's them preachers that drove the women through town," Leon said, still staring out the window. "And they've got Slim Dickson and Fuzzy Taylor with their hands tied behind their backs. And they're comin' here."

"What?" Sheriff Talbot jumped up from his chair and hurried to the window beside Leon. "What the hell?" He reached for his hat hanging on a hook near the door and glanced at the clock behind his desk. "And right at suppertime, don't you know? Calvin Tully said he saw that one called Perley Gates at his stable this mornin', and he bought some horses from him. I didn't believe him. I thought it was just somebody that looked like that fellow." He took another long look at the rider at the rear of the column. "It's him all right." He walked outside to meet them.

"Reverend Smith, Mr. Gates," Talbot addressed each of them. "What have you got there?"

"These two men attacked Reverend Smith, here, while I was in town buyin' some supplies. The reverend was suffering from some food poisonin' from some deer meat that had turned. They struck him in the head and left him for dead and destroyed our camp, stole everything we had, including our horses. We had no choice but to apprehend them and bring them in to face the charges."

"I'm familiar with the two men," Talbot said. "Two lowdown, sorry beings worse than these two never were born. I had them in my jail a week ago, and I ordered them not to show their faces in this town again."

Slim spoke out then. "Sheriff, I'd like to say that we ain't comin' back to town on our own."

"I can see that you blitherin' idiot," Talbot responded. "But you ain't got no business bein' anywhere near Tyler. I told you to take your sorry selves to some other part of Texas."

"We'll go all the way outta Texas if you kick us outta town this time, Sheriff," Fuzzy said.

"You just bought yourself some more jail time," Talbot said. "And maybe a date with the circuit judge when he comes to town. Which one of you assaulted the reverend?" Both men immediately pointed to the other. "That's what I thought. Leon, open that back cell." Perley untied their feet and helped Talbot pull them off their horses, leaving their hands tied behind their backs until Talbot and Leon had locked them in the cell.

"You gonna get us some supper, Sheriff?" Fuzzy asked.

"I don't know," Talbot said. "It's gettin' so late, I might not get any myself."

"My hand needs some doctorin'," Slim complained.

"Later," Talbot replied.

When they went back outside, Perley told them which packhorses belonged to his prisoners and said that their weapons were on the packhorses. "Do you need a hand with them? I reckon you take 'em to the stable."

"Yes, I take 'em to Tully's and I sure would appreciate your help takin' 'em back down there. I'd like to get 'em down there in time to get some supper before the dinin' room closes at the hotel."

"Well, let's go do it," Perley said. "The reverend and I would like to get some supper, too."

"Leon, lock the door, I'll be at Millie's. Follow me!" Talbot exclaimed, stepped up on Slim's horse, and he led the charge back the way the column had come a few minutes earlier.

When Calvin Tully saw who was following the sheriff, he was totally confused. "You want me to take care of these two saddle horses and these two packhorses, but they ain't leavin' them two saddle horses and them two packhorses with me?"

"That's right," Perley answered him. "You see, the reverend and I are only gonna be in town long enough to get some supper. We're just gonna look for a place to leave the horses while we eat. And then we'll just make a camp somewhere up the road."

"You can just leave 'em right here while you eat, if you want to. I don't close up till well after dark, anyway," Tully offered. "You'll walk to the dining room, and there ain't no good place to leave that many horses by the hotel."

"That's mighty neighborly of you, Mr. Tully," Perley said. "We'll take you up on that, won't we, Reverend?"

"Yes, sir, we sure will," Possum replied. "And the Lord's blessin's on you, sir." His response brought a gentle smile of appreciation to the face of Calvin Tully and a devilish grin to Perley's.

They stepped inside the hotel dining room barely a few minutes before Millie Graham turned the *Open* sign to *Closed*. "There you are," she greeted the sheriff. "Melva and I were just saying it wasn't like you to miss supper. And you brought two guests with you."

"They helped me get here before you closed," Talbot said. "I was runnin' close. This is Millie Graham. She owns the dinin' room. Millie, this is the Reverend Smith and Pearly Gates." He paused after introducing Perley, waiting for her reaction to his name, but she didn't respond. He figured she wasn't really interested enough to let their names register. He would have to tell her about it later.

"Pleased to meetcha, Millie," Perley said. "I oughta tell you that we're just joinin' the sheriff for supper. We ain't really his guests, so be sure you charge us for our supper."

A pleasant young woman named Melva was their waitress, and she was prompt to anticipate their needs before they had to ask. Perley attributed it to the fact that they were eating with the sheriff. He was particularly interested in watching Possum, since this was the first he was going to eat since his quickstep with the rancid deer meat. He was pleased to see his friend's ravenous appetite seemed to have returned and he looked himself again. Perley had been concerned with how old Possum had suddenly looked when he was in the grips of the food poisoning. Certainly he'd had the long, gray-spiked ponytail hanging between his shoulder blades on the day Perley first met him. But he never thought Possum an old man — just an older man than he was. "I'm sorry. I reckon my mind was somewhere else just then. What did you say?"

"I said, I expect you and the reverend are on your way back to the academy," Sheriff Talbot repeated.

"The what?" Perley replied then quickly recovered his wits. "The academy, right, that's where we're headin'." He glanced at Possum who was giving him a "wake up" look, and he wondered how much longer he was going to be able to carry on this fairy tale they had created for the town of Tyler. Maybe he was the one who was getting older, not Possum. Regardless, he realized that he was feeling a little guilty about playing these people for fools. He hadn't meant for it to go any further than the one incident in Rinehart's Store to spare Elmira Miller the shame of being told to get out of town. And now he had Possum handing out blessings. He looked at Possum then and said, "Partner, it's time we went home."

"Amen," Possum said.

Chapter 15

They said goodbye to the folks at Millie's Dining Room, then said another one at Tully's Stable when they picked up their horses. They left the dun gelding that Tully had passed on before as a token of their appreciation and started out leading just the two packhorses. After leaving town, they picked the first decent-looking stream they came to and made their camp for the night.

They reached Sulphur Springs a day and a half later, at noontime. "We're right on time for dinner," Perley said. He nodded toward the little establishment wedged in between a saloon and the hardware store. "Varner's Vittles," he read the sign aloud. "Maybe we'll run into the sheriff. He said that was his favorite place."

"That's right," Possum said. "And maybe they can tell us how to get to the academy." That brought a groan from Perley.

There was a wide area behind the buildings, grown up knee high in grass with a stream on the other side. It looked to be a perfect place to leave their horses while they visited Varner's Vittles. They didn't unload the horses because they planned only to be gone long enough to eat, and then they intended to move the horses to a deep creek a couple of miles north of town to rest them.

Varner's Vittles proved to be as down-home as its name. Jake Varner was the owner and manager, and his wife, Polly, did the cooking, as well as all the cleaning up, except washing the dishes. That responsibility was given to their only child, a one-eyed daughter of fifteen, whose name was Violet. Jake was sometimes asked how his daughter lost her eye, and he explained that Violet didn't lose her eye; she never had one on the right side of her nose. She was born with an empty socket on that side of her face. According to Jake, it never made any difference to Violet. "She never had but one eye, so she don't know if the world looks different to other folks or not." There was a common saying around town, however, that when you ate at Varner's Vittles and you got a plate with a little dirt on one side of it, that was Violet's blind side. Otherwise, she was not a homely girl, but because of her uniqueness, she was not courted by any of the young boys in town. The matter did not concern Violet herself, but it caused grief to her mother. Polly was convinced the boys had a fear that marriage to Violet might produce a long line of one-eyed young'uns.

Jake gave Perley and Possum a big welcome. "Welcome to Varner's Vittles, fellers. This is your first visit with us, ain't it?" Possum said that it was and told him that the sheriff recommended the establishment. "That's right," Jake said, "Sheriff Cooper don't hardly miss a day eatin' here." He chuckled and added, "Tell you the truth, I ain't sure it's the cookin'. I think he's sweet on Polly."

Overhearing him, his wife scolded, "Shut your mouth, Jake. Tellin' strangers things like that . . . They don't know you're the biggest liar in Sulphur Springs."

"You know that ain't true," Jake came back. "Everybody knows Mayor Sam Grant's the biggest liar in town." That brought a big round of chuckles from most everyone seated at the one big table. "Shove over there, Sid," Jake said, "and make some room for these two newcomers." To Perley and Possum he said, "Plenty of room, set yourselves down right there on the bench. It won't be crowded till after you eat, but we'll help you get up if you have a little trouble." He turned to tell his wife, "You must be gittin' famous, honey. That makes three newcomers comin' to eat today." He nodded toward a man concentrating on the plate before him, obviously uninterested in the lighthearted conversation.

They wedged in beside the man Jake called Sid, and Polly brought two plates piled high with slices of roast beef and mashed potatoes. "There's beans and field peas on the table, biscuits coming out of the oven now," she said. One of the customers held an empty serving bowl up, and she took it to refill, then asked Perley and Possum, "You want coffee?"

The meal was served homestyle, and it was good. They could see why the sheriff liked it. And when they were about half finished, Jake announced, "I see the sheriff comin'. Anybody who wants to go out the back door better get out now."

That remark brought another round of chuckles, and someone at the end of the table said, "Most likely, he's comin' for you, Jake."

Perley and Possum enjoyed the experience. "It's almost like eatin' with the boys in the cookhouse back at the Triple-G, ain't it?" Possum joked. "Only difference is the cookin's a little better than what Ollie puts out."

Sheriff Virgil Cooper came in the door then to a general reception of "Howdy, Sheriff," from almost everyone, including Perley and Possum.

"Howdy, howdy," the sheriff returned the greetings cheerfully. "You got a good crowd here today, Jake. I hope you saved a little bit for some of us slowpokes. Afternoon Polly, Violet," he offered as well. Then he looked around the table to decide where best to wedge in, and he recognized Perley. "Perley Gates!" he blurted in surprise. To the diners at the table, it sounded the same as if he had uttered an exclamation like *heavenly days!,* and they waited for him to explain. He immediately shoved Sid over again and sat down next to Perley. "I didn't know you were back in town. I declare, as sheriff, I'm supposed to know when boys like you two hit town."

"We just got here, Sheriff," Perley said, "and this was the first place we went. We wanted to see if the food was as good as you told us. And you weren't lyin'. Right, Possum?"

"That's a fact, Sheriff," Possum responded. "Be hard to find food as good as this anywhere else."

"See, I told you," Cooper said. "Best place to get your money's worth. Did you get your two wagons full of soiled doves down to Nacogdoches all right?"

That got everybody's attention. Perley cringed. "Yes, sir, we delivered them safely. But I'd appreciate it if you'd let these folks know that Possum and I ain't in that business."

"Oh, of course," Cooper said, realizing then the picture he'd painted of the two men. "I shoulda thought before I opened my mouth. No, folks, these two was like Good Samaritans. They come up on a couple of wagons — some whores were tryin' to drive to Nacogdoches, but they had a broke wheel. Perley and his friend fixed the wheel so they could bring it to Wyatt Jordan to sell 'em a new one. Then he put 'em on the road to Nacogdoches." He turned to Perley. "Least that's what you said you was gonna do."

"Well, turns out they had some more trouble, and Possum and I ended up havin' to guide 'em all the way down there. That's the reason it's took us this long to head back home."

"I swear — thank you, Violet" — he interrupted himself when she brought him a plate — "if that ain't somethin'. No, folks,

Perley Gates ain't in the business of transportin' prostitutes around Texas. He's just the fastest man with a handgun in the whole state and maybe the country, I don't know." Possum cringed. He saw the instant distress in Perley's face and knew he wanted to strangle Cooper. But Cooper wasn't finished. "Baptist preacher I know, Harvey Poole, saw Perley in a duel with a gunslinger named Quirt Taylor. He said it was like watching lightnin' strike."

Cooper was getting so pumped up with outright embarrassing admiration for Perley's talent that Perley had to interrupt him and ask him to stop. "Please, Sheriff, these good people are gettin' the wrong picture of who I am. Possum can tell you — I'm just a cowhand on a cattle ranch north of here, and that's all I am."

Cooper remembered then that Perley did not want to be known for his speed with a handgun, that he preferred keeping it to himself. "I'm sorry. I reckon I was runnin' off at the mouth without thinkin'. I apologize. No hard feelin's?"

"Of course not, Sheriff. I reckon Possum and I better be gettin' along, too. I sure have enjoyed this dinner, Mrs. Varner." He got up from the table. "That'll give you a little more room to enjoy your dinner, Sheriff. It was good seein' you again, and nice to meet you folks."

"You'd think anybody that fast, you woulda heard of 'em." The remark came from the other stranger at the table, who had been quietly eating his dinner up to that point.

"It would depend on the person and the circumstances, I reckon," Perley replied, since it was obvious the remark was aimed at him. "You ready, Possum?" They walked to the front counter, preparing to pay for their meal.

"I got it, Jake," the sheriff called out. "I owe 'em a dinner."

"You heard what he said," Jake told Perley when he tried to pay. "In this town, we don't argue with the sheriff. I'm glad you enjoyed your meal. I hope you'll come back to see us if you're back this way again."

The stranger got to his feet, too, and walked up to pay for his meal. "Hope you enjoyed your dinner," Jake said politely.

"Yeah, the food was all right," the stranger said, "but the show was better. You coulda charged extra to hear the sheriff talk about the famous gunslinger nobody's ever heard of, shot down by some jasper with a name that sounds like the Pearly Gates."

Possum had been sizing up the outspoken

stranger while Perley was trying to pay their bill, not only from what he was saying, but from the weapon he wore and the holster he used. And he was pretty sure he had sized him up correctly. He stepped over close to him. "You got a name?"

The stranger reacted as if he was being approached on the street by a beggar. "Yeah, old man, I got a name. Maybe you heard of it: Jack Glass."

"Jackass?" Possum replied, surprised. "Well, that fits. Listen, jackass, it's plain to see that you're thinkin' about puttin' the pressure on Perley to shoot you. But just let it rest, all right? Perley don't wanna shoot you, 'cause up to now, he ain't got no reason to shoot you. So play it smart. Don't give him a reason to. And I'm gonna tell you something that you might wanna think about. I've known this man for a few years now, and I can tell you that the more he's pushed, the faster he gets. Keep that in mind and you'll do everybody a favor, especially you. So the best thing now is to just let me and Perley walk away. All right? Nice talkin' to ya."

When Glass walked out behind Perley and Possum, Jake went over to talk to Sheriff Cooper. "Wasn't that a kick in the behind? That feller just comin' up outta nowhere.

You reckon you oughta go make sure he don't start nothin' with Perley? He was sure mouthin' off about him."

"He ain't broke no laws, so far," Cooper answered. "Even if they agreed to have a duel, I wouldn't arrest 'em for it. But you're right — I'd best go outside to make sure there ain't no outright murder. I think just my presence outside would keep that from happening." *Besides,* he thought, *if they decide to face each other, I don't want to miss it, right here in my town.* "I'm gonna go out there to keep an eye on 'em." Out the door he went.

Outside, he saw Perley and Possum walking down the boardwalk on their way to an alley that they could cut through to the open field behind the buildings. About twenty paces behind them, Glass was in step with them, taunting Perley with insults followed by challenges. But Perley continued to walk, his back unprotected. The sheriff heard Perley yell that he was not going to shoot with him. Then, finally, Glass could see that Perley was almost to the alley and his chances were fading. So he gave his ultimatum. "You turn and face me, or I'll shoot you in the back. Either way, you're a dead man."

"Possum, give me some room," Perley said

quietly. Knowing what he meant, Possum stepped aside and turned around to watch Glass. In that moment, Perley just hoped he would be fast enough to do the job, but he wasn't sure. In the next moment, he heard Possum cry, "Perley!" Then it happened like it had always happened before, he turned and fired before his conscious mind had time to think what he was doing. Only then did it register that Glass was crumpled over, his gun halfway out of his holster, and Sheriff Cooper was running toward them.

Possum was close beside Perley then. "Perley, you all right, boy?" Perley nodded.

Cooper came running up then, yelling excitedly, "Damn, damn, damn! I saw the whole thing! He pulled on you when your back was turned! Just like watchin' lightning strike!"

Perley couldn't understand the sheriff's childlike excitement. He had just killed a man. Possum would remind him later that he had rid the earth of a poisonous man, and the earth would thank him for it. "Let's just get outta here and get on the road to Paris," Perley said. So they climbed on their horses and rode through the open field all the way to the end of the buildings before coming out on the road. Behind them, they could still hear Sheriff Cooper ranting about the gunfight and the fact that he had witnessed it. "That makes two towns that I can't go back to," Perley remarked to Possum, "Sulphur Springs and Tyler."

They rode only about three miles to the creek they planned to camp by that night. That would leave them with a shorter ride to strike the south fork of the Sulphur River the next day, where they planned to rest the horses while they cooked some breakfast. That morning, when they reached the south fork of the river, they returned to the spot where they had encountered the five women who had caused such a catastrophic change in their simple trip to buy cattle from George Weber. "I wonder if Elmira's took over that feller's business down there yet," Possum speculated. "I already forgot his name."

"Walt Tatum and the Shamrock Saloon," Perley remembered for him. "It wouldn't surprise me none."

Continuing on, they didn't stop at the north fork of the river, since it was only about ten miles from the south fork, but continued on for another five miles or so before stopping for the noontime rest. They figured that left them only about eighteen miles to the Triple-G and planned to be home that night. They had been gone for weeks, but it seemed like months, considering the fact that they had originally planned three days for the trip — four at most. When they reached Paris that afternoon, as when they had started on the trip, Possum asked Perley if he wanted to stop. "We could even eat supper here if you feel like it," Possum suggested. "It's about time for the hotel dinin' room to open for supper." He paused to wait for Perley's answer. When Perley hesitated, Possum said, "And we'll most likely be too late for supper by the time we get to the ranch."

Still Perley hesitated; he was not looking forward to facing Becky Morris after their last parting. He had to remind himself that it wouldn't be thoughtful on his part to cause Possum to miss supper because he was reluctant to meet Becky. Her last words with him had to do with the fact that he always seemed to be gone somewhere, and she never knew when he was coming back. And this trip might even seem deliberate on his part. He had told her he would be gone for a short time; now he hesitated to count up the days he had been gone. But it wasn't fair to make Possum go without supper, so he said, "You're right. We'd best get some supper here."

"Good," Possum responded. "You had me

worried there for a moment."

Lucy Tate looked out the dining room window to see who was riding around to the back of the hotel, leading packhorses. She paused, startled, then took another look when she realized it was Perley and Possum. She automatically turned to see where Becky was, as if she might sense Perley's presence. But Becky was busy folding a stack of clean napkins, unaware that Lucy was staring at her. Lucy was not sure what to do — tell Becky that Perley was on his way to the dining room or just let her be surprised when he walked in? She wasn't sure which was best. After he'd left that day when he'd killed a man right outside the dining room, he had disappeared. Even his brother, John, did not know what had happened to Perley — or Possum either, for that matter. He'd been in the dining room a couple of days before and told them he had no idea where they were but assured them that the two would eventually show up. And, he added, they would have some wild tale to tell, explaining why they were gone, as usual.

Lucy still couldn't make up her mind whether to alert Becky or not, so she went into the kitchen to tell Beulah. "Are you sure it's Perley?" Beulah asked.

"Of course I'm sure," Lucy answered. "It's Perley and Possum, and they're on their way here. They're tying up their horses beside the hotel. Should we tell her or just let her be surprised? She'll probably be shocked out of her britches."

"I think it would be best if she had a little warning, so she can pull herself together," Beulah said, and she immediately went to the dining room door. But she was too late; Perley and Possum were standing in the open front door, staring at Becky, who was struck speechless.

Possum broke the shocked silence in typical fashion. "Evenin', Becky, what's for supper?"

She could only manage one word at first. "Perley," she uttered, barely above a whisper. After an awkward moment, she said, "I thought you were gone forever."

"I'll always come back until you tell me not to," he said.

"I'm gonna set down at this table over here," Possum inserted. "Maybe you or Lucy can pour me a cup of coffee when you get a minute." He didn't wait for a response and proceeded to seat himself at a table near the kitchen door. He gave Lucy and Beulah a big smile as he took off his hat and hung it on an empty chair. Beulah tore herself away from the doorway where she and Lucy were still watching the young couple. In no time at all, she reappeared with a plate piled high with food and a cup of coffee. She placed them down quickly in front of Possum, then hurried back to her observation post at the kitchen door. Distracted as she was by the meeting of the two young people, she didn't notice the rag bandage around Possum's head.

"Did she mention the telegram yet?" Beulah asked Lucy.

"I don't think so," Lucy whispered. "It's hard to hear what they're sayin'."

"How are things in Nacogdoches?" Becky finally summoned the courage to ask.

Her question surprised Perley. He didn't expect any questions about any of the places he and Possum had visited. "Whaddaya mean?" he replied. "Why are you askin' about Nacogdoches? That's a long way away from here."

Recovering from the shock of his sudden reappearance, her hurt and anger returned. "Fred Farmer was in here one day last week. He said he took a telegram to Rubin that you sent. He said John read it out loud, and you said that you were taking five women to Nacogdoches."

"Damn," Perley swore. "John shouldn't

have read that telegram out loud." He bit his lower lip, frustrated. "And Fred didn't have any business tellin' anybody what I said in a telegram to my brother. They weren't five women. They were whores. At least four of 'em were. The other one was a thirteen-year-old girl named Junie." He paused when he realized what he had just said. "I didn't mean to be so blunt." Completely flustered by then, he begged her indulgence. "I need Possum to help me explain what happened. Come on over to the table and let him tell you what happened."

"I'm working," Becky said. "I can't just ignore my customers."

Listening as hard as they could, Beulah and Lucy volunteered to cover for her. "You go ahead and get the whole story out of him, girl," Lucy said. "I'll take care of your tables."

Still reluctant, Becky went to the table with Perley and sat down. "What happened to your head?" she asked.

"Just a little accident," Possum answered. "I weren't watchin' where I was goin' and ran into a low-hangin' limb."

Then he and Perley told her everything that happened on the Sulphur River, and how they ended up taking the two wagons to Nacogdoches. Possum swore that Perley never had any intimate activity with any of the women. Becky surprised them when she responded, "I know that. It's not in Perley's nature to have truck with whores. And besides, he's too shy to make any advances on a woman."

"Well, if you knew all that, why were you so mad at me?" Perley asked, confused.

"Because you went away again and didn't tell me you would be gone so long," she said. "You sent Rubin a telegram. You could have sent me one. I didn't know if you were alive or dead."

"I never thought about sendin' you a telegram," he confessed.

"See," she said. "That's why I was mad." She gave him a stern look and scolded, "You weren't involved in any more of those shoot-outs with gunmen, were you?"

"No, ma'am," he immediately replied, and looked at Possum, who was wearing a wide grin. Perley quickly looked away.

"See," Becky said. "You can't even lie with a straight face. Are you going to eat supper?"

"What?" he replied when she changed the subject so suddenly. "Oh, yes, I'd like to have some supper."

She got up from the table and went into the kitchen to fix a plate for him. When she returned, she was carrying the coffeepot as well. She placed the plate down in front of him and refilled Possum's cup. Then she got a clean cup and filled it for him. "I hope you enjoy your supper," she said, very businesslike. "I need to check on my other tables." She walked off with the coffeepot.

"Whaddaya think, Possum? You figure I'm back in with her again?"

"I think you just got a damn good look at how it's gonna be after you tie the knot with her. I ain't never seen a horse broke as easy as she just broke you. You'll know for sure if she starts puttin' off the weddin' for this reason and that reason. She'll have you so heated up, you'll agree to everything she demands."

"How do you know that?" Perley asked.

"It's in their nature," Possum replied. "I know some stuff about women."

"Is that so?" Perley came back. "Then how come you ain't got any lady friends?"

"Like I said, because I know some stuff about 'em."

Becky continued to check on them while they ate and sat down to talk for a little while when there was an opportunity. To Perley, she seemed like the old Becky, and it felt quite comfortable. Before it got too late, however, they declared that they had to get the horses back to the ranch. She wanted to know when he might be in town again. "I don't know for sure," he told her. "We've been away from the ranch so long, I don't know what's goin' on. But I'll make some excuse to have to come to town."

She walked him to the door and embraced him tenderly before releasing him to follow Possum to the horses. *You remember that when you get one of your urges to ride off to who knows where,* she thought, following advice that Lucy had lent. She remained standing on the small porch outside the door of the dining room and watched as they rode back out to the road. Perley stood up in the stirrups and waved as they went by. *God, he is awful adorable,* she thought.

She walked back into the dining room to find Lucy and Beulah standing there waiting for her. "Are you all right, honey?" Beulah asked.

"Of course I'm all right," Becky answered. "I just don't know if it's possible to tame a wild hawk and make it think it's a canary, and if it could ever be content to be a canary. I wonder if, in all good conscience, you have the right to try to tame a wild hawk."

Lucy looked at Beulah, confused. "What is she talkin' about? Hawks and canaries, are you sure you're all right? You're not makin' any sense."

"Yes she is," Beulah said. "Go get some coffee for Edgar. He's been trying to get your attention for five minutes." Lucy swore under her breath but hurried away to get the coffeepot and fill the postmaster's cup. Beulah put her arm around Becky's shoulders. "Don't none of us know what's gonna happen to us tomorrow, so maybe you ought not worry about it. At least you know you're dealing with a man with a good honest soul, who would never intentionally hurt you. You're both young, so there ain't no need to hurry with any life-binding decisions."

Chapter 16

Johnny Pepper walked into the Shamrock Saloon in Nacogdoches, thinking it was about time he checked out the new establishment. Some fellow named Walt Tatum had opened it several months ago, but Johnny heard that Tatum had a new partner, a woman, and she brought a couple of working girls with her to liven up the place a little. He stood in the doorway for a moment to take a look at the room. He noticed Sheriff Clayton Steel's deputy, Eddie Price, standing at the end of the long bar, talking to the bartender, so he nodded and gave the deputy a smile. He was aware that Price knew who he was, but he was smug in the knowledge that the sheriff's department had no paper on him. He also knew they didn't trust him because he was married to Broadus Tarpley's daughter, Rena. And in Nacogdoches, any connection you had to the Tarpley family meant you were guilty of some crime. Johnny rather enjoyed that stigma.

He walked over to the bar, and Ernie, the bartender, stepped away from Price to serve him. "Howdy, what can I get you?" Ernie asked.

"Gimme a shot of whiskey," Johnny replied, then turned toward Price and asked, "How do, Deputy?"

"Johnny," Eddie Price acknowledged.

Johnny tossed the shot back and turned around to look the customers over. He didn't see anybody he knew, so he shifted his gaze over to a table in the corner where a man was sitting with two women. *They must be the women the new partner brought in,* he thought. As he gazed at the table, one of the women looked back at him and gave him a smile. He returned the smile and she promptly got up from her chair and strolled over to the bar. "Howdy, handsome," Viola Swan greeted him. "That smile reminded me of a lonely puppy. Are you needing some company?"

"I might be at that," Johnny said. "Why don't we set down and talk about it?"

"You wanna buy me a drink?"

"Yeah, I'll buy you a drink." He turned to Ernie and said, "Give us a bottle of that same stuff. It didn't taste half bad." He paid for the bottle and followed Viola over to a table. She wasn't a bad looking woman, even with the gap right in the middle of her front teeth. They sat down at the table, and he poured the drinks. "You one of the new women in the Shamrock?" Johnny asked.

"That's right," she said. "And we had a time of it before we finally got here." She told him about the broken wheel on one of their wagons and how two strangers came along and got it fixed for them. She went on to tell him about their capture by three outlaws and how the same two strangers came to rescue them. "Then they brought us all the way down here, safe and sound."

"Well, you and your friends was mighty lucky to run into them two fellers, weren't you?"

"I'll say we were," Viola replied. "What is your name, sweetie?"

"Johnny," he said, "Johnny Pepper."

"Johnny Pepper," she repeated. "I knew you'd have a cute name. I'm partial to catchy names. One of those fellows I was tellin' you about had a name like that. Perley Gates was his name. I know what you're thinking, just like up in heaven, but it ain't spelled the same. And the fellow with him had a funny name, too. He was an older man than Perley, though. Had a lot of gray in his hair and a ponytail hangin' down his back." She chuckled and said, "His name was Possum Smith. So Johnny Pepper is gonna be one of my favorite names."

"That's some story," Johnny said. "Are them two fellers still around town?"

"No, I wish they were. They were in a hurry to get back home, but something else happened. Some outlaw the sheriff had locked up broke out of jail, and when he escaped, he stole Perley's horse outta the stable. So Perley and Possum went with the sheriff's posse after him."

"Was the outlaw's name Monk Tarpley?" Johnny asked, suddenly more interested than before.

"Yes, something like that. I know everybody around here was sayin' they'd never catch him if he got to the river. I forgot what river."

"The Angelina," Johnny supplied.

"That's the one," she said. "Well, he made it to the river, so the posse turned around and came home. But Perley and Possum didn't. They crossed the river and kept going after that outlaw. I don't know what happened after that. I know they never came back here."

"Do you know where their home is?" Johnny asked, making an effort not to seem too interested.

"No, not exactly," she said. "I know they work for the Triple-G Ranch, a long way from here. It's north of Sulphur Springs. That's where we first met them: Sulphur Springs."

"Well, Miss Viola, I want you to know I'm really glad I came in here to meet you today. I just wish I didn't have to go somewhere right now."

She looked genuinely disappointed. "You mean you ain't gonna go upstairs with me for a little visit?"

"No, not this time, but we'll try it next time I'm in town," he said. "What do you charge me upstairs?" He got up out of his chair.

"Two dollars for a quick visit," she said. "But on a slow day like this afternoon, I'd let you come up for a dollar. Whaddaya say?"

"Like I said, I ain't got time today, but here's two dollars for the good time I know I woulda had." He leaned over and planted a kiss on her mouth, then headed straight for the door.

"What did you do to him?" Ernie asked when she got up and walked over to the bar. "He went out the door like you lit a fire in his behind."

"I didn't do anything, and he gave me two dollars, anyway. I didn't even have to go upstairs to get it. I wish I had more business like that."

"I declare, what are you doin' home?" Rena Pepper was startled when her husband walked in the door of their little house. "I thought you said you wasn't gonna get back in time to take me over to Papa's."

"I said I was afraid I might not, but I'd try to make it, so I just made it." He had not really planned to attend the funeral service Rena's father was havin' for his brother's family. He was aware that Broadus Tarpley had little use for him, and he cared less for Broadus. The whole Tarpley clan was shy of a full load of brains he liked to say when he taunted Rena.

"You smell like whiskey," Rena said.

"I stopped at a saloon and had a drink with a feller I wanted to talk to about a job he's plannin'. That's where he said to meet him."

"What kinda job?" Rena asked.

"It don't make no difference. I didn't take it. You about ready to go to your papa's?"

"Yes, I'm ready. I'm glad you made it. I wouldn't want everybody to think you don't care about Uncle Clyde and the boys."

"I wouldn't either," Johnny said. "I'm gonna take care of my horse. Then I'll hitch the mule up to the wagon and we'll go."

"Yonder comes Johnny and Rena in the wagon," Elmo said from his position by the front door of his Uncle Broadus's house. He had taken it upon himself to announce every guest that came. He had called out quite a few names of the Tarpley kin that had settled between the Angelina and the Neches. Everyone had brought food and several of the female relatives were helping prepare everything.

"Well, whaddaya know about that?" Cletus said to Marvin. "Johnny Pepper showed up for the supper. I woulda bet against it." Johnny was never going to be accepted by the Tarpley clan. At best, he was tolerated. He wasn't really kin to either the Tarpley family or the Jessup family, the only two families that counted. And it was an unspoken agreement that the first time he laid harsh hands on Rena, he would be dealt with appropriately. This in spite of Rena informing them that if that ever occurred, she would deal with it herself.

"How you doin', Johnny?" Marvin greeted him when he and Rena came into the parlor.

"I'm doin' just fine, Marvin," Johnny

returned. He nodded in Cletus's direction and said, "Cletus." Cletus nodded in return.

They were spared from having to try to make conversation when one of the ladies came into the parlor and announced, "Food's ready. Come in and fix you a plate before it gets cold." A second announcement was unnecessary.

They filed into the dining room, where the women had set a chair with cushions on it for Clyde's grieving widow, Atha, to sit. Everyone started filling their plates until Broadus asked for a few moments of quiet while the Reverend Matthew Tarpley said a prayer. The preacher made it short but managed to remind them all that a regular funeral service would be held for the dead on Sunday at the community church, even if there would be no burial. "If some of you here today need directions to the church, I will be happy to assist you." His announcement was met with a few quiet chuckles.

While the food was being consumed, a few people said some kind words about the deceased, citing some occasion when Clyde or one of the boys had lent a helping hand or performed a needed service. Nothing was mentioned concerning their horse and cattle rustling, nor the robbing of stage and trains. When the supper was finished, the women gathered to clean up the mess while the men retired to the parlor to smoke. This was the moment that Johnny Pepper had been waiting for. He sidled over to the corner of the room where Broadus and his two sons were holding court.

"I hope I ain't interruptin' anything important, Mr. Tarpley," he said to Broadus. "I just wanted you to know how sorry I am about the death of your brother and his sons — and Bud, too."

" 'Preciate you sayin' that, Johnny," Broadus said.

"I heard that you and Cletus and Marvin found where they was killed, and you buried 'em."

"That's a fact, Johnny," Broadus answered curtly, wondering what the hell he was getting at.

"If you're thinkin' about going after the two buzzards that killed 'em, I just wanted to tell you, you can count on me. I'll go with you."

Broadus looked genuinely surprised. Marvin and Cletus exchanged looks of raised eyebrows. " 'Preciate the offer, but we already found out there ain't no use to try."

"You ain't goin' after the men who killed your brother and your nephews?"

"Damn it, you make it sound like we

didn't wanna go after 'em," Broadus responded. Marvin and Cletus both moved in close to Johnny, but Broadus waved them back. "We was gonna try to trail 'em, but they woulda had a two-day head start on us. We'da never caught 'em. And we didn't know who they were. Didn't have no names, didn't know what they looked like, didn't know where they was headin'. So how you gonna chase somebody like that?" Broadus was just about ready to turn Marvin and Cletus loose on their brother-in-law.

"You shoulda talked to me before you decided to quit," Johnny said smugly. "Hell, I know who killed 'em. I know their names. And I know where they're goin'."

The whole room went deadly quiet, which was broken by Broadus Tarpley's booming voice. "What the hell are you talkin' about?"

"Two men you're lookin' for, right?" Johnny began. "One of 'em was a younger man. His name is Perley Gates, like the heavenly gates, but spelled different. The other one was an old man with a gray horse tail hangin' down his back. They ride for the Triple-G Ranch, up above Sulphur Springs, and it's my guess that's where they're heading."

Broadus was almost in shock. "How the hell do you know all that's true?"

" 'Cause when I heard about what happened to Clyde Tarpley and his boys, I decided to do a little diggin' and find out what's what. And I found out those two fellers, Perley Gates and Possum Smith, guided a bunch of whores down to a new saloon in Nacogdoches. They was gonna go right back north again, but somethin' happened." He paused to notice that he had everybody's complete attention. "What happened was Monk Tarpley broke out of the Nacogdoches jailhouse, stole a couple of horses outta the stable, and took off for the Angelina. Well, I found out that one of those horses Monk stole belonged to Mr. Perley Gates, and he don't stand for nobody stealin' his horse. So him and Possum Smith went with the sheriff's posse chasin' Monk. It was just like it always is, they chased Monk till they got to the river, but the posse turned back then. All except Perley and Possum, they didn't turn back. And I don't have to tell you the rest of it, do I?"

No one spoke for a long time, until finally Broadus spoke. "Now I'm gonna ask you a question, and I wanna make sure you've got enough sense to tell me the truth." He paused another second or two. "How much of that story did you make up?"

"Not a dad-blamed word of it," Johnny

replied. "I'da said somethin' sooner, but I figured you'd most likely do the same thing I did. Tell you the truth, I was surprised to hear you was havin' this gatherin' today. I thought you'd be on your way to Sulphur Springs to find the Triple-G and settle that debt."

Broadus looked at Marvin and Cletus, who were staring back at him, still not sure they could believe every word out of Johnny Pepper's mouth. They knew what he was going to say. "We'll mourn my brother and his sons, and Cousin Bud. Then tomorrow mornin', we'll be headin' up to Sulphur Springs."

"Well, that suits the hell outta me," Cletus declared. "That weren't settin' too well in my craw, givin' up on settlin' that score."

"I'll go along to help," Johnny volunteered, "if you want me to."

"You're welcome to come with us," Broadus said, "seein' as how you was the only one who figured it all out." It pained Broadus to say that, but he figured to give the devil his due.

"You just didn't have no idea about them two fellows bringin' them whores down to Nacogdoches," Johnny replied. He knew how hard it was for Broadus to have said what he did, and he was enjoying his father-in-law's pain. "I was in town when Monk broke out, so I knew about that one feller's horse gittin' stole. You'da most likely figured it all out, same as me." He glanced at Marvin and Cletus to judge their reaction, satisfied that it looked the same as their father's. "But if you can use my help, I'd be proud to try to do somethin' to honor my wife's uncle's passin'." *And I'll be honored to show you almighty Tarpley trash that I can outride you, outshoot you, and outdraw you,* he thought.

"Like Pa said," Marvin offered, "you're welcome to come along.

" 'Preciate it, Marvin," Johnny replied, then focused his gaze on Cletus, unwilling to let him off without a similar invitation.

"Won't hurt to have another gun on hand," Cletus said. It was as close to an invitation as he could force himself to offer.

"All right then," Broadus concluded. "I reckon we'll get ready to get started tomorrow mornin'. We'll bring everything we need to cook with, Johnny, but I expect you'll need to bring a packhorse, too, for anything else you're gonna need." They talked then about supplies they would need and agreed that they could carry enough to live on until they reached Tyler, where they could buy supplies for the long haul. "How are you fixed for money?" Broadus asked Johnny.

"I can pay for what I need," Johnny replied. He was still flush with his share of a bank job in Crockett with Henry Jessup's gang. "I'll kick in to pay for some of the supplies for all of us."

"Can't ask for much more than that, I reckon," Broadus commented, frankly surprised by Johnny's sudden change in attitude toward his wife's family. "Can you be ready to go first thing in the mornin'?"

"I'm always ready," Johnny replied at once. "I'll be here, ready to travel."

"Come here for breakfast, if you want to," Broadus told him. "Bring Rena along with you."

"Yeah, I'll do that, if she wants to come, and she probably will," Johnny said.

So, it was set for the following morning. Once again, four of the Tarpley clan would set out on a quest for revenge against Perley and Possum, although one of the four was actually a Pepper.

As Broadus suggested, Johnny met with them for breakfast. Rena came along with him to lend a hand cooking the breakfast and loading the packhorses. The posse did not actually depart until the later part of the morning, but they were in no particular rush. Thanks to Johnny Pepper, they knew who they were going to kill and approximately where they would find them. It was left up to Rena to issue the only negative. "You be careful," she said. "Don't forget what happened to the last four who went after those two."

Chapter 17

"I swear," Sonny Rice blurted, "look comin' yonder!" He got up off the empty nail keg he was using as a stool. "It's Perley and Possum!"

"You sure?" Ollie Dinkler remarked. "It just might be their ghosts comin' back. You know you were a lot younger when they left here." He got up from his stool. "Wonder if they've et supper. I'd better see if there's any heat left in my stove. Perley!" he called out. "Welcome back. You hungry?"

Perley waited until they got a little bit closer before answering. "We stopped in town and ate when we saw we weren't gonna make it back here in time, Ollie. Looks like you've cleaned everything from supper, so I reckon we did the right thing."

"What happened to your head, Possum?" Ollie asked. "Did that gray horse kick you in the head?"

"Nope," Possum answered. "He run me

into a low-hangin' limb." He thought the story he gave Becky was as good as any. He had no desire to tell them he was so sick he let a man walk right up to him and knock him in the head.

"You stoppin' in town to eat didn't have nothin' to do with Miss Becky Morris, did it?" Sonny asked as Perley stepped down from his horse. " 'Course you was gone a while. You might notta recognized her after she got that much older."

"There were a couple of kinda familiar-lookin' ladies workin' in the hotel dinin' room," Perley said. "There was one of 'em that coulda been her. We only ended up eatin' there 'cause we couldn't find a place that had what Possum had a cravin' for."

"What was that?" Ollie asked. "One of my fine suppers?"

"No, he had a cravin' for some deer meat," Perley said. "He gets cravin's like that every once in a while, and when he does, won't nothin' else satisfy him."

"Deer meat?" Sonny asked. "Why deer meat?"

"You'll have to ask him," Perley answered. "I swear, I don't know why he loves it so much."

"I reckon we'd best take care of these horses," Possum said. He was not interested in telling that story just yet, and he didn't appreciate Perley's bringing it up.

"You're right about that," Perley said. "These horses have been workin' pretty hard the last few days." Sonny offered to give them a hand, and they led the horses over to the barn. Perley and Possum pulled their saddles off Buck and Dancer while Sonny started unloading the packhorses. "I wanna give all four of 'em some grain," he said as he rubbed Buck's neck. He was interrupted then by an outcry from Sonny. "Oh, I shoulda told you about that," Perley said, figuring Sonny had discovered the extra rifles and handguns the packhorses were carrying.

"What in the world . . . ?" Sonny started. "Was you in a war while you were gone? Where were you all this time, anyway? I think Rubin just about gave up thinkin' you'd be back."

"Is that a fact?" Perley asked. "What did John think?"

Sonny chuckled before he answered. "John said you'd show up sooner or later and the first thing you'd have to do is clean the cow pie off your boots."

That caused Possum to chuckle. "You can say that again."

"Did you really go all the way to Nacogdoches with some women?" Sonny asked.

"Oh, you know about that?" Perley asked.

"It was in the telegram you sent Rubin," Sonny said.

"Damn," Perley swore. "What did he do, walk it around the ranch and read it to everyone?" Sonny shrugged. "Possum and I will tell you the whole story, but right now, I'd best go tell it to my brothers before it gets any later. You wanna go with me, Possum?"

"Nope," he replied. "I think I druther stay here and feed the horses some grain."

"Good," Perley said. "That way I can blame everything on you." He left the barn and walked up to the house. He opened the kitchen door a crack and called out, "Knock, knock."

Lou Ann came to the door and exclaimed, "Perley!" She stepped back, opening the door wide. "Come in! Let me call Rubin. Are you hungry? Do you want some coffee or something?"

"Have you still got a pot workin'?" Perley asked. She nodded, so he said, "I would like a cup of coffee."

She quickly poured him a cup and handed it to him. "Boy, is he gonna be glad to see you," she said and went to the hallway door. "Rubin! Perley's here!"

From another part of the house, they heard Rubin call Henry, his ten-year-old son. A couple of minutes later, Rubin walked in the kitchen. "Well, I reckon we can cancel the funeral service we had planned. I sent Henry to get John. I know he won't want to wait till morning to hear your story."

"You want some coffee, hon?" Lou Ann asked her husband. He said yes, so she poured a cup for him. "I'll leave you now, so you can fight. I'll leave a cup here, too, in case John wants one. There's plenty left in the pot. Glad to see you back safe and sound, Perley," she said as she went out the door.

"Here's that paper you wanted George Weber to sign," Perley said, handing it to Rubin. "Did the cattle get here in good shape?"

"Yeah, they looked fine," Rubin said, and looked at the signature on the paper. "Good — doesn't hurt to have a record of these things." He put the paper aside and looked Perley in the eye as if about to deliver a lecture, thought better of it, and just shook his head. "Perley, do you know how long you've been gone?"

"Not exactly," Perley said. "A long time. I ain't counted up the days. Why, did something happen that I shoulda been here for?"

"Damn, Perley, don't make light of it. You have family here that worries about you when you just disappear and nobody knows where."

"Whaddaya mean, nobody knows where? I told you in that telegram where I was going. I ain't got any control over what happens in life. The only choice I've got is how I react to what does happen. Same as you. Same as anybody. Sometimes you can't avoid being right in the middle of something you don't want any part of at all. So you just play the hand you're dealt. I always try to play it like I think you or John would play it. It doesn't always work."

They suddenly felt John's presence and looked back to see him standing in the doorway, listening to the conversation. He chuckled and said, "Makes sense to me." He walked on into the room then. "Glad to see you made it back safely, Brother Perley. Rubin, are you trying to play daddy to Perley again? Has it ever worked for you? Any coffee left in that pot?"

"Lou Ann said there was plenty," Rubin answered.

"Even got a cup out for me," John said, and poured himself a cup. "Now, I'm all ears, Perley. I wanna hear the whole damn story, every day of it. Don't leave nothin' out. You're the only one of the three of us who can travel the world outside this ranch and Paris, Texas, Rubin and I being married. And that's something we maybe oughta talk about, too. So I wanna know what I missed on this trip."

Perley had to laugh at his brother's blunt description of his life. Rubin, as expected, just shook his head in exasperation over both his brothers. "Like John said," he finally confessed, "I'd like to hear why you and Possum decided to go to Nacogdoches with a bunch of women."

"It wasn't something we wanted to do," Perley explained. "It was just our bad luck we showed up at that spot on the Sulphur River; or their good luck, if you wanna look at it from their side." He went on to tell them how they came to be the women's protectors as well as their guides. Rubin's concern grew with Perley's accounting of having Buck stolen, and consequently, his and Possum's introduction to the Tarpley family.

When Perley finished his report, both his brothers were amazed that he had survived. The difference in their reactions, however, was easily apparent when judged by the devilish grin on John's face in contrast to the deep frown of concern on Rubin's. It was John who stated the obvious first. "I swear, Perley, you're like a magnet for trouble."

"Sometimes, I feel that way, myself," Perley conceded. "But I think it wouldn't make much difference if it hadda been you or Rubin takin' that money to George Weber."

"That's where we disagree," Rubin was quick to reply. "Things happen to you that don't happen to other people in the same situation. Don't you realize that?"

"You two are makin' too much outta this," Perley protested. "Things like I just told you about are happenin' to everybody who ain't spendin' every minute of their lives tendin' cattle. That's the only difference."

John was obviously enjoying the discussion, which seemed to further irritate Rubin, whose serious nature seldom allowed for humor. Aware of this, John looked at him and said, "I honestly believe it's because of the day Perley was born on."

"Oh, that's nonsense," Rubin said at once. "I don't believe in stuff like that."

John looked at Perley and asked, still grinning, "When's your birthday?"

"April first . . . why?" When John didn't answer with anything more than the same grin, Perley realized what he was referring to. "Rubin's right," he said. "That's just horse crap." He got up from the table. "I can see I've held you two old-timers up past your bedtime. I'm headin' for the bunkhouse."

His brothers got up, too, but Rubin had another question. "You feel like there might be any more trouble from that Tarpley clan you talked about?" He couldn't help but feel there might be huge repercussions. Perley and Possum had killed four men. That was not a small thing, to have taken four lives, and he worried about the effect it might have on his younger brother.

"Well, I wouldn't think so," Perley said. "It wasn't like we had any choice. Can't say for sure, though. We killed those four because they came to kill us. And as far as I know, they didn't know who Possum and I are or where we're from." He moved to the back door, but Rubin had one more issue to discuss.

"Perley, we need to talk about your plans for you and Becky sometime. John and I don't have any idea what you're gonna do. Whether you're thinkin' about buildin' a house, like John did, or what you've got in mind. But we need to know what we can do to help you get settled after you're married."

"I 'preciate it, Rubin, but to be honest

with you, I ain't sure what our plans are right now. Just before Possum and I left to go to Weber's, I almost thought Becky had changed her mind about marryin' me. Tonight, she seemed like she was back the other way. I reckon we'll come to an agreement pretty soon, and then I'll know what to do." Eager to change the subject, he asked, "Where'd you put the Herefords you got from Weber?"

John told him they were on the south range, close to the headquarters. "They look like they're carryin' more meat than our longhorns, so we thought we better keep an eye on 'em."

"I think I'll ride out and look 'em over in the mornin'. I wanna see if they look as good on our range as they did on his." Perley tried not to show it, but he was as concerned as Rubin or John about his relationship with Becky. He had to believe that it was the fact that he had been forced to take another man's life that caused her to question the wisdom of marrying him. He was afraid that if she knew how many times he had been forced to kill or be killed, she would not be able to deal with it.

It was good to be back in the bunkhouse Perley thought, even if the boys were all wanting to hear about his and Possum's trip. There were mostly questions about the two wagons and the women who drove them. "No wonder you took them women all the way to Nacogdoches," Charlie Ramsey said. "I'll bet you collected your guide's pay every night."

"That's all right for Perley," Ralph Johnson said, "but it's a wonder it didn't kill Possum."

"Sorry to disappoint you, boys," Perley said, "but we did not touch a hair on those young ladies' heads."

"There's lots of different ways of doin' it," Sonny cracked. It brought a big round of chuckling and lewd comments.

"Nope," Perley insisted. "Didn't happen."

"Why?" Sonny asked. This time, it was a serious question.

"Possum had his reasons, I had mine," Perley answered. "Aside from that, we had other things to worry about."

"Like finding Possum some deer meat?" Ralph asked. That brought another round of guffaws and requests for details.

"That's another story that there ain't nothin' to," Possum said in an effort to put it to bed quickly. "Perley shot a deer, and we ate on it for a couple of days. But I ate some of it after it had turned and got sick as a dog. End of story."

Perley decided they deserved more than that for their entertainment. "That's the short version of the story. We were on the way back home, and we had gotten as far as Tyler by the time Possum was too sick to ride. So I left him one day at our camp and went into town to buy some things we needed. While I was gone, two fellows found our camp and thought Possum was dead." He went on to tell the story of how they ended up arresting the two men and taking them to the Tyler jail.

"You had to tell it, didn't you?" Possum grumbled.

"Well, they deserved some kinda story, since we were gone so long," Perley told him.

Perley ate breakfast with the cowhands in the cookshack, as was his custom. After breakfast, he left Buck with Ralph Johnson to get new shoes, and he cut out another horse to ride out to take a look at the Herefords. He didn't really have any reason to doubt that George Weber might not have sent his best-looking stock. He just wanted to get his first look at a herd of Hereford cattle grazing on the Triple-G. He found them near a small pond that John had made by damming up a small creek. As far as he could tell, the cows looked to be in fine condition. He tried to imagine what a calf would look like that was the result of a mating between one of the Herefords and a Texas longhorn. *I wonder if John and Rubin know what they're doing,* he thought. He gave the flea-bitten gelding he had gotten from the corral a light kick and rode around the small herd. A random thought of Becky Morris crossed his mind, and he pictured her in the apron-front dress she wore at work. *I reckon I better not ever tell her I was looking over some cows and I thought of her,* he thought. And while he was having nonsensical thoughts, he decided to have another. He had recently spent some time in Tyler, on two separate occasions. Becky's father, a widower, was supposed to live in Tyler, although she said she had not heard a word from him in about seven years. *I wonder what he would have said if I had looked him up and told him I wanted to marry his daughter. He would have probably asked what I do for a living. "I coulda told him, 'Why, Mr. Morris, I mostly just run errands for my two older brothers, and often have to shoot somebody.'"*

I got no business getting married, he thought. He turned the gelding around and headed back to the barn. He decided he was going into town to have a serious talk with Becky. *She has to be out of her mind to want to marry someone like me.*

When he rode back into the barnyard, he saw Buck still standing outside the barn, tied to a rail of the corral. When he saw Ralph coming out of the barn, he asked, "When are you gonna get Buck shoed?"

"I just finished him up," Ralph said. "Gettin' ready to take him back."

"I'll take him," Perley said, and pulled the flea-bitten horse up to the corral beside Buck. Then he pulled his saddle off and put it on Buck, led the other horse into the corral, took the bridal off, and came back to put it on Buck. Buck jerked his head a couple of times to let Perley know he didn't appreciate the taste left on the bit by the other horse. He had told Becky at supper that he would find some reason to come into town that day. It was not a busy time of the year on the ranch, so there was nothing important he had to do. The Gates brothers' hired hands could take care of any routine jobs, he told himself. So he made up his mind. He led Buck over to the cookhouse and told Ollie he was going into town in case anyone might be looking for him.

"I'll tell him," Ollie said with a chuckle,

referring to Possum. "He went to help Sonny and Charlie move part of the herd to some new grazin'."

"Good," Perley said. "At least one of us is workin'. I'll most likely be back for supper."

"Howdy, Perley," Paul McQueen, the blacksmith and acting sheriff, called out to him as Perley passed by his shop. "Glad to see you back in town." Perley pulled Buck to a stop to say howdy. "You had your brother worried there for a while when you were gone for so long."

"Musta been Rubin," Perley said. "He's the worrier in the family. Possum and I were on a little trip to Sulphur Springs we figured would take us a couple of days. We got delayed a little longer. Gave Rubin something more to worry about. Hope he didn't bother you with it."

"No, not at all," Paul replied. "He just mentioned it."

Perley was a little bit early for the dining room to be open for dinner, so he decided to kill a few minutes with Paul. "You stayin' pretty busy with your blacksmith work?" Paul said that he was. "I'm surprised the town council hasn't been naggin' at you again to take the sheriff's job permanently."

"They say something about that every

once in a while," Paul admitted, "but I swear, we don't have that much trouble in town." He chuckled then and said, "Except when some drifter wants to try you out in a face-off."

"I'm sorry about that last little mess just before Possum and I took off. Next time it happens, I'm just gonna send for the sheriff."

"I'll most likely just tell you to go ahead and handle it," Paul said with a chuckle.

"My brother John told me I was a magnet for trouble. I'm beginning to think he's right. I think the best thing is for me to stay outta town."

"Then Becky Morris would probably want me to go bring you in."

The comment surprised Perley. "Why do you say that?"

"Come on, Perley," Paul japed. "The whole town knows you two young people are supposed to get together and get hitched. My wife told me that the women are gettin' mighty impatient for it to happen."

Perley was shocked. He had assumed his relationship with Becky was known only by the women in the hotel dining room, and their intimate thoughts known only by Becky and himself. He was suddenly tempted to get back on his horse and go home, but he was afraid Paul, or someone else who saw him, might say that he had been in town. He'd hate for her to find out that way. "I sure didn't know anybody but Becky and I knew we liked each other." He climbed back up into the saddle. "Well, I reckon I'd better get goin'," he said.

"Where you headed?" Paul asked.

"Up toward the hotel, I reckon."

"Hope you enjoy your dinner," Paul said with a wide grin.

"Hey, sweetie," Becky whispered to him when he walked into the dining room. She had learned not to greet him that way out loud, since the last time she did landed him in the middle of a shoot-out. "Glad to see you made it back today, like you said you would."

"You know I'd spend more time here with you if I could," he told her. "But I have to earn my keep at the ranch. I have to get back by suppertime tonight for a meeting with Rubin and John about those Hereford cattle we bought." He hoped she wasn't reading his eyes, because it was an outright lie. He told it because he had just been away from the ranch for so long, and he felt guilty for that. Now he realized it was the first time he had ever lied to Becky, so he added that to his short list of sins. Killing his fellow man was at the top of that list, but it didn't seem like he would ever avoid that sin unless he dug a hole somewhere and jumped in it. He waited for her in her room until she was finished with all the cleanup after the noon meal, and they spent the two hours talking about their marriage plans. And yet they had still not set the date. He suddenly realized that she was the one who could not commit to a solid date.

When it was time for her to go back to the dining room to prepare for the evening meal, they kissed goodbye, and he rode back to the ranch. When they parted, he told her that he was not going to be able to come back to town the next day, but he would try to make it for supper the day after that. He said he was going to be riding night herd. Actually, he just wanted to spend more time with the men and take part in more of the ranch duties. In effect, he told himself, he had to get accustomed to a life of ranch work, and no more adventures with Possum. He had to laugh when he thought of that. Possum was getting long in the tooth, anyway. He thought that spoiled deer meat had killed him on this last trip.

Chapter 18

"That looks like a store at the crossroads up yonder," Cletus Tarpley declared. "Might be a good place to catch up some of our supplies."

"I reckon we'd better, if we're figurin' to have anythin' to eat tonight," his father said. "Looks like a good time to hit it. Don't look like nobody else around."

They walked their horses off the road and tied up at the hitching rail out front. "Clinton's Store," Marvin read the sign for them, and they dismounted and walked inside.

Abner Clinton looked the four strangers over carefully from behind the counter. They had a look about them that made him cautious. So much so that he rested his hand on the double-barrel shotgun he kept on the shelf under the counter. He relaxed a little bit when Broadus said, "Good afternoon to ya. We're runnin' low on some supplies and saw your store here. Maybe we can get what we need right here."

"Well, I carry a pretty good supply of most basic goods," Abner said, "long as you ain't lookin' for somethin' out of the ordinary."

"No, sir," Broadus replied, "there ain't nothin' out of the ordinary about us. I know we need some flour and some coffee. What else are we about out of, Marvin?"

"We need some sugar," Marvin said, "and some bacon. Have you got any ground coffee?"

"I can grind 'em for you," Abner said. "The beans is already roasted. You just tell me how many you want, and I'll throw 'em in the grinder."

"Ten pounds, I reckon," Broadus said.

"The way the four of us drink up that coffee, you might as well get twenty pounds of it, Pa," Marvin said.

"Make it twenty," Broadus told Abner. "And some molasses, if you've got any. Are you writin' all this down? 'Cause my boys can start loadin' this stuff on the horses." He reached in his pocket and pulled a roll of money out and held it in his hand. It had the proper effect on Abner as the order grew on the counter and Cletus, Marvin, and Johnny were hustling back and forth between the counter and the horses. Abner began suggesting items they might enjoy, like dried apples and hardtack. Broadus was receptive to his suggestions. "That oughta 'bout do it, I reckon," Broadus finally decided. "What's the bill come to, so far?"

"I make it fifty-two dollars and fifty cents," Abner said. "Let's just round it off at an even fifty and a thank you for the business."

"Now, I call that mighty neighborly of you," Broadus said. "What is your name, friend?"

"I'm Abner Clinton," he said. "This is my store."

"Well, Abner, it's a pleasure doin' business at your store. I forgot one thing, though. I need about twelve foot of that clothesline rope off that spool over yonder." Abner jumped right to the task and gave him a generous measure. "By the way, when we leave here, if we take that road there to the east, where does that go?"

"That road'll take you to a little settlement called Beantown," Abner answered, "about fourteen miles."

"That's where we wanna go. See, boys, I told you this was the crossroads where we oughta turn to go to Beantown. Thank you, Abner."

"There's one more thing we need, Pa," Cletus said.

"What's that, son?"

"Money. We're runnin' awful short of it," Cletus said.

"You're right, I almost forgot it. Thanks for remindin' me." Broadus turned back to Abner then, who stood fumbling under the counter, a sick expression on his face. He looked then at a grinning Johnny Pepper, who was holding his double-barrel shotgun up for him to see. Johnny had reached under the counter and found the shotgun when Abner went to cut the clothesline. Johnny's six-gun was in his other hand, and Cletus and Marvin had drawn their weapons as well. Broadus leaned over the counter then and said, "Let's see what you've got in your cash drawer, Abner," as he opened the drawer. "I swear, you ain't been doin' all that good, have you?"

"Damn you, you dirty scum," Abner swore, devastated to have been taken so completely. "Leave me the little bit of cash I've got in the drawer."

"Now, don't disappoint me, Abner. This has been such a nice polite little trade between me and you. It might not look like that to you right now, but you're gittin' the best half of the trade. All we got is some supplies and a little bit of cash money, but you got your life. Ain't that a whole lot more? 'Course that's dependin' on you not doin' somethin' dumb right now — somethin' I'd have to kill you for. Now, put your hands behind your back." Abner failed to obey, so Broadus pressed the barrel of his pistol hard against his forehead. "I said, put your hands behind your back!" he ordered. This time Abner complied. "Cletus, gimme a good tight knot on them hands. Marvin, you and Johnny go see who else is in this store. Bring 'em in here."

Johnny and Marvin went through the door in the back of the store to find a dumpy little red-haired woman working over the stove. Busy with her cooking, Helen Clinton wasn't even aware she had visitors until she pulled a pan of biscuits out of her oven and turned around to place them on the table. Startled to see two strange men in her kitchen, she dropped the pan, then tried to catch the biscuits trying to escape. Johnny and Marvin jumped in to try to help her catch the biscuits. They kept all but a couple of the biscuits from hitting the floor. Unable to speak, the shocked woman just stared, wide-eyed and open-mouthed, as she watched Johnny pick up a biscuit from the floor and take a bite of it. "Mrs. Clinton?" Marvin asked. She nodded, eyes and mouth still locked open. "Your husband wants you in the store." He stood aside to let her pass in front of him, then he reached over and picked up a biscuit before following her into the store.

"Don't harm my wife," Abner pleaded, lying on his side on the floor, hands and feet tied together.

"Don't worry, old man," Johnny replied. "She ain't my type. I'm all right with old, fat, and ugly. It's redheads I don't like." Cletus laughed, in spite of an effort not to.

"Don't pay no attention to his crudeness, ma'am," Broadus told her. "As long as you behave, we ain't gonna do no harm to you or your husband. Now lay down on the floor behind your husband and put your hands behind your back, and my boy is gonna tie 'em together. It'll be just like it was when you was first married and went to bed, and you'd make a chair for him on a cold night."

Too frightened not to, she did as she was told. Cletus took the rest of the clothesline and looped it tightly around her wrists, then looped the rest of the line around both their ankles. "There you go; snug as two little bugs in a rug. Most likely you can work yourselves free if you really try to get out of it. If you can't, then maybe another customer will come along, or maybe not. We might be your only customers today. Let's go to Beantown, boys. It's been a pleasure doin' business with you, Abner."

Marvin and Johnny ran back into the kitchen. "What the hell are you doin'?" Broadus exclaimed.

"I ain't leavin' those biscuits," Johnny yelled back. He and Marvin put all the biscuits in a dishtowel and tied it like a bag. Marvin saw a jar of jelly on the table, so he grabbed that, too.

They climbed on their horses and left the store at a lope until they were back on the road north. "I thought you wanted to go to Beantown," Cletus shouted as they passed through the crossroads.

"He wants them to think we went that way, genius," Marvin said. "But nobody's gonna believe it, anyway."

"I wish I'da thought to ask him how far it is to Sulphur Springs," Broadus said. "Let's put a little distance behind us before we find a spot to rest the horses. Then we'll have some of that fresh coffee and some biscuits and jelly."

They knew the distance from Tyler to Sulphur Springs was roughly fifty miles. And they guessed they had ridden about fifteen miles when they had come upon Abner Clinton's little store. So, they reasoned, the horses should be fine for another five miles or more before needing a rest. But they happened upon a good spot to stop before going quite that far, so they pulled off the road at a nice little spring. From there, it should be one-day's ride to Sulphur Springs without too much strain on their horses. "Then somebody oughta be able to tell us how to find the Triple-G Ranch," Broadus said.

"One or both of them two fellers might even be in town," Marvin speculated. "That'ud make it short and sweet, wouldn't it? Just cut 'em down and get outta town before anybody got a good look at us."

"Yeah, it would," Johnny replied, "if we knew what they looked like." There was a long gap of silence following his remark.

"Whaddaya talkin' about?" Cletus asked. "You know what they look like."

"What gives you that idea?" Johnny asked.

"You, that's what!" Cletus replied. "You said you knew who they was. You knew their names, where they was workin', everythin' about 'em. Ain't that the only reason we're on our way to Sulphur Springs?"

"I never said I ever saw 'em," Johnny said.

"You said Perley Gates was a young feller, and Possum Smith was an old feller with his hair hangin' like a horse tail down his back," Marvin said.

"Well, that's what I was told," Johnny said.

"I never said I saw 'em."

"I swear, I oughta kick your butt," Marvin said.

"You oughta try," Johnny responded, and backed away to face him squarely, his hand hovering over the butt of his six-gun.

"Just hold it right there!" Broadus commanded. "You two cool down. We ain't gonna start shootin' each other, damn it! We're family!"

"Johnny Pepper sure as hell ain't family," Cletus remarked.

"He's married to your sister, so that makes him family," Broadus said, "so don't you forget it." He didn't have much use for Johnny Pepper, either, but he didn't want to make his daughter a widow. Looking at Johnny, he said, "That's a helluva thing to find out at this stage of the game, that we wouldn't recognize the two we're after if we saw 'em on the street somewhere. That was the main reason we wanted you to come along with us. We've come too far to turn back now. We'll just have to be a little more careful and make sure we find the right fellers."

"It's gonna make it an even fight," Cletus said. " 'Cause they don't know what we look like, either." He looked at Johnny then and asked sarcastically, "He ain't ever seen you, has he, Johnny?" Johnny didn't bother to answer.

"When we get to Sulphur Springs, somebody oughta be able to tell us how to get to the Triple-G. Then, I reckon we're just gonna have to watch 'em for a while and see if we can spot the two we're after."

It took them longer to get to Sulphur Springs, than they had estimated the day before, so they arrived well after the supper hour. Most of the shops and businesses were closed; the saloons were the only places open. They decided to have a drink or two before looking for a place to camp while it was still light out. The saloon they picked was the Happy Times. Inside, they found a small crowd of evening patrons. Broadus told his two sons and Johnny to sit down at a table and he'd get a bottle. He went to the bar where he was greeted by Ed Curry, the bartender. "Evenin'. What can I get you?"

"Gimme a bottle of rye whiskey," Broadus said, "and four glasses." When Ed put them on the bar, Broadus paid him, then said, "Me and my boys are on our way to the Triple-G Ranch. Supposed to be north of town somewhere. Any chance you can tell me how to get there? We never been there before."

"Triple-G," Ed repeated. "Can't say as I've ever heard of it. Sorry I can't help you. Maybe somebody else can. Hey, everybody listen up!" He yelled. "Feller here is tryin' to find the Triple-G Ranch. Anybody know where that is?" Nobody did. "Sorry, mister, looks like we ain't no help a-tall. You know who owns it? Maybe they've been in here."

"I don't know who owns it," Broadus answered. "Feller named Perley Gates works for him, though."

Ed's eyes lit up then. "Perley Gates," he repeated. "I know that name." Practically everyone in Sulphur Springs was familiar with the name, thanks to Sheriff Virgil Cooper's fascination with the man. "The man you wanna ask is the sheriff. He knows who he is, and I wouldn't be surprised if he knows where that ranch is."

That left Broadus with an uncomfortable decision to make. The last person he wanted to go to for information, or anything else, was the sheriff. "Much obliged," he said. "I might do that." He took his bottle and the four glasses to the table where the boys were waiting. "Drink up, boys, courtesy of Abner Clinton and his redheaded wife."

"Triple-G must not be a very big ranch, if

ain't nobody ever heard of it," Marvin said. "We might search for six months to find it if it's just one of them little ol' farms they call a ranch." His comment started a conversation on what they should do next, since it was obvious their planned execution wasn't going to be as easy as they first thought. So engrossed were they in their discussion, in fact, that none of them noticed the man who walked in the saloon and went over to talk to the bartender. He and Ed talked for a few minutes, both occasionally looking toward the four men at the table. Finally the man left the bar and approached the table. Only then did Marvin notice. "Watch your mouth," he warned the others.

"Evenin', boys," the man said. "I'm Sheriff Cooper. Ed tells me you're lookin' for Perley Gates and the Triple-G Cattle Company."

Four right hands dropped casually down to rest on four gun grips, but Broadus answered calmly. "That's right," he said. "We was hopin' to talk to him about raisin' some cattle. We're from down San Antonio way, and we heard the Triple-G was just a little north of Sulphur Springs, but it seems like nobody here ever heard of it."

"Well, that ain't so surprisin'," Cooper said. "Somebody didn't give you very good directions. The Triple-G is north of Sulphur Springs all right, but a little farther north. From what I understand, it's a few miles north of Paris, and Paris is thirty-eight or forty miles north of Sulphur Springs."

"Well, I'll be . . ." Broadus started. "How 'bout that, boys? We thought we was there, and we're a full day's ride short. It's a good thing we ran into you, Sheriff. Can we buy you a drink?"

"Thank you just the same," Cooper said. "I 'preciate it, but I don't drink much when I'm on duty."

"I expect we'd best get up from this table, boys. We've gotta make camp and cook us up some supper."

"You'll be takin' the road straight north outta Sulphur Springs," Sheriff Cooper said. "There's a good campin' spot about two miles outta town by a nice little creek. Lotta people camp there. Hope you don't have any trouble finding the Triple-G. I imagine you just keep on the same road outta Paris, 'cause the Triple-G is between Paris and the Red River."

"Thanks again, Sheriff. You've saved us a heap of trouble," Broadus said.

When the sheriff returned to the bar to talk to Ed, three pairs of eyes zeroed in on Johnny Pepper. "What the hell are you all starin' at me for? I told you that ranch was north of Sulphur Springs, and it is," Johnny declared. He had no intention of confessing that all the information he had given them had come from a whore in the Shamrock Saloon.

"North of Sulphur Springs," Cletus repeated slowly. "Hell, it's damn-nigh in Oklahoma Injun Territory."

"Don't even get started, Cletus," Broadus warned him. "We've got to get outta here and go make our camp for the night." He picked up the bottle he'd bought, and they all filed past the sheriff, still at the bar. They all nodded to Cooper as they passed.

They found the creek the sheriff had recommended and were satisfied that he hadn't lied. The creek was deep and clean, and there was good grazing for the horses. That was enough to improve Broadus's disposition for the moment. He anticipated better luck in finding Perley Gates and Possum Smith when they reached the town of Paris. If the sheriff in Sulphur Springs was familiar with the ranch called the Triple-G, surely people in Paris would be also. It might take some time, but unless he was in hiding, they would eventually find Perley Gates and his friend with the ponytail.

CHAPTER 19

As Perley had promised Becky when he rode in to have dinner with her, he showed up for supper two days later. He had spent those days pitching in wherever he saw work going on, whether he was actually needed or not. He wanted to get used to a routine of finding the work needing doing and doing it along with the men. It had taken Possum to have the necessary talk with him, and he started in his usual subtle way of counseling. "Perley, what the hell is wrong with you?"

"What are you talking about?" Perley replied.

"You know what I'm talking about. The last two days you've been runnin' around here like a chicken with his head cut off. 'Lemme help you with this. Lemme help you with that.' What's the matter with you? You act like you're afraid you're gonna get fired. What's goin' on? Is it this marryin' business that's got you gun-shy?"

"I don't know, Possum. I reckon I'm trying to get used to workin' on the ranch all the time. And I don't want the other men to think I'm a slacker."

"Perley, you ain't just another hand. You're part owner of this ranch. You can do what you wanna do. You pay their salaries. You ever see Rubin throwin' hay down or muckin' out a stall in the stable? Hell no, you don't. John actually works some with the cattle, but only when he wants to. You ain't gotta prove nothin' to nobody. And I'll tell you somethin' else. Becky fell in love with you when you were the old Perley. You'd do well to get him back. Now get on your horse and go on into town for supper."

Although he never admitted it, Perley always listened to Possum's infrequent words of wisdom. And he'd thought a lot about Possum's saying that Becky fell for him when he was his old carefree self. So he had decided to stop worrying about his somewhat easygoing approach to life, and woo her as the old Perley. And he had to admit, it seemed to go well with her. That night's visit with her had been much less stressful for him.

He walked down the steps by the outside door of the dining room in time to see four riders coming down the street leading packhorses. When they got closer, he didn't recognize any of them in the fading light of day. One in the lead, an older man, called out to him. "Is that the hotel dinin' room?"

"Yes, sir, it is," Perley answered. "But they've already closed for the night."

"Damn, I was hopin' we could have us a good set-down supper tonight," one of the other riders, a younger man, complained.

"If you're wantin' some decent food," Perley said, "you can't go wrong at Patton's Saloon. It might not be quite as good as the hotel, but it's pretty darn good. Patton's got a lady there that does the cookin'. Her name's Sadie Bloodworth, and she'll give you your money's worth."

"Well, thank you, young feller," Broadus said. "We'll give it a try. Patton's Saloon, you say?"

"That's right," Perley said. "Halfway down the street on your left. You can get supper there almost till midnight." The four men rode off down the street with no reason to pay any special attention to the bay gelding the young man was untying from the hitching rail. He climbed up into the saddle and said, "Take me home, Buck." The big horse wheeled away from the hitching rail and headed toward the north end of town.

"Maybe I shoulda told 'em to tell Sadie that Perley recommended her, so she'd treat 'em right. Maybe not, though, since I quit eatin' anywhere in town but the hotel. She mighta took it out on those poor fellows."

Broadus and the boys pulled up in front of Patton's and tied their horses. "I reckon they'll be all right here," he said. "Don't look like there's anybody much in town."

"Looks pretty calm to me," Marvin said. They walked inside to find only a few customers scattered about the room.

They walked up to the bar and Benny Grimes greeted them. "Evenin' fellers. What can I getcha?"

"Young feller up the street told us we could get some supper here," Broadus said.

"That's a fact," Benny said. "Just set yourselves down at any of them tables over there, and I'll go tell Sadie she's got four hungry customers. You wantin' anything from the bar?"

"Yeah," Johnny spoke up, "give us a shot of whiskey." Benny promptly set four shot glasses on the bar and filled them. Johnny grinned and tossed his back right away, oblivious to the annoyed look he got from Broadus for ordering for the group. He put the glass down hard on the counter and nodded to Benny to fill it. Then he picked it up again and walked to one of the tables across from the bar and sat down. Irritated by Johnny's tendency to lead, Broadus walked over to another table and sat down. His sons followed him. Johnny shrugged, got up, and went over to sit at their table. He didn't need to make a crack about their preference for the other table. He got the message: Broadus was the boss, and Cletus and Marvin better hope nothing happened to him real soon because that would be the day Johnny Pepper would start calling the shots. He looked forward to any challenge Cletus or Marvin might make to prevent it. In the meantime, he would humor the old man for the sake of his daughter.

Benny walked over to the kitchen door to tell Sadie, and in half a minute, she came out the door. Benny pointed to the four men, and she came over to their table. "Benny says you're wantin' to eat," she said. "Supper tonight's stew beef, potatoes, and beans and biscuits." She saw that they all had a shot of whiskey, so she asked, "You want coffee or water with your supper?" They all opted for coffee. "I'll be back in a jiffy," she said, and returned to the kitchen. As she promised, she was back shortly, carrying a large tray with the four plates of food and four empty coffee cups. One more trip with the pot to fill the cups and she said, "If you need anything else just holler. My name's Sadie."

When she walked away, Johnny remarked, "That's a big woman. She must like her own cookin'."

"That feller was right," Marvin said, "it taste pretty good to me. I was ready for somethin' cooked by a woman." He took a biscuit and rubbed it around in the gravy before taking a big bite of it. "I believe these biscuits are as good as Ma's." He cocked his head toward Broadus and said, "Don't you go tellin' Ma I said that." His father laughed.

"I wish your ma had taught her daughter to bake decent biscuits," Johnny said. "Rena can't bake a biscuit without it turnin' out to look more like a cracker."

"I've et Rena's biscuits," Cletus remarked. "I thought they was pretty good."

"That's because you ain't never had a decent biscuit," Johnny said.

"So now you're tellin' me my ma's biscuits ain't no good? Is that right?" Cletus demanded.

"I didn't say nothin' about your ma," Johnny responded. "I said you wouldn't know a good biscuit if you got hit in the side of the head with one."

"I got a good mind to hit you in the side of your head with somethin' harder than a biscuit," Cletus threatened.

"Why don't you try that," Johnny replied, and pushed his chair a little farther back from the table, prepared to get up.

"Damn it, you two!" Broadus snapped. "We rode all this way up here on some serious business, and you're fixin' to have a shoot-out over a biscuit? You'll have the sheriff in here on us in a minute. You're a disgrace to those poor souls we've come to avenge. If you don't care no more about rightin' the wrong against my family than what you've showed so far, then get the hell on back home, and let me do what I came to do."

"Sorry, Pa," Cletus apologized. "I didn't mean no disrespect to Uncle Clyde's family."

"Yeah, sorry, Mr. Tarpley," Johnny said, but not very convincingly. "I reckon some of us has got wound up a little tight."

With conversation killed for the moment, everyone concentrated on the plate in front of him until it was cleaned of all traces of gravy. Sadie returned once again to refill the coffee cups, and Broadus told her she had done a good job with the cookin'. "Now I'd like another drink of that whiskey to settle my belly," Broadus told her. She relayed the request to Benny, and he walked over to the table with a bottle. Broadus watched Benny fill the glasses, then he asked, "You ever hear of the Triple-G Ranch?"

"Sure I have," Benny replied. "The Triple-G Cattle Company."

"Is it close around here somewhere?"

"It's straight out the north road, six or eight miles to the gate leading to the headquarters buildings is what I understand," Benny said. "I ain't ever actually been out there, myself." He corked the bottle. "Is that where you fellows are headin'?"

"No," Broadus answered, "We're headin' up toward Oklahoma Territory. I just heard the Triple-G was up this way somewhere, and I wondered about it."

"Well, if you're headin' to the Red River, you'll be passin' through a piece of Triple-G range."

"We got no business with 'em," Broadus said. "I was just curious to know where they was located. I expect we'd best settle up with you for our supper and the whiskey. We've gotta find a decent place to camp tonight before it gets much darker." Bennie figured up their bill, and Broadus paid for everybody, still operating out of Abner

Clinton's cash drawer. "We ain't never been to Paris before. Don't be surprised if you see us again. We might hang around for a day or two to see what kind of town you've got here."

"What did you tell him that for, Pa?" Marvin asked when they walked out the door.

" 'Cause I already told him we was just passin' through on our way to Oklahoma," Broadus explained. "We still don't know what Perley Gates or Possum Smith looks like. We might have to hang around town to find out, and he might get suspicious."

"Oh," Marvin responded. He suspected that his father didn't want to admit that he made a mistake telling Bennie they were passing through in the first place. But he didn't feel like this was the time to say so.

They rode on out of town, looking hard at the few people left on the street with the coming of the evening. At this point, their only clue to finding the two men they hunted was to happen to luck upon a young man with an older man with a ponytail down his back. Their odds of that were slim. So they continued on the road to the Red River until they came to a sizable creek after a ride of about two miles. "We ain't gonna find much better'n this," Marvin said, and his father agreed. So they pulled off the road and rode back upstream until they found a clearing in the trees. They unpacked the horses and released them to water and graze, then started collecting wood for a small fire, since they didn't have to cook anything for supper.

Their intent, as they sat around their little fire, was to decide the best way to find their two intended victims. When they'd begun the mission, they'd had a simple plan for once they found the Triple-G ranch, which was to scout the cowhands tending the cattle until they spotted Perley Gates and Possum Smith. Then they would draw a bead on each man and pull the trigger. It was as simple as that. But that was because they were under the impression that Johnny Pepper could identify the two men. Now that they knew that to be untrue, the question to be answered was how to identify Perley and Possum, either together, or apart. It might turn into a sniper war against the entire crew of the Triple-G, until they killed every one of the men and assumed that Perley and Possum were among the dead. The problem with that was that the hunted could become the hunters, and the Triple-G would outnumber them. They talked it over from every angle, but in the end, they had to come to the only possible conclusion:

They were going to have to hang around town and get a positive identification from someone who knew the two men. They felt sure that Perley and Possum must come to town sometime.

"I've made up my mind, boys," Broadus finally announced. "I've got the money to stay here a while. I'm goin' to take a room in that hotel, and I'm gonna hang around that saloon until those two walk in. Then as soon as I get somebody to tell me it's them, I'll follow 'em, and as soon as I get a chance, I'll shoot 'em down."

"What are you talking about, Pa?" Marvin wanted to know. "You talkin' about just you stayin' in town? What about the rest of us?"

"That's up to you," Broadus said. "I've got enough money for all four of us to stay in the hotel and put our horses in the stable. But I ain't tellin' you that you gotta do it. I could use your help, but it might be better if you stay outside of town. Once I know who they are, we'll follow 'em and shoot 'em outside of town. I think we got a better chance of gittin' both of 'em that way."

"I think that's the best way to do it," Cletus said. "Pa stays in town until he spots them, then we can all tail him when he leaves town and shoot them."

"I agree," Marvin spoke up. "I can't see

how that can go wrong. I druther stay outside of town."

"Well, I hadn't," Johnny declared. "I wanna stay in town where I can see what's goin' on. It'd be better if there was two of us askin' people about them two. I can pay for my room in the hotel. Then if somethin' happens where you get caught in a trap or somethin', I'll be there to help you out."

"Whaddaya think, Pa?" Marvin asked. They had grown so accustomed to Johnny being contrary to everything they proposed, they were not surprised he wanted to go against their wishes. "Maybe it ain't such a good idea for two people tryin' to identify those two."

"No, it ain't," Broadus replied. He looked at Johnny then and said, "Remember when you wanted to come on this trip with us? I told you you were welcome to come along, but I was callin' the shots. And you said that was the way it would be. Well, I'm still callin' the shots, and I'll do the talkin' to the people in town about Perley Gates and Possum Smith."

"All right, all right," Johnny responded, not oblivious of the looks he was getting from both of Broadus's sons. "You can do all the talkin'. But I'm still gonna stay in town. I'll pay for my own room, so it won't cost you or Abner Clinton a damn nickel."

Broadus glanced at his sons, and when their eyes met, they exchanged a look that could be read as a prediction that only three of them might return home after the executions of Perley and Possum. "It's your money," Broadus said. "Spend it in the hotel, if that's what you want, but don't check in at the same time I do. Same thing at the stable; ain't no use to let everybody know we're ridin' together. They already know it at the saloon, so it don't make no difference there." He got up from the fire. "Well, I reckon we pretty much know what we're gonna do tomorrow, so I'm goin' to bed." He walked over a little way out of the firelight to relieve himself of the coffee he drank at the saloon, then retired to his bedroll.

"I reckon that's a pretty good idea," Marvin said, and he followed the same routine as his father had. Cletus was not far behind.

"I reckon I'll go to bed, too, long as everybody else is," Johnny announced. "I think I'll play it safe tonight and sleep with my six-gun outta the holster, just in case there's any snakes crawlin' around these bushes." *Especially them two-legged kind,* he thought.

■ ■ ■ ■

Morning broke the next day with all four assassins sleeping peacefully after an uninterrupted night. Marvin was first up and brought the fire back to life, as was usually the case, then went to the edge of the creek to fill the coffeepot. There was no hurry to get started anywhere, so he didn't bother the others, preferring to have that first cup with nothing but his own thoughts. It wasn't long, however, before the other three started stirring. Johnny crawled out of his blankets next. He visited nature, then got his cup out of his saddlebag and poured himself a cup of coffee. "I swear, Marvin, you're just like havin' a wife along," Johnny remarked.

"I didn't hear no gunshots durin' the night," Marvin said. "Reckon you didn't see no snakes." *Ain't nothing like a long trip together to really get to know your in-laws,* he thought.

"I expect they knew what was waitin' for 'em if they came crawlin' around my bedroll," Johnny replied. *I ain't worried about no snakes in that hotel tonight,* he thought.

When Broadus and Cletus roused themselves from their blankets, Marvin got out a frying pan and started slicing some bacon into it. He happened to glance up in time to catch Johnny — it served to remind him that he was glad Johnny was going to be in the hotel that night. He and Cletus would most likely spend the evening planning Johnny's death. *What in the hell was Rena thinking when she married Johnny Pepper?* he thought.

While they waited for their breakfast to fry, Broadus told them his plans for that morning. He was going to go to the hotel first and rent a room, then he was going to take his horse to the stable. After that, he was just going to walk around the streets, visit the stores, see who was in town. He'd eat dinner in the hotel dining room, then spend a good part of the afternoon in the saloon and just hope somewhere along the line, he'd get lucky.

"Well, there ain't nothin' for me to hang around here for," Johnny said. "You didn't want us to check in at the same time, so I'm gonna saddle up and go on back to town. I'll see you in town, Pa," he said, emphasizing the last word. "You can have my share of the bacon." He saddled his horse and left them to grumble about it.

"I swear," Broadus said, "if it weren't for your sister, I wouldn't hesitate to cut that guy's throat."

"I ain't sure we wouldn't be doin' Rena a big favor if we arranged a little accident for Johnny before we head back home," Marvin suggested.

"I don't know what you've got in mind, son," Broadus replied, "but I don't want you or Cletus to think about callin' him out, man to man. He's an awful hard pill to swallow, but he's fast with that .45 he loves. And there ain't no use in one of you boys takin' a chance against him. We need to wait on that deal anyway, at least till after we take care of what we came up here to do." He nodded at one of them and then the other. "We're clear on that, right?" They both said they were. "Good," he said. "I'll ride back out here later this afternoon to let you know if I'm havin' any luck."

"Maybe you can eat dinner with Johnny, if he ain't too busy," Cletus japed.

"That'll be the day," Broadus replied.

David Smith, desk clerk at the Paris Hotel looked up when Broadus Tarpley walked in the front door. An imposing figure, even in spite of recent long days in the saddle, Broadus strode up to the desk as if he intended to buy the hotel. "Mornin'," he said. "I'm gonna need a room for a day or two."

"Yes, sir," David responded courteously,

"we can fix you right up. You have anything special in mind?"

"Nope, nothin' fancy," Broadus replied, "just a clean room with a good bed. I've been in the saddle for a number of days, and I'd like to take a rest."

"Well, I've got just the room for you, Mr. . . ." He paused and waited for Broadus to give his name.

"Johnson," Broadus said, giving him the first name that popped in his head.

"Mr. Johnson, right," David repeated, and wrote it down on his register. He paused again to give Broadus a smile. "You're not kin to our owner and mayor of the town, Otis Johnson, are you?"

"No, 'fraid not," Broadus answered with a chuckle. "That's one of the problems with havin' a common name like Johnson."

"I know exactly what you mean," David said. "My name's David Smith."

They both chuckled then, and in spite of his caution, Broadus couldn't resist asking, "You kin to a feller named Possum Smith?"

"No, I'm not, but I do know there's a fellow who works for the Triple-G Ranch named Smith, and they call him Possum. You know him?"

"No, I don't," Broadus answered. "I just heard the name the other day." He scratched out the name, *B. Johnson,* on the register, and David handed him a key.

"Hope you enjoy your stay, Mr. Johnson," David said. "I put you in room number four, at the top of the stairs on your right. The washroom is straight down that hall, past the door that says *Dining Room,* all the way to the end of the hall."

"I'll throw my saddlebags in the room," Broadus said. "What time does the dinin' room open for dinner?" David told him eleven thirty. "Fine. I might as well eat some dinner before I take my horse to the stable." He looked at the big clock on the wall. It was almost noon, and the few strips of bacon he'd had for breakfast had long since departed his belly. So he went up the steps to room number four and threw his saddlebags on the bed, took a quick look at the room he just rented, then went back downstairs.

CHAPTER 20

Broadus walked into the dining room, entering from the hotel hallway. He was greeted by Lucy Tate who called his attention to the table where firearms were left and assured him that no one else could wear one while eating unless they were officers of the law. He made no objection to the rule other than to say he felt naked without it. "We hope you're gonna enjoy your meal so much, you won't feel like shooting anybody," Lucy said. "Sit anywhere you want, and I or Becky will take care of you."

"Thank you, ma'am," he said, and started into the dining room, only to stop suddenly when he saw Johnny Pepper sitting at a table against the far wall, grinning at him. He immediately turned toward the opposite wall and sat down at a table next to the kitchen. *That sorry dog,* he thought. *He heard me say I was going to eat here. Probably thought we'd sit at the same table.* It seemed that his son-in-law was determined to irritate him and his sons. He would pretend not to know him, and hoped Johnny had sense enough to do the same.

His thoughts were interrupted then by the arrival of Becky Morris at his table. "Good afternoon," she greeted him. "Are you going to have coffee?"

"Yes, ma'am, I am," Broadus replied. "Whaddaya servin' today?" he asked, no longer sure he had an appetite for anything after finding Johnny there.

"Beulah made meat loaf today," Becky replied. "Think you can handle that? If you can't, we can give you some sliced ham. They both come with potatoes and gravy. Either one of those appeal to your appetite?"

"Meat loaf, huh?" Broadus replied. He loved meat loaf, and he hadn't had any in a long time, and that was one that Atha had made. Hannah couldn't make meat loaf, and she was too proud to let Atha teach her how. He felt his appetite coming back as rapidly as he had just lost it. "I'll take the meatloaf," he said.

"I think you'll be glad you did," Becky said. "I'll get you some coffee." She left and was back in a matter of seconds with his cup of coffee. Minutes later, she returned to set a plate before him with a generous slice of meat loaf covering one half of the plate, the other half covered with a pile of mashed potatoes and a serving of red beans, all covered with gravy. For a few moments, he forgot the irritation seated on the opposite side of the room and gave his full focus to the plate in front of him.

Thankfully, Johnny made no attempt to catch his attention, although Broadus could see him out of the corner of his eye, constantly looking toward him. *Mind your own business!* Broadus wanted to yell at him. He thought he had made it plain that they were not to act like they knew each other anywhere but in the saloon. He worried that if Johnny kept staring his way, other people in the dining room would begin to notice. He managed to finish his plate of food, however, and Becky came to check on his progress.

"Did you save any room for apple pie?" she asked as she filled his coffee cup once more. She was standing with her back to the outside door, so she couldn't see the young man who came into the dining room at that moment.

Lucy walked by her just then and said, "Perley just walked in." Then Lucy called out to him, "Howdy, Perley!"

Broadus almost choked and lost a mouthful of coffee in his plate. He looked at once toward Johnny, who had obviously heard the name as well. *Don't do nothing, you blame fool,* he thought. *Don't let on you know him. You can't do nothing in here. You ain't even got your gun, and he's still wearin' his!* But Johnny was quivering excitedly. Whatever was about to happen, Broadus was helpless to stop it. His only choice was to remain seated and play dumb. Then, to his horror, Johnny got up, dropped some money on the table, and walked straight to the weapons table, where Perley was in the process of unbuckling his gun belt. Johnny picked up his belt and strapped it on, staring into Perley's face as he buckled it.

Perley started to step around him, but Johnny reached over and caught his arm. "Are you Perley Gates?" Johnny asked.

Surprised, Perley answered without thinking whether he should or not. "Yes, I'm Perley Gates."

"Then maybe you better put that gun belt back on. My name's Johnny Pepper and I've been sent here by the Tarpley family to kill you. I'm willin' to give you a chance to face me like a man, but if you don't, I'm gonna shoot you down like a dog. Your choice. If you ain't out in that street in one minute,

I'm comin' in here and killin' you, and anybody that tries to help you. Which way you want it?"

Literally struck dumb for a moment, Perley was not prepared for the notice of his death sentence. He looked at the cocky stranger for a moment more, then said, "I'd rather not have it either way. I'd rather you just go on back to where you came from and forget about killin' me."

"You want it right now then," Johnny decided. "Suits me." He pulled the six-gun from his holster, preparing to perform the execution. Only a few people in the dining room were aware of the drama unfolding by the front door. One of them, Broadus Tarpley, was as stunned as Perley was.

Perley realized at that moment the man was crazy enough to do what he threatened. "Wait!" He exclaimed. "I'll go outside with you and face you in the street, man to man, like you said. Innocent people might be hurt in here. We'll go outside."

Johnny still had his gun out and pointed at Perley. He continued to hold the gun on him as Perley walked out the door in front of him. "If you try to run, you're gonna get it in the back," Johnny said.

"I'm not gonna run," Perley said. "Let's just get away from the dinin' room before we decide what we're gonna do."

"Are you stupid?" Johnny demanded. "How many times do I have to tell you?"

"I just want you to know it's not too late to change your mind about this duelin' business," Perley said.

"I swear, I'm gonna shoot you down where you stand!" Johnny blurted, and cocked his pistol.

"Wait! Wait!" Perley exclaimed. "I'm goin'. Where do you want me to stand?"

"You just stand right where you are," Johnny told him, then he backed up, keeping his eye on Perley every second, in case he decided to cut and run. When he had put about twelve paces between them, he stopped, released the hammer on his .45, and dropped it in the holster. Just like the last time Perley was called out of the dining room, the windows on the front wall were now crowded with the spectators. One in particular had a special interest in the spectacle. Another was back in the kitchen, unable to watch. Out front the two combatants stood facing each other without moving. "All right, Perley," Johnny finally said, "you just draw that weapon when you're ready to shoot."

"Right," Perley said, but did not draw his weapon. Still they stood there, waiting and watching each other. Finally, Johnny became disgusted with what he deemed outright cowardice on Perley's part and decided to put him out of his misery. He reached for his .45 and almost cleared his holster when he was slammed in the chest by Perley's shot.

The sheer look of disbelief on Johnny's face would remain in Broadus's mind forever. Like Johnny, he had never seen anything approaching the speed of the move he had just witnessed. He could not really say that he saw the move. Maybe his eyes were playing tricks on him. He saw the gun in the holster and Perley's hands in the air. Then he saw the one hand still in the air but with the gun in it. He couldn't say that he actually saw anything happen between those two positions. He shook his head to clear it of those thoughts. One thing for sure: The assassination of Perley Gates would have to be in ambush or at long range. He was thankful that his two sons had no ambitions toward fame as fast guns. Nothing could beat good ol' back shooting.

On the positive side of his first day in Paris, he could now identify Perley Gates, and he had solved the irritating problem they had with Johnny Pepper. It was better that he was shot by someone outside the family when it came to telling Rena the news of her husband's demise. He would tell her of the brave effort he made to avenge her uncle and cousins, and how grieved her brothers were that they were not there to avenge him. The next problem to work out was Possum Smith. Was he, like Perley, a fast-gun artist? And where might they track him down? He remained at the window and watched as the sheriff approached Perley, and he was struck by the way the sheriff appeared to question him. Through the windowpane, he couldn't hear the actual conversation between the two men. But from the window of the dining room, it looked the same as if two friends met on the street and stopped to talk about the weather. A few minutes more passed before a man pushing a handcart appeared, and Perley helped him pick up Johnny's body and put it on the cart. The man pushed the cart back down the street, and Perley and the sheriff came toward the dining room door. Broadus went back to his table then and sat down. It struck him as a most unusual way to handle a shooting. He was not sure it was wise for him to hang around any longer, but he didn't think there was any way anyone there could connect him with Johnny Pepper. Thank goodness

Johnny didn't come over to join him at his table. At least that was one thing he did right, and the only thing that didn't annoy one or all three of them.

"Did you want some more coffee?" He looked up to see Lucy Tate standing there with a coffeepot. "I know Becky was taking care of you, but she took a little sick spell and had to go sit down a while." She couldn't help noticing his plate filled with coffee but decided not to ask about it.

"Yes, ma'am, I would like one more cup of that coffee. That meat loaf was mighty good, I wish my wife could fix it like that."

"I'll tell Beulah that, she'll be happy to know you liked the cookin'," Lucy said, and started to leave, but paused when Broadus spoke again.

"That was some shootin' just now, with that fellow, Perley Gates. Does that happen here very often?"

"No, just once in a while," she said.

He nodded toward the front door, where the sheriff and Perley were talking to Beulah. "The sheriff don't seem to be goin' too hard on Perley for the shootin'."

Lucy smiled. "Paul knows Perley didn't start it. Perley doesn't start shoot-outs, he just finishes 'em."

While Broadus sipped his coffee and

watched, Perley walked through the dining room to the kitchen, and the sheriff walked out in the middle of the room and called for everybody's attention. "Does anybody in here know who that man was that just got killed?" Sheriff McQueen asked. His question was met with a lot of head shaking and murmuring among the customers. No one had ever seen him before.

"Well, I guess that's about all I can hold," Broadus said. "Do I pay you, or somebody at the desk up by the door?"

"I'll take it at the desk," Lucy said. "Any one of the three of us women work the register." She left the coffeepot on the table and walked with him to the front, where he paid her and strapped on his gun. "Come back to see us," Lucy said as he walked out the door. He nodded in reply as he headed for the black Morgan gelding waiting at the hitching rail and took the north road out of town. He had a lot to tell his two sons, camped at Two Mile Creek.

Perley walked into the dining room looking for Becky, knowing she was upset over the second shooting he was involved in right there at the hotel. She had barely gotten over the first one when this had to happen. He didn't know what to expect this time.

Lucy told him that Becky had gotten physically sick when the stranger called him out as soon as he walked in the door. "She fled to the kitchen," Lucy said.

Perley started to go there, but the sheriff asked if he was certain he had never encountered the dead man anywhere before that day. "I was taken completely by surprise," he told Sheriff McQueen. "The man said his name was Johnny Pepper and that the Tarpley family had sent him to kill me." Johnny Pepper sounded like a made-up name, so the sheriff asked the customers if anyone of them had ever heard of anyone by that name, but no one had. When Sheriff McQueen seemed to have no more questions for him, Perley went in search of Becky.

Becky wasn't in the kitchen when Perley got there. Knowing only one other place to look for her, he went out of the kitchen to the back hallway, where the women's rooms were located. He rapped lightly on her door and waited, but there was no response. He tried the doorknob, but the door was locked. He was pretty sure she was in there. There was no place else she was likely to run to. He rapped again, this time a little harder. "Who is it?" her voice finally came through, and it sounded to him like her cheek was pressed against the door.

"Becky, it's me, Perley. Please open the door."

After a long pause, he heard the key turn in the lock. The door opened, and she stepped back to let him in. She had been crying. Her eyes were red, and her face was streaked red where she had tried to dry her tears. "Oh, Perley, you don't need to see me like this." He pulled her close to him and she pressed her face against his shoulder. Once in his strong embrace, she broke down in a fit of sobbing. He held her tight up against him, feeling her whole body convulsing with her efforts to stop her sobbing. He held her tightly until she finally began to relax to the point where she could speak without starting to cry again. "I don't know if I can do this or not," she finally confessed. "It's always going to be like this until one day you're going to walk away and not come back to me."

Once again, he found himself at a loss for words. What could he tell her? That this was the last time something like this would happen? He thought the time before this would be the last time. Now the simple fact that this Johnny Pepper had mentioned the name Tarpley was evidence enough that he was not finished with them. He remembered the Nacogdoches sheriff, Clayton Steel, telling him that the territory between the Angelina and the Neches rivers was infested by the Tarpley family, thicker than fleas on a dog's back. And they lived by their own code of law. Evidently they had placed a death sentence upon him for protecting himself when the four Tarpley men came after him. No doubt there was a vengeance threat against Possum's life as well, and he greatly regretted that. He had to get back to the ranch right away to make Possum aware of the threat. The more he thought about it, the more he began to wonder — how did Johnny Pepper know his name was Perley Gates? And how did he know to come here to look for him? Since he knew these things, he probably knew about the Triple-G also. What if there was another assassin scouting the ranch right now, looking for him and Possum?

All these thoughts raced through his mind as he held Becky in his arms. She still pressed her face tightly against his shoulder, as if never wanting to leave the haven of his arms. Yet he could sense the battle going on inside her brain with a decision that was difficult for her to make. He was afraid it was going to be a decision that would destroy the future happiness for both of them. In a little while, he could feel her beginning to relax, then after a few moments more, she released him and stepped back. "I'm sorry," she said softly. "I'm sorry I'm not a stronger woman." Then as if to remind herself, she said, "I'm glad that you're all right. Did you know this man was coming to kill you?"

"No, I didn't even know he knew my name or where I was."

"See," she said, "you have no warning that these people are going to come looking to kill you. I love you with all my heart, Perley, but I can't live with the uncertainty of never knowing if you will come home to me or not."

"Don't say that, Becky," Perley begged. "It's not gonna be like this forever. I'm gonna be workin' right there on the ranch every day, just like John and Rubin. I've already started doin' some of the everyday chores around the ranch. You're just gonna be married to another Triple-G ranch hand. You'll be tryin' to talk me into goin' somewhere."

She stepped back to arm's length and looked at him. "Oh, sweetie. You're Perley. You can't change who you are. And it would be wrong for me to try to change you. You would soon learn to hate me for breaking

349

your free spirit."

"I can guarantee you one thing right now," he insisted, "I'll never hate you. I'll always love you. That's just the way it is. I ain't got no choice."

"And I'll always love you," she said, "no matter what happens. Now I guess you came in to eat dinner, so go on back to the dining room and Lucy can get you started. I'll be in as soon as I wash my face and change my blouse. All right?"

"All right," he said, although he wasn't sure where they stood as far as their marriage was concerned. He would do as she suggested, but he had lost his appetite for dinner, since he now had a reason to worry about Possum. He knew better than to mention that to Becky at that point. It was too much in support of her problem with his life. So he went back to the dining room and told Lucy that Becky would be back as soon as she freshened up a little.

In her typical crass fashion, Lucy said. "Oh, she has to freshen up a little bit, does she? How 'bout you? You don't need to freshen up, too?"

Not in a mood to tolerate her humor, he said, "Just bring me a cup of coffee, please, and a plate of whatever you're servin' today."

"Coming up!" she said cheerfully, in spite of his humorless reply, and went to the kitchen to fill his plate.

"Is he all right?" Beulah asked as she poured a cup of coffee for her.

"I don't know," Lucy answered. "Whatever they did back in her room made him kinda grouchy." She picked up the cup of coffee and took it and the plate of food out to him. As she went out the dining room door, Becky came in the kitchen from the back hallway.

"How you doin', honey?" Beulah asked. "You okay?"

Becky looked at her and sighed. "Yeah, I'm okay. I just had a little breakdown, I guess. Did you get Perley something to eat?"

"Yeah, Lucy fixed a plate for him and took him some coffee," Beulah told her. "There ain't many folks left in there now. Why don't you sit down and visit with him?"

"We've already talked some," Becky said. "I can help Lucy start the cleanup."

"Suit yourself," Beulah said.

She went on into the dining room and started clearing dirty dishes off some of the tables before Lucy told her not to bother. "I'll help you clear a few of these tables," Becky told her, "in case we get some late arrivers. Then I'll sit with Perley for a minute or two." Lucy shrugged in response.

Watching Perley out of the corner of her eye, she finished clearing the tables she had started, then she went to his table. "You need more coffee?"

"No, thanks, I reckon that'll do me," Perley said.

"You're eatin' like you're in a race to finish," she said. "Are you in a hurry to get someplace?"

"No, I'm in no hurry," he lied. "I was just hungry, I reckon — ah, hell, I am in a hurry. I need to go find Possum and tell him to be careful, just in case."

"You're right," she said. "I think you'd better go and do that." He gave her an apologetic look and got to his feet. "Beulah's up front, you can pay her," she said. He nodded and turned to leave, but she stopped him. "And Perley, be careful. All right?"

"I will," he said and hurried out of the dining room. As soon as he went out the door, both Beulah and Lucy turned to face Becky, their faces an open question.

"It's too complicated to explain," Becky said, and she picked up Perley's dishes and took them into the kitchen.

Chapter 21

Broadus rode up Two Mile Creek to find both his sons in the camp. "I thought you boys might be gone huntin' or fishin' to find somethin' to eat," he said when he pulled his horse up short of a healthy fire.

We done that this mornin' after you and Johnny left," Cletus said. "We figured we'd have somethin' to eat besides bacon and hardtack."

"Have any luck?" Broadus asked.

"I reckon so," Marvin said, "if you take a look at what's hangin' in that tree down near the water."

"Did you get a deer?" Broadus asked.

"A little doe," Cletus answered, "and she's got some tender meat on 'er, too. You wanna try a slice?"

"No, thanks, I filled my belly up with meat loaf, and it was good. Not like that stuff your mama calls meat loaf, and don't you tell her I said that. But you know what

I mean."

He seemed in good spirits, and Marvin called him on it. "How'd it go in town? You act like you're in a pretty good mood. Did you run into Johnny?"

"You think I'm in a good mood, do ya?" Broadus replied. "Well, there's some good and there's some bad news to tell ya. In the first place, I know who Perley Gates is, and I know what he looks like. Me and Johnny ate dinner at the hotel, but we wasn't together. He was already there when I got there, so I sat down at a different table. Everything was fine, and then this young feller walks in, and some folks speak to him, callin' him by name, Perley. Well, you oughta seen your brother-in-law, him and his fast-gun talk. He walks right up to Perley Gates and calls him out. Tells him if he don't meet him in the street, he'll shoot him down in the dinin' room." He paused then to make them beg.

"Well, doggone it, Pa, what happened?" Marvin prodded.

"It saddens me to tell you your brother-in-law won't be ridin' back to Angelina County with us."

"No foolin'?" Marvin reacted.

"No foolin'," Broadus replied.

"Well, what's the bad news?" Cletus asked.

"The bad news?" Broadus repeated. "You remember that Johnny was always fast with that handgun of his. Well, he drew first on Perley Gates, and he never cleared his holster before Perley put a bullet in the middle of his chest. It was like a crack of lightnin'. And that's the bad news — leastways it was for Johnny."

"Maybe for Johnny," Marvin said, "but it ain't for me. I got better sense than to call a stranger out to face off against me. If you're wantin' to kill somebody, it don't make a bit of sense to give them a chance to kill you first."

Cletus chuckled. "I reckon if Johnny was here, he'd agree to that now, wouldn't he, Pa?"

"I reckon," Broadus answered. "I'm glad you boys are smart enough to know that."

"So, now we gotta find out what Possum Smith looks like," Marvin said. "I wonder if he's in town today, too."

"If he is, he wasn't with Perley at the hotel dinin' room," Broadus said. "I expect we're gonna have to move our camp on farther outta town. Then we're gonna have to start scoutin' that Triple-G spread to see if we can spot Possum. We might end up havin' to shoot every older feller we see with a gray horse tail down his back."

"That sounds like a good target to me," Cletus remarked. "If we spot him, shoot him in his horse tail."

"We know for sure that Perley's in town today," Broadus said. "So we need to go into town and see if we can find him, maybe in the saloon or somewhere. Then we'll keep an eye on him, and as soon as he gets somewhere where there ain't nobody to see us, we'll put a bullet in his back. Might have to wait till he heads for the ranch and follow him outta town."

"That sounds like our best chance of takin' care of him," Cletus said.

"If we go back to that saloon, ain't they gonna remember that Johnny was with us when we was in there before?" Marvin asked.

"I thought about that, too," Broadus said. "And I think we can talk our way around that pretty easy. We can say he was a stranger who came up on our camp the night before and rode on into town with us. Remember when we bought them drinks at the bar, then set down at a table to eat some supper? He took his drink and set down at a table, but we took our drinks and went to a different table. Anybody that asked about it, we can tell 'em we was trying to get shed of him, but he came on over to set with us. We can tell 'em, hell, we liked to never got rid of him. And another thing, he was by himself when he got a room at the hotel." Marvin and Cletus agreed that the story would most likely hold up, so that was the plan they intended to follow.

The three men of the Tarpley family who planned their activity for the night could have saved themselves a lot of speculation had they known Perley Gates had passed Two Mile Creek while they were still talking about the shoot-out. On his way back to the Triple-G, Perley's head was swimming with thoughts of all that had happened since he'd ridden into town that morning. Might there be the front sight of a rifle lined up between his shoulder blades even as he traveled the familiar road to the ranch? When he thought about it, he couldn't blame Becky for suddenly pulling away from a union with someone whose best odds of returning home every night were fifty-fifty. Already, he had put a target on Possum's back, the result of his refusal to come back without his horse. Was Buck's life more important to him than Possum's? He'd have to think about that, he told himself. Maybe he should have refused to allow Possum to go with him into the Tarpley rat's nest to rescue Buck. It was impossible to refuse Possum anything that Possum considered his duty. "Damn," he swore to Buck. "I wish I knew if Johnny Pepper was a lone assassin or if there are others."

Link Drew met him at the barn when he rode in, and as he usually did, volunteered to take care of Buck for him. "Thanks, Link," Perley said. "I worked him a little harder coming back today. He could use a portion of grain. Do you know where Possum is?"

"Nope," the boy answered, "but Ollie will be ringin' his bell pretty soon, so he'll probably come for supper."

"You're right," Perley said. "I forgot what time it was." He started toward the cookhouse but paused when he saw three riders coming from the eastern section of the range. He easily identified Possum as one of them, even though he was riding a chestnut horse instead of Dancer. That told Perley that he had been working the cattle today. Sonny Rice and Charlie Ramsey were the two riders with him. They pulled up at the barn and dismounted, then pulled their saddles and bridles off.

"I didn't expect you back from town this early," Possum said as he turned the chestnut loose. "You have another misunderstandin' with Becky?"

"I reckon you could say that," Perley said. "There's a lot more that you need to know. I killed a man today."

That captured Possum's full attention. "You what? How did you kill him? Were you called out by somebody?"

"I was, right in the damn dinin' room again," Perley replied. "But what I wanted you to know was when he called me out, he said he was sent by the Tarpley family to kill me."

"Damn, another one of them Tarpleys. How the hell did he find you?"

"I don't know, but I got to thinkin' about it on the way home. He was in the dinin' room when I walked in, eatin' dinner. Lucy and somebody else called out my name to say hello. And right after that is when this fellow walks right up in my face and ask me if I was Perley Gates. I wish now I'da said no, but I told him I was. And that's when he said face him in the street or he was fixin' to shoot me in the dinin' room."

"And he told you he was a Tarpley, come to make you pay for killin' them four that came after us?"

"No," Perley said. "He told me his name was Johnny Pepper and that he was sent by the Tarpley family."

"But you shot him instead," Possum said, "so no sweat. Right?"

"I wish. But that killer didn't know for sure who I was till he asked me. And I don't know if he was by himself or just one of who knows how many. He knew to come to Paris to look for me. How did he know that? There were two of us that rode through there and took my horse. There might be somebody else lookin' for you and me. So you've got to be careful and be mindful of what kinda target you're makin'. If what I suspect is true, then this jasper who told me his name is likely the only one that wants the chance to shoot you face to face. I don't know if there was anybody with him today. But if there was, then they know I'm their target. What I'm countin' on is that they ain't identified you yet; they're still lookin' for you. But they most likely have a general description of the two of us. So, if I was you, I'd take some shears and cut that ponytail off your back."

"What?" Possum exclaimed "Cut my hair off? It'll be a cold day in hell before I let somebody cut that braid off!"

Perley had expected some reluctance, but not the violent refusal. "Come on, Possum, it's just hair. It'll grow back, and it could keep you from getting' shot in the back by some Tarpley maniac."

"It took me too many years to grow that ponytail, as you call it. I ain't got that many years left to grow it back. And it's my lucky piece. It's what's kept me from gittin' shot in the back up to now." He paused and fumed over Perley's suggestion for a couple of minutes. Then when he had calmed down a little, he said, "Besides, we don't know for sure there is anybody with that one you shot. We need to find that out first thing. We need to go back in town and ask around if there's been some strangers who hit town and they're still hangin' around. What I'm sayin' is we need to be the ones doin' the huntin', instead of the ones bein' hunted."

"That makes a lot of sense to me," Perley said. "I'd sure like to keep them away from the Triple-G. I'm afraid we might have some snipers hidin' out around our range, taking potshots at every rider they see. I've got to tell Rubin and John about the possibility of sniper trouble out here. And I reckon it's best to let everybody know about the trouble I've managed to stir up, so we can all be careful till we find out if there's a threat or not. I'll go back into town in the mornin' and maybe that'll bring the rats outta their holes."

"When you talk to Rubin and John, tell

'em I'll be goin' into town tomorrow, too," Possum said.

"I don't know, Possum." Perley hesitated. "Right now, they don't know what you look like. I 'preciate you wantin' to help, but you're better off back here."

"You need somebody to watch your back," Possum said, "so I'll be goin' into town in the mornin', and I don't want to argue about it." Ollie started banging on his iron triangle at that moment. "So, let's go eat supper," Possum said.

"As part owner of this ranch, I'm orderin' you to stay here tomorrow," Perley said.

"I quit," Possum said. "Let's go eat supper."

"I should know better than to try to talk sense to you," Perley complained.

"It's a wonder to me that you still ain't figured that out yet," Possum replied.

"I think I'll go up to the house and tell John and Rubin what's goin' on," Perley decided. "I'll get something to eat there. They always have supper together at the main house. I expect John will wanna talk to the men about it."

CHAPTER 22

Supper was a big affair on the Triple-G. It was mainly for the benefit of Perley's widowed mother, so that she would always be part of both Rubin's and John's families. Perley popped in unannounced occasionally because he knew there was always plenty of food prepared. With Rubin's wife, Lou Ann; John's wife, Martha; and Alice Farmer all helping to prepare the meal, Perley knew he could eat and there would still be leftovers. Alice had been Nathaniel and Rachel Gates's cook for many years and was treated like family. She had been in their employ longer than her husband, Fred, who besides being Triple-G's oldest cowhand was the only married cowhand on the ranch. He was also the only cowhand who slept in a small back room of the main house.

"Perley!" Lou Ann exclaimed when he came in the kitchen door. "Are you gonna have supper with us tonight?" When he said he thought he might, if that was all right, she said, "You know there's always a place for you. Mama Gates will be delighted to see you. It's gonna be ready in about fifteen minutes. Rubin and John are in the study."

"Thank you, Lou Ann, I'll go aggravate 'em. Evenin', Martha, Alice," he said as he passed through the kitchen and walked up the hallway to the study. "Is this a closed meetin'?" he asked when he walked into the room.

John chuckled and said, "It was a meeting for adults, but I reckon we can try to dumb it down a little bit to include you."

"Glad you came to supper, Perley," Rubin said. "You know how Ma lights up every time you show up."

"I figured it was about time I brought you something more to worry about."

"Well, now, you wouldn't be Perley if you didn't do that," John responded. "It ain't got nothin' to do with yours and Possum's latest little trip to Sulphur Springs, when you took the shortcut through Nacogdoches has it?"

"I'm afraid that it does," Perley said. "And I might as well get right to it. I told you about the four men that came after Possum and me. Well, today another one of that clan down there in Angelina County showed up at the hotel dinin' room and called me out. I killed him."

"Damn," Rubin swore. "Was there anybody else with him?"

"I don't know," Perley said. "That's what I'm gonna try to find out tomorrow." He went on to tell them the whole story of the encounter with the assassin named Johnny Pepper, and the fact that Pepper didn't know who he was until someone called out his name. As he had told Possum, he didn't expect any more challenges for a face-to-face duel. "Pepper was a typical fast-gun assassin lookin' to make a name for himself. If there are other killers lookin' for me and Possum, they'll most likely be back shooters. And I'm afraid if they find this ranch, they'll be sneakin' around lookin' for a back shot. And they ain't gonna worry if they've hit an innocent man or not." He paused then, for he could see that he had hit a nerve with both his brothers.

"I swear, Perley. . . ." That was all Rubin could say when he pictured the possible chaos that could result.

"I'm sorry, Rubin," Perley said, "for bringin' this trouble back home with me. I'm goin' into town in the mornin' to see if I can bring another rat outta his hole. Possum's goin' with me. It we don't flush anybody out in town, we'll start patrollin' our range to see if we turn up any signs of snipers." He was interrupted then when Rubin's son, Robby, came to the door to report that supper was ready.

"Tell your ma we're comin'," Rubin told him, then looked back at Perley and shook his head.

"I think it would be a good idea to tell the men about it and why they need to be on the lookout for strangers," Perley suggested. "It might not be a bad idea to double the fellows workin' night herd tonight, so they can kinda watch out for each other."

"I think that's a good idea," John agreed. "I'll go with you to talk to 'em right after supper."

"Let's go eat now," Rubin said. "No need to get the women upset."

Supper was unusually quiet on this evening. So much so, that Lou Ann commented on it. "I declare," she said, "everybody's so quiet tonight. It's usually like a holiday party whenever Perley comes to supper. Tonight it's more like a funeral service."

Perley thought that a poor choice of similarities on this particular night. "I expect it's because the food's so good everybody wants to concentrate on every bite."

"That's such a sweet thing to say," Rachel said. "These young women worked hard to cook up this nice meal for everybody."

"Mama Gates is right, Perley," Martha said. "And speaking of sweet things, when are you gonna tell us about a wedding date for you and Miss Becky Morris?"

"That ain't a proper thing to talk about at the supper table," Perley said, trying to appear shy when, in fact, it was the last thing he wanted to think about at this time. Unfortunately, Lou Ann wanted to hear more about the wedding, too, and pressed Perley to give them an update on the progress. "To be honest with you, things are at a standstill right now, so there really ain't no news to tell you," he said. He was thankful when John said he couldn't drag his supper out because he wanted to talk to the men before those who had night herd rode out. Perley finished in a hurry, too. He complimented the cooks and thanked them for the supper.

They caught the night herders before they rode out, and John asked Perley to tell the men what the situation was. He told them of the shooting in town that day and the fact that they weren't sure if there was still a threat or not. "But to play it safe," John said, "we're gonna double the night herders tonight, so you can keep an eye on each other. It'll be the same as when you've got cattle rustlers in the area. Just keep your eyes peeled. They're after Perley or Possum, but in the dark, they might take a shot at anybody."

It was sobering news to the all the cowhands, and especially worrisome to an older hand like Fred Farmer. "I'll be ridin' around the herd for most of the night, myself," Perley told them, "but I'll let you know it's me if I run up on you. Like John said, this is just to play it safe. I think the risk will really be greater in the daytime, when a shooter can see a target to shoot at. At least it would be for me if I wanted to get a shot at a man with a ponytail hangin' down his back. I'd have a better chance of pickin' him out when it's daylight." He looked at Possum to see if he was listening, but Possum just shook his head.

"Well, that makes me feel a little bit better about ridin' night herd tonight," Charlie Ramey remarked. "But now I'm scared to get on a horse in the daytime." It was good for a laugh as the men climbed on their horses and headed out to watch the herd.

The night passed peacefully. Perley rode a

wide circle around the cattle — wide enough to allow for vantage points that might conceal a man with a rifle. He had a feeling all along that it was a useless sacrifice of sleep, but he would not have been able to forgive himself if one of the men had been shot. Possum rode night herd with Sonny Rice, so Perley stopped to talk to them a couple of times during the night. When they rode back in for breakfast, Perley asked Possum if he needed some sleep before riding into town. "Shoot, no," Possum replied. "This ain't no different than a regular cattle drive, where you don't get enough sleep to fill your pocket. I'll be ready, as soon as I get some breakfast."

The two Tarpley brothers woke early the next morning and roasted some more of the fresh venison for breakfast. It was a small doe Cletus had shot, and it was a shame to waste so much of it, but they had smoked all night what they had room to carry on their packhorses. The rest they had dragged off into the bushes for the buzzards to find. Their father had gone back to town to sleep in his room at the hotel, thinking it might cause some suspicion if he rented a room but didn't use it. At least that was the reason he gave them. But they suspected a warm bed and the hotel dining room might have affected his decision. "This is a good campin' spot," Martin declared. "I wish we could just leave the packhorses here and come back here tonight."

"I reckon we'll just take the packhorses to the stable, and leave 'em there till we're done lookin' for them two fellers in town" Cletus said. "If we don't find Perley and Possum in town today, Pa said we're gonna go look for that Triple-G Ranch, so we wouldn't be comin' back here, anyway." They packed up their horses and rode back to the road, then headed to town. They led their string of four packhorses straight to Walt Carver's stable.

"You just wanna leave them four packhorses here for the day?" Walt asked.

"That's right," Marvin said. "See, we're supposed to meet somebody here in town today, and I don't know if we're gonna stay here tonight or not. And we don't want these horses to stand around all day loaded down. Then if we stay here all night, we'll wanna leave our saddle horses here, too. We can do that can't we?"

"Sure," Walt said, "You can unload 'em and leave your packs right over there in the back corner of the barn and turn the horses loose in the corral. You want me to feed 'em anything, or just let 'em water?"

"Nah, they're all right with just water," Marvin said. "They've been grazin' pretty good the last couple of days. If we end up stayin' the night, we'll feed 'em some oats then."

"All right," Walt said. "I'll take care of 'em. All I need is some names."

"Names?" Cletus replied. "What for? They ain't got no names. They're just packhorses."

"I mean your names," Walt explained, "so I'll know who to charge for which horses."

"Oh," Cletus replied. "Tarpley," he said before he thought about it. He looked at Marvin, who was displaying a deep frown, but it was too late to fix it.

"Right, Mr. Tarpley, I'll take care of 'em for ya'."

They unloaded the horses and stacked their packs in the corner of the barn that Walt had pointed out. Then they turned the horses out into the corral. "Now we don't have to worry about 'em," Marvin said. "Let's go find Mr. Johnson."

Cletus knew Marvin was berating him for dropping their name. "Dagnabbit, I couldn't help it. It just slipped out before I thought about it. He ain't gonna remember it, anyway. He didn't write it down nowhere.

Where do you reckon we oughta go look for Pa? He didn't say no place to meet him, did he?"

"No," Marvin answered. "Maybe he's still in the hotel, or the dinin' room. He might not want us to come lookin' for him in there, same as when he didn't let on he knew Johnny Pepper when he walked in."

"We could do the same thing," Cletus suggested. "Go in there and set down at a different table if he's in there."

"And do what?" Marvin asked sarcastically. "We done et breakfast. And I don't know about you, but I'm too full of deer meat to hold another bite of anythin' else. Let's go to that saloon. They already know we came together." That was as good a suggestion as any, so they got on their horses and rode down the street to Patton's.

"Well, here they are," Broadus announced when Marvin and Cletus walked in the door of the saloon. "I told Benny you boys would show up here for a shot of whiskey this mornin' and maybe some breakfast if you didn't have no luck huntin' yesterday."

Both Marvin and Cletus were momentarily stunned to find their father sitting at a table eating breakfast with Benny Grimes, the bartender. The saloon was empty of other customers. "Ain't no tellin' what he's told him," Marvin whispered to Cletus, "so just let him do the talkin'." They walked on over to the table and Marvin said, "Mornin'," and that was all he would risk.

"Mornin', boys. I came on over here from the hotel to see if I could get some breakfast, and Sadie fried me up some eggs she was already fixin' for Benny. I told her that you boys went deer huntin' yesterday and that's the reason you didn't stay in the hotel with me. Did you have any luck?"

"Yes, sir," Martin answered then. "We got a nice little doe. We smoke cured a good bit of it so we'll have somethin' besides bacon to eat. We don't need no breakfast, and that's a fact."

"I was tellin' Benny how you boys love to hunt," Broadus continued. "But I've got somethin' to tell you that'll tickle you some. Yesterday that drifter that took up with us before we hit town, that Johnny Pepper blowhard, well, he was in the hotel dinin' room when I was eatin' dinner. And this feller came in." He looked at Benny then and asked, "What did you say his name was?"

"Perley Gates," Benny said.

"That's right," Broadus continued then. "Anyway, he called this Perley Gates out right there in the dinin' room. They went outside and Perley Gates cut Johnny Pepper down like a dead cornstalk."

"You ain't foolin'?" Cletus asked, ready to go along with the farce. "Well, I ain't surprised. He sure talked a big game, though, didn't he?"

"Yes, he sure did," Broadus agreed. "I reckon the devil's already tired of hearin' about how fast he is with a gun."

"He ain't the first gunslinger that found out just how fast he really is when he called Perley out," Benny said. "Everybody around Paris knows that, and poor ol' Perley wishes nobody knew it." He started to expound on Perley's natural ability with a handgun when he looked toward the door and said, "Speak of the devil. . . ." All three Tarpley men turned to see the cause of his interruption.

"Perley Gates," Broadus uttered unconsciously, then was quick to ask, "Who's that with him?"

"That's Possum Smith," Benny answered. "Mornin', Perley, Possum. Ain't used to seein' you in here this early in the day."

And there they were, the two men they had come to town to kill, as if to present themselves for their execution. Both Marvin and Cletus dropped their gun hands on the grips of their six-guns. Broadus was prone to make the same move as they, but he whispered, "No!" For he had witnessed Perley Gates in action. He had no idea about Possum's skills, but he knew Perley would likely take two of them out, even if he caught a bullet in the process. "Patience," he told his sons when Benny got up and walked over near the bar, in case Perley and Possum had come in for a drink. "Remember what I told you." Broadus spoke quickly and softly. "Not head on. We'll wait for a better chance."

"Don't let us interrupt your breakfast," Perley said to Benny. "Possum and I are a little earlier than usual. It's too early to start drinkin' likker, anyway."

"How 'bout some coffee?" Benny asked. "Sadie just made a big pot of it when Mr. Johnson came in for breakfast."

"That sounds more to my likin' right now," Possum replied. "I'll go get it. You just set back down and finish eatin'." He didn't wait for Benny's protest but proceeded to the kitchen.

"Say howdy to Mr. Johnson and his sons," Benny said to Perley. "I don't know the boys' names."

"I'm glad to meet you Perley. Broadus Johnson is my name, and these are my sons, Marvin and Cletus." He wished he could tell him their real last name. He would have liked Perley to know who it was who killed him when the time came.

"Pleased to meet you," Perley replied. "I believe I saw you in the hotel dinin' room yesterday."

"As a matter of fact, you did," Broadus said. He paused when Possum came back with two cups of coffee and handed one to Perley.

Perley had a hunch that just occurred at that moment, so he thought he'd give it a shot. "Did you enjoy the supper Sadie cooked night before last?"

Broadus was confused by the question. "How's that?"

"Your supper night before last. You ate here at Patton's, didn't you? I was gonna ask you if I steered you right. But you're back for breakfast, so I reckon it wasn't too bad." Broadus was still obviously confused, so Perley enlightened him. "When you rode into town night before last, you were too late to eat in the hotel dinin' room. You asked me if there was someplace to get supper. Don't you remember? I told you Patton's."

"Well, I'll be . . ." Broadus started. "That was you?" Perley nodded. Broadus was at a loss for words for a few moments. It seemed like fate wanted him to find Perley Gates, otherwise it wouldn't keep throwing him in his path. *Fate, the devil, whoever,* he thought, *I'll be glad to accommodate you.*

"Where's the other fellow?" Perley asked then. Again, Broadus looked stumped, so Perley said, "When you rode into town the other night, there were four of you. What happened to the other fellow?"

Broadus forced a chuckle. "You did," he said. "That was the feller that called you out, Johnny Pepper." Then he retold the story he had created about Johnny Pepper riding into their camp and hanging around until they reached Paris. "So, I reckon we've got you to thank for takin' care of that problem for us."

"Unfortunate thing, that duel with six-guns," Perley said. "It ain't the kinda thing the folks here in Paris like to see. I'm sorry I had to have a hand in it."

When he said it, Possum couldn't help thinking what Lucy had told him about everyone in the dining room rushing to the two front windows to watch Perley shoot Johnny Pepper down. But he decided not to mention it.

The conversation shifted away from the recent gunfight when Raymond Patton, the owner of the saloon, came into the barroom. "I thought I heard some talkin' goin' on down here, so I thought I'd better get down here to get my breakfast before Sadie cooks up all her fresh eggs."

"You know Sadie ain't ever gonna let that happen, boss," Benny said.

Patton said good morning to Broadus and his two sons, then he said, "Perley, Possum — don't usually see you boys in this early."

"I expect not," Perley said. "We had a couple of things we had to do this mornin', so we came in a little early." He hoped Patton didn't ask what they were because he couldn't think of anything that made sense. Luckily, Patton had something else in mind.

"I heard about that business in the hotel dining room," he said. "I'm glad to see you came out all right. I swear, Beulah Walsh is gonna start banning you from eating in the dining room. She's havin' more gunfights than I'm having in this saloon — not that I'm complaining."

"I'm gonna leave before I get banned from here," Perley said. "Here's for the coffee, Benny." He put two nickels on the bar. "We'll be back tonight for a shot of something stronger. We ain't goin' back home till in the mornin'. Come on, Possum, we gotta go to the stable."

"You don't owe nothin' for the coffee," Patton called after them, but they were already out the door.

When they got outside, Possum asked, "Whaddaya gotta go to the stable for?"

"I just wanna ask Walt some questions," Perley told him. Then he asked Possum a question. "What did you think about Mr. Johnson back there and his two sons?"

Possum shrugged. "Whaddaya mean? I didn't think nothin' about 'em. What did you think about 'em?"

"I'm thinkin' that maybe we mighta just had a cup of coffee with three fellows that rode all the way from Angelina County to kill you and me."

"You really think so?" Possum wasn't so sure. "You think them two weren't really his sons?"

"Oh, I don't doubt that. I expect they're his sons. Shoot, they even favor him. The other one, the one I killed, he didn't look like he belonged in the family. I just wanna talk to Walt Carver, ask him a couple of questions."

"Might as well. We ain't got nothin' else to do but walk around and try to look like a big target," Possum said.

"Mornin', boys," Walt greeted them when they pulled their horses up in front of the stable and dismounted. "What can I do for ya?"

"Mornin', Walt," Perley returned. "I just wanted to ask you about a couple of things."

"If it's about the horse and saddle that belonged to that Pepper feller you shot, I ain't got nothin' to say about that. Sheriff Paul McQueen decides what happens to that."

"Hell, Walt, I don't care about that fellow's stuff," Perley said. "I just wondered if you got some strangers with four horses, and maybe some packhorses, in the stable night before last."

Walt shook his head. "Nope, I got two horses that night from strangers, a saddle horse from that feller, Pepper and a saddle horse from a Mr. Johnson."

"But no packhorses? Are you sure?"

" 'Course I'm sure," Walt insisted.

"This Mr. Johnson and Mr. Pepper came into the stable from who knows how far away with nothin' but what they had in their saddlebags," Perley declared. "Don't make sense to me."

"I had two young men already this mornin' that left four packhorses for me to keep just for the day. They wasn't sure if they'd be here overnight or not. I heard 'em talkin' about what their pa decided."

Perley turned to Possum and said, "There you go, Mr. Johnson's sons brought in the packhorses, and there was four of 'em, just like I saw night before last."

"Nah, I don't think so," Walt said. "They weren't Mr. Johnson's boys. Their names was Tarpley." It was as if Walt had fired a gun between them. Perley and Possum both recoiled at the sound of the name.

"That kinda puts the frostin' on the cake, don't it?" Possum said. "Mr. Johnson's sons are named Tarpley, and they brought four packhorses with 'em."

"I reckon Pepper's name mighta been Tarpley, too," Perley speculated. "Most likely wasn't a hired gun, though. 'Cause if he was hired to kill us, the other three likely wouldn'ta come with him. So, now, they'll be waiting for a good chance to catch one of us when we ain't careful."

"Makes for a good argument for us to go back to Patton's and shoot 'em down, don't it?" Possum suggested.

"Yeah, I reckon it would," Perley answered him. "Only trouble is, they ain't made no attempt to kill anybody, so we'd end up swingin' on a rope for murderin' a man and his two sons. And the fact of the matter is, we don't know for sure what they came here for. They say they're just passin' through. Maybe they are."

"I don't know about you," Possum said,

"but that don't sound like a good plan to me — to wait around for them to shoot us so we can prove they're out to kill us."

"Maybe with a little help from Walt we can get 'em to show their hand without us havin' to get shot. I reckon we're gonna have to let Walt in on the whole story, or he might not wanna help." They both turned and stared at Walt, whose face was one big question mark.

So they told Walt the whole story of their adventures in Angelina County, and their unfortunate dealings with the Tarpley family, their escape from the four who followed them and died as a result, up through Johnny Pepper's challenge to shoot it out with Perley. When he had heard it all, Walt was more than willing to help any way they thought he could. So they were ready to prepare their trap. For the immediate present, however, Possum reminded Perley that they had agreed to meet Jimmy Farmer and Link Drew at Henderson's store. "Right," Perley said. "They oughta be gettin' there about now."

Chapter 23

After leaving the stable, Perley and Possum went to Henderson's General Store to meet the two young boys. It was a big occasion for them to drive a team of horses pulling a wagon into town to pick up needed supplies. Jimmy and Link had proved to be responsible young boys, so John Gates agreed to let them drive into town and bring back supplies unescorted. Although he allowed it only after he learned that Perley and Possum would be in town for the day. Perley had a duplicate list of the supplies needed and the money to pay for them. When they arrived at Henderson's, they saw the wagon in front of the store. "Well, they got the wagon to town all right, looks like," Possum remarked. "Let's see how they're doin' with the list."

When they went inside, they found the two boys standing in front of the counter and Ben Henderson behind the counter. He and his wife, Shirley, were hustling around the shelves, pulling the items as Jimmy read them off. "Howdy, Perley, Possum," Ben sang out when he saw them.

"Howdy, Ben, Shirley," Perley said. "Looks like you got a big order workin' there. I hope those young men have got enough money to pay for all that."

"You're supposed to have the money to pay for it," Jimmy said. "Pa just gave me the list."

"I ain't got any money," Perley teased. "Possum you got any money?" But he could never carry a tease very far, so he said, "I'm just foolin' with you. I've got the money. How you doin' with that list? I've got one just like it. Read me what you've called out so far." Jimmy read off the items that were already on the counter. "That works with what I've got here."

"He reads very well," Shirley Henderson said. "He's doing just fine, so leave him alone to take care of his order."

"Yes, ma'am," Perley said, respectfully. "He's probably readin' it better than I could."

After the order was filled and Jimmy and Link had carried all their purchases out and loaded them in the wagon, Jimmy came back inside while Perley paid the bill. "We're all loaded up, Perley," he said. "So I reckon we'll head on back. I reckon I shoulda brought some jerky or somethin' with us, since we won't be back in time for dinner."

"Yeah, looks like you ain't got time." Perley said. "I kinda thought you and Link would eat with Possum and me at the hotel dinin' room, but if you're in a hurry to get back . . ."

"We ain't in no hurry!" Jimmy interrupted. "We'll eat with you."

"Pull the wagon over to the waterin' trough beside the hotel, then come on in the dinin' room. They'll be all right there while you eat."

"Thanks, Perley!" Jimmy said, and ran back out to the wagon. "I told you Perley would buy us some dinner in town," he told Link.

"Well, howdy, boys," Beulah greeted Perley and Possum when they walked into the dining room. She seemed surprised to see them.

"Howdy, Beulah," Perley replied, and he and Possum placed their guns on the table. "I hope you cooked up something good for dinner. We're expectin' a couple of distinguished guests to join us."

"Is that so?" Beulah replied. "In that case,

I'd best get back to the kitchen to make sure everything's ready to serve." She hesitated to say anything more but decided to, anyway. "Becky's in the kitchen. I'll tell her you're here." She turned at once and headed for the kitchen while Perley followed Possum over to a four-place table close to a window.

After a couple of minutes, Becky appeared in the kitchen doorway carrying two cups of coffee. She paused momentarily by Perley's usual table near the kitchen, expecting to find him there, then glanced up from the cups she was carrying and proceeded to the table near the window. It seemed to be an unconscious reminder to her that things were different now. "Good afternoon, Perley, Possum," she greeted them politely. "Beulah said you were expecting two guests."

"That's a fact," Possum answered, and pointed toward the door. "Here they come now." She turned to see the two grinning young boys heading toward the table. She smiled in spite of herself.

"Welcome to the Paris Hotel dining room," she said to them. "What can I get for you to drink with your dinner?" They both wanted coffee, just like Perley and Possum. "Aren't you afraid it'll stunt your growth?" Becky teased.

"No, ma'am," Link answered. "I been drinkin' coffee ever since I was young."

"That long, huh?" Becky responded. "Well, I'll go get you some right now, and you can be deciding what you're gonna eat with it. You can have ham and baked beans or meat loaf." She went to get their coffee.

"Look out the window," Perley said. "You can see your wagon over there, so you won't have to worry about it while you eat."

Already back with coffee for the boys, Becky overheard his remark. "I wondered why you didn't sit down at your regular table," she said as she put the cups down. She knew it was a small thing, but it somehow made her feel some comfort in knowing the change in tables was not symbolic of a change in his attitude about everything else.

The boys chose meat loaf because it was something they never got at home. They both ate in the cookhouse with the men. Even though Jimmy's mother and father lived in the main house, Jimmy slept in the bunkhouse. Link Drew had always lived in the bunkhouse, ever since Perley brought him home with him after Link's parents were killed. And Ollie Dinkler never made a meat loaf for the crew of the Triple-G. Perley tried to sell them on the baked beans because he said Ollie cooked beans every day but had never fixed baked beans like Beulah was offering. Becky kept their coffee cups filled, and the two boys were enjoying their rare visit to the hotel dining room when Possum tapped Perley's arm and nodded toward the door.

Broadus Tarpley removed his gun belt and placed it on the table reserved for that purpose. While he waited for Cletus and Marvin to do the same, he looked toward the dining room, suddenly tensing when his gaze fell on the table of four by the window. When Cletus turned around and saw what had stopped his father, he started to retrieve his gun from the table. "Leave it!" Broadus ordered in a whisper. "We'd never make it outta town." All their horses and packs were in the stable, and if they shot the two men down, the whole street between the hotel and the stable would probably turn into a shooting gallery. "This ain't the time or the place to do what we need to do, so just enjoy your dinner. We'll take care of business when the time and the place suits us. They told me this mornin' that the woman who runs this place is makin' meat loaf again today, and I don't want nothin' to spoil it for me. Go on and pick out a table,

I wanna speak to our friends."

Cletus and Marvin walked over to the side of the room opposite the windows while their father stopped by Perley's table. "Well, we bump into you and Possum again," Broadus said. "Looks like you've picked up some new men. These young men belong to either one of you?"

"Howdy, Mr. Johnson," Perley responded. "No, these two young men work for the Triple-G. They just came into town to pick up some supplies. I'm afraid I don't have any offspring, and Possum has so many scattered all over Texas that we wouldn't know how to get in touch with 'em."

"Ha!" Possum snorted in response to Perley's attempt at humor.

"Well, you can see that I'm havin' dinner with my sons. When I saw these boys settin' at the table with you, I thought you or Possum mighta been doin' the same. So I reckon we won't see you at Patton's tonight, after all. You'll be goin' back to the Triple-G with these boys."

"No, we'll be here tonight," Perley said. "These two bobcats don't need anybody to escort them home. Do ya, Link?"

"No, sir," Link answered.

"No, Possum and I will be stayin' in town tonight," Perley continued. "We've got some business we need to take care of in the mornin', so it's easier to just stay here."

"Is that a fact?" Broadus responded. "Me and my boys are stayin' in the hotel tonight, too. I stayed there last night. It was a pretty comfortable bed."

"We won't be stayin' in the hotel," Perley said. "We'll be sleepin' in the stable with our horses. This ain't the first time we've slept in the stable. Walt let's us sleep in the first stall and puts our horses back in one of the other stalls. He's glad to do it because he likes to take a little extra time in the mornin' when he knows we're there to watch things. He always puts down fresh hay for us, so we roll up in our blankets and sleep like we were on a feather bed. Ain't that right, Possum?"

"Just like a feather bed," Possum echoed. "Only trouble is, I sleep harder than I do in the bunkhouse, and it's harder to wake up in the mornin'."

"I know what you mean," Perley said, laughing. "Affects me the same way."

"I declare," Broadus remarked. "You make it sound so comfortable, I'm tempted to check out of the hotel and check in the stable." He forced a chuckle. "But my boys are gittin' tired of sleepin' with their horses. Well, enjoy your dinner." He went over to join his sons.

"I swear, Pa," Cletus said when Broadus sat down. "I wouldn't stoop to passin' the time of day with the buzzards that killed our kin. I don't understand why you do."

"You don't, do you?" Broadus replied. "Well, I'll tell you why, since you can't figure it out for yourself. I just found out that they ain't going back out to the Triple-G tonight for sure. They're staying in town. But they ain't stayin' in the hotel like we figured. They're stayin' in the stable tonight. I even know which stall they'll be sleepin' in. That's why I stoop to pass time with the buzzards."

"I reckon he answered your question for you," Marvin said.

"Yeah, and you was thinkin' the same thing I was," Cletus came back at him. "You was just too scared to say it."

"I weren't too scared, I just had better sense than to say it."

"Quit actin' like a couple of six-year-old young'uns," Broadus scolded, "or I'm gonna be eatin' in here by myself. I swear, them two little boys settin' over there with them act more like adults than you do."

"That sounds to me like what we've been hoping for," Marvin said. "Right, Pa? I mean when we figured they'd be stayin' in

391

the hotel, we was worrying about how we could get to 'em without waking up everybody in the hotel. If they're sleepin' in the stable, we oughta be able to kill both of 'em and come back to the hotel if we're careful. And nobody would know we was out of our rooms."

"That's what I'm plannin' to do," Broadus said. "And to make sure they're sleepin' good I'm plannin' to buy 'em a bottle of likker tonight at that saloon to take with 'em. Because I know they'll be leavin' early, if they're sleepin' in the stable. I want 'em sleepin' so good tonight till we can just walk right in and cut their throats just like you was killin' a hog. And there won't be no noise to wake up anybody in town."

"How do you know they'll be in that saloon tonight?" Cletus asked.

"Because they said they was this mornin' when they came in there and said they didn't want no likker until they came back tonight," Marvin answered him. "We're gonna get it done tonight, ain't we, Pa? Then we can get to hell outta this town and get back to Angelina County."

"Yes, ma'am, we're ready," Broadus said, answering Lucy's question before she asked it. "I'm gonna have that meat loaf, and if there's any of it left over, I'm gonna have it again tonight for supper."

"I declare," Lucy replied, "you must love meat loaf. What about you two?"

"I reckon I'll try it, too. He said it was better'n what our ma makes," Cletus said. Marvin made it three, so she went to the kitchen to fix their plates.

When Lucy went in the kitchen, she found Becky busy fixing a plate for a lone customer who walked in after the Tarpley men — or the Johnson men, as they were registered in the hotel. "How you doing, honey?" Lucy asked. "How's Perley tonight?"

Becky paused slicing ham to look up at Lucy when she replied, "He's all right, I guess. He's treating Link and Jimmy to dinner before they drive the wagon back to the Triple-G. That's why they didn't sit at his regular table — so the boys could keep an eye on their horses." She felt it important to explain that to Lucy, in case Lucy might attach some other meaning to the change.

"Well, that's mighty nice of Perley, ain't it?" Lucy said. "That's the kinda thing Perley does." *When he ain't shooting a hole in somebody,* she thought, then scolded herself for thinking it, knowing what a peaceful man he was. "Peaceful, but unlucky as hell," she murmured to herself.

"Nothing, I was just mumbling about

something I forgot to do," she lied when Becky asked what she had said.

The boys finished their dinner in short order and were ready to go back to the ranch. They were excited about driving the wagon back with no adult supervision. They thanked Perley for the dinner treat and made their exit. Perley and Possum watched them through the window as Jimmy backed the horses away from the watering trough and turned them toward the street. Then he handed the reins to Link, and Link drove the horses forward. "Were you ever that young?" Perley asked Possum.

"I remember being as young as Jimmy," Possum said. "I think I was about fourteen when I was born. 'Cause I don't remember much before that except bein' hungry all the time."

"You two look like you need more coffee," Beulah said when she walked by their table. "Ain't Becky takin' care of you?"

"We told her we'd had about all we could hold for a while," Possum said. "We're ready to go, just too full to get up and move." He looked at Perley then, who seemed to be a million miles away. "How 'bout it, partner? Are we ready to go?"

"Yep, I'm ready," Perley answered. "Lemme say goodbye to Becky." He got up out of his chair.

"For a minute there, I thought you went to sleep with your eyes open," Possum said.

Perley ignored his remark and went to the kitchen door and looked in. Becky was putting some dirty dishes into a big washtub. "I'm sorry we didn't get to visit a little bit," he said. "I can see you're pretty busy. Maybe tonight at supper you'll have a little time."

"I'm sorry, Perley," Becky answered. "It just got awfully busy all of a sudden. You say you'll be here for supper?"

"That's right," Perley said.

"Good. Maybe we'll get more time to visit then," she said. He hesitated, standing there for a long few seconds, trying to think of something appropriate to say. And when he could not, he turned and walked away. It crossed his mind that maybe he didn't know Becky at all — at least not the Becky he saw today.

Possum was waiting for him at the front door where he was talking to Beulah. "She won't let me out the door unless I pay her for four dinners," Possum joked. "I told her you were the big shot who invited those two little eatin' machines to have dinner with us."

"That right?" Perley responded. "Well, I tried to sneak out the back door, but Becky was guardin' it." He gave Beulah the money for the four dinners and picked up his six-gun from the table. "We'll see you for supper tonight," he told Beulah. "Just me and Possum, though."

"Always look forward to seein' you two," Beulah said. Perley paused before stepping out the door to take a cautious look out into the street, then reminded himself that the assassins were still in the dining room.

Once they were outside, Possum wanted to know where Perley's mind wandered off to for that short time just before they left. "What's eatin' away at your mind?" he asked. "Is it Becky that's got you fogged up?"

"Sorry," Perley said. "I was thinkin' about something that was troublin' me some. It wasn't Becky. I'm still in a fog about the way she seems different lately. There ain't no doubt about that. But back there a little while ago, I was thinkin' about what we're plannin' to do tonight — set up a trap for Tarpley and his sons."

"What about it?" Possum asked, thinking they had a perfect solution for the Tarpley problem.

"I was thinkin', the first time they sent four of them after us, we ended up killin' all four of 'em. So they sent four more to find us here in Paris. I already killed one of them, and when we kill the other three tonight, then what? Are they gonna keep sendin' killers up here till they get the job done? According to the sheriff in Nacogdoches, there's so many folks by the name of Tarpley in that part of Angelina County, they'll never run out. So it crossed my mind that maybe we should involve the law in this and try to capture those three tonight instead of just killin' 'em outright."

Possum was at once skeptical. "You mean tell the sheriff what's goin' on? And tell him to put 'em in jail?"

"Maybe Paul could help us arrest 'em, then hold 'em there till some deputy marshals come and get 'em," Perley said. "Maybe then the Tarpley vengeance might be shifted offa us and put on the law. And the Tarpley family could spend all their time tryin' to break those three outta prison instead of worryin' about us."

"So that nest of killers down there would forget about us and go after the marshals," Possum said. "I swear, Perley, you're one of the smartest men I've ever known. But that's the dumbest thing I've ever heard of. Them people down there was raised knowin' that if you keep tryin' to grab a rattlesnake, you'll most likely wind up gettin' bit. Now they've already got bit reachin' for this snake once. And when they get bit reachin' for it again, they're more likely to decide it best to leave the damn snake alone."

"Maybe you're right," Perley admitted. "I forgot what a philosopher you are, though. I reckon we ain't got much choice but to take care of the problem ourselves."

"That's right, partner," Possum said. "We'll let 'em show their hand, then we'll end it." Possum was sure he knew there was one more thing that troubled his friend, although Perley would never bring it up for discussion. He did not have an aggressive bone in his entire body. For some reason, this mild-mannered, young man was born with the lightninglike reflexes of a rattlesnake. He had been forced to kill too many times, but every time it was in reaction to a threat to himself or others. And it always happened so fast that he had no conscious thought about what he was doing. It was just his natural reaction to a threat. Possum felt certain Perley was reluctant to deliberately kill someone before they actually made a move to take his life. Possum might have been even more concerned had he known how accurate his diagnosis was. For thoughts of that nature had crossed Perley's mind, and he wondered if his actions would be fast enough when they were deliberate. With the assassination they were planning for that night — and in his mind, it was just that — they would be the aggressors. He was going to have to shoot someone attacking a dummy made of hay, maybe in the back. It would not even be like waiting in ambush for someone coming to attack you head on, like the ambush at the gully on the Neches River. He warned himself then to stop thinking in terms of failure to react. This time, he wouldn't count on his natural reflexes. He would make himself act.

Chapter 24

Most of the afternoon was spent at the stable, working on the dummies they were making out of old horse blankets and rags in an effort to make them appear to be real bodies. When they were satisfied they had done the best they could, they put them out of sight in the back of the stall until that night. After that, they decided on the best places to take cover and wait in ambush. Walt Carver was very cooperative in helping them set up their ambush after hearing the whole story behind it. He was the only person they had told about the trap they were setting for their would-be murderers, and he considered that a special distinction. He not only cleared the first stall; he left the second and third stalls vacant as well, to keep any horses from catching a wild shot. When Perley and Possum decided they were as ready as they were going to get, they thanked Walt again and said they would see him at about six o'clock.

The first two parties to arrive at the hotel dining room when it opened for supper were Perley and Possum and the Johnson Party. Beulah Walsh was pleased to see them because both parties had eaten a big dinner only a few short hours before. She figured it was a tribute to her cooking. Perley and Possum sat down at Perley's usual table and Broadus led his sons to the table closest to theirs. "Looks like we're keepin' to the same schedule," Broadus offered cheerfully, in contrast to the sullen expressions his sons maintained. "I like to eat my supper pretty early in the evenin'," he continued. "Then I'm going straight from here to Patton's Saloon. I like a drink of likker after I eat a good supper."

"I reckon we are keepin' the same schedule," Possum said. " 'Cause that's where we're headin' from here. We'll have to get along pretty quick to the saloon, though, if we're gonna get a drink. We're sleepin' in the stable tonight, and we don't wanna get locked out." He chuckled then, looked around as if making sure no one overheard, and said, " 'Course, Walt don't ever remember to lock that little door in the back of the barn." Possum couldn't help noticing that he was making all the small talk from their table. Perley was just sitting there as mute as Marvin and Cletus Tarpley. And Perley usually did the talking. Possum remembered that at dinnertime earlier, Perley had painted a verbal picture of the way Walt fixed the stall up for their comfort. Now he sat almost stone-faced as he sipped the coffee Becky brought them. Possum wanted to ask him what the hell was the matter with him, but he couldn't because the Tarpley trio was too close to their table and might overhear.

Before they finished eating, Becky sat down at the table for a short visit. "How was the stew?" She asked casually. They both answered that it was good. "Beulah put a lot more onions in it than usual," Becky said. "She was wondering if you liked it better with more onions." She directed her question to Perley.

He shrugged indifferently, "Tastes about the same to me as it usually does, I reckon."

"I'll tell her you liked it just as well," Becky said.

"Forever more!" Possum blurted, his patience with the two young people near exhaustion. "I can't stand no more of this! Tell Beulah the stew was better the way she fixed it before. It was all right tonight, but the onions gave it a little too much bite to suit my taste. Becky, you love Perley. Perley, you love Becky. Get that straightened out between ya or I'm done with both of you!"

His little outburst, although he attempted to confine it to the table, brought a genuine smile of amusement to Broadus Tarpley's face as he and his sons got to their feet to leave. It added a double measure of satisfaction to his lust for vengeance against Perley Gates. His death would also leave a grieving woman. He felt happy he could introduce Becky to the sorrow that Atha felt and that Rena would know when they returned home with news of Johnny's death. "Come on over to Patton's," he said before he walked away, "I wanna buy you a drink."

"We're gonna take you up on that," Possum called after him. "Come on, Perley, we've got business to take care of tonight. Give Becky a kiss if you love her or shake her hand if you don't. We got to go."

Becky and Perley got up from the table and faced each other, saying nothing for a few seconds. Then Perley extended his hand toward her. With an expression of complete despair, Becky reluctantly took the hand he offered. Perley locked it in his hand and yanked her forcefully toward him, then planted a big kiss on her lips. "I'll explain all this tomorrow," he said just for her ears alone. Then he released her and strode out the door after Possum.

"Way to go, Perley!" Lucy Tate yelled as he went past her. She turned to face Beulah, who was wearing a grin from ear to ear. "Ain't that the sweetest thing you ever saw?"

"Well, I'll be go to hell," Beulah exclaimed. "Lucy, you got tears in your eyes. That's another miracle tonight, I ain't ever seen Lucy Tate cry."

"It's them damn onions you put in that stew," Lucy claimed.

"That's another thing," Beulah said. "I got a bone to pick with Possum Smith, sayin' my stew had too much bite in it."

"I swear, Pa," Cletus Tarpley protested. "I don't know why we don't just turn around and shoot the two of 'em down in the street right now. They're comin' along right behind us, and they wouldn't know what hit 'em. And we'd be done with what we came all the way up here to do."

"Damn it, Cletus, I already told you why not. We've got horses in the stable, saddlebags in the hotel rooms. What in blazes do you think the sheriff and every citizen with a gun would be doin' while we was runnin' around the town tryin' to get all our stuff together?"

"I reckon you're right," Cletus declared. "I weren't thinkin' for a minute there. It woulda just been so easy to catch 'em walkin' right toward us in the middle of the street."

"You ever wonder why you don't get to call the shots in this family, little brother?" Marvin asked.

"You go to hell," Cletus answered.

"In due time, I expect," Marvin said.

"When we go in this saloon, I want you two to try to act like you're half growed up," Broadus said. "And go easy on the likker. They're the ones I wanna get drunk, not you. I wanna finish this business tonight and get on the road to home in the mornin'."

"I'll drink to that," Marvin japed, "but not too much. Right, Pa?" Broadus showed no appreciation for his attempt to be funny.

"Howdy, Mr. Johnson," Benny Grimes greeted them when they walked in. "What can I pour for you?"

"Just whatever you're pourin' outta that bottle there will do just fine for the three of us," Broadus answered. "Then I wanna buy a bottle of the good stuff, better'n this watered-down whiskey you're pourin' at the bar."

"I can sell you a bottle of the same rye whiskey the boss drinks," Benny told him.

"It's supposed to be eighty-six proof. That's the best we've got. We don't cut none of the whiskey we buy after it gets here. I just open the bottle and pour, so I expect that whiskey I just poured in your glasses is better than fifty percent pure."

"Don't get me wrong," Broadus said. "I ain't complainin' about the whiskey. It suits me just fine. If it was any stronger, I probably couldn't handle it. I just want a bottle of the good stuff for a special reason." That seemed to appease Benny, who appeared to be getting ready to defend the saloon's whiskey quality. He opened a cabinet on the wall behind the bar and took out a bottle of rye whiskey, which he handed to Broadus. "You can take a look at that and tell the seal ain't never been broke on that cork."

"Good, good," Broadus replied. "That's what I want. Perley Gates and Possum Smith oughta be comin' in right behind us. Pour 'em a drink outta the same bottle you poured ours and I'll pay for 'em."

Perley and Possum walked into the saloon a moment later, and Broadus waved them over to join them at the bar. When they walked over, Benny poured them a drink of whiskey and told them Broadus paid for it already. "Well, thank you kindly," Perley said. "I'm payin' for the next round."

"Fair enough," Broadus said. "But I invited you for a drink, and the boys and I got to talkin' about it. Seein' as how you have to get to the stable pretty quick, you ain't gonna have no time to enjoy a few drinks of likker. So we decided to buy you a bottle of the good likker for you to take to the stable with you."

"Well, I can't think of anything Possum and I did to deserve this," Perley said when he took the bottle from Broadus. "It is a fine idea, though." He held the bottle up and admired it. "I can hardly wait to hit the hay now, Possum." Then he said to Broadus, "But let us pay you for this."

"Nope, it's already done and paid for," Broadus said.

"Thank you again, then," Perley said, holding it up for Possum to admire it. "We can just drink ourselves to sleep, partner. Whaddaya say?"

"Sounds to my likin'," Possum said. "Thank you, sir."

They remained at the bar for a while longer and a couple of drinks more before Possum reminded Perley that sometimes Walt locked up the stable a little early if he got a little extra hungry. "He don't eat when normal folks eat, anyway, 'cause he can't close up too early."

"All right," Perley said, pretending to regret having to leave so early. He held the bottle of whiskey up. "We'll think of you fellows when we're havin' a drink with the horses."

"Hope you enjoy it," Broadus said as Perley and Possum left the bar and headed for the door. He turned to look at his sons then. "One more drink of this cheap stuff and we'll go back to the hotel and wait. You can have another drink later tonight outta what's left in that bottle of the good stuff they're carryin'."

Walt was waiting for them when they arrived at the stable. "I figured you boys oughta be showin' up pretty soon," he said. "Do I need to get outta here right now?"

"There ain't no hurry," Possum told him. "They'll wait till late tonight before they show up. They wanna be sure we're asleep. You can just go to supper when you usually do, if you druther. Who knows? You might have a customer before you close up."

"You want me to leave the stable door unlocked?" Walt asked.

"No," Perley answered him. "That might make 'em suspicious. Let's leave that little door in the back of the barn unlocked, all right?"

"Whatever you say," Walt replied. "You sure you don't want me to let Paul McQueen know what's goin' on?"

Possum answered him quickly, afraid that Perley might start thinking about trying to arrest Broadus and his sons. "No, that would just be one more person in a space that's already crowded. Perley and I will be real careful when we have to shoot, too, so there are no horses hit, or we don't end up shootin' each other. It might get confusing in here with another body to watch out for."

"All right," Walt said. "Sounds like you know what you're doin', so I'm gonna get on outta the way. Good luck to ya. The back door's unlocked." He started toward the door. "Oh," he remembered, "I put some more wood in the stove and set the coffeepot up ready to boil. All you need to do is set it on the stove."

"Much obliged, Walt," Possum called after him. "We can use some of that." Then he paused to see if Perley was going to say anything about Walt's suggestion to tell the sheriff. He didn't want to take any chance the three Tarpley men might be sentenced to a short stay behind bars, then released to come after them again. He intended to give them a trial in his mind. If Tarpley sneaked in the stable and shot the two dummies to pieces, that was attempted murder, and the verdict would be death by him and Perley. Justice would be served. He waited, but Perley didn't say anything, so he went back into the stall to position his dummy. He placed it so it could be easily seen from the front of the stall, but on a side of the stall that had the open barn behind it and no chance of a horse being hit. He liked the arrangement, so he proceeded to place Perley's dummy in line with his. "Looks like the real thing when you turn the lantern down," he said to Perley when he came back from starting the coffeepot brewing. "Whaddaya think?"

"I don't like it," Perley answered.

"Why in the world not?" Possum demanded. "Even in this light, they look like real people sleepin'. What's wrong with 'em?"

"You need to turn one of 'em around," Perley said. "You got my head next to your feet. I ain't gonna sleep all night smellin' your feet."

"How do you know which one is which?"

" 'Cause that one is the better lookin' one," Perley said, pointing to one of them.

"Doggone, you're right, that one is me.

But I ain't gonna change 'em. They look perfect to my eye. Let's go check on the coffee."

After they had a cup of Walt's coffee, they felt confident that any lingering effects of the whiskey they had consumed were totally destroyed. "I swear, I ain't sure I'm man enough to drink another cup of that coffee," Possum declared. They went back to the stable then to decide where they were going to position themselves to receive their visitors. They reasoned that the three assassins would come in the small door at the back of the barn. They would then walk through the barn to the double doors into the stable. The first stall they would come to would be the ambush stall. There was no place Perley and Possum could hide near the stall so they decided they would have to hide in the barn and wait until the three men walked past them. Then they would follow their assassins into the stable. They would have no protective cover, but if they were quick enough, they wouldn't need cover. Add that to the element of surprise they anticipated, and they felt they would have a total advantage. There was nothing left to do now but wait, and that was the hard part. Perley picked up a bucket and took some oats to Buck, then he did the same for Dancer. After that, it was more coffee, which was even stronger after sitting on the stove that much longer. When the sun finally sank and took with it all traces of daylight, they closed the two big doors in front of the stable and dropped the bar in place. The stable was officially closed for the night.

If anything, the waiting was more exasperating for the three Tarpley men killing time in the hotel. Broadus sat in the one armchair in his room, checking the Colt Army .45 he wore. Cletus and Marvin were sprawled on his bed. "How much longer do you think we need to wait?" Cletus asked.

"We gotta give 'em time to work on that bottle I bought 'em," Broadus told him. "What's your hurry? You got someplace you gotta be?"

"Yeah, that saloon," Cletus said. "I'm hungry again. I wonder if that old woman that cooks for them has got anythin' good to eat tonight."

"You can get you some of that deer meat we smoked outta our packs after we make our social call at the stable," Marvin suggested.

"Maybe so," Broadus said, "but we might be in a little bit of a hurry about that time."

Finally, after Marvin had drifted off to sleep, Broadus got up out of his chair and said to Cletus, "Poke your brother. It's time to go." Cletus lifted one leg and gave Marvin a stout kick in the seat of his pants.

Almost rolling off the bed, Marvin grabbed the foot of it. "What's wrong with you, you blame fool?"

"It's time to go, Brother, dear, or would you druther stay here and sleep while the men take care of business?"

"Cletus," Broadus said, "stick your head out the door. See if there's anybody in the hallway. I'd just as soon nobody noticed us leavin' the hotel." When Cletus took a look and said the hall was empty, Broadus led them to the end of the hallway and took the back steps down to the first floor. A quick look told him nobody was in the hall to the back door of the hotel, so he quickly led them outside that way. To avoid bumping into anyone on the street, they walked behind the buildings until reaching the last one. Then they walked to the road leading to the stable.

Up in the hayloft of the barn, Perley squinted in an effort to see the three figures approaching in the darkness of a moonless night. When he was sure, he went over to the ladder and called down to Possum.

"They're here!" Then he scrambled down the ladder to the barn floor, and he and Possum went to their respective hiding places. The spot Perley had chosen to hide in was behind three bales of hay stacked just inside the front double doors of the barn. His back was almost against one of the doors. He waited and listened. And he realized at that moment that they really were coming to kill him and Possum. Before that moment, even while making their elaborate preparations to receive them, it seemed unlikely the man and his two sons would actually show up. He heard them then at the front doors.

"They're locked," Marvin whispered, "with a bar across both doors. We ain't gonna get in this way."

"Remember what he said about the door on the back of this barn," his father whispered. "Maybe he forgot to lock it again."

"If he didn't," Marvin whispered, "we might have to break it down or tear out a window. And that's liable to wake 'em up."

Perley heard them hurrying away from the doors. He gave them a few seconds to make sure they didn't hear him before he alerted Possum again. "They've gone to the back door," he said with a loud whisper. "Get ready!"

"We're in luck," Marvin said, still talking in whispers. "He forgot to lock it." They filed inside as quietly as they could manage. Once inside, they stopped to listen and to adjust their eyes to the heavier darkness inside the barn. It struck them as pitch black immediately, but gradually their eyes adjusted and they could make out objects enough to avoid bumping into them. "Look up to the front," Marvin whispered. "There's a light up there near the door into the stalls." It appeared to be a lantern with the wick turned way down. He figured it was intended to keep you from breaking your neck when you stepped off the barn floor onto the ground floor of the stable.

"Most likely stays on all the time," Broadus speculated. "Just keep your eyes open."

They continued a cautious approach toward the front of the barn until they could see the lantern hanging on a large post that was part of the support for the hayloft above. Creeping steadily through the barn, their guns drawn, they made it to the front when, suddenly, Broadus grabbed hold of Marvin's arm to stop him. When Marvin and Cletus both looked at him, he said nothing but motioned toward the first stall. There in the eerie light provided by the lantern, they saw the two sleeping bodies.

Cletus raised his pistol to fire, but Broadus stopped him. He shook his head and drew the knife he wore on his gun belt. He held it up for them to see and grinned when the blade caught the reflection of the lantern. They understood and holstered their six-guns and drew their knives as well.

As soon as the three men moved past their hiding places, Perley and Possum came out behind them. Their guns drawn, they walked silently in step with Broadus and his sons as they prepared to cut the throats of their sleeping victims. Since there were three assassins and only two victims, a shoving match occurred between Cletus and Marvin over who was going to slit the throat of the one victim left for them. Marvin, being the bigger of the two, managed to shove Cletus out of his way and prepared to finish the figure rolled up in the blanket. Lacking the maturity of a man half his age, Cletus reacted by drawing his gun and firing a shot into the sleeping figure in an act of spite.

Enraged by his son's childish behavior, Broadus was left with no choice. He roared in anger and lunged at the other figure, stabbing it violently with his knife, over and over, until he realized he was not making solid contact with a body. "What tha — ?" he blurted out, knowing in that instant that he was a dead man. It was confirmed an instant later when he turned to receive Possum's bullet in his forehead. Reluctant to shoot when their backs were turned and they were attempting to slit the throats of two sleeping figures, Perley now had no choice. Cletus, whose gun was already in hand, turned to fire at Possum. So Perley put one round into his chest, then fired one into Marvin's chest when he attempted to draw his weapon. Both shots happened before Possum could get off another round.

Neither Possum nor Perley spoke for a couple of minutes. Possum was silently giving thanks that Perley had not hesitated to shoot because he knew Cletus was already preparing to shoot him. Perley knew that he had saved Possum's life, but he also knew that he didn't consciously fire at Cletus, then consciously fire at Marvin. He had done it automatically, with no thought that he recalled. He turned to find Possum staring at him. "You all right?" Possum asked.

"Yeah," Perley answered, coming back to the present. "I reckon there ain't no doubt about what the Johnsons had in mind to do, is there?"

"At least, they were gonna be quiet about it and not wake up the neighbors," Possum said. "I woulda kinda liked to seen the expression on the ol' man's face when he tried to cut the throat on that dummy. But his boys couldn't keep from fightin' about which one was gonna get to slit a throat. Other than that, they seemed like a right peaceful family. If you hadn't acted as fast as you did, though, I'd be layin' in the hay beside 'em. I thank you for that."

"I expect we oughta go get the sheriff and tell him what happened," Perley said. "I started to say we could drag the bodies outta the stable. But maybe we oughta leave everything like it is so he can see what happened." Possum agreed with that, so they decided to go wake the sheriff. It was not necessary, however, because they heard him outside the front door.

"Walt!" McQueen called out, "Are you in there?"

"Hold on, Paul," Perley called back to him. "I'll open the door." He lifted the bar off the doors and pushed one open far enough to let the sheriff walk in.

"Perley," McQueen said, surprised. "What's goin' on?"

"You got here awful quick," Perley said. "We were just fixin' to go get you outta bed."

"I don't go to bed this early. I was makin' my last rounds around the town when I heard the gunshots. Sounded like they came from here."

"They came from here all right, and if you'll go look in that first stall, you'll see what happened," Possum told him.

McQueen walked into the stall and stopped abruptly when he saw the bodies sprawled at odd angles on the hay. Confused, he asked, "That's that Johnson fellow and his two sons, ain't it? Who do you reckon did the shootin'?"

"We know who did the shootin'," Possum said. "It was me and Perley, except for that one bullet hole in the blanket. Cletus did that when he thought he was shootin' one of us."

The sheriff was totally confused, so Perley and Possum told him the whole story that led up to this attempt on their lives here in the stable. When they finished, McQueen wanted to know why they didn't tell him about it before all this happened. "Because we couldn't prove for sure that Johnson's name was really Tarpley, or that he was here to kill us, until we had proof. Reckon this is enough to make you believe us?"

"I reckon," McQueen said, scratching his head to help himself think. " 'Course, if it was anybody but you and Possum, I could allow that Johnson and his boys mighta just come to get their horses when they was ambushed. Like I said, if it was anybody but you and Possum."

Possum had to chuckle. "But it came to your mind anyway, didn't it? Lemme help ease your mind a little bit with some questions you could have. What the hell was those three doin' in the stable that time of night in the first place? Walt closed the stable a long time before you heard them gunshots. Number two, why would we make up two dummies to look like we was sleepin'? Number three's a good'un. Why did their daddy say their names was Johnson, but his two sons told Walt their name was Tarpley? Tarpley is the same name of them four that came after Perley and me and got theirselves killed for it."

"You can save your breath," McQueen protested. "I already said I figured it happened like you said."

Perley smiled to himself. *Possum Smith for the defense,* he thought. In spite of Paul's insisting on the contrary, Perley was sure he had questioned the obvious setup, if only momentarily. But Possum set him straight.

Chapter 25

"I reckon it's too late to go get Bill Simmons to come get the bodies," Perley said. "I expect Walt would like to have 'em gone from the stable."

"It might not be too late," the sheriff said. "Bill Jr. was in Patton's just now when I stopped by there to check on 'em. He usually picks up the bodies for his pa, anyway. I'll go see if he's still there. If he is, I'll tell him to get his cart, and he can haul 'em over to his pa's barn." He walked back over and looked at the dummies they had created and shook his head. "Pretty good job. Well, I don't see that there's anything more for me to do here. I'll send Bill Jr."

"Much obliged, Paul," Perley said, then walked back into the stall where Possum was still standing over Broadus Tarpley's body. "Paul didn't seem to doubt anything we said about this little party tonight," Perley said, "especially after you told him the facts."

"It was really because he knows you don't never lie," Possum replied. "Everybody in town knows you don't never lie. It's a reputation you need to get rid of. It's just gonna come back to bite you one of these days."

"I'll keep that in mind, like I do with all your wise advice." He was about to say more but was interrupted by a voice in the back of the barn.

"Perley, is everything all right?"

"Yeah, Walt. Come on in and see what a mess we made."

"I heard the shootin' a while ago," Walt said as he came in from the back, looking right and left until he sighted the three bodies lying in the fresh hay he had put in the stall. "Damn," he drew out slowly. "They really done it. They came to kill ya. I didn't want to walk into the middle of something, so I watched the stable from over there by the creek. When I saw Paul McQueen leavin', I figured it was okay to come on in. What are you gonna do with those three dead men?"

Possum couldn't resist. "Oh, they're yours. You can do whatever you want with 'em. They'll be gettin' stiff after a while, and you can stand 'em up in the corner somewhere."

Perley couldn't let him go on when he saw the look on Walt's face. "He's just japin' you, Walt. The sheriff's gone to see if he can get Bill Jr. to come get 'em tonight."

Nearly forty-five minutes had passed before Bill Jr. arrived with his handcart to pick up the bodies. The cart, while handy to use in a hurry, was designed to transport only one body at a time. Bill Jr. wanted to make only one trip with the cart, however, so with Perley and Possum's help, he piled all three on the cart. He secured his lifeless cargo with rope to make sure he didn't lose one on the way to his father's shop. That was not the major problem, however; with the two extra bodies, the cart became extremely heavy to push. Perley volunteered to help him push it, but Possum had a better idea. He borrowed some harness from Walt and hitched one of the packhorses up to the cart. Perley went with them, then he and Possum brought the horse back to the stable. When they went back inside, they found that Walt had removed all the hay that had blood on it and tidied up the stall. "There ain't many hours left to sleep, but I'm goin' home now and try to get a little shut-eye. What are you boys gonna do?"

Perley and Possum looked at each other

for an answer. They hadn't thought about what they would do after this encounter with the Tarpleys. "We got no place else to sleep but right here," Perley said.

"Well, ain't that what we was supposed to do?" Possum asked. They both looked at Walt then. "That's all right with you, ain't it, Walt?"

"Sure, that's all right with me," he replied. "Just twenty-five cents apiece is what I charge to sleep in the stable."

"Hell, you're boardin' our horses," Possum complained. "And because of what we did here tonight, you'll most likely pick up some extra horses and tack. You ought not charge us nothin' to sleep with our horses."

Walt looked at Perley and winked. Then to Possum, he said, "I'll sleep on it and let you know in the mornin'."

They were awakened the next morning by the sound of Walt opening up the doors to his stable and barn. "You fellows gonna sleep all day? I hope I ain't disturbin' you, but I've got a business to run here. I've got customers comin' in this mornin' to get their horses, and I've got horses to take care of, including yours. I'd appreciate havin' these two front stalls back to put to better use than trappin' rats."

"I swear, Walt," Possum grumbled, "you can be downright aggravatin' sometimes."

"Walt's right," Perley said. "We've got things to do, and we'd best get started." He crawled out of his bedroll and pulled his boots on after checking to make sure there were no mice homesteading in them. Then he rolled up his bedroll and tossed it toward his saddle. "How much do we owe you, Walt?"

Walt looked at him and smiled. "You don't owe me nothin', Perley. I'm glad I was able to help you take care of those three killers. And there weren't no harm done to the stable."

"Well, that's mighty neighborly of you, Walt," Perley responded. "But what about our horses, and for Possum and me sleepin' in the stable? You usually charge me for that."

"Not this time, I reckon," Walt said. "I feel like I had a part in takin' those three down, and I was the only one you told your plan to. So lettin' you use the stable was my part in it."

"Thank you, Walt," Perley said, and extended his hand. Walt shook it, then turned to Possum, who was waiting to do the same. "Now, we'll saddle up and get outta your way so you can get something done."

Perley knew they had to ride out to the Triple-G that morning to let Rubin and John know it was no longer necessary to take extra caution in the normal routine of the ranch. And there was no need to have the night herders doubling up anymore. The threat was over. But their first stop was to be the hotel dining room for breakfast.

Becky had good-naturedly suffered through a heavy dose of teasing ever since Perley's exit from the dining room the night before. They interpreted his dramatic embrace with Becky as he was about to go out the door as solid evidence that he had decided to take her forcefully if he had to. So they were tactless in their questions about how she was going to saddle break the wild young stallion. After all, Perley seemed to drift with every breeze that swept across the grassy plains. To be expected, Lucy was the most relentless. "What I'm wondering," she asked, "is what are you gonna do about Possum?"

"What are you talking about?" Becky answered. "I'm not going to do anything about Possum."

"Well, you're gonna have to do something about him. Anything you do with Perley, Possum's gonna be right there, too. You know, Possum's getting up there in years.

He's gonna need a lot more care than Perley. It ain't gonna be long before Possum will probably need constant care, spoon-feedin' and stuff like that. It'll be like havin' a baby. You ain't gonna have any time for Perley."

"Lucy, you're sick. Do you know that?" Becky finally told her.

"Behave yourself, Lucy," Beulah scolded. "Here comes Perley now."

"Is he by himself?" Lucy asked quickly. "Or is Possum with him?"

"Possum's with him," Beulah answered.

Lucy looked at Becky with a wicked grin. "Kiss my foot, Lucy," Becky said and went to the kitchen to get their coffee.

When they walked into the dining room, Perley and Possum were both a little surprised by the unusually cordial greeting they received from Lucy and Beulah. Perley was at first disappointed when he didn't see Becky, but a moment later, she appeared in the kitchen doorway carrying two cups of coffee and smiling sweetly. "Mornin', Perley. Mornin', Possum." She placed the coffee on the table and stepped back to watch them seat themselves. "I'm happy to see you this morning. Are you gonna have your usual?"

"Mornin'," Perley returned. "I don't see

no reason to change as long as Beulah keeps cookin' it the way she has been."

"I guess I'd best go get it started then," Beulah said, then turned to go to the kitchen.

Lucy, like Beulah, had been standing there, watching to see if the two young people were going to act like a couple who had decided to marry. When she saw no change in their usual shyness toward each other, she decided to inquire about something else. "I heard some gunshots from somewhere in town late last night. Beulah said she heard 'em, too. Did you boys have anything to do with that?" Her question brought a frown to Becky's face, but only for a moment before she replaced it with her smile.

"Now why would you think we had anything to do with it?" Perley asked. "Might be you were just havin' a dream." He was disappointed to hear her question, afraid any talk about that might send Becky back into her sour mood.

"Yeah, right, and Beulah was having the same dream at the same time I was," Lucy said. "Paul McQueen ain't been in for his breakfast yet. I guess I can ask him." As if on cue, McQueen walked in the door then. Lucy turned, and when she saw who it was, said, "Well, good mornin', Sheriff McQueen. We were just talking about those gunshots we heard late last night."

"Yeah, at the stable," McQueen replied. "Perley tell you all about that little trap him and Possum set up?" He nodded to them and asked, "I reckon Bill Jr. picked up the bodies all right?"

"Yep," Possum answered, "he got 'em."

Becky looked immediately at Perley, a question on her face, but said nothing. He didn't speak, either, but formed the words silently for her, *I'll explain.* She nodded in return. Lucy pressed the sheriff for details about the cause for the shooting, and he told her that Perley and Possum had set up an ambush for three men who were in town to kill them. Becky was horrified. She looked at Perley, who was still trying to signal her to wait until he could explain it all. And then McQueen said, "You know who they were. They were stayin' here in the hotel. The Johnsons. Mr. Johnson and his two sons — they ate in here, didn't they?"

"Well, for goodness sakes," Lucy responded in complete surprise. "They seemed like ordinary people. The boys didn't say much one way or the other, but Mr. Johnson was always polite and friendly.

Wasn't he, Becky? Wait till I tell Beulah." She went straight to the kitchen where Beulah was finishing up Perley and Possum's breakfast. "Have a seat, Sheriff. I'll bring your coffee," she called back over her shoulder.

Perley had always been able to let Lucy's playful remarks bounce off him with little concern. This time he wished he could strangle her. When he looked at Becky now, she looked away. Feeling much the same way she was acting now, he thought he might just get up and walk out and head back to the ranch. But he told himself that would only do more harm. *Besides,* he thought, *she owes me the chance to say my side of this thing.* So he remained silent and started to eat the breakfast Beulah brought out to him. Becky continued to check on him and Possum and keep the coffee cups filled, but no more than any other customer. Finally, when she came to take away their dirty dishes, he said, "Bring Possum some more coffee and tell Lucy to take care of your tables. You and I need to have a little talk before I leave. All right?"

"All right," she answered. She filled Possum's cup again and told Lucy she was leaving for a few minutes. When Lucy naturally asked where she was going, Becky answered,

"None of your business. I won't be long." She walked back to the table then, took Perley's hand, and led him into the kitchen. Walking past a surprised Beulah Walsh, she led him through the kitchen and out the door to the back hallway. Perley thought she was taking him to her room, but she stopped there in the hallway. After she closed the kitchen door, she turned to face him and said, "Now, I want to hear the whole story."

Perley decided she had a right to know it, so he told her about the Tarpleys and how he and Possum had become involved with them. "It was all on account of my bad luck," he explained, "when Monk Tarpley stole Buck. We were ready to start for home, but I couldn't let him take my horse. There wasn't any need for bloodshed. I left him a horse when I took Buck. The Tarpleys were the ones who started the bloodshed. Possum and I just defended our lives." As she had demanded, he told her the complete story of their escape from Tarpley revenge up through the presence of Broadus Tarpley and his two sons in Paris. "They came here to kill Possum and me. We had to defend ourselves. The reason we set the ambush was to make sure we were right. That's the whole story, and now I've got to go home to tell Rubin and John that it's over and things can get back to normal at the ranch. If you've got any questions about any of it, I'll answer them as honest as I can."

"Just one," she said. "When are you gonna marry me?"

With no hesitation, he answered, "As soon as I can find a preacher to tie the knot."

"If you're thinking that's going to give you more time to put it off, you're forgetting about the new church on the Sulphur Springs Road and the Reverend Ronald Blessing."

"Are you sure he's a real preacher?" Perley asked.

"Presbyterian," Becky replied.

After telling Becky he'd be back to see her as soon as he could, Perley and Possum rode back to the Triple-G to report the happenings of the night just passed. Unfortunately, there was no guarantee that the three just killed would be the last to be seen of the Tarpleys. Perley had no explanation for Broadus having found out where to find him and Possum, or even how he learned his name. The only thing he was sure of was that Broadus and the three who came with him could not identify him until someone called his name. If, as Sheriff Clayton Steel had told him, the Tarpleys and their kin were thick as fleas down in that part of Angelina County, Perley wondered how many families he and Possum had touched. At least two, he figured, and maybe three, if Johnny Pepper wasn't a Tarpley. He discussed the possibilities with Rubin and John at length, but they could only arrive at the conclusion that there was nothing they could do to prevent future contact. Perley apologized for bringing his ill luck home to Triple-G. His brothers told him not to worry about it. Things happen the way they're supposed to, and they would deal with them when they occurred.

After Perley went back to the bunkhouse, Rubin said, "It ain't his fault these things happen to him. It just seems when bad luck is lookin' for a place to squat, he looks like the perfect spot."

"You're right," John said. "It ain't his fault, but we're liable to pick up some of this last cow pie on our boots. It'd be a pretty good idea to keep a sharp eye out for any drifters riding our range."

In extremely high spirits, Becky Morris walked down to Ken Stallings's dry goods store during the free time she had after cleaning up the dining room from the noon meal. "How do, Becky?" Ken greeted her when she walked in. "What can I do for you?"

"I just wanted to visit a minute or two with Evelyn if she's here at the store," Becky said. Ken and his wife often ate Sunday dinner in the hotel dining room after church, and she and Becky had become quite friendly.

"She sure is, Becky," Ken answered. "She's in the back room pricin' some new bolts of cotton cloth. Evelyn!" he yelled for her. "Becky Morris is lookin' for ya!"

Evelyn came to the door and said, "Hello, Becky, you lookin' for me? Come on back here." When Becky went back in the storeroom, Evelyn asked, "You need some help?" She was accustomed to helping the women when they needed undergarments and other things they'd rather not discuss with Ken.

"I wanted to talk to you about your church and the preacher there," Becky said. "I know he hasn't been there very long, but do you think he would perform a wedding for someone who's not a member of the church?"

"Oh, Becky!" Evelyn lit up immediately. "Are you and Perley finally gonna do it?"

Becky flushed bright red. "Does everybody in town know about Perley and me?"

"My, goodness, yes," Evelyn replied. "When are you gonna do it?"

"We haven't set a date yet, but I really want us to be married by a real preacher. That's why I wanted to ask you if you thought Reverend Blessing might marry us. I don't want to just jump over a broom or anything like that. I want to be really officially married."

"He's only been here about eight months," Evelyn said, "and he hasn't performed any weddings that I know of. But I don't know why he wouldn't."

"I was worried about Perley's reputation with a gun. Reverend Blessing hasn't been here long enough to know the kind of person Perley really is."

"I see what you mean," Evelyn remarked. "I think maybe if some of his church members told him what kind of man Perley is, he wouldn't object to performing the ceremony." She paused to giggle. "Besides, with a name like Perley Gates, how could he refuse? When we go to church Sunday, I'll talk to the other members, and I'm sure they'll all put in a good word for Perley."

"Thank you so much, Evelyn," Becky said. "I knew you would help."

"So you're finally gonna get married," Evelyn said, eager to talk about it some more. "And by Reverend Ronald Blessing," she went on. "There aren't many eligible single women anywhere around this town. But when they find out about Reverend Blessing, they're all gonna be joining our church."

"Is he not married?" Becky asked.

"No, he's not, and that's a question all the women in the congregation are asking. He's tall and handsome, looks like a Greek god when he stands up at the front of that little ol' church and tells us to love thy neighbor. Dark wavy hair with little touches of silver just over the ears — he's got more than one wife thinking *what if* ?" She glanced quickly at the storeroom door. "Not me, of course, but he really is something. He's going to build that shabby little building we're worshiping in now to a church that people all around will come to see. That's where all the collection money is headed, as well as the new-building fund drives we've had. He's not even spending the money on building a parsonage. He says the church is the most important thing. A house to live in can come later. So he's living in a tent behind the church. Even as busy as he is raising money for the church's future, I'm sure he'll arrange for a ceremony for you and Perley."

Feeling even more optimistic now, Becky thanked Evelyn again and went back to the hotel. She couldn't wait to tell Perley what she had found out. Maybe they should go to the church together to meet the preacher, so he could get to meet Perley before he decided to perform the ceremony.

Chapter 26

The Reverend Ronald Blessing was of interest to the men in his congregation as well as the women, especially two men who were also outstanding members of the town council. Amos Johnson, owner of the hotel as well as mayor; and Wilford Taylor, president of the First National Bank of Paris, sat down to discuss an issue that the mayor found disturbing. "Thank you, Thomas," Wilford Taylor said when Thomas Deal, one of his tellers brought two cups of coffee into Taylor's office for them. "Now, Mr. Mayor," Taylor began, "what's on your mind?"

"Nothing really serious at the moment, but something that struck my mind last Sunday, so I thought as a deacon in the church, maybe I should look into it to make sure our new pastor knows what he's doing."

"He strikes me as very capable," Taylor said. "Seems to know his Bible pretty well and delivers a powerful sermon."

"I know, and I agree," the mayor said. "But when I watched them take the collection plates back on the table beside his stand he uses as a pulpit, I wondered what he does with that money to keep it safe. So I'm asking, does the Presbyterian Church have a bank account in your bank? Can you check on that for me?"

"Don't have to," Taylor said. "No, the church doesn't have an account here."

"Then where is he keeping all the money he's collected in the last eight months from the collection every Sunday for the building-fund drives he's organized?"

"You think he's dishonest?" Taylor asked.

"No, no, I'm not sayin' that," the mayor was quick to reply. "What I'm concerned about . . . is he just that trusting in the Lord to guard the money for him? It's not that unusual for a preacher to think he's exempt from the crimes committed against ordinary men just because he's a man of the cloth."

"Well, I don't know, Amos, I never thought about it, to tell you the truth. He might be guilty of ignorance when it comes to handling money, and too wound up in the hellfire and the hereafter. He's scraping out a living out there by that little church, saving every nickel and dime. Maybe he thinks he'll have to pay for a bank account. Hell, if that's the case, I'll tell him the church won't pay any fee. Better not to risk losing all the money he's collected."

"I thought you'd say something like that," the mayor said. "It should make the congregation of the church feel a whole lot better, knowing that money isn't hidden underneath that little church building."

"I'll call on Reverend Blessing myself," Taylor said, "and tell him he's got an account in the bank. I'll do it this afternoon."

"I'm glad I came to talk to you about it," the mayor said. "Thank you, Wilford."

Wilford Taylor drove his buggy down the Sulphur Springs road until reaching the path leading to the church. There was smoke coming from the chimney of the rough little building, so he guessed he must be calling on the preacher at suppertime. "Hello, the church!" Taylor called out. "Reverend Blessing!"

In a matter of seconds, the preacher appeared in the door of the church. "Why Mr. Taylor," Blessing called back. He stepped on out of the front door and came to meet his visitor. "You caught me cookin' myself a little something to eat. I don't have much on the stove, but you're welcome to share it."

"Oh, no thanks, Reverend," Taylor replied. "I won't be but a minute or two. Do you need to take a look at whatever it is you've got on the stove? I don't wanna cause you to burn your supper."

"I'll take the pan off the stove," Blessing said. "I'm using the church stove to fry some bacon. I hope that's all right. You want to come inside?"

"No, we can talk out here. Of course it's all right for you to use the church stove."

"Thank you, sir. It's a lot easier than cookin' over my campfire. What brings you out to see me?"

"There's something we need to be thinking about," Taylor said. "We need to take some of the funds we've been collecting and at least build our preacher a house to live in."

"Oh, I know that will be grand," Blessing said, "but we must build God's church first."

"I guess we can discuss that later. I don't want to keep you from your supper. The reason I came by today is to tell you the church has a no-fee bank account. I don't know what you're doing with the money you've collected, but I think it'll be a lot safer in the bank, don't you?"

"Maybe," Blessing replied, "as long as the bank doesn't get robbed. I've got the money in a safe place."

"The mayor came to me about this," Taylor explained. "He said the congregation will feel a lot better if they know their money is in the bank."

Blessing didn't respond to that for a moment, but then he said, "I think I understand what you mean, and you're right, of course. We'll put it in the bank."

"Good. If you want me to, I can take it back with me right now, and I'll send someone with a deposit slip tomorrow to show how much was deposited. All right?"

"It's going to take me a little longer than that," Blessing said. "The money's buried pretty deep. Would it be just as good if I dig it up after I eat and bring it into the bank in the morning?"

"I don't see why not. Come in to see me in the morning, and I'll get you all set up with the bank. And I apologize for interrupting your supper."

"Oh, that's no bother. Thank you for coming to tell me. I guess it would be best to have that money in the bank. I'll see you in the morning." The preacher stepped back from Taylor's buggy and stood watching until it pulled back onto the road back to town. "Well amen to you, Brother Taylor, and to you, too, Paris, Texas. I was hopin' it would last a little longer, but it was good while it lasted. It's time for the good reverend to travel and spread the gospel somewhere else." He started packing up his tent and his belongings right away, in an effort to have as much daylight as possible before having to camp for the night. Last, but most important, he lifted the one loose board in the floor next to the stand that served as his pulpit and pulled the canvas bag out. "It ain't as much as I planned on takin' outta this shabby little church, but it's enough to get me started somewhere else."

Paul McQueen was just about to step out the door of the sheriff's office when Wilford Taylor pulled up in front in his buggy. "Mr. Taylor, what can I do for you?" Paul greeted him.

"Sheriff, I'd like a word with you, and it's strictly between you and me. I've just got a little suspicion about something, and I'd be mortified if it got out and I was wrong."

"Oh?" Paul replied. "Well, sure, Mr. Taylor. You wanna come in the office?"

"No need to do that," Taylor answered. "You looked like you were on your way somewhere, and I don't want to hold you up."

"I was just fixin' to go to the hotel to eat supper," Paul said. "I'm not in any hurry. What have you got a suspicion about?"

"I had a meeting with Amos Johnson a little while ago, and it caused me a little concern." He went on to give the details of his discussion with Johnson that resulted in his visit to Reverend Blessing. "On the way back from the church, it started worrying my mind that Blessing didn't want to give me the money to deposit in the bank. Said it was buried too deep, but he said he'd bring it into the bank in the morning. I don't know, Sheriff, I just got a feeling that he might not show up at the bank or anywhere else tomorrow morning. If he's so inclined, he should be in possession of a large enough sum of money to disappear. And that money belongs to the people of the church who donated it. I'm sure you understand why I don't want anyone to know I suspected him if I'm wrong." He paused to force a chuckle. "Who knows, I might get struck down by a bolt of lightning for even making such an accusation."

"Well, that would be a pretty rotten trick to pull on the folks who donated money to his buildin' funds," Paul said. "I'm one of those folks. So you want me check on him to see what he's doin'?"

"I know you always take a late-night check on the town before you retire for the night," Taylor said. "I thought maybe you could include the church tonight, just to make sure everything is quiet there, anything suspicious going on, and so forth. Just be discreet about it. It would be terrible if I'm wrong."

"I understand," Paul assured him. "It'll just be between you and me, and I won't even let him know I'm checkin' on him."

"Thank you, Paul. Hop in, and I'll give you a ride to the hotel."

"Lemme lock my door," Paul replied. Then he did so and climbed in beside Taylor.

"Evenin', Sheriff," Lucy greeted him when he walked into the dining room. "You oughta be happy tonight; Beulah's fryin' pork chops."

"You're right about that," he said, taking a quick glance around the room. "I see Perley sittin' back there near the kitchen. I think I'll go join him."

He walked on back toward the kitchen. "Howdy, Perley, mind if I join you?"

"Howdy, Paul. Have a seat."

Paul settled himself in a chair and asked, "What brings you in town tonight?" Then he said, "Never mind," when Becky came out of the kitchen with a plate of food to set before Perley.

"Good evening, Sheriff," Becky greeted him. "I'll get you some coffee. You want pork chops?"

"I sure do. Those look pretty good. I might even ask him for one of his while I'm waitin'."

Becky laughed and said, "I'll try not to be that long with yours." She went to get his coffee.

"You stayin' in town tonight, Perley?" Paul asked.

"No, hadn't planned to. I'll be goin' back to the ranch later," Perley said. He had promised Becky that he would hang around until after the dining room closed for the night so they could have some private time to visit. Consequently, he was in no hurry to finish. The conversation between him and Paul naturally landed back on the subject of the Tarpleys and the ambush in the stable.

"How'd you get away from the Triple-G without Possum?" Paul asked.

"I told him this shindig tonight was for couples only, and he couldn't find a gal," Perley joked.

They both took their time to finish supper, with Becky stopping frequently to visit whenever her other customers were in no need of attention. When they finally called it quits, Perley walked outside with the sheriff, since he felt he was in the way of the women cleaning up the dining room. "You could walk the town for me," Paul suggested, joking. "You know the routine," he reminded Perley of the time he had acted as sheriff temporarily. Perley remembered the time, and he also remembered that it was a job that didn't suit him at all.

Paul said so long and went back to his office, leaving Perley to wonder what to do to kill time while waiting for Becky to finish work. He had a key to her room in his pocket, but he didn't want to sit in that room and wait. He decided a better choice was the front porch of the hotel. So that's where he went after he stuck his head back in the dining room to tell Becky where he'd be. It was peaceful there in the evening as darkness descended upon the town. He was surprised, then, when Paul McQueen rode by the hotel and out the Sulphur Springs road. Paul never made his rounds on horseback, and never that far out of town. This left Perley's mind right away, however, when Becky joined him on the porch. "Oh," she sighed, "it's so much more pleasant out here. It's a beautiful night." She pulled a chair over beside his, gave him a quick kiss, and sat down to enjoy the night air.

The sheriff walked his horse slowly up the path to the church, his eyes focused on the rough building ahead. No lamp burned inside. As he approached the building, he realized that the tent that normally stood behind it was gone. "He's on the run," Paul muttered to himself. "Wilford Taylor was right." He continued on up to the church to be sure, and when he pulled his horse around behind it, there was little doubt. Blessing's horses and all evidence of his tent and camp were gone. Paul slid down off his horse and walked inside the church. There was still a fire dying out in the stove, but it offered no reason to be alarmed, so he left it to burn out. He lit the lantern that always hung near the back door, took it off the hook, and went outside to see if he might spot tracks to show him which way the preacher fled. In the light provided by the lantern, he could see no hoofprints going out the path, only prints — mostly his own — coming in mixed with the tracks left by Wilford Taylor's buggy. Blessing had run, but not out toward the road. So Paul went across the little stream behind the church, and that was where he found tracks leading into the woods.

Where the hell is he going that way? he wondered. *No path or anything, just woods. This lantern ain't gonna be enough.* As if hearing his plea for help, a full moon appeared, poised to climb out of the distant treetops. "I need help," he declared to the night in general. "That lowdown slick-talkin' piece of dung slickered us all out of our money." But he knew he didn't have time to raise a posse. That would have to be done in the morning and Blessing would be too far by then. *I need Perley.* That thought struck him squarely. Perley had a lot more experience at tracking and being tracked. He didn't wait another moment but jumped back on his horse and galloped the short distance to the hotel, hoping and praying that Perley hadn't gone home yet. He only knew two places to look for him. If he and Becky were not still on the porch, her room in the hotel was the only other possibility, and he didn't know which room was hers. But if the porch was vacant, he was determined to knock on every door in that hallway behind the kitchen.

Luck was with him, for he found Perley and Becky on the porch steps, saying goodnight. He didn't waste time with detailed explanations. "Perley! Good! You're done! I'll take him now, Becky. Perley, get on your horse and follow me. Quick," he added.

Perley, caught up in Paul's excitement, gave Becky a quick kiss and jumped on Buck. He wheeled the big bay around and galloped off after the sheriff. "Perley!" Becky protested, frustrated.

When they got to the church, Paul led them right across the stream in back of the building before he dismounted. Then he told Perley why he had literally been snatched out of Becky's loving arms to go on a wild goose chase in the woods. "You mean the preacher, the Reverend Ronald Blessing, ain't a real preacher a-tall?" Perley asked, amazed, and thinking of what Becky was going to say when she was told.

"No, he ain't," Paul said. "And the worst part is he's run off with over eight months' worth of the congregation's donations and offerin's."

"Damn," Perley responded. "That is bad. When did he run off?"

"Just before suppertime, I reckon. Wilford Taylor saw him here this afternoon, so however long it took Blessing to pack everything up after Taylor left. I need you to help me figure out which way he went, 'cause he didn't go out the way we just rode in. I had that lantern lit, and I couldn't find any tracks leavin' here but those heading straight into the woods."

"Yeah, well, I expect the reverend has done this same thing before, so he's most likely got him a back way outta here when days like this come along."

"I know we ain't set up to track somebody," Paul said. "No food, no coffeepot, no blankets, but I figured we only had one chance, and that was a slim one. I figured we had to move fast and catch him where he makes camp tonight. He didn't have that many hours of daylight to travel, so I'm hopin' he ain't that far, if we can just pick up a trail."

"Well, let's start lookin' around in these trees and see if we can find someplace where his horses tore up some pine straw, just to give us the general direction." They split up and started searching among the trees. They searched for about twenty minutes before Perley called out, "I think this is where he went!" Paul hurried over and Perley pointed to a complete hoofprint standing out in the moonlight, where some small critter had scratched the pine straw away. "Probably lookin' for bugs," Perley said. He pointed then and said, "If you look through those bushes that way, you can see that it's a game trail. It's just grown over a little."

"Damn, I believe you're right," Paul agreed. "That must be his emergency exit."

"Or leads to it," Perley said. "Let's follow it and see where it takes us." With Perley leading the way, they followed the small game trail until reaching a stream that they figured was the same stream that ran behind the church. They were rewarded with some distinct hoofprints on the sandy bank. "There's his escape route," Perley pointed out. "That path on the other side, followin' the stream." He stopped to get his bearings, looking at the sky to see if he could find the north star. When he couldn't, he took a guess, anyway, because it made sense. "He's headin' west. I'm thinkin' this trail we're on now is gonna lead us to the road to Honey Grove."

"So he's headin' to Sherman from there, I reckon," Paul speculated.

"That would be my guess," Perley said. "But if what you said was true, about him not gettin' away from the church till maybe just about suppertime, there's a pretty good chance he'll stop before he gets to Honey Grove. Moonlit night like this, we oughta catch him before he breaks camp again."

"What if he decides he can just keep goin' in the moonlight?" Paul asked.

"Then we'll be like a couple of dogs chasing their own tails. So I hope he stops for the night." They started out again and after about two miles, the game trail crossed over a road that could only be the road between Paris and Honey Grove. They checked the game trail on the other side of the road just to make sure Blessing took the road and didn't continue on the trail. From that point on, they watched for possible campsites, with special attention to any stream or creek they came to. They weren't sure how much farther they traveled the Honey Grove road when they caught sight of a tiny red glow in a grove of trees beside a fair-sized creek. "I believe we found him," Perley said.

They left the horses near the road and went into the camp on foot, Perley on one side of the creek, Paul on the other, since they couldn't tell from the road which side of the creek the camp was on. When they got closer, they saw that the camp was on Paul's side of the creek. He looked across at Perley and signaled with a wave of his arm, then pointed to what appeared to be a sleeping figure close to the fire. Paul didn't wait. With his pistol already in hand, he advanced into the camp and approached the sleeping figure. From his position on the opposite side of the creek, Perley was tempted to yell for him to be more cautious. The memory of his ambush of the Tarpleys in the stable was still fresh in his mind. But it was too late by then, and if he yelled, it might cause Blessing to react too soon. So he made his way cautiously across the creek to try to get to a backup position.

"All right, Blessing!" Paul yelled. "On your feet! This is Sheriff McQueen, and you're under arrest." The sleeping figure did not respond to his command. Paul was about to repeat his order when he heard the voice behind him.

"Sheriff McQueen, if you don't drop that gun right now, you're gonna get a bullet in the back." Blessing stepped out from behind a tree where he had been sleeping when Paul dropped the gun. "I kinda figured you'd try to catch up with me. I oughta just shoot you and be done with it. If you hadn't dropped that gun when I told you to, you'd already be dead."

"I'm offerin' you the same advice, Blessing, or whatever your name is," Perley said from behind him. "Your choice: Go back to Paris sittin' in the saddle or layin' across it. It don't make no difference to me." Blessing froze. He hadn't counted on the sheriff having time to mount a posse, so he thought he'd be alone, if he came at all.

"Who the hell are you?" Blessing demanded, still facing Paul's back, and still holding his six-gun.

"I'm Perley Gates. Pleased to meet you, and if you don't drop that pistol right now, you're gonna find out if they'll let you in the real Pearly Gates. I'm bettin' they won't." Blessing dropped his weapon right away. He had never met Perley, but after eight months in Paris, Texas, he knew his reputation. "Paul, if you wanna take charge of your prisoner, I'll watch him while you're doin' it."

Paul picked up his and Blessing's guns, then he backed Blessing up to a tree and handcuffed his hands behind it. As soon as that was done, Perley holstered his .44 and went back to bring his and Paul's horses to the campsite. "It ain't gonna be but a couple of hours before daylight," Paul said. "We might as well rest our horses till then. I don't know exactly how far we are from Paris, but it couldn't be more than about six or eight miles. So it'll be a short ride back to town. I wanna look through his packs to make sure we're carryin' the church's money back with us."

"Might as well see what he's got for

breakfast while we're at it," Perley suggested. "I hope to hell he's got some coffee. Excuse me, Reverend, for the cuss word." He pulled Buck's saddle off, then joined Paul in searching the packs. Paul found the canvas sack containing the church's money, so he packed that back where he found it. "I'm glad you thought to bring something to eat to our little party, Preacher," Perley said to Blessing. "We got off on such short notice we didn't have a chance to pick up anything."

Blessing, silently watching them look through his packs, finally spoke again. "Well, I tried to work a little money scheme on you folks, and you caught me at it. But I never did no harm to nobody, never tried to pleasure myself with any of your women, although I won't deny I had more than a few opportunities. Fact is, I think I gave a lot of your folks some comfort and encouragement in my sermons. What I'm gettin' at is this: I've been caught before, and I was run outta town. Now that you caught me, you've got all your money back. I'm appealin' to you now, why do you have to take me back to jail? Why can't you just run me outta town? And then you'd never see me again. What good is it gonna do to lock me up and go to the expense of feedin' me for however long before you let me go?"

"Tryin' to cheat the congregation outta their hard-earned money might be considered doing some harm by most folks," Paul responded. "And givin' 'em false hopes with your slick preachin' might make 'em give up hope for the future."

"Well, I'm truly sorry for that," Blessing said. "I never meant to cause anybody any real harm."

"You know, I'm tempted to let him go at that," Paul said to Perley just as they found the coffee. "He is right. If there wasn't any money lost, that's most likely what I woulda done, just run him outta town and tell him never come back. And we've got the money back so it's the same thing. He's right — the town would like to not have to feed him for however long we're gonna have him in jail."

"I see what you mean," Perley said. "I think that's up to you. He ain't guilty of any violent crimes, no armed robbery or shootin' or such. I can see why you'd rather not have the bother of him. Like I said, it's up to you."

"I think I'll let him go," Paul said, "but I ain't gonna tell him till we're ready to mount up and go back."

So they made use of Blessing's supplies

and made some coffee and fried some bacon. Then they unlocked him from the tree and guarded him while he ate. When the horses were rested, Paul announced it time to saddle up. He walked Blessing over to his horse, and when he was about to step up into the stirrup, Paul said, "I've decided to let you go free. Just don't ever show your face in Paris again. All right?" He dropped his gun back in his holster and stepped back to let him climb up into the saddle.

Blessing looked stunned, but he recovered immediately. "You mean that, Sheriff? You ain't just japin' me?"

"I'm not foolin'," Paul said. "You're free to go, anywhere but Paris."

"I declare, Sheriff McQueen, you are a truly Christian man. I thank you, sir. Please, may I shake your hand?" Paul shrugged and extended his hand. Blessing stepped forward to reach for it, but his hand went right by Paul's and drew Paul's six-gun from his holster. But he didn't shoot it. Instead, he looked down in surprise at the small hole in his shirt and the gun dropped from his hand. As blood began to spread around the hole, he looked at Perley in shocked disbelief. "I believe you've killed me," he gasped, staggering a couple of steps, then collapsing.

Paul quickly picked up his gun and brushed the dirt off before replacing it in his holster. He didn't say anything for a few seconds while he realized what his carelessness might have cost him were it not for Perley's reactions. When he recovered, he went over and checked on Blessing, then looked up at Perley and said, "He's dead. You musta hit him in the heart."

"Whaddaya wanna do with him?" Perley asked.

"We'll take him back to town and let Bill Simmons bury him. He gets paid to do it." So they picked up the preacher and laid him across the saddle and started home. The church had recovered their money, but they were going to have to find a new preacher. Perley couldn't help wondering if the Lord might be telling him not to get married.

ABOUT THE AUTHORS

William W. Johnstone is the #1 bestselling Western writer in America and the *New York Times* and *USA Today* bestselling author of hundreds of books, with over 50 million copies sold. Born in southern Missouri, he was raised with strong moral and family values by his minister father, and tutored by his schoolteacher mother. He left school at fifteen to work in a carnival and then as a deputy sheriff before serving in the army. He went on to become known as "the Greatest Western writer of the 21st Century." Visit him online at WilliamJohn stone.net.

J.A. Johnstone learned to write from the master himself, Uncle William W. Johnstone, who began tutoring J.A. at an early age. After-school hours were often spent retyping manuscripts or researching his massive American Western History library as well as the more modern wars and conflicts. J.A. worked hard and learned, later going on to become the co-author of William W. Johnstone's many bestselling westerns and thrillers. J.A. Johnstone lives on a ranch in Tennessee and more information is at WilliamJohnstone.net.

The employees of Thorndike Press hope you have enjoyed this Large Print book. All our Thorndike Large Print titles are designed for easy reading, and all our books are made to last. Other Thorndike Press Large Print books are available at your library, through selected bookstores, or directly from us.

For information about titles, please call:
(800) 223-1244

or visit our website at:
gale.com/thorndike